Creatus

Carmen DeSousa

Creatus - Bonus Edition
Copyright© 2016 by Carmen DeSousa
Published by Carmen DeSousa
ISBN-10: 1-945143-19-3
ISBN-13: 978-1-945143-19-9

www.CarmenDeSousaBooks.com
PO Box 253
Delmont, PA 15626
U.S.A.

Cover Design: Sherwin Soy

This Special Edition Includes:

The Prequel - Creatus (They Exist)

Creatus – Book One

Sneak Peek at Creatus Rogue – Book Two

A Note From The Author...

Dear Friend,

This bonus edition includes the prequel to the Creatus series, *Creatus (They Exist)*, Book One - *Creatus*, and a sneak peek at Book Two - *Creatus Rogue*.

If you've already read *Creatus (They Exist)*, please don't think you've purchased the same book. *Creatus (They Exist)* is included in this special edition so that readers who haven't read the prequel won't miss anything.

While the Creatus series isn't my first book, it's technically my first born. Years before I started writing professionally, I wondered about all the myths about superheroes and monsters, questioned why since the beginning of the written word, man has told stories – many similar – about sentient beings who are stronger than humans, live longer, and eat differently, but have also managed to stay hidden. After much research, I believe I have figured out some of their secrets, discovered how they have managed to stay hidden.

If you haven't read the prequel, which is now the first part of this book, remember it is a prequel, so it will not give away many of the secrets of the creatus race. And please know, creatus aren't any of the mythical beings you've read about. Instead, it is from them we obtain our fairy tales — and our nightmares. They are the reason we believe in superheroes — and monsters. Because ... they exist.

I hope you enjoy discovering their secrets as much as I loved writing about them.

Happy reading,

Carmen

Creatus (They Exist)

In every myth, there's a modicum of truth.
Believe ...

Chapter One

Bored beyond belief by the instructor's dull and repetitive lecture, Derrick leaned back in his chair, wishing he could skip this part of his training. He'd already gone through extensive preparation and instruction, and by all accounts, had his Medical Degree in Internal Medicine. As with the rest of the residents at his family's small hospital, though, he needed to complete his education in the US and receive an accredited degree.

The double doors of the auditorium burst open, and a young woman barreled into the didactic session. A backpack slung over one shoulder, causing her to walk with a slight tilt, and her long platinum hair fighting to escape her ponytail captured everyone's attention from the speaker, especially Derrick's.

The instructor didn't miss a beat, though, as he droned on about malpractice suits, state-of-the-art procedures that the training hospital would be putting into effect, and finally the importance of being on time if you wanted to be selected to be a resident upon finishing the program.

The last topic, Derrick was certain, was aimed at the young woman who was now nervously jotting down everything the lecturer was saying.

Derrick couldn't care less about a position within the prestigious Boston hospital. He knew his future and what role he was destined to fill. He would be an attending physician at his family's small hospital, and his father had hinted that he'd be overseer. The council had already mentioned him stepping in; it was just a matter of him being ready.

The discourse ended, and Derrick moved quickly, cutting off escaping students so he could bump into the woman. Not that he was supposed to fraternize with anyone in school, but she'd caught his eye so completely he had to talk to her.

While tapping on her cell phone, the young woman juggled her books in the crook of her arm as she rushed toward the exit. *Busy woman*, he thought.

"Need some help?" He reached for the books in her arms before she could object.

"Hey ..." She looked like a viper ready to strike, but then her pupils dilated as she stared up at him. "I'm sorry ... do I know you?"

"No." He offered her a smile, hoping to settle her nerves. He didn't speak to many women, but when he did, he always got that same staggered expression. "But you looked as though you needed a third hand."

"I don't think I could manage if I were an octopus."

He laughed. *Beautiful and a sense of humor.* Most of the women he knew were too serious. "Funny. Are you off to another lecture?"

"No ... I'm late for work. I keep telling my boss not to schedule me on Tuesdays and Thursdays, but he doesn't listen, and then — sorry. TMI. I tend to ramble on, something the professors keep fussing at me about. Thanks. I sent the message, so I can carry my books now. I'm not up on all these new gadgets." She waved her phone. "This is my first cell phone. I can't afford it, but I really needed it. " She smacked her hand over her mouth and reached for her books. "See ... I never shut up."

Derrick couldn't help but smile. She was so cute. "I'll walk you to your car. That way if your boss replies, you can respond quickly."

Her eyes narrowed this time, a look he *wasn't* accustomed to; the few women he talked to trusted him completely. Even the female professors said he had a wonderful bedside manner. "Umm ... it's okay. I take the *T.*"

"Would you like a lift, then, so you aren't late?"

She shook her head. "No. Thank you. I appreciate it ... but I don't even know you."

"Derrick Ashton." He offered her his hand.

The young woman hesitantly extended her slender, creamy-skinned hand. Her hand looked so small and delicate in his larger, olive-skinned hand. "Nice to meet you, Derrick. I'm Janelle Heskin. But still ... "

Derrick released her after a second and lifted his hands in front of him. "I'm harmless, I swear. They wouldn't have accepted me into medical school if I had a record, and I'm here because I want to help people, and you looked like you needed help."

She laughed. "That makes sense. Okay, but I have a bottle of pepper spray, and I'm not afraid to use it."

"Keep it handy, but I assure you, you won't need it. I only want to help." Derrick turned and headed toward his Navigator, hating that she'd see him driving in a fancy new vehicle after her comment about not being able to afford a cell phone. He'd bought it because of the leg and headroom. At six-four, he didn't fit comfortably into too many vehicles, and when his brother was home from school, he appreciated it too. At six-six, his brother barely fit through some doorways.

Derrick held open the passenger door, allowing Janelle to step up. "Nice," she said as he opened the driver's side door. She ran her hand over the soft leather. "Your parents do well, I take it."

"Yeah, but I don't live off my parents' money." He hated when people automatically assumed that. He knew he looked young, but he'd always been a hard worker, and he put in plenty of hours at the clinic. Everyone in his family worked from the time they were sixteen.

"Oh ... okay ..." She paused for a breath, then said, "Just head toward East Somerville."

He cringed without meaning to.

"I know it's not the best neighborhood ... but —"

"Sorry ... that was rude. As I said, I worry about people, especially beautiful young women who walk home alone at night."

She attempted to mutter *yeah right* under her breath, which was impossible; he had excellent hearing. Although he knew she didn't mean for him to hear that, he wanted to laugh at her denial. How could she not think she was beautiful?

Resisting commenting, he just peeked in her direction. "So, what time do you get off work? Would you like to grab something to eat afterward?"

She released a soft exhale. "Derrick, you seem like a really nice guy, but didn't you notice that I'm a lot older than you? How are you even in medical school? I know what you are ... you're one of those young princes from overseas, aren't you? From Romania maybe? You have such dark hair and eyes, like a gypsy."

He laughed. "I'm not so sure if that was a compliment or if I should be offended, but you're not even close." He continued to chuckle as he pulled out his wallet. "I was born in Massachusetts, I assure you, and I'm older than you think." He was also ten years older than his driver's license indicated, but he couldn't share that with her.

She peeked at his date of birth. "Twenty-five? I'm twenty-five! You barely look eighteen, while I probably look thirty," she groaned.

He furrowed his brow. "Most people say I look at least nineteen, so I'm above the legal age to date. That's why I showed you my license, though. No one ever believes me," he said through a laugh, attempting to set her at ease. "And you don't look thirty. Twenty-nine tops," he said, grinning.

She smacked his arm. "Hey, that's just mean to kick a girl when she's already feeling inferior."

"Maybe that's why I can't get a pretty young woman to have dinner with me."

"I'm *sure* you get turned down all the time. Not!"

He chuckled softly. "Actually, you're the first woman I've asked out in a year."

She released a non-believing puff of air. "I'm flattered. But honestly, I really don't have time to date. And ..." She paused, reaching into her backpack and pulling out her wallet too. She flipped it open and held it out for his inspection. "I have an eight-year-old daughter."

He stole a peek into the rearview mirror, then glanced at the picture of Janelle and her daughter. It appeared to be one of those shots taken at a cheap photo box booth in the mall. Her daughter had the same color hair, identical features, same smile. Even with the seventeen-year difference, they looked more like sisters than mother and daughter. "Nice try, but you failed to deter me. How about we study together at a coffee shop."

She released a long sigh. "You're sweet —"

"Oh, no ..." He laughed harder than before. He felt so natural with her. "Not sweet, anything but sweet."

She smiled but then pointed to a diner at the end of the block. "You can drop me off at the back entrance."

Derrick pulled into the alley behind the structure, hoping she didn't walk home from here. He stopped near the back door, next to an overflowing dumpster that reeked. It took everything he had not to pinch his nose. As with most people, the stench didn't bother her. Few had a sense of smell as acute as his.

"Thank you, Derrick. I really appreciate the lift." She reached for her backpack and moved to get out.

Not wanting her to leave, wanting her to know he wasn't feigning an interest, he touched her arm. "Seriously, what time do you get off work?"

With her eyes still cast on the door, her escape, she sighed softly. "Thank you for the ride, Derrick." She opened the door and hopped down, closing it behind her.

He waited while she walked inside, then pulled around to the front of the restaurant to read the hours of service. Unable to keep the smile off his face, he drove away. "I'll see you at ten, Janelle, even if you don't see me."

Derrick sat on the ledge of one of the taller, more vacant rooftops in the city. Not a difficult thing to find in Somerville, but practically impossible to find in Back Bay where he lived. Most of the Victorian Brownstones and new condominium towers had converted the rooftops into getaways, whereas most of the Somerville properties were basic tenements.

Janelle had finished with her last table fifteen minutes ago, but she was still sweeping and doing other menial tasks. He couldn't help but admire a young woman who attended medical school, worked a full-time job, and then went home to an eight-year-old daughter. When did she find time to study?

"Good night, Bob. Don't forget. No Tuesdays or Thursdays, okay?" Janelle called as she walked out the back door of the diner — no escort.

"Yeah, yeah. See ya, Elle!"

Derrick smiled. *Elle.* Cute, but he liked Janelle. He watched as she rounded the building, following her track down the street. As she turned the corner, he took off in a sprint and leapt onto the next building so he'd be able to see where she headed.

Janelle scanned the area cautiously, her hand stuffed inside her pocket. Probably holding the pepper spray. Good, but not good enough. He knew he wasn't supposed to do this. The family had enacted the policy years ago. It was too dangerous to *watch* and *protect*, as his father and grandfather used to do, but how could he sleep at night knowing this young woman could become a statistic any day?

She stopped in front of a brick building but didn't go inside. Instead, she glanced up and down the street as she pulled out her cell phone.

Derrick peeked over the side of the building, making sure it was clear, then slid down the fire escape to the pavement. While he'd waited for her to get off work, he'd gone to his condo and changed into all black clothes, typical *watching* gear. No, he wasn't supposed to *watch*, but sometimes his family had to when one of their own was committing crimes, something that hadn't happened here in New England in years, but he'd helped other families across the country.

A few seconds after her phone call, Janelle was still standing on the street. *Did she have a date?* he wondered. Is this why she turned him down?

The door flung open, and a miniature version of Janelle bopped down the brick steps. Watching the happy child reminded him of playing Ringolevio with his cousins and brother. Base had always been the brick steps leading to the front door of his parents' house.

The child held up a paper for Janelle. "Look what I made you today, Mommy."

Janelle accepted the black-and-white image. From the quick glimpse he'd caught, it appeared to be a charcoal drawing. "Wow. This is beautiful." Janelle surveyed the street again, and then stooped in front of the young girl. "Honey, did you trace this?"

The girl whipped her head back and forth. "Uh-uh."

"Baby, you have talent."

"Really?"

Janelle squeezed her daughter's shoulders. "Really, really. We need to get you to some art classes, baby. I'm impressed." Janelle held the paper under the streetlight to get a better view.

Derrick smiled. She wasn't patronizing the child. If she hadn't traced it, she *was* good.

Janelle took her daughter's hand and strolled down the street. "So, what else did you do today, Kristina?"

How could he not protect this beautiful, loving mother and her child from the crime surrounding them? He thought about what had happened to his mother. She'd understand. His father would understand too. But they wouldn't know. He wouldn't get involved with Janelle, not that she'd let him anyway. He'd just be her friend.

Derrick followed, but remained far away. If anyone approached them, though, he'd break every rule his family had made. He'd never stand by idly. Two blocks down, both of them stepped into another building. Now he knew where she lived, and it was only a few blocks from her work. Next time they spoke, he'd find out what nights she took off, which he suspected were typically Tuesdays and Thursdays, and he'd just privately escort her home. He could spare fifteen minutes of his day to protect a woman who obviously didn't have anyone else helping her.

Nothing could ever come of them; his family would never approve. She was too old, or he was too young, they'd say. Whether he wanted to admit it or not, he knew they'd be right.

And then there was Tori. He knew what she wanted, but it'd be five years until she returned to the States permanently, and as much as he liked her — loved her — he wasn't *in love* with her.

He'd only seen Janelle walk into a room, and his soul had practically leapt out of his body. His father'd said he'd know. He'd said his soul would know whom he was destined to be with before he did. It wasn't looks either. Although the two women were polar opposites, Tori was one of the most beautiful women on the planet. He'd never had a problem with wanting her, but he knew better than to screw around with her head. He had to wait until he felt something inside his head and heart, not his loins. Otherwise, her uncle and father would make sure he never felt anything again, he was certain.

Chapter Two

"Morning," Derrick called as Janelle stepped off the bus.

Janelle turned. "Oh ... umm ... hi." She shook her head. "Were you waiting for me?"

Derrick shrugged, handing her a cup of Dunkin'. "I figured since you didn't have time to have coffee with me, I'd bring it to you." He took a pull off his water bottle.

She rested her hands on her hips. "Well, where's yours? How can we have coffee together if you already drank yours?"

"Oh, I don't drink coffee."

She laughed. "You're a bit odd, Derrick."

He smiled in response. "So I've been told. Can I walk with you?"

"We can sit. I have a few minutes today. I'm not always so frazzled."

"You don't look frazzled at all. I'd be, if I were a single parent, working a full-time job, and going to medical school. How do you do it?"

Janelle walked to a squat brick planter surrounding the hospital, which enabled the area to have something other than a parking lot surrounding the mass complex of buildings. The trees and shrubs added color to the otherwise monotonous shades of beige and red brick surfaces. Unlike some of the architectural masterpieces in the Boston area, the hospital buildings were just tall and square, boring, nothing to catch the eye.

She sat down and lifted her coffee cup in salute. "Plenty of caffeine and the ability to go days without sleep."

Derrick sat too, angling his body so he could look into her eyes. She had beautiful hazel eyes, the color of peridot with golden flecks that seemed to dance in the sunlight. "No one can go days without sleep; they only think they can. It catches up with you. It's extremely unhealthy."

She lifted her eyes, but resisted a full-out eye roll, it seemed. "Why thank you, Doctor. So why exactly are you here? I told you, I'm flattered, but you still look as though you're barely out of high school, and as handsome as you are, I simply don't have time to add one more thing to my schedule."

"Ouch. Another compliment and slap in one sentence. You're good at those. Are you sure you're not a law student? You'd be good at cross-examining."

She closed her eyes and shook her head again. "I'm serious. You're such a handsome man ... women must throw themselves at you."

He laughed. "No ... but again, thank you. I don't want anything from you, Janelle. I swear. I just want to be your friend."

"Oh, so you're a sucker for a damsel in distress, is that it? I assure you, my hands may be full, but I'm no damsel."

"Wow ... you're tough." He lifted his hands in surrender. "Okay ... no rescuing. No dating ..." he paused, "but who couldn't use a friend? It's actually better that you aren't interested in me. We can really be friends, then."

She bit her lip, but a chuckle still escaped. "You're incorrigible."

"Heard that one too. So, how about it? Can we be friends? I could use a study partner."

She nodded slowly, so Derrick took the close and ran with it. "What's your number? I'll program it in my phone. That way when I have a question I can't answer at three a.m., I'll have someone I know who's wide awake."

She read off her number, then took another sip of coffee. "We'd better go. It probably won't look professional if I'm late again."

Derrick stood and picked up her backpack.

"Umm ..." She just stood there, a blank stare in her eyes, as though no one had ever helped her. Had nobody truly ever offered her a hand, or was she one of those women who took offense when a man tried to be a gentleman?

Whether she liked it or not, he had to be who he was, as much as he could anyway. He glared at her. "Yes?"

"Never mind. Thanks."

Janelle strolled silently beside him as they made their way to the main entry. "I have clinic duty today, so this is my exit."

"Ah ... fun," Derrick said. "I get to shadow."

"More fun." She accepted her backpack from him, but didn't turn away. "So, should I expect to see you later?"

"Are you working this afternoon?"

She shook her head and smiled. "No. Today I get to study without pulling waitressing or mommy duty. The sitter has Kristina until five o'clock, so I have about three hours."

"Meet me up front at two o'clock then." He was supposed to take over the nightshift at his family's hospital, but someone else would cover him until he arrived. His father knew he got caught up at school sometimes. Nothing could come of this, he reminded himself for the hundredth time. He just wanted a friend.

"Okay ..." She didn't sound completely at ease with their impromptu engagement, even though she'd opened the door for his request, which he just realized came out like a statement, not a request.

"See you then." Derrick smiled and turned. It felt awkward, as though he was supposed to kiss her goodbye. Friends didn't kiss each other goodbye, though. He was thirty-five, and he felt like an adolescent who'd just secured his date to the senior prom. Of course, not only did he look nineteen, his family tended to mature slower too, so he did have the mentality of a twenty-something male, not always good when you were trying to procure a *friends only* relationship.

How could he ignore the way his heart leapt every time she said his name ... how his soul knew from the first moment he'd seen her? It was as if there was a connection somehow. He needed to call his mother. Something was off about this. It wasn't normal. Not yet, though. First, they'd have an innocent study session over lunch. She hadn't agreed to lunch, but he was sure she wouldn't mind.

Derrick glanced at the clock over the patient for the tenth time since he'd followed the attending physician into the room.

If the doctor hadn't been training, he would have been long gone by now. Instead, he asked the patient tons of questions that the man had probably answered a hundred times over. The symptoms were cut and dried; any first-year resident could answer, and Derrick had no desire to be a star pupil, so he rarely spoke up.

"Mr. Ashton, do you have an appointment elsewhere?"

Derrick blinked. "Yes, sir."

"Then, go."

As always, Derrick took his close. He'd deal with the repercussions later. He glanced at his watch. "Damn." He skipped the elevator and made for the stairs. He listened and then did something else that would get him in major trouble if he was caught, possibly even endanger his entire family, but he was on the first floor in a second.

He pushed through the metal door and slid down the foyer a few yards toward the front entrance. Since he looked nineteen, he could act like it sometimes.

Janelle was pressing keys on her phone when he calmly walked out of the hospital. "Oh, I thought you were going to stand me up."

"Not a chance." He took her backpack from her, slung it over his shoulder, then reached for her hand, pulling her toward his Lincoln. Her hand was warm in his, but her pulse quickened. He was making her nervous. It'd felt so natural that he hadn't even thought about it, but it was wrong of him. He'd assured her they would just be friends, and he couldn't take a chance that anyone in his family would think otherwise.

He released her hand as he held open the door and resisted watching her step up inside. He walked around to the driver's side and inhaled a deep breath before entering. They'd have lunch, study, and then that'd be it. He wouldn't bug her to go out with him again.

"So ... Janelle ... have you ever had sushi?"

"Sushi? As in raw fish?"

Derrick dipped his head, resisting a chuckle. Sushi had only become popular in the last few years in Boston, but he and his family practically lived on it, since it was one of the few meats they could eat in public without being stared at. "There's more to it than that, but yes. I'll help you order."

"I usually just grab a smoothie and go to the library, Derrick."

"My treat. You'll love it, I promise."

"Okay."

He buckled his seatbelt and took off.

As soon as he pulled in front of the building, Janelle's eyes darted to the six-story brick exterior, then back at the waiting valet. She peered down at her jeans and T-shirt as the valet opened the door. She stepped out, but Derrick was certain she planned to make a run for it. He darted around the vehicle and handed over his keys without his normal spiel about being kind to his vehicle.

"Derrick ... "

He rested his hand on the small of her back. "You look great, and I promise I'll have you home before five."

As they walked inside, her eyes shot up to the two-story entry and the waterfall, then back at him. "I'm not dressed ... I don't have this kind of money —"

Derrick pointed to the lounge. "We'll sit in here. It's casual, and it's more fun to watch the chefs as they make the rolls anyway. Come on. I haven't had anyone to go out with in a while."

She shook her head but allowed him to escort her to a booth in the bar area.

He knew it was a mistake, but he didn't care. All the time he'd spent with Tori, as many times as they'd made out, he'd never felt even remotely like this. *Just friends ... they could only be friends.*

"So tell me about yourself," Derrick started. "I'll give you a list. Just answer whatever you want. Where'd you go to college? Are you from Boston? Do your parents live here? Do you have any siblings?"

It worked. She laughed. He'd hoped to ease her tension. "What is this, the dating game?"

"I don't play games, Janelle." *Liar* ... he was playing the riskiest game of his life.

"I think you do, Derrick."

He'd managed to put her on edge again. He picked up her hand. "I'm sorry. Let me rephrase. I've never played games ..." He sighed. "Where did you go to college?" He quickly got back on track.

"Believe it or not, Harvard."

"Really? So your parents do well?" He threw her question from yesterday back at her.

"No ... they weren't well-off. And they died in a car wreck when I was seventeen. A little-known fact about Harvard, though: if you're smart enough — and determined enough — you can get in. As an orphaned child, I applied for every grant I could find, and I do have a mountain of student loans that will hit after I'm working for eighteen months, but it'll be worth it. Anything I can do to give Kristina a better life will be worth it." Her jaw tightened as though she were holding back emotion.

"I'm so sorry," Derrick offered. They needed a lull in the conversation so she didn't get too uncomfortable. He signaled the waiter, who had politely brought them water and then walked away when Derrick motioned him off. The waiter headed back toward them. Derrick didn't bring women here, but he was a regular. "Would you like me to order for you?"

Janelle nodded. "Yes, please. I wouldn't have a clue."

"Are you allergic to anything, or is there anything you don't like?"

"Nope. I'll eat just about anything you put in front of me."

Perfect. The woman was perfect ... except for one small detail — okay, one *large* detail. He ordered for both of them, then went back to his questioning.

"And your daughter ... what about her? If you don't mind my asking, that is. I hope you receive assistance from her father."

Janelle sighed. "Kristina, thankfully, slipped through the cracks."

Derrick tilted his head. "What do you mean? As in, you made a mistake?"

"No. Never. I've dedicated my life to her and my education. I told you, I don't have time to date."

"So, what are you saying?"

"Kristina isn't really my daughter. She's my sister. But luckily, the authorities didn't pay much attention until I was legally old enough to be her guardian. Otherwise, they would have taken her away from me. So, I've raised her as my own, told everyone, including Kristina, that my parents had claimed her on her birth certificate because I was so young when I had her. The schools don't question me because I have all her records, along with my parents' death certificates. Either way, I'd be her next of kin now."

"You've taken care of all of this since you were seventeen?"

She nodded and a tear slipped down her cheek. "Not that you'd ever meet Kristina, but if you ever do, please don't tell her. She might be angry with me. And I only did it because I didn't want her to grow up thinking she was an imposition. She hasn't been. She is as much of a daughter to me as if I'd had her."

"I promise." Derrick thought about how loving Janelle had been to Kristina last night. How she took the time to look at her drawing, said that they'd get her to art classes. Most young parents weren't that attentive. She really loved her. It also explained how they were so alike in their physical appearance. Most mothers and daughters couldn't pass for twins because of the father's influence on their genes. But since they had the same biological parents, it made sense that he'd thought Kristina had looked like a miniature version of Janelle last night. "Although, I would like to meet her someday."

"Maybe."

The waiter brought out their plates, providing another break in their conversation. His meal was exactly how he always liked it. Mostly, he didn't explain to every waiter that he wanted sushi, but he didn't want all the accompaniments; he only wanted the fish.

Derrick picked up a set of chopsticks. "Allow me to make your first one." He drizzled a drop of soy sauce to add flavor, a thin slice of ginger, then peeked up at her. "Do you like wasabi? Horseradish?"

She offered him an assuring nod.

He added just a dab and then held the sushi roll out in front of her. As sexily as he'd imagined, she leaned forward and took the bite off the chopsticks. If he knew it, why had he put himself in this situation? What was wrong with him? He sucked in a breath, then absently set the thin strips of bamboo on her plate. "Now, you try," he said as casually as possible while his heart thrashed in his chest.

He ate his food quickly. They needed to get back. He'd made a mistake. He couldn't do this.

"You okay?" she asked.

He smiled. "Yeah. How could I not be?" He sucked down his water, then pushed away the plate. "You like it?"

"It's very good." Her tone was clipped. She'd recognized his hesitancy.

"Do you plan to stay in Boston?" he asked, attempting to get back to normal conversation.

"It's okay, Derrick. I know I have a lot of baggage. I tried to warn you. We can just go."

He sighed. "Janelle, don't ever let anyone tell you that. You are an incredible woman. To have done so much for Kristina and yourself, when so many others would have just laid down and cried, *poor me*. I'm honored to have met you. It's just —"

She reached across the table. "You don't have to explain anything. Life is complicated. Obviously if a man as good-looking as yourself hasn't dated in more than a year, you have a reason. You don't have to explain anything to me."

He smiled at her. "I'm not gay."

Janelle's face turned bright red. So that had been what she was thinking. He could have let her think that; it would have been an easier explanation, but he didn't think he could hide his attraction to her, and there was no way he could tell her the truth.

"It wouldn't matter to me one way or another. As I said, I still want to be just your friend. Can you do that, Derrick? It's clear that you made that point for a reason. And I assure you, as attractive as you are, I just don't have time for a man in my life, so let's just keep our secrets, okay? You don't owe me anything."

He turned his hand so hers was resting in his. "Okay. That's probably the best for both of us. Just friends." But her pulse quickened in his hand, and his own heart rate matched hers beat for beat.

Derrick parked outside Janelle's apartment. She was supposed to pick up her daughter only a couple blocks away, but she hadn't directed him there, so maybe she didn't want him to know where she was. It was good that she was wary. It'd keep her safe.

He got out of the vehicle, even though she hadn't waited for him to open the door for her. He couldn't just drop her off at the curb; it felt ungentlemanly-like.

He walked her to the bottom of her steps, and she turned. "Thank you, Derrick. It was excellent and definitely not in my budget."

He stood motionless for a second. He wanted to kiss her; God, he wanted to kiss her. *Friends don't kiss*, he reminded himself. *They don't have sex either, and they definitely don't fall for each other.* He stepped back, smiling. "My pleasure."

Dejection was clear in her eyes, even if she tried to cover it with a smile. They weren't meant to be. He spun away as his eyes burned, a feeling he'd never experienced. He'd never been unhappy in his life.

As he entered the vehicle, he turned to see her watching from the top step. He hadn't even kissed her, and yet, he'd broken her heart too. Two short interludes and he'd felt more than he'd ever felt for any woman.

He pulled the vehicle into drive and sped off. He was only going around the block. He'd slip on his hoodie and he'd be ready to *watch*. From now on, that's all he'd do. Keep her safe. It was the least he could do for the wonderful woman he could never have.

Chapter Three

D errick!" his brother's deep voice echoed through his earpiece. "Dude, I just landed. I'll get my luggage and meet you out front."

"You're at Logan? Why didn't you tell me?"

"It's spring break, dude. I did tell you. I emailed you, left you messages. Where've you been?"

"Hanging around. Okay. On my way."

The line clicked. His brother had always been matter-of-fact like in his style. He was looking forward to seeing Michael. He didn't think it was possible, but he actually missed his bratty brother. Five years difference in age wasn't a lot as an adult, but as a teenager, it'd been annoying on many occasions. Especially since his larger and heavier brother always wanted to challenge him, as did Mike's best friend, Jonas; and Ry, Jonas' brother. For that matter, Tori liked to wrestle too. Growing up around almost all guys, she'd always been rather tomboyish.

He'd spoken to Tori at least once a week over the last few months, and she'd always seemed distraught and mentioned coming home, even though she knew that was out of the question. She'd asked him on more than one occasion if they'd attempt a relationship when she returned from London. He'd deflected as often as he could. She still had almost five years. All he could hope was that she'd meet someone while she was there.

Derrick circled until Mike texted him an *OK*. He pulled up to the airport arrivals and couldn't keep from sighing. They were all here, and they were all behaving like college kids as they wrestled with one another outside the terminal. Yeah, it was spring break, but they were professors, not students.

"Dude!" Michael called through the window as Derrick pulled up in front of the group.

And if he called him *dude* one more time, Derrick might just grant his brother's wish of another wrestling match. Derrick hopped out and walked around to the sidewalk. He accepted a pat on the back from Jonas and Ry and then a hug from his brother, who quickly stepped back after a second, knowing Tori would want her time.

"Hey, Tori."

She uncharacteristically leapt into his arms, pressing her lips against his. Her mouth worked its magic, parting his lips, and then her tongue touched his. She was an incredible kisser, but he couldn't do this.

He pulled back, gasping for air. "Wow. What a great reception." He took the bag propped up beside her and hauled it to the cargo area.

Clearly, Tori wasn't buying his attempt. He was certain she'd felt what he'd felt. Nothing. He loved her; she was one of his closest friends, but he'd felt nothing. Shouldn't he? Shouldn't a kiss from a woman you'd kissed a thousand times, but hadn't in almost a year, make your toes curl, your heart pulse, and other parts of your anatomy react?

He walked to the passenger side and opened the door for her. She got in, but didn't even look at him. The three men crawled in the backseat, chattering about which club they'd hit first.

"Man, am I glad to be back in Boston!" Michael hooted out the back window.

Derrick raised the rear window and activated the child locks. He glared in the rearview mirror at his immature sibling. "Try to control yourself, brother. You're not really a college kid on spring break, even if you look like one."

Michael wiggled his eyebrows. "The ladies don't know that. To them, I'm a twenty-year-old college student from abroad. I can even speak in a British tongue, and they eat up that stuff."

"You are also underage according to your driver's license, and you barely look as though you're out of high school."

"Never stopped me before. Besides, I have a big brother who'll let me use his ID."

Derrick raised a brow. "You have another brother I'm unaware of?"

"Are you kidding me, man?"

"Nope. If you want to stay at my place and drink, fine. I know your real age. But I'm not giving you my ID. You get busted, I get busted, and there goes my career."

Michael punched the back of his seat.

"You put a hole in my new leather, and I won't buy you any wine either," Derrick chided.

Michael huffed, but Jonas and Ry laughed, smacking his brother upside the head. Tori sat in the seat next to him without saying a word.

Derrick reached over and picked up her hand. He didn't say he was sorry; he didn't say he'd try. He just held her hand, hoping he could feel something. Just a flutter ... anything. If he could *fall* for Tori, everything would be fine. It'd remove all doubt.

She squeezed his hand, letting him know that she forgave him. She always forgave him. She knew what she wanted. What she'd always wanted. The hang-up was his, not hers.

Derrick peeked in the rearview mirror before he changed lanes, and locked eyes with Jonas. They'd never gotten along well; they merely tolerated each other. He was an okay guy, but he was a hothead, and losing your temper could get the family in trouble. Of course, falling for someone outside the family could get you in trouble too, so who was he to talk?

He and Janelle had stuck to their promise, though. In the last month, they'd met several times a week over coffee — and water — and studied. They had lunch a few times, but no more five-star eateries, she'd insisted. They talked and had fun, but he kept his distance. Then, on the nights she worked, he made sure that she and Kristina got home safely. She never went out, so he never had to worry. She pinched every dime.

Derrick stopped by a liquor store and purchased two cases of wine, the only type of alcohol that he and his family could drink. Chardonnay, because it went with everything, and merlot, because Tori liked merlot.

As soon as they reached his apartment, Tori grabbed a bottle of merlot and headed into his kitchen. She went directly to the drawer that housed the corkscrew, then pulled a wineglass off the rack. She deftly removed the cork, filled the glass, downed it, then filled it again.

Derrick followed her into the kitchen, placing his hand over hers. "I'm sorry. You took me by surprise."

She tucked the bottle under her arm and looked up at him. "Bring your own bottle and meet me on the roof."

He knew he didn't have a choice. He opened a bottle of chardonnay, downed a glass, and then filled another. Unlike his brother, he rarely drank, but he needed to loosen up.

He followed a few minutes later. Michael and his buds had already cranked up the music on some video channel, so they'd have fun all by themselves. They'd probably leave the apartment after they had a few, but as long as his brother didn't have his ID, he didn't care. Even drunk, Michael could outrun any of *The Boys* at Boston PD.

Derrick pushed through the door to the rooftop. Tori stood at the ledge, looking out over the Back Bay skyline. The night air was cool, but she'd removed the sweatshirt she'd been wearing earlier, displaying her finely sculpted arms. He walked up behind her and set the bottle on the wall.

In a relaxed, unhurried manner, she turned to him. The wine must have started working. He couldn't deny that Tori was all kinds of beautiful. Sleek black hair that almost reached her slender waist. Legs that seemed to go forever, wrapped in close-fitting, faded-in-all-the-right-places jeans and a body-hugging, white tank top that showed off her ample chest. Any man would jump at the chance to have her, and she wanted him.

The two glasses of wine he'd downed warmed his insides. He stepped forward and wrapped his arms around her.

She draped her hands around his neck and molded her body against his. "Let's try this again." She touched her lips to his, and he accepted her this time. He moved his hands through her hair. He wanted her. He wanted her badly. Maybe if they …

She pressed her hips against his, pulling him with her as she backed up against the wall.

Coming to his senses as his body lit up with a hunger to consume her, he retracted from her lips. "Tori ... "

"Maybe if we ..." She kissed him harder, and her hands gripped him powerfully. "Maybe if we just tried ... maybe we'd *fall*."

Everything in him wanted to experience her fully, but he knew he couldn't allow that to happen. He couldn't lie to her. His brother could whisper plenty of sweet nothings into a woman's ear. Michael had no problem taking what he wanted. Derrick couldn't seem to clear his head.

"No, Tori. It's not right."

"Then let's just enjoy it. It doesn't matter if nothing happens. I know this is me pressing this. I don't expect anything from you."

He pulled back. "No ... "

"Derrick, I'm a thirty-year-old virgin. I've waited for you for twelve years. At what point do we just go for it?"

He pressed his hand to her cheek. "Why? Why me? Tori, you have five more years in London. Most of us meet our soul mates in school. Why are you waiting for me?"

She narrowed her eyes. "Because I love you ... "

In the nicest tone he could muster, he reminded her, "Love isn't enough. You know that. I love you too. But I'm not going to take advantage of you."

"Even if I ask you to?"

He smiled. "Even if you ask me to."

She dropped her head against his chest. "I've missed you."

Derrick brushed her hair off her shoulder and pressed his lips to her neck, inhaling. "I missed you too. I really have. You're my best friend." And damn, he wanted her, but he couldn't do it.

She lifted her head. "I wish I wasn't. Then maybe you'd be willing to take advantage of me."

Derrick laughed. "That still wouldn't happen, Tori. I'm just not that kind of guy. I think you're confusing me with the other Ashton downstairs."

"Yeah," she laughed, "Mike's a slut, and he doesn't seem to know how to turn it off."

Derrick pressed his forehead against hers. "I know. I really am glad to see you, Tori. It's been so boring here without you — or Mike, as hard as it is to believe I'd ever admit that. Don't tell him, though."

Her dark eyes glistened in the dim light. "Maybe I could just come home now."

"You know that's not possible."

"Will you wait for me, Derrick?"

"What other woman would I choose? There's no one like you. The few women my age came home from school attached," he lowered his gaze at her, "which is normal."

"You didn't come home attached," she said, smiling.

"That's because I left the only girl I ever cared about, ever even kissed, in London."

Tori pressed her body against his again. "Then let's just go to your room."

"There are three other men in my apartment. Not happening."

She moved from underneath his arm. "I'll go remedy that right now."

Derrick reached for her. "No. Can we just talk?"

She sighed. "You are *so* not a guy."

He directed her to a bench situated between a few potted evergreen shrubs. The night was clear and cool, and she had to be freezing. He pulled her into his arms. "Believe me, I'm a guy, and you, as always, are the most beautiful woman I've ever seen. But tonight, this week, nothing is going to happen between us. And yes, I will wait until you come home, and I *will* try. But we're not going to have sex until I feel it in my heart first."

"But, Derrick, I've heard that the only way to really *fall* is to have sex."

"Did my brother tell you that?"

She lowered her head.

"Tori ... I know you don't have a mom, but maybe you should stop hanging out with just us guys. That is not true. My mother, and my father, assured me I'd feel it in my head and heart before I felt it anywhere." Tired of having this conversation every time they talked, he sighed. "Besides," he nudged up her chin so she'd look at him, "What if we did *fall*? How could I live here without you while you're in another country for five years? You know that'd be impossible."

"If we fell, maybe I could stay."

"No ... you have to complete your training. It's the law. We're all required. We don't have so many laws that we can't abide by them. And since I'm going to be overseer —"

She bolted upright. "You are? My uncle didn't tell me that."

"Shh ... it's not public yet. But according to my father, they'll announce it at the next meeting. Since the four of you are home, it'll probably be this week."

Tori kissed him quickly. "I'm so proud of you, Derrick. Are you ready? It's a lot of responsibility, being in charge of all the families in New England. And my uncle said the overseer always has enemies. Even though he's part of the council, he said if there were any rogues who didn't want to follow our ways, they always blamed the overseer if they banished them."

"I can handle it."

"I have no doubt about that. After all, you're the strongest in the family."

Tori nuzzled against him, and he automatically wrapped his arms around her. He did love her, and he would wait for her to come home. He didn't have any concern that another creatus woman would turn his head. Only one woman had captured his heart and mind, Janelle. But ... Janelle was human.

Chapter Four

Derrick stood proudly beside his father. It was an honor, even though everyone assumed he'd step right in as overseer with his father and uncle as part of the council. And then, Tori's uncle, Dean, who'd always been like an uncle to him.

Michael and Tori whooped and clapped, as did all the other families within their family. Well, except Jonas. Jonas just stared at him, lightly tapping his hands together. Derrick didn't think he was actually jealous of him, so it must be something else. Jonas' gaze wandered around the room and fell on his brother and Tori. Ahh ... that's the problem. Jonas wanted Tori, and Tori only had eyes for him. Of all the eligible bachelors, he'd prefer it to be anyone but Jonas. If it were anyone but Jonas, he'd probably step in and see what he could do to get them together.

His father adjourned the meeting, but nodded at Derrick as though he wanted him to stay. Derrick sat, but watched a sullen-looking Tori gaze back. She'd evidently had plans for after the meeting. Derrick glanced at his watch. He had plans too. The town of Harvard was a little more than an hour's drive from Boston, so he needed to get going soon.

The room cleared and Dean approached him. "Congratulations, Derrick. You know I've always thought of you as one of my own, and I can't think of a better man for the job." He gestured to the door, even though no one was there, then sat down beside Derrick, his mouth close to his ear. It wasn't easy to keep secrets among the family. "What about you and my niece? Anything new on that front?"

Derrick's face heated. "We've been close for years, sir, but no, she still has almost five years of school."

"Nothing stops love, son. Tori wants you ... we've spoken several times." He pulled back to look at him. "But you don't know?"

Derrick looked to his father. Thirty-five years old, and he felt like a teenager being interrogated by his girlfriend's father, and Tori wasn't even his girlfriend, even if everyone thought she was. Never once had he told her that. He'd always been honest. He'd only promised that he'd wait. "No, sir. I don't."

Dean narrowed his eyes, then lifted his chin at Derrick's father. "Lyn, haven't you explained the birds and the bees to your son?"

The three men laughed. Derrick didn't find his love life, or lack thereof, funny.

Matthew Ashton sat down on the other side of Derrick and smacked him on the knee. "I assure you, Dean, my nephew knows all about how things work. He's just sensible. Aren't you, Derrick? We didn't choose him as overseer lightly. He knows the laws, so he's keeping them. I wouldn't want my wife across the Atlantic either."

Derrick nodded, silently thanking his uncle, who just so happened to be the attorney in the family. He handled the law within and outside family business. His practice also took on other family law issues, just as their clinic treated humans. They still had to live and work in the human world.

Lyn Ashton stepped in front of Derrick and offered him his hand, pulling him up from the chair, away from the inquisition. "Let's go eat, gentlemen, or Sabrina will be out looking for us."

The two men strolled off, and Lyn held Derrick back again. His intelligent eyes trained on Derrick's and he moved closer. "What is going on with you?"

Derrick narrowed his eyes, tilting his head, asking what he meant without speaking.

"You've stared down at your watch fifteen times since we started," Lyn said. "And you've been late to take over the nightshift several times in the last few weeks, and you're never late for anything."

Derrick closed his eyes. He couldn't lie to his father, but this wasn't a conversation for here. "Can we talk tomorrow?"

"Do you have school in the morning?"

"No."

"Then let's meet for breakfast on the wharf. It's private enough."

Derrick nodded, but cringed inside. How had his father known? He didn't think he was just upset; he knew the conversation was private too. His eyes darted to his watch again. "I have to go. Will you apologize for me, please?"

His father nodded, but then shook his head. "Be smart, Derrick."

"I will, Dad."

The next morning, Derrick strolled along the wharf, taking in the sounds. He loved coming here. The smells from the harbor, the cry of the seagulls, the salty taste in the air always reminded him of when he was a child without a care in the world. Truly, he had no cares right now. Other than Janelle. He worried about her safety, he worried about her health, and he hated that he couldn't be with her. That's what his father had seen in his eyes: hopelessness. He'd always been happy, always been carefree. Suddenly, he was morose.

What good was life if you couldn't be with the one you loved? And he did love her; he knew he did. He didn't have to kiss her or make love to her to know he loved her. He just had to spend a few days a week working, studying, and eating with her to know how he felt. Maybe it was because he knew he couldn't have her.

Nice try, Derrick. If that were it, he'd be like Michael, interested in everything that walked upright and was female.

Derrick heard his brother's laugh before he saw him. He dropped behind the seawall, wondering what his brother was doing here — and so early. He'd been up past four again last night.

"Derrick," his father called.

Derrick pulled himself back onto the wharf. His father had brought his brother. Why?

Lyn Ashton motioned both of them to the park. "You know the family is counting on you. Both of you."

"What do you mean?" Derrick asked.

"We need a new position, and although Michael won't be back for a while, we think he's the right man for the job. As overseer, you could reject him or the new role within the family, but I think you'll agree we've needed this for some time. We also want Michael to finish his medical degree, as we still need medical staff. But we think he'd be better suited as head of national security. He has an eye for noticing things."

"Hell, yeah, I do!" Michael resounded.

His father glared down at his youngest son. "That'll be enough with the language. I didn't rear my sons to talk like that."

If it were possible, Michael looked contrite. Not many men took down Michael; he was a beast. But his father could knock him to his knees with a few words and a pointed gaze. Good. His brother had been getting on his last nerve this week.

Lyn shifted his scrutiny back to Derrick. "He saw you, Derrick."

"What?" Derrick bolted off the bench.

"Sit down."

Derrick plopped back down, but glared at his brother. He couldn't believe that he'd ratted him out. He probably thought it was for his own good, and Derrick was sure Michael hadn't told anyone other than his father, but still. His own brother? How could he?

"Who is she?" his father continued.

Derrick shook his head. "No one. Just a fellow student," he lied lightly, but it was the truth. As much as he didn't want her to be just a friend, Janelle and he had done nothing but talk.

"Are you seeing each other?"

"No ... not in the way you mean. We go to school together and have had a few study sessions."

Michael raised his head. "And you've been following her home after work ... in watching gear."

"Is that true?" his father demanded.

He released a breath. "I'm not *watching*, Dad. I know the law. Only her. She has an eight-year-old daughter and lives alone in a horrible part of town ... She might as well have a sign on her back that says *rob me*."

"Derrick ..." His father released a long breath. "We can't interfere —"

"You of all people —"

"Don't interrupt me, son, and times have changed. And the two of you, you're special. We can't afford ... if anyone found out ... we'd lose both of you."

"Okay ... I'll figure out something. I'll figure out how to get her out of there ..." He stood again, only this time respectfully. "I just need a few weeks, and then I'll figure out how to get her the money to move."

His father shook his head. "No ... it has to stop now. If anything does happen ... there are cameras everywhere. No. I'm sorry, son."

Derrick ran his hands through his hair, but he didn't have to second-guess what he was about to say. "Then I quit. I'll leave the family."

Lyn rested his hand on his shoulder. "Derrick, what are you thinking? Have you fallen for her?"

"No, I swear we're just friends, but there's a connection. I can't explain it. I don't know what it is, but I can't ... I can't abandon her."

Lyn squeezed his arm. "I don't want you to continue, but I don't want you to leave either. I'll get back with you tomorrow. See if I can come up with anything."

"Thanks, Dad. She doesn't work tonight, so I'll stay away."

His father walked off, leaving Michael and him standing in the park. So much for breakfast, and now he had to deal with Michael. He was supposed to meet Janelle for lunch today. He could at least cancel that. It'd hurt, but his father was right. The longer he let this go, the harder it'd be. They really were just friends, but he knew if he wasn't careful, that status could change at any given time. Her heart had started to race more often when he got close to her, and she'd brushed her hand up against him more than a few times the last time they'd studied. Something about having to whisper, feeling her warm breath on his ear, made the library more dangerous than a romantic restaurant.

"So, Bro, what do you want to do today? Maybe we could go back to your place and discuss ideas for my new position. I have a few things I want to run by you. Stuff I can start working on while I'm at school even."

Michael wanted to do something other than get drunk and pick up girls? "Sounds good, man. Let me just make a call."

Derrick strolled away from Michael, but then, even though he thought it was impersonal, he decided he'd text Janelle. No matter how low he spoke, Michael would hear him.

Sorry. In a meeting. Can't make lunch. D. He knew it'd be a few minutes; she was slow. He'd shown her how to use T9, but she hated it.

It's OK. I'm going to pick up a shift at work anyway.

She also refused to abbreviate, said her education wouldn't allow it. He was surprised she'd even shortened *okay.* But she was going to work? That meant that he'd lied to his father. Well, at the time he hadn't lied. Just one more night.

OK. Stay safe.

Always. :)

Derrick snapped his phone closed and headed back to Michael.

"So tell me about this new chica. You dog —"

"Mike, I'm really not in the mood, and I'd rather this not get to anyone else. I've done nothing wrong. Hell, I haven't even kissed Janelle. We're just friends. But if this got back to Tori ... "

"You think she'd finally throw in the towel?"

Derrick shook his head, resisting laughing at his brother's apparent excitement at that prospect. So Tori had at least two potential suitors other than him, and he was sure there were others at school from other parts of the world who'd jump at the chance to be with her. If she'd take her focus off him, maybe she'd see that. But, Michael or Jonas? He didn't want her with either of them. Neither was good enough for her.

"No, I don't think she would, but it'd still upset her, and the last thing I want is to hurt Tori."

"I know, man. She's a great woman. I just wish — let's go."

Not wanting to talk about this anymore, Derrick was fine with not knowing what Michael wanted to say. He'd listen to what Michael had for ideas, and then he'd figure out how to get away for fifteen minutes.

Chapter Five

Derrick took the same path he always did as he followed Janelle home, watching that she made it to her second-story apartment before one of the crackheads that lived a block away robbed her for the few bucks she might be carrying. He also kept an eye on the man who'd spent only six months in jail on a rape charge.

Janelle Heskin was smart, though, so she'd make it out of here soon enough. Not soon enough for his liking, but all he could do was watch. She wouldn't understand if he gave her the money to move, and she'd never accept a handout. Maybe his uncle could set up a grant for medical students. Through some dummy corporation they used to buy safe houses. That'd work.

"Caught 'cha!" Michael said, plopping down in front of him.

Derrick shoved him out of the way, then charged around the next building, moving quickly so he'd lose his younger brother. He wasn't supposed to run, but it was dark, and he was dressed all in black. Most residents were too oblivious to pay anyone attention anyway. One of the reasons he felt compelled to watch over Janelle. If she even had a car, he'd feel better. She didn't think walking a few blocks was unsafe, but it was. Not only because she was outside in the open, but because she did it regularly. Druggies knew how to get quick money. They staked out homes where they knew they'd find guns and jewelry, and they knew waitresses walked out with cash, enough to buy a night's worth of partying.

He reached the next block, and Michael landed in front of him with a soft thud.

"Get lost, Mike!" Derrick grunted, making a dash for his Navigator parked at the end of the block.

Michael jogged up alongside of him. "You said you weren't coming tonight."

Derrick stopped and crossed his arms, tucking his fists closely to his side so that he wasn't tempted to punch his little brother, who was actually larger than he was. "Since when is it your job to monitor my movements?"

Michael grinned. "Since you agreed to put me in charge of national security."

"Not to watch me, Mike. Your job is to watch the authorities."

Mike harrumphed, but it came out like a growl. "I wouldn't have to monitor the authorities if certain creatus didn't show off their abilities. No one has questioned our existence in years. I think Dad wanted me to watch you."

Derrick walked toward his vehicle again, turning his back on his brother. In a flash, Mike was at the passenger door. Even though he didn't want to, Derrick hit the *unlock* button. "Look who's talking."

"Yeah, well, if I didn't have to keep an eye on you ..." he trailed off, then reached for the stereo, turning on some new age rock station Derrick hated. Probably just to irritate him.

Michael had a lot to learn, the reason creatus stayed and taught in their private schools until they were thirty-five.

"I only watch her when she picks up her daughter and walks home."

"How about when she goes out at night ... "

"She hardly ever goes out at night." *Thank goodness*, he thought.

"But somehow you're there when she does."

"Are you stalking me, Mike?"

His brother grinned again. "Just trying out some new toys."

"Whatever it is ... get rid of it," Derrick demanded. "I'm not your concern."

Michael rolled his eyes. "Such a grouch ... Let's go out. We haven't gone out alone since I got here. For that matter, we didn't go out together when I was home for a couple of weeks last summer either."

Derrick scanned his mirrors before changing lanes, then glared at his brother. "That's because every time we go out, you hook up with a woman and ditch me."

"I always find a woman who has a hot friend. It's not my fault you're a prude."

"Thought you didn't like humans, Mike."

"I'm not dating them ... "

Derrick sighed. His brother *was* a male slut. "That makes it okay?"

"Yeah."

"Whatever."

Although his family should discipline Michael for his aberrant ways, they didn't. As long as he didn't befriend humans and bring them home, no one chastised him. The only concern his family had was getting too close. Because if a human didn't fall ... if they ever left ... Derrick couldn't even imagine. He'd never heard of his kind killing a human unless they were a rogue. But ... creatus kept to their own kind. Most of them socialized as briefly as possible with humans, so there would never be a chance of falling in love with someone who might not ever fall completely.

Derrick decided just to go home. He didn't feel like doing anything. The last thing he wanted was to be out hitting the bars after he'd told Janelle he was too busy to have lunch.

As soon as he pulled into the parking garage, his phone chimed: *We're going for ice cream. If you're close, want to come?*

Janelle was inviting him out ... to meet her daughter even. He'd been right. She was softening to him. He wanted to, but he couldn't. He promised his father. But ... he couldn't let them go alone either. He'd just watch, then come right back.

Sorry. Still in meeting. Have fun. :)

Her text came back immediately; she'd been waiting. *It's okay.* No smiley face. Not like her. She knew it was over. She'd said she only wanted to be friends, but she knew he'd pulled back.

Derrick stopped by the elevator instead of parking. "I have to go do something."

Michael narrowed his eyes. "What happened?"

"Nothing. I just have to do something."

Michael threw the shifter into park and pulled out the keys. "No." He jumped out and darted for the stairwell.

Derrick shot out of the vehicle and bounded over it, landing in Michael's path. "Give me the keys."

Like an immature brat, Michael raised the keys above his head.

No way would he jump for them. "Give me the keys, Michael. I won't ask again."

"Where're you going?"

"You know where I'm going."

"But you told Dad —"

Derrick had warned him. He released his fist into Michael's jaw. His brother's arms came down, but he still didn't release the keys. Instead, he squared off with him. "Let's go."

Derrick shook his head. "I have no wish to fight you, little brother."

"Haven't you noticed, Derrick? I'm not the little brother anymore."

Michael hadn't been smaller for a long time, but maybe he was speaking of physical strength. He was fresh out of martial arts class, so he was antsy to practice his skills.

"Give me the damn keys, now!" Derrick seethed. "I'm not going to grapple with you, Mike. If you make me fight you, I'm going to take you out in one punch. Do you hear me? That last hit was a love tap. I've had nothing to do in the last year but study and train. I haven't gotten sloppy, believe me."

His brother stuffed the keys in his back pocket. "You'll have to take them from me. I'm not going to let you ruin all of our lives for a crush. Bang her and get her out of your system."

Derrick launched for his brother's throat, slamming him against the wall. He didn't want to kill him, though, so he grabbed enough of Michael's shirt in his left hand so that his head wouldn't hit the wall, and then released his fury so that he could get the keys.

Michael dropped, as he knew he would. He'd proven to him and his friends repeatedly that he was the strongest. He was tired of proving himself. He felt like that old show *Tarzan*, and that he should now be pounding on his chest as a warning to all who'd challenge him. He reached into his brother's pocket and grabbed the keys.

Kneeling down in front of Michael, he tapped his cheek. He pulled the house key off the key ring and stuffed it into his hand. "Sorry, Bro, but you asked for it. Go put some ice on that."

Derrick bounced up and darted for his vehicle.

Chapter Six

Kristina cowered against the damp building, looking to her mother for direction. Even at eight, she could see the wild gleam in the man's eyes.

Pepper spray in hand, her mother pushed her toward the street. "Run, baby!"

A knife glinted in the man's hand as he knocked the pepper spray out of her mother's hand, then waved the blade in front of them. "I just want the jewelry and your money, lady. Don't make me hurt you or the kid."

Her mother took her eyes off him for a fraction of a second. "Run, Kris —" Her mother's words cut off as the man slammed the knife into her mother's chest and then reached for Kristina, but she ran as her mother had instructed.

As she fled, she heard her mother's cries. How could she have left her, especially when it was all her fault? She stopped in the middle of the street. She had to stop him. Her legs felt heavy and sluggish as she ran back down the alley toward the mugger, tears blurring her vision. Kristina watched in horror as the dirty man knelt over her mother, trying to pull off her mother's ring, the one Kristina's grandmother had given to her mother.

"Stop!" Kristina cried.

Out of nowhere, a silhouette of a man landed in between Kristina and the thief. When he stood, a sliver of light from the street revealed that he was dressed in black and much larger than the man who'd attacked them. An anguished scream shredded the air as the new man tore the thug away from her mother, slamming him into the concrete. He knelt down over her mother, checking where the man had forced the knife, but she didn't move. The kind man lifted her to her feet. Her mother gazed up at him. Her mouth opened, but nothing came out. She stumbled forward, and the man directed her toward Kristina.

Seeing the blood drip from her mother's mouth and seep through a rip in her dress, Kristina screamed, "Mommy!"

Her mother's eyes and mouth opened again, but still, she said nothing.

"Go!" the man in black shouted. His voice was deep and strong, his eyes dark as he reeled toward the man on the ground, pulling him up by his hair.

Kristina wrapped her arms around her mother's waist, doing her best to hold her upright. As they staggered away, one lone wail filled the air and then silence. She hoped it was the bad guy, not the one in black. Normally his dark hair and mysteriously deep eyes would scare her, but she'd felt safe when he looked at her, as if he knew her.

Her mother collapsed in her arms. The blood had soaked through her dress, turning it bright red.

She looked back to the alley where the mugger had pushed them off the sidewalk. They'd just been going to get ice cream. "Help me," she pleaded to the man who'd saved her. He was leaning over the bad guy, his fingers touching his neck. "My mother's dying ... "

The man in black looked up at the sound of her cry, but didn't move. "I'm sorry. There's nothing I can do."

She blinked the tears out of her eyes, and he was gone.

Chapter Seven

Derrick stood at the edge of the building. Wanting to cry, wanting to scream, wanting to die. None of it came, though. He just watched as the little girl cried over Janelle's lifeless body. He'd failed. Because of Michael, he'd failed. He hoped the man would die, but when he'd checked his pulse, he still had one.

Movement caught his eye, and Derrick watched as the thug rolled to his side, moaning, holding his head. The girl. He couldn't let him hurt Kristina. The beast crawled until he could get his footing, but he didn't seem to notice the crying girl. He stood on wobbly legs, and then finally ran.

Derrick blocked his phone number on his cell and called 9-1-1. He wanted to chase the man, but he couldn't. He couldn't leave Kristina. She had no one. At eight years old. How would she survive?

A wail of sirens filled the air, but still Derrick waited.

What had the girl seen? She'd looked right into his eyes. Could she identify him?

Blue and red strobes flashed off the brick walls, lighting the area. A cop jumped out of his patrol car, but held back behind the engine, assessing the scene. He rattled off a series of ten-codes, then slowly made his way to Kristina.

His back to the wall, the officer squatted near Janelle's head and touched the side of her neck. Shaking his head, he pulled the girl up beside him, and she screamed.

"Mommy! I can't leave my mommy! It's all my fault. It's all my fault!"

The officer kept his eyes on the street as he tried to soothe Kristina. "It's not your fault, sweetheart, but I need to make sure you're safe." He pulled her gently but forcibly to his patrol car. He closed her inside while she continued to scream.

More lights lit up the street and alley, but Derrick couldn't leave yet. What would the girl say? What would his family do?

Paramedics leaned over Janelle, but knew just as he did. Nothing could have saved her. If he'd been inside the hospital, in the O.R., he couldn't have saved her. He felt nauseated, something else he'd never felt. He never got sick. When more officers arrived, the first cop made his way back to Kristina. He opened the door and held on to her, letting her cry.

Derrick should be there for her. Janelle would have wanted him to protect her. She'd wanted to introduce them, and that caused another jolt to his insides. If he'd said *yes*, she would have waited, and even if Mike had still fought with him, she probably wouldn't have left when she did.

"My Dark Angel saved me," Kristina whispered to the officer.

Derrick clasped his hand over his mouth. "Oh, my God."

Those words would doom his family.

The officer knelt down in front of her. "Your *dark angel*? Was he a black man?"

"Don't think so."

"Did he hurt your mommy?"

She whipped her head back and forth. "No. He tried to save her. He was mad at the bad guy."

"Do you remember what he looked like?"

She shook her head. "The bad guy? He looked mean. Dirty."

"Okay. We'll get you with a sketch artist. Someone who draws faces."

"I draw," she whispered, and Derrick's eyes stung again. She'd drawn Janelle that beautiful picture just a little over a month ago. "My mommy ... was ... gonna get me lessons."

The officer opened the front door for her. "He's a nice man. Maybe he'll let you draw too."

"My mommy's in heaven, isn't she?"

"Yes, sweetie. I'll protect you. I have a daughter who looked like you, but she's almost all grown up. I won't let anyone hurt you."

The officer drove off, and Derrick prayed Kristina would be okay. Social services would step in, but as beautiful as she was, most couples weren't looking to adopt an eight-year-old girl with three dead family members.

Derrick headed in the direction that the scumbag had gone. He was exhausted and wanted to go home, but he needed to find him and make him pay, and he couldn't go home. Michael was there, and he'd probably kill him.

He searched the alleys, dumpsters, boxes, any place degenerates like him might hide. The man — murderer, he didn't deserve to be called a man — hadn't gotten anything, so he still needed money to get his fix, so more than likely he'd look for someone else to mug. Although ... Derrick had hit him hard enough that he probably had a concussion.

Derrick made three loops of Somerville, then sank to his knees. Janelle was gone. She'd only been a part of his life for little more than a month, but he'd looked forward to their afternoons together. Her smile, the way she knew immediately what he was thinking. He could still feel her soft skin in his hand. But he'd never even had a chance to kiss her. And based on their conversations, she'd never been with anyone. She'd been taking care of Kristina for so long, right from high school to college, and she mentioned a couple of times that she'd never allow a man in their house with Kristina home. The woman was a saint. And that loser had taken her life ... stolen her from Kristina, who'd never know how great she really was, all that she'd given up for her.

Derrick made the trek to his vehicle, but just slumped behind the wheel. He had no strength to go anywhere. A tap on his window brought him up fast. No one had ever snuck up on him before.

Michael stood outside the door. His eyes were red, and his normally-happy face drooped downward. "I'm so sorry, Derrick. Please open the door." Derrick opened the door and rolled out. Michael caught him and held on to him. "I didn't mean ... I'm sorry."

The tears still didn't come for Derrick, but his heart felt like it'd been torn in two and could never be repaired. "How did —"

"I saw it on the news. A beautiful woman like her. The reporter was all over it. Again, how could I have known? I just ... I don't know what else to say. I'm sorry."

Derrick fell back against his vehicle, his head dropping to his chest. "I loved her. I'm pretty sure she was the one ... "

"Where's her daughter? The news said her eight-year-old daughter witnessed the attack."

"She's safe ..." Derrick closed his eyes. "But I couldn't save Janelle. He stabbed her in the descending aorta."

"You saw her?"

"I was too late ... I watched her fall to the ground after that degenerate shoved a knife into her chest. For what ... a few bucks ... jewelry he'd get twenty bucks for on the street. I took him out before he could hurt her daughter, but I was too late to save Janelle."

Michael grabbed him by the shoulders. "They saw you?"

Shaking his head, Derrick shoved Mike away from him. "Are you serious right now? Do you think I give a rat's ass if that scumbag saw me? You think he's going to run to the police?"

"The girl?"

"She saw a shadow ... nothing more. No one will believe her, even if she says someone saved her."

Michael shook his head. "Derrick, we can't have that. We have to make sure."

Derrick launched at his brother, this time encircling his hands around his throat. "You touch her, I'll kill you. Anyone. No one touches her."

He released his grip, and Michael stumbled backward. "I understand you're hurt, but you're not acting like an overseer right now, Derrick." With that, his brother took off.

Derrick spent the rest of the evening hunting the loser who'd taken his friend. He didn't sleep, afraid that Janelle's face would haunt him. The way she'd looked at him when he lifted her ... Not as if to say, *I'm dying*, but it appeared she wanted to admit, *I made a mistake*. She'd actually looked guilty for dying. Maybe because of Kristina, because now she wouldn't be able to give her what she'd wanted to give her. Janelle had given up what should have been some of the best years of her life to take care of Kristina, and now she was gone. Derrick shook his head at the senselessness of it all.

When his father called, he wanted to ignore him, but knew he had to answer. He just wanted to leave Boston, leave his family. Just go somewhere and be alone, but then, he really would suffer. He had to keep his mind busy, and he needed to find Janelle's murderer.

Derrick sat motionless beside the council, his head in his hands while he listened to the family shout back and forth over Kristina's fate.

"Let me make myself clear," his father said in a deep and commanding voice, one Derrick hadn't heard in years. "This session is not about whether or not Kristina Heskin dies. We are not in the business of killing eight-year-old girls. This hearing is about Derrick and the part he played. We will deal with the repercussions of his actions if there are any, but we can't be sure if she saw anything, and even if she did, it's not the girl's fault. Understood?"

Murmurs of disagreement and approval rumbled through the room. Derrick heard nothing but the low drone, as if he were inside a wasps' nest. His skin felt like it too. Every fiber in his core ached, and he hadn't slept for days.

"This will be a democratic vote. Simply cast a *yes*, meaning Derrick stays or a *no* meaning he forfeits his position as overseer. A blank ballot means you waive your vote." After everyone wrote down a decision, his father passed around the box. Derrick didn't really care, but as overseer, at least his mind would stay occupied.

Dean read off the votes as Matthew wrote them down. Derrick didn't bother keeping track. It was as fair as a system could get. One person collected, another called off, while both watched the third man write down the information.

"It's a seventy-thirty split," Matthew announced, "and the *ayes* have it. Derrick remains overseer."

Derrick exhaled, but again, he wasn't sure that this outcome actually made him happy. It did tell him one thing ... his kind were hopeless romantics. Almost all of them understood his need to protect Janelle. If he had to guess, he'd say that the thirty percent were probably the younger members of the group, the ones who'd not fallen yet. No, he hadn't fallen for Janelle, but he'd felt it in his head and his heart.

"Meeting adjourned," Lyn said, walking over to him. "I need you here for a little while today. Your mother wants to talk to you after everyone leaves."

Derrick nodded and caught Tori's gaze out of the corner of his eye. She didn't stay, though. The moment he caught her looking, she fled.

Dean approached him. "She's hurt. It's not that she hates humans, nor do I, in general. But neither of us can forget that an inebriated human took her mother from us. My sister was a great woman; she didn't deserve to die, and still, everywhere I go — every restaurant, every bar, the mall, for God's sake — serves alcohol. The consumers aren't calling taxis, and they aren't just drinking two drinks either. So, she's a little upset that you'd befriend a human and put us all in danger."

"Janelle's parents died in an accident caused by a drunk driver too. Should she have hated every human because of him?"

"I don't know, Derrick. I just know that I lost my sister way too early in life, and Tori lost her mother. And she might as well have lost her father too. He's nothing without the love of his life; you know that."

Derrick didn't bother to comment. He did know that. He hadn't even fallen, and he felt as though he didn't want to go on without Janelle.

Dean leaned toward him. "I still voted for you to stay, though. I still think you're the best man for the job."

"Thanks, Dean. That means a lot to me, and I'm sorry. I never meant to hurt Tori."

"She'll get over it. All women do eventually." Dean slapped him on the back. "Okay. I'll see you next week."

Derrick waited for his father. They stood outside until everyone left, including Tori, without saying goodbye. He felt bad, but he felt bad for her, not him. He didn't have the strength to regret that she was upset with him. She didn't understand how he felt about Janelle, and he could never explain how much he cared, as that'd only hurt Tori more.

He followed his father into the house. His mother was waiting. She never came to the meetings. The family had asked that she didn't years ago. He guessed as overseer he could change that, but she didn't seem upset by it.

She wrapped her arms around him. "I'm so sorry, honey. I wish there was something I could say that would make it all go away, but I know I can't."

His mother knew pain, so he could accept her condolences as genuine. If she could heal, so could he. Sabrina backed away and took the seat next to his father.

"Where's Michael?" Derrick assumed if they were having a family meeting that he'd be here.

"I asked him to stay away. This doesn't concern him. This doesn't concern anyone but us and Kristina Heskin."

Derrick soared out of his seat. "Dad! Not you too. I thought —"

"Derrick," his father spoke softly, "you really need to control your outbursts. It isn't becoming of a leader to lose his temper."

Derrick nodded. His father was right; he was always right. But ...

"Michael told me that Kristina saw you, is that correct?"

"Yes, but —"

"Derrick, I won't warn you again. You're a grown man. You need to start acting like one."

"Yes, sir."

"Your mother and I have discussed this and spoken with your uncle about the legal issues, and we'd like to adopt her."

Derrick shook his head in disbelief. First that they were willing to accept Kristina into their lives, and second, that he didn't want that. It wouldn't be fair. She shouldn't have to live with their secret. "No. I'll watch her."

His father narrowed his eyes.

"Not in that way. I'll just listen ... make sure she didn't see anything, make sure she doesn't talk. If she does, then yes, we can pursue this option, but I'd rather give her a chance at a normal human life. It's what Janelle wanted."

"You're sure?"

"Yes."

Chapter Eight

It'd been months, and Kristina hadn't mentioned a word, so Derrick was confident she wouldn't. He couldn't understand it, though. Weren't all children inquisitive? She'd said *Dark Angel*, so it was clear she'd sensed that he didn't just stroll up behind her. Why wouldn't she be telling everyone?

Today would have been his last day until he found out she was being transferred to a foster home. He drove to the home, which was only about three miles from Boston. The neighborhood where the home sat had beautifully manicured patches of green around stately homes, most of which had been converted into duplexes and apartments. The home itself was a three-story, plain rectangular building with a basement. According to the records he'd pulled up, it housed up to sixteen children ages eight to fifteen, so Kristina would be the youngest. He didn't like the idea of her being with fifteen-year-old juveniles with issues; most of the adolescents weren't in homes because their parents had died. Many were unwanted or came from abusive homes, where the youths had witnessed behaviors that they would likely imitate. The home did offer psychiatric services, so at least she'd get help in coping with Janelle's death.

The other thing he didn't like was the neighborhood surrounding the home. Even the home itself had bars on the first floor windows of the building. He was certain they weren't there to keep the children inside, but to keep the riffraff out.

The high school was down the street, another sure sign that it wasn't the safest area. The government tended to build schools in areas where the property values were the cheapest.

Parking down the street, he waited until she arrived and was shown her room. He honed in on her quiet voice, listening as she nervously greeted her roommates, and then later cried herself to sleep.

His heart ached for her. Would it be better to allow his parents to adopt her? He'd always been happy. His family was wonderful. They also lived in the country. She'd like that.

No, he couldn't destine her to live with a family where only his parents would accept her. She'd never fit in, and it was possible that one of the younger members of his larger family would hurt her. Not purposely, of course, but they often didn't know their own strength.

Derrick drove back to the clinic and tried to move on with his life. He'd check in from time to time, but he had to let her live her life. He couldn't chance her seeing him again and recognizing him.

The weeks passed, and although he tried not to check in on Kristina, he continued to drive by the home. He typically just parked down the block and worked on his homework while he got a feel for how she was progressing in her new home. It was the one thing Janelle had wanted, for her to have a better life.

The child, who'd been soft-spoken and joyful from the first night he'd seen her with Janelle, had already started turning into a sullen girl. It wasn't because of the adults who ran the house; it was the other children. As suspected, Kristina was too young and sweet to be with a houseful of older children. Her petite stature and platinum hair made her look like a princess among the older, larger students.

At first, they just asked her for details of how her mother was murdered, but then they started asking about her father. Kristina deflected the questions, ignoring most of them, and tried to disappear into drawing.

"What's this?" Derrick heard a shrill voice and a snap of paper.

"Give that back!" Kristina shrieked.

The older girl laughed. "You think an angel is going to save you. God didn't save your mother. Why would he save you?"

So Kristina had drawn a picture of an angel saving her. That wasn't good. Had she seen his face? Was she good enough to capture his image?

A loud crack cut through his thoughts. "I said, give me that!"

Screams shredded the air, but they weren't from Kristina. "The new girl hit me!" the girl shouted, her feet thumping against the wood floor of the old building.

"Let me see. What did she hit you with?" an older woman asked in a calm, controlled voice. Derrick had researched the women who ran the house. They were all clean, no records.

"I don't know, but there's a lump on the back of my head."

"Kristina," the woman called.

More footsteps. "Yes, ma'am," Kristina's soft voice.

"Did you hit Camina?"

"Yes, ma'am."

"We don't hit others. You know that. This is your only warning. If you hit anyone again, you will be sent away. Do you understand?"

"Yes, ma'am."

"Go on up to your room. You will have extra chores for a week."

Kristina walked off without a word, and Derrick couldn't help but smile. Maybe she'd do all right. He couldn't imagine the sweet little girl he'd seen with Janelle hitting anyone, but the other kids had done nothing but pick on her from the day she'd arrived.

The next day, Derrick decided to show up after school. The older girls may know better than to hit one another in the house, but that wouldn't keep them from retaliation on the walk home from school.

Seeing a gang of kids up ahead, Derrick parked his vehicle alongside the road and hopped out. A cluster of students circled another group. This wasn't good.

He jogged up, listening to the insults.

"At least we know who're daddy is. At least I gotta momma."

Whoever was in the middle of the group was on the ground as the girls kicked.

"Hey!" Derrick called, and the crowd broke up and started to run. All except the one girl who lay on the ground, her hands covering her face — Kristina.

He stooped over her. Her dirt-covered face had white lines down the sides where her tears had streaked through the black and brown smudges. Her eyes were swollen shut, so she couldn't see him as he picked her up and pulled her to his chest. "I'm sorry," he couldn't help but say, so she'd know someone cared. "You'll be okay."

He carried her to the home and set her on the front porch. He rang the bell, then disappeared around the side.

"Kristina, oh my Lord, child," the woman shrieked, "Call 9-1-1, Gail!"

Another set of feet ran across the house.

The next day, Derrick listened as the other girls claimed that Kristina had started the fight, and so she was shipped off to the next home.

The cycle of new homes, verbal and physical attacks, and defending herself went on for years, and Derrick again questioned his decision, hoping he hadn't made a mistake.

At least he didn't worry about anyone in the homes hurting her anymore; she'd learned to take care of herself. But her taking care of herself usually meant that she was sent away again. Most homes had a strict policy of *it didn't matter who started the fight*; if the kids were caught fighting, they were evicted.

Derrick ran his normal drive-by, happy that she seemed to be doing okay in this current home. She was thirteen now, and she no longer bore the sweet, innocent look of the girl he'd seen five years ago. She'd dyed her hair with streaks of purple and orange, started wearing all black, and didn't take any crap from anyone.

He glanced at the time and then headed to Logan. Tori, Michael, and the rest of his friends were flying in from London for the last time tonight, and he had to figure out how to make it work with Tori. He had no desire for any other woman, so he didn't understand it. She'd come home twice a year, and they'd always had fun, always made out until they fell asleep in each other's arms. He just couldn't bring himself to have sex with her, though he knew it was what she wanted, what he wanted really. Maybe it would happen then. And then he could forget about what might have been with Janelle.

Chapter Nine

This time when Derrick arrived outside the airport, he went right to Tori. He grabbed her up and swung her around. He'd missed her so much in the last three months, and he really was going to try.

"Much better," she said with a seductive smile. She reached up and locked lips with him, but they had to get going. Airport security wouldn't let you sit but a couple of seconds anymore.

"What about me, Bro?" His brother released a hearty laugh. "Aren't you gonna swing me around?"

Derrick grabbed his brother in a bear hug, but he wasn't about to swing him around. "I missed you, Mike. It's good to have you home."

"Sure ya do. You just miss my magnetic personality, since you're such a stiff."

"Yep. That must be it." He opened the hatch and helped load all the luggage inside. "Hey, Ry ..." Derrick reached for the youngest in their group, giving him an authentic hug. He'd always liked him. He had to go back to London for a couple more years, but he'd enjoy hanging out with him over spring break. "Hey, Jonas." Jonas hugged him too, but

Derrick could feel the tension, and based on Tori's greeting, she'd kept herself for him.

The group piled in his Navigator, and Derrick started for his place, knowing they'd all make their way to their respective homes on their own. Tori and Michael, though, usually hung out with him.

Michael leaned over the center console. "So, I made us reservations ... "

Derrick glanced over his shoulder. "Reservations?"

"Yep, I already called Dad. He approved vacation time for you; he's gonna cover your rounds. I figured since Ry is only here for a week, and we're all going to have to start our internships, we should take off a few days and enjoy ourselves. I booked us at the Mount Washington Resort. If we're lucky, we should still be able to get in a little skiing."

"I wish you would have told me," Derrick said.

"Why? So you could have thought up an excuse not to come?"

Derrick grimaced into the rearview mirror. "Fine. When are we going?"

"Tonight. No time to back out. Just swing by your place and pack a bag, and let's go. We're all packed." He laughed, seemingly proud of himself.

Derrick glanced over at Tori, noticing she tried to hide her smile. Obviously, she knew about Michael's plans.

He could escape for a few days. Kristina seemed to be doing well at this new home. How much trouble could a thirteen-year-old girl get into in a few days? He had to start pulling back. He couldn't watch over her forever.

Derrick grimaced when they checked in. Why should he have been surprised? His brother had booked only one room for Tori and him.

She nuzzled up against him as he signed in. "If it's a problem, Mike said I could stay in his room."

"Not a problem and I'm definitely not letting you stay with my brother." Derrick leaned over and kissed her. He'd said he'd try, and it appeared his brother wanted this too. Tori was back for good now. He didn't have to worry that if they fell for each other she'd have to go away for months at a time. She was the logical choice, the perfect woman for him. Beautiful, sexy, smart, and she loved him. They'd been friends since they were children; this was just the next step.

After unpacking their bags, they made their way to the rear of the hotel that overlooked Mount Washington. The sun had already set, but the streaks of pink and red it'd left behind provided a magnificent backdrop for a romantic evening. Even the heavens wanted him to fall, it seemed.

Tori trailed him down a heated path to the pool. Snow-covered trees and shrubs surrounded the area. Even the gate and posts had a dusting of the white powdery flakes. The hotel could have graced the pages of a fairy tale in a majestic faraway land. So close to Boston and yet so far from his daily routine and concerns.

Throwing her robe on a nearby chaise, Tori glided into the water. Her body, as always, was perfect. Her olive skin, smooth and blemish-free, looked even darker than usual beneath her white bikini. Her silky hair reached the top of her bikini bottoms, the longest he'd ever seen it. Derrick followed her in cautiously. She'd take him to the precipice this evening, he was certain. Would he go over, or would he be able to resist her as he'd done in the past? Should he even try?

She dunked her head and then came up in front of him, glistening, beckoning a kiss, but he held back, allowing the desire to build. He needed to want her completely. He needed to starve himself of her touch until he couldn't take it anymore, until his heart cried out for her, and then maybe he'd fall.

Her lip jutted out slightly. "Don't you like the suit? I know you like white."

He smiled. "What's not to like? You look like a goddess, Tori."

Slightly appeased, she bit her bottom lip, looking seductive again. "But you don't want to kiss me?"

"Oh, yes. Definitely. But, I want to let it build up until later."

"Mmm ... I like the sound of that," she purred in his ear. "Tonight, I'm going to make you forget everything in the world but me."

He gulped. How could she scare him? What was he afraid of? "There isn't anyone but you, Tori. You know that."

"I want to make sure of it."

After swimming, they changed and met the others for dinner. Mike, now twenty-five to the world, took it upon himself to supply the wine for dinner. Derrick filled his glass repeatedly, hoping to clear his mind, to release his inhibitions. His kind didn't usually marry; they *fell*. Once they made a conscious decision to spend the rest of their lives with each other, their souls connected in a palpable way. The feeling, supposedly, was electrifying, a sensation that couldn't be faked or mistaken, according to his father. When you fell for your soul mate, you knew it. Usually just a kiss would start the reaction, and then, once you made love, your souls would connect forever.

Derrick knew Tori was his perfect match, but he'd yet to feel the spark, so he was scared. What if his soul mate had already died? Was it too late for him? His father assured him that one would not fall without the other, so even if

Tori knew what she wanted, she wouldn't fall for him without him falling too. It was so convoluted that sometimes he wished it wasn't a factor of their kind. Maybe it was because he was different from most creatus. Maybe that was why his brother could sleep with any woman he wanted.

He filled his glass again, emptying the bottle.

Michael set another one in front of him. "I'll keep an eye on you, Bro. Lighten up and have fun."

"That's what I'm afraid of. I don't know if I can trust you as my keeper."

Tori squeezed his knee, and he jumped. This was ridiculous. He was forty years old, for God's sake. He emptied another glass, letting the warmth course through his veins. It felt good. He never did this.

After dinner, Tori and he strolled to the fire pit. They skipped the complimentary cheese offered by the hotel, but accepted the free wine. Derrick slid into one of the Adirondack chairs, and Tori lowered herself sideways across his lap.

Michael had found a cute strawberry blonde to keep him company, but Ry and Jonas just discussed London and the differences between it and Boston. Derrick couldn't make out any specifics. All he could think about was the beautiful brunette on his lap.

He wrapped his arms around her shoulders and pulled her closer. He'd been watching those lips all night and couldn't wait to taste them. The merlot she always liked tinted her lips, making them even redder and tasting of different berries along with the hint of spice, mocha, and oak. His body came alive with want and need.

"Let's not stop," she whispered beneath her kisses.

Her comment woke him, knowing the men around them had heard her announcement. His gaze darted up, catching

Jonas watching them; even Ry had a scowl on his face. Did all the men want her? Why did she keep waiting for him?

"Tori —"

"Shh ..." she cut him off, standing up and taking his hand. She didn't allow him to pull free, and if he did, it'd look rude, so he followed.

They rode up the elevator silently, then she trailed him to their room.

"Tori ... "

"Derrick, for me, please?" She backed him up to the sofa beside a crackling fire. "I'm thirty-five, and I'm ready. I know I want to be with you forever, but even if it doesn't happen, I'll understand. I still want to make love to you."

"Tori, I'm drunk. I can't. It's not right —"

She pushed him back onto the seat and straddled him. "Then we'll just kiss in the privacy of our room, and whatever happens, happens." She pressed her lips to his again and started unbuttoning his shirt.

Images flashed through his mind of Tori in the pool, in the firelight, on top of him. She was beautiful, his best friend, and she wanted this. His body soared to life. Maybe he could force it. Then, she'd be happy, his family would be happy, and maybe he could escape the demons that haunted his nightmares nightly.

Chapter Ten

Damn that girl! Derrick seethed. She was so smart, and yet she did the stupidest things. Why in the world was she out this late? You'd think watching Janelle die would have been enough to scare her, but it was almost as though she had a death wish.

The men had stalked Kristina ever since she'd left her friend's house, but they'd held back, waiting until no one else was around. They didn't care that she was only fifteen. In fact, that had them salivating.

"Don't spook her," the one said. "I don't want her screaming. Just get her in the van, and we'll have fun back at the club."

Oblivious in her miniskirt and tank top, Kristina strolled down the dark street, texting, not aware of her surroundings. How she'd even conned her foster parents to sign for a phone for her was beyond him. She'd always been good about working, though, so she probably agreed to pay more than it cost the woman. Kristina had been babysitting for neighbors since she was thirteen, always talking about how she was going to move south as soon as she saved enough money.

She'd probably do it, too. Then how would Derrick protect her? He couldn't very well leave his family to protect a bratty fifteen-year-old.

Derrick took off in a sprint and leapt onto the next building. He had a pretty good idea where the other man planned to intersect with the van, so he'd get there first. Hopefully, when the others saw the van wasn't there, they'd put off their attack.

One look revealed he was correct. He glanced around and then pounced. The roof crushed under his weight.

The slimeball jumped out of the driver's side. "What the fu —" Derrick grabbed him from behind, cutting off his air in a rear naked choke, and then threw him into the back of his van. He went to the front of the vehicle and shoved it back a hundred yards so it collided with a dumpster. From the end of the alley, passersby wouldn't be able to see the black van, and it'd be a while before the man woke up.

Derrick waited for Kristina to pass the alley, then grabbed the other two men, who'd peered down the darkened street, looking for their comrade.

Careful to exert just the right amount of force, so as not to kill them, he smashed their heads together and threw them on the ground.

He darted around the building and watched Kristina enter her apartment building. The girl would be the death of him, he was certain.

"Tell me about these new gadgets, Mike," Derrick said as he slammed through his brother's office door. "I need one that will track a cell phone. You got that?"

"Yeah, man. I got that. But, why?"

"Just a hunch," Derrick said.

"I thought that was my job, tracking down hunches. What'd you see? Do you have an idea who the vigilante is?

It's starting to tick me off. *The Boys* at Boston PD don't care that someone's trying to clean up the streets. And now there've been sightings ... people saying an angel saved them." Mike narrowed his eyes.

Derrick shook his head. "Not me! You know me better than that. I've only protected Kristina. Besides, from the reports you've shown me, I think whoever's doing this is just looking for an excuse to fight. He's having fun terrorizing humans. I have nothing to prove. No, I need the device for something else. As I said ... just a hunch. I just want to have a little fun tracking someone."

Mike harrumphed. "You, have fun? Yeah, right."

"Just give me the damn program, Mike."

"Touchy ... okay." Michael typed a few keys on his keyboard. "What's the number?"

"Just give me the name of the program, and I'll take care of it."

His brother leaned back in his chair and sighed. "Oh, no. No ... Not happening."

Derrick threw up his hands. "Fine. I'll go find it on my own. Of course, maybe I'll get in trouble by hacking into some private government-controlled website ..." Derrick turned and strode toward the door.

"Get back here. But, dude, please be careful."

"You going to run and tell Dad on me again, Mike? That was rather childish, don't you think?"

Mike shook his head, dropping his eyes to his keyboard. "I like my job, and I like you as my boss. I'd rather you not be banished."

Derrick sat across from him. "I have to keep her safe. I owe it to Janelle."

Mike nodded. "I guess I understand." He printed out the info and handed it to him. "Just be careful, okay?"

"Always am." He stood up to leave again. He needed to get back to the hospital.

"Hey, how's Tori?"

Derrick shrugged. "You spend more time with her at school than I do at the hospital."

"That's not what I meant."

"I know what you meant, Mike, and it's none of your business."

Derrick walked out. He was so tired of the family butting into his love life. Why was it so important that he fell for Tori anyway? Maybe he was broken. He'd tried really hard not to blame his brother, the reason he was certain Michael had agreed not to tell his father that he was *watching*.

He wouldn't do anything to endanger his family, but he had to keep Kristina safe. When she was old enough to take care of herself, he'd stop. He certainly couldn't continue to watch her for the rest of her life. He just needed to get her through these teen years, as Janelle would have done if she were still alive. Then, he'd be able to move on with his life, knowing he'd given Janelle the one thing she wanted.

Chapter Eleven

Kris let the screen door slam behind her, knowing that her foster parents hated it. Good, she hated them.

"Where ya going, Kristina?" Liz called from the porch.

"Out!"

"It's a school night, young lady. You be home by ten."

Kris lifted her head in acknowledgement, but then hopped in her friend's Honda Accord. Yeah, like that was gonna happen. Tonight was the night of her first frat party. Not many sixteen-year-old girls could claim that privilege. She'd posted it all over Facebook, so her friends would be expecting some juicy pics. Her current guardians would be lucky if she came home by three.

She exhaled a long breath as she collapsed in the passenger seat of her best friend's car. "OMG! Freedom!"

Beth shifted the vehicle into drive and drove away from the lopsided parallel parking job she'd done in front of her foster parents' apartment building. She pulled her eyes off the road for a second. "Wow. I like the dress —" Her friend lifted the hem of her dress, running her fingers over the embellished silk. "Is that the Sherri Hill? Where'd ya get the cash?"

Kris propped up her feet on the dash, displaying her new platform sandals with four-inch heels and twinkling crystals.

"Dang ... girl. Did you rob a bank?"

She smiled. "Not exactly."

Her girlfriend arched an eyebrow. "You didn't!"

"I did."

"How much did you get?"

"Two thousand dollars on eBay. Enough to take off if I want."

Her friend shook her head, huffing out a breath. "Yeah, right! Where would ya go?"

Kris shrugged. "Anywhere? Somewhere warm. I hate Somerville. We get a few weeks of sweltering heat in the summer, and then the rest of the year is just cold and wet."

"I don't know, Kris. I don't know if I could have sold my mother's jewelry. Didn't you say one of the pieces belonged to your grandmother?"

"Yeah. But if my mother hadn't been wearing that stupid ring, that dirtbag probably wouldn't have jumped us when I was eight. I'm better off without it." Kris reached for the stereo and cranked up the alternative rock station. "Anyway, shut up! I wanna rock tonight."

Within minutes, Beth pulled up in front of the red brick manor with gray trim and made a phone call. "We're here ..." Her voice took on her silky, sweet tone she reserved for her boyfriend. She clicked *end* and angled her body toward Kris. "Jason said he'd meet us here and park the car."

Kris faked a swoon against the passenger door. "You're so lucky. Jason's soooo sweet."

"Well, from what he tells me, his suitemate can't wait to meet you, so I'm sure he'll be just as great."

"Squee! So cool! I'm so excited."

"Chill, girl. We're supposed to be smooth and calm. Know what we're doing, you know? Act like college girls."

Jason ran across the grass and pulled open Beth's door. "Go on up to the front door, and I'll be right back." He pecked Beth on the lips and then jumped inside the Honda and peeled off.

Beth and Kris sauntered up the front stoop, staring up at the four-story dorm, which looked like a mansion. Most of the students who walked by didn't give them a second glance, but Kris caught the glower from a few girls. She'd always stood out among the dark-haired girls in Boston with her long blond hair, especially since she'd added streaks of eggplant and fuchsia.

Jason took the front steps two at a time, then scooped up Beth, planting a kiss on her lips. He set her down, then shifted his gaze to Kris, as though examining her from head to toe; well, maybe he didn't get past the hem of her dress. "Looking hot, ladies. Come on, Greg's anxious to meet you." He held open the door, and they followed. The inside of the old brick manor was spacious with red leather sofas and even a grand piano. He smiled as their mouths dropped open. "You think this is nice, wait'll you see our suite."

When he opened the room to their apartment, Kris understood what he'd meant. One side of the room had a full bar built into the wall, and the other side had a terrace overlooking the courtyard. The sky was ominous-looking with its oranges and deep blues, making her wonder whether Boston would get a final snow before springtime. God, she hoped not.

A tanned hottie with dark blond hair combed to one side, wearing skinny jeans and a black T-shirt, stepped into the room. She crossed her fingers behind her back, hoping the guy was Jason's roommate Greg.

He fist-bumped Jason and walked right up to her. "You must be Kristina," he said in an accent that didn't fit New England, as didn't his hair and clothes. *Yummy*, she thought. He was exactly her type — different. He lifted her hand to his lips, and she felt lightheaded.

"Call me Kris," she said. "Only my guardians call me by my full name."

One side of his lip quirked up. "I wouldn't mind being your guardian. I'll keep an eye on you all night." He dropped her hand and strolled behind the bar. "So, what would you ladies like to drink?" Greg looked at Jason. "You already checked their IDs? They're twenty-one, right?"

"Absolutely," Jason said, kissing Beth. "Give them our house specialty."

Greg reached behind him without taking his eyes off her and pulled down two bottles. One with green liquid, the other clear. He flipped the bottles once and poured equal amounts into a short glass, twirled again, and poured another few shots into a second glass. "Two house specials."

Jason grabbed one and handed it to Beth, then walked over to a stereo and cranked up some tunes, pulling Beth to the middle of the room. As soon as the music started, college students funneled into the apartment.

Kris' blind date — she'd have to thank Beth later for setting her up with him — stepped around the bar and handed her the green concoction.

She touched a tiny bit to her lips, tasting the drink. It was strong, but good. "Melon?"

"Yep ... and a few secret ingredients. If I told you, I'd have to kill you though." He wiggled his eyebrows. "Careful, they taste so good they can sneak up on you. I wouldn't want you to get drunk and fall asleep before the party's over." He lifted her hand and directed her out the

French doors to the terrace. "Tell me about yourself, Kris. Where do you go to school?"

She opened her mouth, but then snapped it shut as she'd almost said the name of her high school. Jason knew she was a junior in high school. *Had he really not told his roommate?* she wondered. "Hmm ... there's not much to tell. I live in Somerville —"

He cringed.

"Yeah, I know, but I'm leaving soon."

He stuck out his bottom lip. "Really? Where? We just met."

"I don't know. Someplace warm."

He laughed. "Yeah. Me too. Back to Cali as soon as I graduate."

She licked her lips and smiled. "I like the sound of that."

"Well, Kris, maybe we should get to know each other better before you move away then."

Kris' entire body tingled at the fact that this hotter-than-hot college boy was interested in her. Heck, she may even get to L.A. faster than she thought. His parents probably owned a beach house in Venice.

Greg touched his fingers to the bottom of her glass. "Drink up, babe. There's a lot more where that came from, and we have a lot of partying to do."

She tilted back the glass, savoring every drop. He left her on the terrace to greet more students filtering into the suite, each carrying a dish of food in one hand and a bottle of some kind of liquor in the other.

Kris wandered around the apartment, meeting new people, but kept her mouth shut and mostly just let them talk about professors and what they were gonna do for spring break. Every time she turned around, Greg was close by, offering her a sweet smile. She'd been so lucky he'd chosen her as his date with all these older college girls around.

When she walked back into the main living area, all the couches, chairs, and tables were back against the walls of the apartment, leaving space in the middle for swaying bodies. An eighties dance song belted out of the Bose speakers, and Beth squealed in response, pulling Kris into the middle of the room. Kris kicked off her sandals, and within seconds, Greg handed her another drink and moved up behind her, pressing her closer to her friend. She tipped back the glass, draining it. He handed her his glass, and she pounded it too.

The warmth that surged through her body felt de-lish. She'd needed a release from the strains of her life. A day didn't go by that thoughts about the night she'd lost her mother didn't plague her, and every evening, nightmares inundated her sleep as she attempted to rewrite the events of her past. She had no parents, no siblings. And every six months, or less sometimes, she ended up with new foster parents when her current guardians were finally able to adopt a baby or have their own child. No one wanted a troublesome teenager. Beth was the only person on the planet who even cared about her worthless existence.

Greg slid his hands around her waist and pulled her closer. The room blurred for a second, and she stumbled backward into his arms, feeling as though she might fall.

He steadied her. "You okay?"

"Yeah. Just hot, I guess."

He lifted her hand and pulled her toward the door. "Let's go get some fresh air."

Kris followed behind him gratefully. "That sounds good." Beads of sweat dripped between her shoulder blades even though she could feel the air was cool.

Greg led her down a staircase and outside to the courtyard behind the building. He crossed the common area, walking until they were in the shadow of two buildings at the rear of the complex. The setting sun's orange rays peeked through massive pine tree branches, casting eerie patterns across the lawn as they swayed gently in the breeze. Greg dropped down on a bench and pulled her onto his lap.

Kris' heart immediately thumped out a nervous rhythm. She'd only known him a couple of hours; she wasn't ready for this.

He slid one hand up her shirt and the other between her legs.

She jumped off his lap and staggered backward; he hadn't even kissed her and was already trying to feel her up. "What are you doing? We just met." A wave of heat flashed through her body, and the world seemed to twist and bend around her as she tried to steady herself. Her mind was clear, but the ground felt as though it were moving beneath her, as if she were rocking in a boat.

Greg's face distorted, and she wasn't certain if the devilish sneer was because he was angry with her or if she was hallucinating. He stood up. "I thought this is what you wanted. To get to know each other." He approached her and pushed her back against the brick wall. The grainy material pierced through the thin material of her dress, scraping her back.

She clawed at his hands and arms. "I mean it! Stop it!"

He smashed his hand over her mouth and slammed her harder against the wall. She tried to scream, she tried to push him off, but his body against hers was too strong. It felt as if her arms were floating and her legs could no longer hold her weight.

The loser must have put something in her drink. He tugged up her dress as she struggled to free herself, but he pulled her body away from the wall and then bashed her head back into it. White stars filled her vision as the world began to close around her. She couldn't pass out; she had to fight.

Greg's body soared backward, hitting the wall of the building opposite her. She blinked in an attempt to clear her head, trying to register what she'd just seen. Then her body felt weightless as cool air rushed over her skin. Strong arms cradled her body, but they weren't hurting her; someone was carrying her.

She stared up at the pine trees that rushed by, their long branches reaching out for her, hoping her protector wouldn't let them take her. That wasn't right. Trees couldn't hurt her. She was hallucinating. She struggled to lift her head, to see who'd saved her. "Who ... are ... you?"

"You stupid girl ..." The familiar deep voice filled her ears, resonating through her body as he pulled her against his chest. "I'm sorry. It'll be okay ... you'll be okay."

Hearing his voice sent a thrill through her soul, clearing her mind for a second. Every time she'd tried to convince herself that she'd made him up as a child, her heart argued that he existed. She tried to focus on his face to make out his features, but all she saw were those deep and mysterious eyes that filled her good dreams when she had them. The ones where he whisked her away, as opposed to the nightmares when the thief returned to kill her.

He set her down inside of what must be Beth's car. "Keep the doors locked until your friend comes out."

"It's you, isn't it?" she struggled to speak through the haze that threatened to steal her into unconsciousness.

"Yes, it's me." He brushed her hair from her face, and her world went black.

Chapter Twelve

This can't go on, Derrick." Tori's words reached him in a whisper that only he could hear as soon as he stepped inside the lobby of his building. He turned to see her sitting at the coffee shop.

Not wanting to deal with her tonight, he sighed but then walked over to her, sliding down in the seat across from her.

"You were *watching* again tonight, weren't you?" she said without condemnation, just matter-of-factly.

He bit down on his lip as he glanced at his black jeans and hoodie. How could he possibly deny it? "I have to protect her. She doesn't have anyone else."

"Many girls don't have anyone else."

"You don't understand."

"Try me."

"Tori, please ... let's not do this. When she's an adult, I'll stop. But right now, she doesn't have parents —"

"She has foster parents. Surely —"

"A new foster family every six months or so doesn't help instill values. She's had to protect herself from other kids in her own home, rotten foster parents who only signed on for a government check, and now —" Not wanting to talk about what had just happened, he cut off his words. "What should I do, abandon her?"

Tori shook her head. "I don't know. I just can't live with you disappearing every night."

"Then don't," he snapped. He hadn't meant to sound as harsh as he had, but he was so tired of this conversation when he'd been nothing but honest with her from day one. He'd told her they could only be friends, and she pushed and pushed. "I've never asked you to do anything. We don't live together; we're not a couple. Besides, I'm always at home or the hospital; this was a rare situation. Her date drugged her tonight and then tried to rape her."

"So she saw you?"

"No ... she was drugged, and the degenerate only felt his body slam against a wall."

"Derrick ... "

He stood swiftly. "Don't *Derrick* me ... I'm not your concern." He turned to walk away, but then reeled on her. "If someone had been there to protect your mother from that drunk driver, would you have wanted them to stop him?" He didn't wait for her response. He charged off to the stairwell. The elevator was too slow for him. He had to write a report to send tomorrow. No way would he allow that boy to harm another innocent girl again.

Some would say that Kristina wasn't innocent, that she'd willingly gone to the party and had too much to drink. But he didn't see it that way. Taking advantage of a drunk girl was never acceptable, no matter what the situation.

Dammit, Kristina. Dammit, Janelle, he seethed silently. For not listening to him, for not realizing that they needed to be more careful. He reached his door, but didn't open it. He just fell against it. He was so tired. Not that he required a lot of sleep, but watching over Kristina had become a full-time job. And now she was drinking.

Warm hands wrapped around his waist. "I'm sorry."

"Tori, I can't do this anymore. You have to give up on me."

She inched herself beneath his arm. "I can't give up on you anymore than you can give up on that girl."

That girl ... To everyone else, Kristina was just *that girl*. A girl who'd fallen between the cracks, a girl no one wanted. How could he abandon her too? He closed his eyes and rested his head on Tori's forehead. "I'm broken, Tori. Can't you see that? I'll never fall, which means I'm holding you back from whomever you should be with. We aren't meant to be. Why can't you see that?"

"I don't care."

Derrick ran his hands through his hair, and then reached behind her, opening the door. He took her hand and led her to his bedroom. She didn't have to coax him or get him drunk, as she was fond of doing. He needed a release from the angst inside of him, and he would try. He would do everything in his power to submerge himself in her passion. To feel her, to accept her, to make his heart obey. Everything in his head told him that Tori was the woman for him. Only his heart refused to let it happen.

She tore at his shirt, ripping it off him, clearly feeling the energy in him tonight. He backed her up to the bed, and for once, let his body take over, ignoring the screaming in his head that told him this wasn't right. It *was* right. This is what his kind did. They found their match, the person who completed them, and they made love, they made a life, they had children, and they lived happily ever after. Tori was his match in every way. They did everything together. What was his problem?

Her lips moved away from his mouth, working their way lower as she unbuttoned his jeans. He gently moved her hands away. He couldn't. He just couldn't do it again. He'd caved before, but as much as he wanted to, he couldn't surrender tonight. It wasn't right. Normally at least his head was here, but right now, his mind was elsewhere. As much as the lower half of his body wanted her, he couldn't succumb tonight. He felt nothing sensual for her other than a raw need to fulfill his physical wants. As beautiful as she was, as much as she wanted him to make love to her, his heart had taken over again. Not tonight. No way could he do anything with her tonight.

He clenched his fists, wanting to ignore the screaming in his head telling him this was wrong. Gasping for air from his inner turmoil, he rolled off the bed. He left the room without looking at her, knowing the dejected look he'd witness.

He practically sprinted to his study, to the bag he'd ignored for a while. He needed to release the fury inside of him. Picturing the loser he'd pulled off Kristina tonight, he punched it squarely. He'd wanted to kill him. Probably would have if Kristina had been unconscious. He slammed the bag repeatedly until it exploded, wishing it were the man's insides. It'd taken every ounce of willpower he had not to go back and finish him off after he'd deposited Kristina in Beth's car.

"I think the bag's dead," Tori said behind him.

His heart still pounding out a vicious rhythm, he turned to her. He was finished ... with all of it. All of the games. "Tori, I can't do this anymore. Please go home."

This time, she listened. Without a word, she turned and walked toward the door, but then whirled on him at the last second. "By the way, don't call me Tori anymore. I'm tired of it. It sounds like a little girl, not a grown woman with a Ph.D."

He sighed. "I thought you didn't like your full name."

She shrugged and walked out.

Chapter Thirteen

B ut it's prom," Beth cried over the phone. "What do you mean you're not going, Kris? We bought dresses, my dad's letting me use his Cadillac, the cutest guy in school asked you to go with him ... "

Kris sighed. "I'm not going."

"What's going on? You haven't been the same since the night of the party. What happened? Jason won't tell me. He just said that Greg left school. Talk to me, please. I'm your best friend."

"I just don't feel like going, okay? I gotta go. I have homework."

"Since when do you study? You ace your tests without studying."

"If I wanna get out of this dump, I gotta start putting in some extra work."

"Okay ... but, this discussion isn't over."

"Yes, it is, Beth. I'm not going, so don't bug me about it again. Bye." Kris hung up the phone and stared down at the picture she'd been drawing. The eyes, she almost had them right. When she'd seen him when she was eight, she'd thought for sure that it had just been her imagination, but he'd saved her again. She couldn't make him out completely this time, just his eyes and his voice. She could never forget his beautiful voice. Though, she had been drunk, and she suspected that Greg had drugged her too. She didn't even remember Beth taking her home.

At first, she'd thought she'd imagined the entire night, but the welt on the back of her head hadn't happened from falling or tripping. It'd happened when Greg slammed her head against the brick wall.

When she finished the sketch, she did what she did every time, tore it into shreds and flushed it down the toilet so no one could see it and question her sanity. She reached into her purse and pulled out the wad of cash. If she didn't do something with it, some loser in the house would steal it.

She searched the newspaper ads, looking for something she could afford, circling anything in her price range and local. One caught her eye, a Grand Am. She made the phone call and was out the door in minutes. The car had belonged to a woman who'd passed away, and the daughter just wanted rid of it.

Kris handed the woman the cash, took the title, and she was one step closer to freedom. Now to get a job. She'd save every penny, and then she'd head south.

It took all day, but she found a job at a deli, which also meant free food. The food at the foster home sucked. The first night she pocketed forty dollars in tips. By the time she graduated, she'd have enough.

Kris parked her car and scanned the alley behind her apartment building. Her eyes darted to the rooftop. "You're there, aren't you?" she whispered. She squinted at the nighttime sky. Was it her imagination, or had she seen a shadow? "Why won't you show yourself?"

"Kristina, is that you?" Liz called from the window. "Where've you been?"

Kris had to admit, out of all of the foster homes she'd been in, Liz was the one woman who seemed to care. But it was too late. Too late for her to have a mother or father, brothers or sisters. She peeked up at the rooftop again. Beth had been her only family, but now, she realized she had someone else. No one would believe her, of course, so she couldn't tell anyone, but someone was protecting her.

What if she left Massachusetts, though? Would she ever see him again?

"Here," Billy said in the back of the deli. "Try this. You won't be worried about anything anymore."

"Are you sure it's safe?" Kris asked. "What is it?"

"Just pot, babe. I wouldn't hurt you."

Billy had been kind to her. He'd never come on to her as most of her dates did. He'd always just wanted to hang around and watch TV and get high. She'd never done drugs, but she'd heard pot wasn't bad.

She held out her hand and accepted the thin, tightly-wrapped paper. She inhaled and then choked.

"Take it easy, girl. Just inhale and hold it in." He demonstrated again.

Kris inhaled a few more times, but didn't feel anything. He continued to swap with her, but then she backed up as his face distorted.

"What's wrong?" Billy said, sounding like a cartoon character, but not a funny one, an evil one.

She backed up further, her eyes darting around the room. "What did you give me?" she screamed.

"Relax, babe. I smoked the same stuff. It's clean."

Kris fell to the floor and covered her face, wishing the room would stop spinning. Every time she tried to uncover her eyes, Billy's face moved forward and back again, as though growing and shifting in size. "Make it stop," she cried.

His hands touched her shoulders. "Kris, I don't understand."

"Stop it!" Chills rocked her body and her heart raced.

"I'm sorry, babe. I swear. There's nothing in it." He wrapped his arms around her as she shook violently.

"It hurts. My heart hurts. I'm scared," Kris cried.

He continued to rock her back and forth. "I'm sorry."

It took forever, but finally her body stopped quivering. "I don't want to do that again."

Billy held her. "Okay."

Kris got to her feet and stumbled to her car. The deli had closed hours ago, and Liz would be freaking out. She sat in her car while she waited for her head to clear. It didn't take too long. Maybe it was just a fluke because it was her first time. Everyone else seemed to enjoy it.

Chapter Fourteen

Derrick sat in the back of the library, his head down, ball cap low over his eyes. Kristina had been coming here regularly, attempting to get some college work finished before she went to work.

Obviously, she was safe in the library, so he had no reason to be here. But something had changed. At twenty years old, she was a beautiful woman, a woman he suddenly wanted to meet. He wondered if she still remembered him. He'd managed to stay invisible for the last four years, but he couldn't help but wonder if she'd even recognize him. The thought that she wouldn't stung his heart; he wanted her to know him. To know him as intimately as he knew her.

Most days she just read and took notes, but today, she'd been working intently on a piece of paper, had changed out her pencil several times. She was drawing, he realized. She'd drawn since she was a little girl, but he'd never seen one other than the page Janelle had held up. He'd heard Kristina rip up several drawings when she was young and someone had walked into the room. Ever since the one girl had teased her when she was eight, it was as though she was afraid to let anyone see what she'd drawn.

He felt a compelling urge to walk by, but he couldn't. He could never get close enough that she could see him. If she recognized him ... as much as he wanted her to, he knew that would be dangerous — he couldn't think about it. He'd told Michael repeatedly, he'd never allow anything to happen to her. He'd failed once; he refused to fail again. It wasn't in his nature to fail. He had one goal: keep her safe for one more year, until she was twenty-one. Truly, she was a grown woman now, but she was still so vulnerable. She was always trying to find herself, so she still made unwise decisions. Not that he stopped her from making the wrong decisions; he just wanted to be there if someone took advantage of her.

Kristina picked up her phone and glanced at the time.

"Yes, you're late, silly girl. As always," he said under his breath. He couldn't help but smile. She tried so hard, but she was easily distracted. At least she was trying to finish college, trying to make a better life.

The last few weeks had been tough, though. Both Janelle's death and her almost-rape had happened in March, so she didn't do well this time of the year when everyone else was basking in the springtime. And tonight was the anniversary of Janelle's death, the reason he'd decided to keep an eye on her. She hadn't mentioned it to anyone, but when he'd driven by her apartment the last few nights — just to make sure she was safe — he'd heard her screams. He'd learned to tell her nightmares, though, so he didn't rush to her fire escape anymore, ready to kill someone.

She stood and shoved her books inside her backpack, then crumpled up the paper she'd been working on so diligently. She threw it in the trashcan, then darted out of the library.

He couldn't stop himself ... he had to see it. He ambled toward the bin, his eyes darting around the library. Not that it was illegal, but he didn't want the librarians to see him fishing through the garbage. He waited until all eyes were averted, then reached down so quickly that probably no one would have seen him anyway.

He waited a few seconds to make sure she'd pulled out of the parking lot, then walked outside and sat on a bench. He unfolded the wadded up piece of paper, but then gasped at the image.

He'd hoped that when she occasionally gazed up at the rooftops she was looking for him. And he'd been right. She *was* looking for him. Why else would she have drawn this image? But ... he'd also been wrong in thinking she couldn't identify him. She'd remembered every detail of his face, his hair, his eyes. She knew him as intimately as he knew her. She'd only seen him twice, and both times, she'd been under duress. And yet, she'd captured his image perfectly.

He released a long sigh. If Michael ever saw this ... If anyone ever saw this ... As much as he didn't want to destroy the drawing, he walked to the librarian's desk, knowing they had a shredder. Without asking, he slipped the piece of paper he wished he could keep into the blades.

Kristina, he whispered her name as the black-and-white image separated into thin white strips and dropped into the wastebasket. He closed his eyes ... *I want you to see me. I wish I could let you see me. But not yet ... maybe someday.*

His phone chimed. He looked at the message. *E.R. STAT*

He charged off toward his vehicle, glad for the interruption of his thoughts, but hoped it wasn't someone in his family. He hit the call button on his steering wheel, and Roseanne answered after a few rings.

"Roseanne, it's Derrick. I'm on my way. Who's the patient?"

"Mrs. Jones. Dr. Maher wants to transport her to Mass General, but she refuses, says she's been coming to this hospital for years. She'll only speak to you."

Derrick smiled. "She's a stubborn woman, I know. I'm on my way." Mrs. Jones wouldn't see anyone but him or his father. But she did have heart trouble. At least it wasn't someone in the family.

Thankfully, his job kept him busy, so he wasn't tempted to constantly watch Kristina anymore. But he'd probably have to go without sleep tonight. No telling how much she'd drink or what she'd do to commemorate Janelle's death, and he couldn't lose her. Not when he and Kristina were so close to the same age now.

Chapter Fifteen

W hat's your excuse this time, Derrick?" Michael asked, sliding across from him at the back of the pub.

A group of men surrounded Kristina at the bar, buying her shots for her twenty-first birthday. She'd mostly kept out of trouble in the last year, but she still put herself in precarious situations. Never worrying about walking down a dark alley alone, as though she knew he'd save her. She hadn't called out for him in a while, but every so often, she gazed up at the rooftops as though she knew he was protecting her.

"You need to let her go," Michael continued. "You said you'd quit when she turned twenty-one. She's an adult now, even if she doesn't act like one."

"Sometimes she acts like an adult," Derrick said. "She's almost finished college. It's been slow going, but she's trying. It's not easy paying your way on a waitressing job."

Mike snorted. "Especially when you drink away half your tips nightly."

Derrick glared at his brother, even though he knew it was true. Every time he heard Kristina say she'd never do it again, she did. She was just lonely. Not that she had a lack of dates, but she was lonely for someone who cared.

"I want to talk to her."

"The family won't allow it. She's a liability. And if it didn't work ... "

Derrick drilled a gaze at his brother again. "It'd never happen. I think I made myself clear on that. She hasn't said a word all these years. Obviously, she's forgotten."

"What if she recognizes you? You'll only look a few years older to her," Michael said, as if he had to remind him what he looked like.

"I think I'm in love with her."

"Derrick, you don't even know her."

"You're wrong. I know everything about her. For the last year, all I can do is think about her. I know her walk, her scent, her voice ... I know that she only reveals her real self to her best friend. I've listened to her share her dreams with Beth, dreams of what she wants, what she wants to accomplish. She has just as much drive as Janelle had ... but Janelle had a home, parents who loved her." He shook his head. "And I know she fights invisible demons in her sleep, just as I do every night. I know that she blames herself for Janelle's death. I know that she dreams about moving somewhere safer and warmer, where I'll never see her again. I know that she's lonely. And ... I think she's waiting for me."

"Damn, Bro, you're a regular stalker."

"You know it's nothing like that. I've only protected her. But now, it's there. The connection that I never understood, the reason I could never fall for another woman. My heart skips a beat every time I hear her voice. I'm not just worried about her anymore ... I want to meet her — personally. Who knows, I might be like one of the other guys she meets, and she might turn me down flat, and then, you'll win. I'll walk away. But shouldn't I get a chance? We're the perfect age for each other now."

Mike shook his head. "She's still too young, dude. Few humans make lifelong relationship decisions at twenty-one, and she drinks too much. She'd be a liability. Maybe in a few years the family will approve it. And what about Tori? I thought you two were getting along."

Derrick raised an eyebrow. "I hope you aren't still calling her Tori. She hates it." Derrick shook his head. "And we get along fine. Always have. We work together, have fun together, but that's it. I've told her how I feel. I can't help it that my heart doesn't practically leap out of my chest when she walks into the room."

"Every other man's does," Michael said, laughing. "You're insane. She's perfect."

"I know, and I've been honest with her. It's never going to happen, Mike. She, you, and the rest of the family need to realize that. I'm tired of repeating myself. In fact, let's go."

Derrick jumped up with one fleeting look at Kristina, who was too drunk to recognize him right now anyway. All that he could do was hope she'd get home safely. He didn't follow her anymore. He just made sure she was at home. If she wasn't, he just made sure no one was killing her, but he had no desire to listen to her on a date with another man.

When he reached his car, he called his father, letting him know he planned to put in his official request. He didn't care anymore. He knew what he wanted, what his soul wanted, the reason he couldn't fall for another woman. He'd just needed to wait until they were closer in age. Now that she was twenty-one, and he looked twenty-five, they were perfect for each other. Yeah, he'd be alone for a few years if it worked out, but he knew she was the one he wanted forever.

A few more years, the council agreed ... he only had to wait a few more years. He knew that would be better anyway, even if he didn't want to admit it. If she didn't get married, and he didn't fall for someone by the time she was twenty-five, the family agreed that she'd be old enough to make a decision. They were mostly concerned about her drinking, but Derrick was pretty sure she could walk away from alcohol if she wanted. They'd warned him, though ... If they did attempt a relationship, and she didn't fall, if it didn't work, he'd have to accept the consequences. He'd agreed, even though he knew he'd never let anyone touch her, regardless of what she decided.

Chapter Sixteen

Kris scanned the vestibule of her apartment building while she headed to her mailbox. As much as she tried to play off her mother's murder and the attack on her when she was sixteen, it still affected her sometimes.

She balanced her phone and water bottle in one arm while she jiggled the key inside the keyhole. "Stupid piece of garbage," she grumbled, "just like the rest of this place." If she didn't get it just right, the stupid thing refused to open. Meanwhile, her back was open to anyone who wanted to attack her. God, she wanted to get out of here.

After retrieving her mail, she trudged up to the third floor. Her feet ached from being on them all day at the restaurant, but she liked being on the top floor. It felt safe. Her apartment was one of the only places she felt secure.

She dropped the mail on the table and then worked her way around the apartment, watering her plants. She chattered aimlessly to each plant as she checked the soil and removed dead leaves. She felt silly sometimes, but whom else was she going to talk to, and she'd read that her carbon dioxide was good for them. The plants repaid her in their own way, greeting her daily with bright green leaves that reminded her of a tropical locale. Even when the rest of Boston was frigid and dreary, her apartment was warm and cozy.

Someday she'd be able to move south.

Kris set the water canisters in the sink, then plopped down at the table, picking up the first envelope. She sighed ... she knew what it was. She received them from the college almost every semester.

Your records have been placed on hold, which stops future enrollment, blah, blah, blah, the letter from college read. It wasn't the first time she'd had to drop out of a class. As much as she wanted to leave for a warmer state, college was the other reason she couldn't. She'd looked into out-of-state admission costs. She could barely afford what she was paying here, and she really wanted to finish.

The other reason she couldn't leave, of course, was *him. Someday,* she told herself. Someday she'd get attacked again, and he'd be there. Only next time, she wouldn't let him leave. She couldn't be one hundred percent sure that she hadn't made him up. *But twice?* How could she have imagined his eyes and heard his voice twice?

Absently, she reached for a pen. Those eyes ... she knew those eyes. Within seconds of finishing just his eyes, she ripped the paper to shreds. This was ridiculous. She couldn't stay here alone tonight. But she couldn't afford to go out either. Unless ... She hated doing it. She felt like such a tramp when she did it, but the men never seemed to mind. It wasn't as though she asked them.

Making up her mind, she pushed away from the table. No way was she going to stay home alone and wallow in self-pity or dream about some mysterious stranger who refused to show himself.

After showering, she doused herself with her favorite body spray she only used on rare occasions. She couldn't afford to use it daily, and it wasn't as though she'd increase her tips at work by smelling like Malibu Beach. No, she reserved it for going out.

She lined her eyes with dark eyeliner and shadow, then added a light sparkly color at the tips and just above her eyes, the way she'd seen the models in the magazines she perused at the library make up their eyes. Lastly, she slipped into the sexiest dress she owned. She'd bought the sheer, low-cut, backless black dress for prom when she had cash in her pocket after selling her mother's jewelry. She'd never worn it to prom, of course, but she'd reserved it for special occasions.

Tonight wasn't a special occasion; it was the anniversary of the worst night of her life. To celebrate, she planned to get so drunk that she wouldn't even remember her own name, let alone what she'd lost.

Kris didn't come to this nightclub often; it was too large. She preferred a quaint pub, where she stood out among the mostly male patrons. But she wanted to dance tonight, and the dance floor here was massive. She stared up at the majestic staircase that led to the second-story balcony where girls were practically hanging over the edge. The club was like a grand ballroom from the old days, but with a contemporary venue. Its classic splendor and modern atmosphere made for a unique nightlife experience, and she planned to enjoy every second of it.

She didn't go to the bar; she knew how to do this. And she didn't wait for someone to ask her to dance either. She found a spot right below the DJ's booth and let herself go. The dance mix pounded out of the speakers, and she moved to the beat. Lifting her arms, she moved her hips and got lost in the sounds, forgetting that she was supposed to find herself a date. It felt so good.

It took only a few minutes and a looker approached, smiling. He was ultra-hot, but she turned, acting as though he were obviously smiling at someone else. She continued to dance to her own rhythm, but felt him approach behind her. It wasn't unusual to feel another body knock up against you on the crowded dance floor, but two large hands on her hips was another story.

If she were anywhere else, she would have already turned around and shoved him off her. She turned beneath his hands, making sure it was the blond hottie, though. It was.

He smiled. "Want company?" he shouted above the din.

She narrowed her eyes as though she couldn't hear him.

He lowered his head to repeat his words in her ear, allowing her to inhale his cologne. Good. She didn't want to end up hanging out with someone who didn't smell good and take care of himself. Even his breath hinted of mint. "Would you like company?" he repeated. "Or would you rather dance alone?"

She smiled. So he'd come across the women who came here and wiggled their ass, but then got upset when a man dared to approach them. She was a lot of things, but she wasn't a tease. She enjoyed a good time as much as any man did. That didn't necessarily mean sex, but she wasn't afraid to have some fun. "Sure. Although, I'm kinda hot."

"Can I buy you a drink?"

She flashed him a seductive smile. "Sure."

He took her hand and led her off the dance floor toward the bar. "What do you like?"

"Coors Light, in the bottle, would be great."

"Bottle of Coors Light and a Heineken," he told the bartender. He looked back at her. "Want a glass?"

"If it doesn't bother you, I prefer the bottle."

He smiled as he nudged her closer to the bar, away from the swarming bodies. He seemed nice, gentle even. Of course, so had Greg. "Why would it bother me?" he asked.

She shrugged. "One guy said it looked unladylike. It just always seems easier when I'm out."

"I can't imagine you doing anything unladylike."

"Nice comeback," she said, offering him another smile.

He tipped his head as he handed her the bottle. "I try." He paid the bartender, then led her to a table away from the throng of people waiting for drinks and then even held out the counter-height stool for her to climb up. He took his own seat and then held up his bottle to hers. "By the way, I'm Kyle."

She clinked her bottle with his. "Kris."

"You come here often, Kris?"

"Ooh ... and you were doing so well." She laughed.

"Sorry ... lame, huh?"

"Yes, definitely lame, but no, it's a little loud for me. But I wanted to dance."

"Me too." He downed his beer, then motioned the waitress over for another one. "Want a shot?"

"Sure." As long as the server brought it, she didn't care. One rule she never broke anymore, though; she never accepted an open drink from a guy.

"Two more beers and two shots of tequila, please," Kyle requested.

After a few more shots and beers, Kyle led her back to the dance floor, this time for a slow dance. He rested his hands on her hips again, and then just moved them in a small circle. He dipped his head to her neck and inhaled. "You smell great, Kris."

She leaned back to look at him. "So do you."

He moved his hands up her back, pulling her closer.

Kris cringed. This, she didn't want. She just wanted to get drunk, which he'd done a good job of providing the means so far. Every time she reached for her purse, he'd pushed away her hands. The last thing she wanted was to take comfort in a man's arms, even as cute as he was. Somehow, it felt wrong. As strange as it seemed, drinking seemed to be an acceptable way to mourn her mother.

Kyle dipped his head again. "Do you like to get high, Kris?"

She didn't, not anymore. Every time she tried, she had some strange reaction.

"I have some good stuff. My brother gets it from Florida."

"That sounds like fun," she heard herself say.

He didn't wait; he took her hand and led her off the dance floor again. "Let's go. Do you need a ride?"

"I have a car."

He narrowed his eyes. "Should you be driving?"

Was he for real? He acted like a boy scout the way he escorted her to and from the dance floor, away from the scores of people, but then offered her drugs. *Who did that?* "I'm fine," she said.

"All right. I'll walk you to your car, and then you can just follow me home."

Home? She'd just been thinking they'd go to his car. He seemed nice, but ... Hell, what difference did it make? He could rape her just as easily in the parking lot as he could at his place, and somehow, it seemed if he was willing to invite her into his home, he didn't plan to hurt her. Didn't most psychos kill their prey in abandoned buildings — or in between dorm buildings?

No, Kyle was a clean-cut business guy who liked to get naughty on the weekends. His hands hinted that he'd never done a hard day's work in his life. His clothes screamed money. Too bad money had never been important to her; otherwise, she could probably trap some unsuspecting man like him. She'd known a few girls who'd done that. Kyle was probably some high-level consultant or broker. She doubted he was an attorney or physician, based on his nonchalant mention of drugs. But all she wanted from him was a night of escape from her life, from the guilt, from the nightmares.

He trailed her down the street, stopping in front of a sleek black Lexus. "Hop in. I'll drive you to your car."

"Umm ..." she hesitated. "It's just down the street."

He smiled. "I swear I won't bite."

She stood there, so he shoved his remote back in his pocket. "Okay. I'll walk you to your car, then."

Kris couldn't help but laugh. He wanted to get her high, but she couldn't walk down the street. Maybe he thought she'd run. "Fine. You can drive me."

Content in her assent, it seemed, he unlocked the vehicle again and opened the door for her. "Thank you. I'll feel better."

By the time they reached her car, her head had started to spin. She'd drunk more than she thought. Oh, yeah, the shots. She didn't usually do shots. How many had she had? Three ... no, four, and four beers. "How far is your place?" she asked as he stopped in front of her car.

"Just a few miles. You sure you're okay?"

"Yeah ... but drive slowly." She knew it was wrong, but who was out at this time of the night anyway? It was only a few miles. Tomorrow, she'd stop drinking for good. She just needed to get through this one night.

Kris pulled up behind Kyle, but cringed. She wasn't far from home; she'd driven through this neighborhood before, she was pretty sure. It looked vaguely familiar anyway. Too bad his apartment building wasn't as nice as his clothes and car.

Kyle opened her door and held out his hand. "I know it doesn't look like much. I'm working on moving soon, but I assure you it's clean inside."

Needing the support, Kris nodded and accepted his hand. He really was quite sweet. Her vision blurred and she tottered, almost falling into him as he led her up the stairs.

Kyle unlocked the door to his apartment, holding it open for her to enter. He hadn't lied. It was clean and tastefully furnished.

"Let me guess," Kris started, "you recently graduated MIT and landed a great job."

He smiled sheepishly. "Yeah ... something like that."

"So you're smart, you have a great career ahead of you, and yet, you get high."

He shrugged. "It's just pot. I already took my drug test."

Just pot. That's what everyone said.

"You want another beer? I don't have Coors Light, but —"

"Whatever you have is fine. Unopened please."

"Got it."

Kris sat down on the dark blue sofa. It was cleaner than most of the guys' apartments she'd been in, but she still wondered why she was here. What was she thinking? She knew better than this. Still, the thought of going home ...

Kyle sat down beside her. He opened the beer and handed it to her, then scooted closer, burying his head into her neck. "You smell amazing."

Kris adjusted herself so she edged away from him a bit. He no longer smelled as good as he had. The drinking, the dancing, sweat from the other patrons, had all permeated his clothes, and he must have smoked a cigarette on his way home. Buying some time, she took a long pull off her beer. Just what she needed ... more liquor.

Kyle ran his hand over her knee, moving her dress up slightly. At least he hadn't just gone right in for the kill. She hated that. "So ... do you want to fool around a bit or get high?"

She wasn't usually such a killjoy, but neither sounded acceptable anymore. But she still didn't want to go home either, not that she was capable of driving anyway. "Umm ..." she lifted her bottle again, downing it, "maybe another beer first."

He got up from the sofa, fumbled around in the kitchen for a few minutes, and then came back with the ice bin filled with beers. "There ... now I won't have to leave again." He opened another beer for her and leaned into her neck again while she downed it.

He was gentle, but she just wasn't feeling it. She hated strong odors. "How 'bout that hit?" If he got high, maybe he'd be like Billy and not be interested in anything but eating and watching cartoons.

"Uh ... sure." He got up again, and Kris fell back into the couch. What was wrong with her? Why couldn't she meet a guy like him under good pretenses? No liquor, no drugs. He seemed okay. But now that he was sweaty and smelly, she just wanted to leave.

Kyle sat back down with a bong and a bag. He sprinkled a few crushed leaves into the bowl and then reached for a lighter. He held up the bong for her.

"That's okay. Go ahead."

He smiled. "You're wary of doing things first and drinking out of opened containers, and yet, you're in my apartment." He shook his head. "Not sure I quite understand, but I swear I won't hurt you, and this really is primo weed."

Kris shrugged. "I've just been burnt a few times."

Kyle leaned toward her, running his fingers up her jaw. "You're beautiful, Kris, and I just want to have a little fun."

She gulped as he moved to her mouth. He pressed his lips against hers, immediately working to separate her lips so he could enter her. She tried to relax, but she just couldn't take it. She pulled back again. "Thank you."

Her disinterest didn't seem to upset him; he just moved his mouth to the bong instead of her. He held the lighter over the bowl and inhaled. He sat back, holding the smoke in, and then handed her the bong. She didn't want to, but she accepted it from him. She breathed in slowly, holding it in her lungs as long as possible.

Kyle smiled, seemingly content that she trusted him enough to smoke after him.

Kris reached for another beer, counting ... six, seven ... did it even matter anymore?

As suspected, Kyle sat back after a few more hits and flipped on the television, no longer as intent on sexual activity, she guessed. Good ... she just wanted to feel the buzz course through her, and for just a moment, forget.

"No ... take me, not her!" Her own scream woke her up. Kris looked around the strange apartment. The flickering TV gave her glimpses, but she couldn't quite make out where she was. A soft snore from beside her brought her up fast. She looked down at the stranger leaning against her.

Uck ... she cringed away ... trying to move out from beneath him. Thankfully, she was still fully dressed, so at least she hadn't had sex with him. *Umm ... was it Cato, Keith? God* ... she couldn't even remember his name.

She scrambled for her keys and purse on the coffee table. Her shoes. What had she done with her shoes? She fumbled on the floor with her toes, then got down on her hands and knees and felt around. Just a tip protruded from underneath the sofa. He must have inadvertently pushed them back when he'd sat down beside her.

Kris glanced down at the bong, the drugs, the empty beer bottles. Gross ... she was gross, and a rancid smell had her covering her mouth and nose, about to puke. She had to get out of there. Then what? Another day ... another night ... more days of her life wasted away.

She pushed through the door and stumbled into the hallway. She cringed again ... she'd forgotten what a dump he lived in.

What a worthless piece of garbage she'd become.

Chapter Seventeen

Derrick watched as Kristina left the bar and jumped into her Grand Am, ready to follow a total stranger home for a hit.

He still had three more years before he could talk to her, but with such a short time left, he couldn't take a chance that something would happen to her now.

She'd stopped smoking pot years ago, since every time she did it, she had the reverse reaction. Derrick wanted to grab her and show her how to use Google. Not everyone reacted the same way, and if she wasn't careful, one bad batch and she could end up dead. He'd been so good about not watching over her anymore, just making sure she got home safely.

Tonight was a bad night, though, the anniversary of Janelle's murder. She hadn't mentioned it ... she may not even remember, but she always became depressed in March and tended to drink too much. For that matter, so did he. When he heard the man at the bar mention that he had some good stuff at his apartment, he had to follow her.

As always, he tried to tune out if she was going to do anything sexual, but it sounded as though she'd fended off the man's advances rather well. She didn't sleep around, but she didn't seem to care whom she made out with.

The apartment was quiet for a while, and then her scream broke the air, "No ... take me, not her." She was safe ... just another nightmare. He still had them too.

A few minutes later, she barreled out the front of the apartment building. He clambered up a fire escape, repressing a sigh as she tripped on the sidewalk. She stumbled down the block, searching for her car, fussing the entire way, as if her choices in life were his fault.

Derrick lost focus of her for a second as he saw where they were. The same alley. *No!*

From the street below, her words echoed his as he smashed his hand over his mouth, feeling as though he'd puke from the stench and the memory. He couldn't be sure if the reek was from his recollection or if it still smelled like death here. *Not here.* He dropped to the floor of the rooftop, his body racking in pain. *Of all the places ... why did she have to end up here tonight?*

He lost sight of Kristina, but heard her yell at no one in particular. He was dying inside, and she was furious. With him. She blamed him. Only this time, she was right. He'd failed.

She finally stumbled upon her car and sped off. He raced across the rooftops to keep up with her. Normally he'd stop and look before he'd jump to the next building, but she sounded angry and desperate.

"Where are you going, Kristina?" he screamed at the top of his lungs, wishing she could hear him so she'd stop whatever she planned to do. He'd waited too long, and now she hated him for it.

Not caring, he bounded from one building to the next until he made it back to his vehicle. He sped through the streets to catch up to her until he saw that she was heading to the Mystic River, the Tobin Bridge. "Oh, no. God, no!"

Knowing she didn't plan to just drive to Chelsea, he pulled his vehicle over the first chance he got and then shot up to the top of the bridge, hoping she was bluffing. She hadn't seen him in years, since she was sixteen. It'd been six years. Why would she suddenly do this? He raced across the top railing, listening to her threats.

His heart pounded in his chest. *Don't do this, you stupid girl. God, don't do this. I can't save you this time.* Even though the sun hadn't come up yet, there were still too many people around. If anyone saw ... He chewed on his lip, deliberating how to stop her, but then dropped his head in defeat as he watched her plunge a hundred and thirty-five feet into the frigid waters of the Mystic River.

Creatus

It is from them we obtain our fairy tales — and our nightmares. They are the reason we believe in superheroes — and monsters. Because ... they exist.

Chapter One

Kris staggered down the stairwell of the apartment building, cursing aloud for what her life had become. Just twenty-two and she'd poisoned her body so many times she hardly even recognized herself.

A stale stench of sweat and liquor assaulted her senses, causing her stomach to lurch, compelling her to escape the dilapidated structure. The rusty railing swayed beneath her grip, giving her minimal support as she descended the stairs. As soon as she stepped onto the street, she inhaled a deep breath, trying to rid herself of the rancid smell. The smell persisted, which meant it was on her. Sadly, she wasn't sure if the odor belonged to the stranger with whom she'd spent the last few hours dodging sexual advances or if she smelled like the walking dead. How had she let herself become such trash?

"Why did you save me?" she screamed into the black void, similar to her life. She hadn't asked *him* to save her when she was eight years old.

As always, no one answered her ridiculous peal, which was probably just as well. Attracting attention in this part of town wasn't smart. She clicked the key fob for her Grand

Am as she scanned the street. She barely even remembered driving here after she left the nightclub.

The problem with drinking too much, which she did far too often these days, was that as her inhibitions fell, so did her standards. The man from the bar had been cute, but he'd obviously wanted something other than money in exchange for a hit. What else should she expect when she followed a man home whose name she couldn't even remember?

She hadn't planned to go home with a stranger. But when he'd suggested they could get high together, it had sounded like fun, a chance to escape her nightmares and her empty apartment. A chance to do anything but feel the pain she endured by her guilt every time she closed her eyes.

Kris strained to hear the chirp from her vehicle as she weaved along the sidewalk. Her heels lodged in the cracks in the concrete, causing her to trip several times. Somerville was such a dump. She should have used the money from selling her mother's jewelry six years ago on eBay and moved to California. Instead, she'd stayed in this frigid, run-down suburb of Boston. But she knew why she hadn't. She was afraid if she left, she'd never see her protector again. A day didn't go by that she didn't get an eerie feeling that someone was watching her.

Out of nowhere, a chill would travel the length of her spine she'd swear was her Dark Angel's breath on her neck. But every time she turned around, no one was there. So instead of escaping, she'd used the money to buy a P.O.S. car and drugs and started on her debauched journey. She knew she was better than the life she'd been living, but every night she found the answers no one offered her at the bottom of a bottle.

Sometimes she wished her *Dark Angel* hadn't saved her. If he didn't care, why had he bothered?

Not once, but twice.

She was beginning to think she'd conjured up his image to erase the guilt of her mother's death. Her Dark Angel, as she called him since she had no name for the handsome stranger, had accosted a degenerate who'd attacked her mother and her when she was eight, allowing her to escape. Unfortunately, her mother had still died.

When she was sixteen, he'd rescued her a second time. She'd been so excited to go to her first college frat party, but her date had laced her drink with some type of date-rape drug. Seconds after he'd helped her outside to get fresh air, he'd ripped at her clothes. When she'd refused, smacking his hand away, the college sophomore had turned aggressive. He'd smashed her head against a brick wall of the dorm, slamming his hand over her mouth. He would have raped her, and she wouldn't have been able to stop him. The drugs he'd given her had made it impossible to stand, let alone thwart his attack.

But again, out of nowhere, she'd felt the warm embrace of her Dark Angel's arms after he tore the loser off her, the same way he'd wrenched the murderer away from her mother. His mysteriously ebony-colored eyes had gazed into hers as he'd whisked her away. His deep, melodic voice had whispered that she'd be okay. The same aspects she'd distinctly remembered about him when she was eight. But then he'd disappeared again after depositing her inside her vehicle, ordering her to lock the doors until her best friend came out to the car.

She'd never told anyone about *him*. Not even her best friend.

Beth would have said, "Dark, mysterious stranger who watches over you ... yeah, right!" It did sound preposterous and melodramatically romantic, so it couldn't possibly be true. But no matter how many times her brain tried to convince her *he* didn't exist, her heart refused to listen. He'd protected her for a reason, she was certain. Although sometimes Kris wished her Dark Angel had allowed the thief in the alley to kill her too, saving her from a life of loneliness.

The sun hadn't come up yet, but the hue of the horizon was fading from a deep navy to a lighter shade of violet. Another beautiful spring day she'd spend sleeping off a massive hangover she felt making its way to the surface. Another day she wouldn't make it to work, and this time they'd fire her. Her boss had made that crystal clear last time.

Another sharp odor hit her senses, knocking her backward a few steps, stumbling again. The pungent scent of rotting vegetables instantly transported her to the night of her mother's death. For years, she'd been unable to keep fruit for more than a day in her apartment because the scent brought back the painful memories. But this time, it felt as if she were actually there again, as if the scent had literally transported her to that horrible moment when she lost everything.

Kris took a moment to survey the alley from which the reek emanated. Her eyes raked over the faded red brick, a flickering sign at the end, and a dumpster overflowing with garbage from the mom-and-pop grocery store, the source of the insulting pong. Sucking in a breath, she almost retched as the memory hit her fully.

Oh, God! She was in the same alley where her mother had been murdered.

Shaking her head to dislodge the painful recollection, Kris tottered in her high heels. The rough texture of the wall dug into her skin, reinforcing the memory. The image of the thief's face flashed in her head. Even before he'd plunged the knife into her mother's chest, she'd detected the murderous gleam in his eyes.

Nothing would obliterate the memory of him shoving them against that decaying building, the glint of the knife as he'd wielded it erratically. The blood — so much blood. Her mother's blood.

Kris whipped her gaze to the rooftops, knowing her Dark Angel was watching her, knowing he was always close by. "You were there," she cried. "I don't know who or *what* you are, but I want to know why you didn't save my mother!" She gasped out a breath, attempting to contain her cries. "And why you left me alone!"

No matter what she wanted to believe, the memory was real. She hadn't imagined the fact that he jumped off a four-story building and landed in front of her with a soft thump, the sliver of light from the street which revealed that he was much larger than the guy who'd attacked them. Nor had she dreamt up the anguished scream that had escaped his throat as he tore the thug off her mother, the *crack* of the degenerate's skull as he slammed him into the concrete.

As they'd tried to get away, her mother collapsed in her arms. She'd pleaded for the angel to help her. But he'd just stared from where he squatted by the thug, his dark eyes focusing on her as though he recognized her, and said, "I'm sorry. There's nothing I can do to save her." She'd blinked the tears out of her eyes, and he was gone. Kris had buckled in the dark alley, crying over her only parent's lifeless body until the police arrived.

She'd hated him for protecting her but not her mother. Since her mother had never told anyone her father's name and no relatives had claimed her, she'd spent the next ten years of her life in a different foster home every six months or so. Every time she'd gotten into trouble or the couple was able to adopt a newborn, they had tossed her back to the state, and the state pitched her right into another unloving home.

Realizing her Dark Angel wouldn't show unless her life was in danger, Kris yanked off her shoes and started running down the walkway. The icy pavement burned her feet, as if she were running on coals, and the uneven surface caused her to stub her toes. But she had to escape the rancid memory of her mother's death, and she had to force him out of the shadows.

"Where are you?" she shouted, deciding that maybe she did want to attract the wrong kind of attention. Again, no one answered. *Figures*, she thought. *No thieves or rapists around when you need one.*

She pressed the button on her key fob frantically, spinning in the street, her arm raised high as she checked every direction, desperate to find her car. Finally hearing the chirp, she careened toward her vehicle. After fumbling with the door handle, she slumped in the seat, her head sinking against the steering wheel.

"Why did you save me?" she blubbered again. "So I could drink myself to death?" Of course, *her choices* weren't his fault. She'd just hoped that he would feel compelled to rescue her from her stupid decisions, like going outside with that college guy. He'd been right to call her *stupid girl* as he carried her away.

Kris examined her face in the rearview mirror, blanching at her reflection. Even with her creamy skin and golden blond hair, she looked old. Swirled and smeared lines of mascara streamed down her cheekbones, filling in the few creases on her face. She'd obviously been crying in her sleep again.

She vaguely remembered the nightmare that had woken her a mere hour after she'd crashed on the stranger's couch. She'd been attempting to save her mother, trying to grab the knife. The thief had stuck her this time, and she was happy. Happy she'd taken the punishment for asking to go out for ice cream that fateful night. The reward she'd received for making the honor roll was that her mother had died.

Kris turned the key, and the engine whined in protest. Her car was obviously on its last leg too. When she reached the highway, she headed toward the Mystic River, specifically, the Tobin Bridge.

It was time.

She'd realized before that it was the only way, but now she was going to follow through with her decision. The jump itself wouldn't do it. But from what she understood, it'd knock her out. Drowning was supposed to be a tranquil way to die, especially if you were unconscious. Hopefully that wouldn't happen, but he'd left her no choice.

She lifted her phone from her purse and called the one person who'd care. A pang of guilt shot through her. They hadn't spoken much since graduation five years ago, but Beth had asked her to be her maid of honor. Beth was now a teacher at their old high school and a soon-to-be-married woman. It was *Facebook Official*, as Kris would have said a few years ago. Nowadays she couldn't care less about social media, though. The only notifications she still received were Beth's updates. They no longer shared common interests, but she was the one person Kris had ever felt a connection with. Well, except for her Dark Angel. Even though she couldn't see him, she always felt him. Somehow, their souls had connected when he'd saved her. She just needed to get him to reveal himself.

She'd done the rashest things in the last six years to force him into the open, but she'd never been desperate; she'd just been reckless. But no matter how many times she'd put herself in precarious situations, she'd never been attacked again. Maybe that was why she'd decided to kill herself slowly with drugs and alcohol, hoping he'd eventually save her from herself. *Did he feel her pain now?* she wondered. *Would he stop her?*

Kris waited as the rings ceased and the message clicked on. "You know what to do," Beth's chipper voice came through the phone followed by a beep.

"I love you, Beth," Kris said calmly through fresh tears, attempting to suppress any audible cries. She didn't want her friend to hurt in the event she was wrong. "I'm sorry. I really am. But know I'll be happier wherever I am." She clicked *end* and tossed the phone on the seat.

Kris drove her car onto the curb and climbed out onto the upper deck of the Tobin Bridge, the highest bridge in Massachusetts.

"Are you going to let me do this?" she yelled into the darkness that engulfed her, wishing the sun would just come up already. "I've looked everywhere for you, and you refuse to show yourself."

Bitter March winds whipped at her hair and body, turning her pale skin into a checkerboard of red and white. She scrubbed at her arms with her hands to warm them. How stupid. If he was a figment of her imagination, or chose not to save her this time, she'd be drowning in the frigid water of the Mystic River in minutes.

"If you exist, you'll save me. I know you will. But if you don't, I don't want to live anyway."

As the sun's rays peeked above the horizon, lighting the abyss below her, she inhaled a deep breath, closed her eyes, and jumped. The ice-cold air coming off the freezing river enveloped her as she plummeted. She didn't scream; she didn't look down. As much as she hated her life, she hoped it wouldn't end this way. She'd really like to see him one more time.

Her life didn't flash before her eyes as she'd always heard. Just an image of her mother covered in blood and her Dark Angel telling her he was sorry. Those were obviously the only images she'd ingrained into her subconscious as important.

As she hit the water, a second of crushing pain seized her body and then the world turned dark and cold, enveloping her into its chasm.

"Breathe, dammit!"

His deep voice penetrated her brain at the same time the sensation of a red-hot poker seared her shoulder. She gasped for air, but fire radiated through her chest as she attempted to inhale the cool air. She opened her eyes but couldn't see the face above her, only a silhouette of a man. She recognized his voice, though. Her Dark Angel had come for her.

The morning sun glared into her eyes, blinding her as she tilted her head to see him. As she lifted her hand to shield her face, a bolt of pain surged through her arm. "Oww ..." she groaned.

"You dislocated your shoulder and you may have a couple of cracked ribs, but you'll live," said the deep voice she'd longed to hear for six years.

"I'm supposed to be dead," she wheezed.

He cupped the side of her face. "No, you're not. You're supposed to live, Kristina. For me. I just wanted a few more years, you stupid girl."

Remembering how he'd called her *stupid girl* when she was sixteen, she tried to pull in a breath to protest, but it hurt too much. So she used what limited oxygen she had left in her lungs. "Stop ... calling ... stupid."

He spurted out a breath and stood, shaking his head. "I'll be back in a minute. Try not to get into trouble."

Kris sealed her eyes shut, attempting to block out the sun as well as the throb in her shoulder, but then she couldn't help but smile. Maybe she *was* dead, because she could swear she'd just heard him say he'd be back.

Chapter Two

Derrick leaned over Kristina, thankful she was still alive. Her eyes opened and she smiled. She had to be in pain, but she forced a smile anyway. His heart soared. He'd wanted to wait a few more years. But now that he was here, beside her, allowing her to see him, he had no idea how he'd waited as long as he had.

He could have lost her. She could have died from that drop. He'd never believed for a second she would jump. She'd never indicated she was suicidal.

He touched her face again, loving the way her soft skin felt beneath his palm, hating that he was going to have to hurt her to help her. "I'm not going to lie to you; this isn't going to feel pleasant. I need to set your shoulder before I can move you." He removed his leather belt and held it in front of her mouth. "Bite down on this."

Her eyebrows furrowed a bit, a flicker of fear lighting in her eyes, but she accepted the strap without uttering a word. Did she think he'd hurt her on purpose?

Derrick bent her arm at a ninety-degree angle, rotating her arm and shoulder inward, toward her chest. She clenched her teeth together on the leather, restraining her cries, for which he was grateful. It would kill him to see her in agony. Slowly, he rotated her arm and shoulder outward, keeping her upper arm stationary, coaxing it back into the shoulder joint.

She released her grip on the belt and exhaled in relief. "How did you do that?"

"I'm a doctor." He scooped her up carefully and moved her into his vehicle. They needed to talk, but they couldn't remain here. Someone might have seen her jump and would be calling the police.

As if in shock, Kristina didn't say anything else as he strapped her in the passenger seat. She just stared at him, her hazel eyes sparkling in the morning sunlight. Beautiful, mesmerizing, even though wisps of red lined the sclera. He reached into the cargo area of his Navigator and grabbed a blanket, which he handed to her as he dropped behind the wheel. She accepted it without comment, wrapping it around her. He adjusted the temperature controls as he drove out of the parking space at the yacht club where he'd carried her up on shore. She still hadn't spoken a word, so he drove off without explanation. Maybe she was in shock or ticked that he'd called her stupid. It'd been rude, he knew. But why in hell would she jump off a bridge?

Feeling her gaze burning through him, he cast a glimpse in her direction.

"You're ... real," she finally sputtered, a quiver in her voice as she touched his arm. "You're flesh and blood."

Huffing out a chuckle at her words, he attempted to contain his nervousness of her accusation, as if she'd discerned there was something unusual about him. He didn't look any different from any other twenty-something-year-old male.

He'd always assumed that once they met, he could convince her that she'd been mistaken as a child when she told the police officer that her dark angel had saved her.

"Of course I'm real," he said, attempting to add enough conviction behind his words so she wouldn't question him further. He proceeded over the Tobin Bridge and took the exit toward the park underneath the tall structure on Chelsea's side of the Mystic River. After he pulled into a space, he turned to the young woman he'd waited fourteen years to meet. "We need to talk."

Her eyes widened in a mock gesture. "You think?"

Derrick exited the vehicle and walked around to the passenger side, opening the door, but Kristina didn't get out. "Are you coming?" he said as softly as he could force himself. He'd saved her life for the fifth time by his count — of course, she only knew about two of the situations — and the first thing she chose to do was develop an attitude with him.

She assessed the deserted recreational area, her gaze raking across the vacant playground and picnic area, and then looked at him again. "Where are we going?"

"A morning stroll." He motioned his head to the north, raising an eyebrow. "Don't tell me you're afraid of me," he taunted, knowing she always tended to lean toward danger. He swore the girl thrived on putting herself in treacherous situations.

"I'm not afraid of anyone," she retorted, a pronounced pucker of her lips detracting from the power of her words. She proceeded to move her legs to the side, but then cringed at the pain in her side.

"That's what happens when you jump from a hundred and thirty-five feet." He shook his head at her foolishness. "What in the world were you thinking?"

Ignoring him, Kristina inched herself out of the SUV and carefully pulled herself upright. Her good arm cradled her other, but she didn't as much as let out a peep.

"We could stay in the car," he offered quickly, a pang of guilt rushing through him. He was being too hard on her. He'd heard her proclamation, knew why she'd jumped. "But the sunshine will do you good. You picked a beautiful morning to kill yourself, so I thought it'd be nice if our official introduction was a little more memorable than just me saving you." He held out his hand to her.

She scrutinized him, scrunching her eyebrows and crossing her arms, even though the movement caused her to wince again. "What's your name?"

Ah, my spunky girl is coming to, he thought. He smiled, dropping his hand since she obviously wasn't going to accept it. "Derrick," he said, gesturing to the walkway. "Come on, it's just a short walk."

As they strolled along the boardwalk that bordered the Mystic River, a grouping of black-capped chickadees flew about them, searching for offerings, which brought a faint smile to Kristina's face. A local obviously fed them regularly.

The sun was higher now, bathing Boston with a heavenly glow, providing a beautiful backdrop.

Rays of sunlight reflected off the steel and glass buildings, sparkling like diamonds on the horizon. *The City upon a Hill,* as it had been dubbed, conveyed a quiet innocence in the morning. Of course, he knew better. Tonight, the vilest of society would be out to terrorize and take what wasn't theirs. But for the time being, he was with the woman he'd protected from those beasts. The woman he'd also protected from his brother and best friend after she'd seen his antics in the alleyway so many years earlier.

He stopped at a bright sunny spot away from the playground, which would fill with children in the next hour. He aided Kristina to the lawn and then tucked the blanket around her. "I would have taken you to the hospital, but they can't do much more than I did. All they can do is try to make you comfortable. *And* ... they'd commit you for attempting suicide." He shook his head again at the fact that she would do something so reckless, but held his tongue from uttering any more insensitive remarks. "Warm enough?"

She bobbed her head, but then released an uneasy breath tinged with discomfort. She crinkled her nose and then shook her head as if confused. "You look exactly the same."

Derrick broke eye contact and stared off at the river. He figured she wouldn't accept anything but a full explanation, but that was something he couldn't give her yet. "No I don't. It was dark in that alley," he refuted, realizing she wouldn't buy it, but knowing he had to try to convince her otherwise.

"But I saw you," she insisted. "It's been fourteen years, and you look the same age as me."

He turned to her and sighed, wanting to tell her everything. Hoping she'd accept him. "I wanted to wait a few more years. You're too young to know what you want, but you forced my hand."

Her mouth turned up a fraction, revealing she was pleased with herself, but she held a full grin at bay. "I always thought you were a vampire or something."

He cleared his throat, resisting the urge to laugh. "Vampires don't exist. The dead don't walk. And if you don't have a heart pumping blood through your body, you can't do any of the things that supposed vampires do." He raised his brow, inquiring if she caught the gist of his comment. He'd always wondered how books and movies portrayed vampires as sensual and erotic when they purportedly didn't have the necessary body functions required to perform sexual acts. You didn't have to be a doctor to understand that if you don't have a heart pumping blood through your body, vital sexual organs aren't going to function properly.

"I know vampires don't exist," she rejoined. "But ..." she moved her head slowly from side to side as though trying to unite her memory with reality, "the way you came off that roof. And you *do* look the same. Now that I know I didn't conjure up some apparition, I know what I saw. So, what are you? No *normal* human could jump off a four-story building without getting hurt."

He gazed into her eyes, attempting to impress on her the importance of this conversation. "If I tell you, Kristina, your life as you know it is over. You'll have to stay with me forever. My family won't allow you to leave once you choose. That's why I wanted to wait until you were older."

Kristina lifted her chin, steeling herself, a question in her eyes as she struggled to understand, it seemed. "Can you make me what you are, then?"

His jaw practically fell open in response. He hadn't expected her to accept that he was different so easily. "Can you turn an ape into a human? No, I can't make you what I am; I'm a living being like you."

Her body trembled, and she gathered the blanket tighter, as though a chill had swept through her. She'd been fishing for an answer, and he'd caved. Maybe she wasn't ready. He needed to be careful.

But then she squared her shoulders and sat up straighter, as if preparing for the truth. "So, why me? Why did you save me — twice?"

Twice? It'd been more than twice, he wanted to confess. But he understood what she was really asking: *Why hadn't I saved Janelle?*

"I was too late." He balled his hands into fists at his sides. "If I'd only been a few minutes earlier, your mother would be alive. That punk stabbed her in the descending aorta. It was amazing she'd lived as long as she had." He ran his hand across his forehead at the memory, pinching his temple. "So I had to make sure I'd never lose you; I couldn't fail twice."

Her eyes softened, accepting his answer. But then she leaned closer, her brow furrowing as if a thought had just occurred to her. "But how do you always know where I am?"

Derrick focused above her head, afraid to meet her eyes for this tidbit. "I wish I could claim some magical, mythical power, but I can't," he said, trying to make light of his confession. She didn't crack a smile, so he continued, "It was easy the first eight years; I just had to check on you at night, make sure whichever foster home you were with didn't abuse you. But then, you turned into a wild teenager, so I had to find ways to keep track of your whereabouts." He lowered his gaze to her eyes again. "I tracked you by your cell phone. Amazing the programs that are available. I could sit back and wait to see what trouble you would find." He smiled, attempting to diminish his admission.

"So that's how you knew I was at the party," she said, seemingly not alarmed by the fact that he'd kept tabs on her. He thought for sure that she'd think he was some deranged stalker.

He drew in a breath at the memory of Kristina when she was sixteen. He'd seen the two of them on the balcony, heard their conversation. Ignored the first twinge of jealousy as it'd hit him. He'd never thought of her as anything but his charge. But when he'd heard the college kid tell her to drink up and then offer for them to go outside for fresh air, he sensed he was up to no good. He'd waited, though. He'd thought it would be good to let the boy scare her, but he hadn't expected him to turn violent as quickly as he had. "That kid is lucky I didn't kill him."

Kristina dropped her head, apparently not upset, but plainly disappointed for some reason. "So, you're human?" she asked, a note of doubt tainting her words.

He released a breath of relief that the idea didn't repulse her, but then realized she'd obviously ignored his attempt to change the subject of what he was. Offering her a hint of a smile, he said, "Would that disappoint you?"

When he'd failed to save her mother, leaving her parentless, he'd become her protector. But after seeing her with that college kid, he'd started to see her differently. They looked nothing alike, didn't listen to the same music, didn't do the same recreational activities. But he'd always hoped that once they finally met, she would like him. In the last few years, he'd fallen in love with her strength and spirit, even though he didn't agree with her unwise choices to escape reality.

"I just don't understand. How can you be the same age as I am if you're human?"

"I'm not the same age," he said, resisting a sigh. He wanted to tell her, needed to tell her, longed to tell her, but knew he could only reveal so much without knowing if she was the *One*. "I'm roughly twenty-eight in your years, though." Again, he was talking too much, but he had to give her something, and for some reason, he felt as if he could confess anything to her.

She absorbed his answer without commenting. Kristina did senseless things, but she wasn't stupid by any means.

He stared into her eyes for a moment, noticing she didn't look away. "Kristina, if you'll allow me, I want to watch over you while you come down. And then we can discuss everything else. Okay?"

Her brow furrowed again. She hated anyone to tell her what to do. He'd overheard many arguments between her and her foster parents over the years. Of course, in her defense, most of them had never treated her as their child, but rather as a paycheck. Just another kid they fed in order to pad their pockets. "Come down from what?" she snapped.

His breath came out as a puff of smoke in the cool air at her reaction. He was surprised she was even able to have the conversation they were having. Based on her dilated pupils, even in the bright sunlight, she was still a tad bit high from her recreational activities only hours earlier. "Trust me; in about two days, you'll know what." He tilted his head in query. "Do you trust me, Kristina?"

A gentle smile lifted her cheeks, the first indication of the sweet woman he knew was hidden beneath her hard outer shell. He'd seen her soft side, the side she only shared with her best friend, Beth. "I don't even know you, but yes, I do trust you. Even with my life a couple times, obviously."

Derrick rested his hand on the side of her neck, his heart thrumming at the chance to be near her. She didn't flinch at his touch; in fact, she closed her eyes and leaned into it. Soft golden beams of morning light saturated each strand of her hair, casting a delicate glow around her face. "You're a beautiful woman. So smart, so sweet. Why have you done this to yourself?" He ran his fingertips along her face from her temple to her jaw, then brushed her long blond hair off her shoulder, happy that she had at least stopped adding the purple and pink streaks. Another attempt to stand out in a world where she felt all alone, he assumed. She could have been anything she wanted, but she'd spent the last six years abusing her body.

She pressed her hand against his. "You forced *my* hand," she answered. "I was looking for you."

Chapter Three

Derrick paced the floor of his apartment, his phone clenched in his hand as he listened to his brother's babbling. As usual, Michael was unable to keep his opinions to himself. They'd gone through the same thing last time.

His brother took a breath long enough that Derrick thought he might get in a word, but then started yapping again before he could speak. "Mom and Dad will be fine as long as you clean her up, but Vic's going to be ticked. Me? What do I care? She's just another human you're infatuated with —"

"That's enough, Michael," Derrick cut him off, breaking into the one-way conversation. "The reason I called was to tell Dad I wouldn't be in to work this week. I didn't ask for your opinion." Derrick stared out at the Boston skyline through the wall of windows on the one side of his apartment, his blood boiling at his brother's callousness. His brother was one of their kind who'd be happier if they were the only superior beings on this planet.

Michael released a long, drawn-out breath. "I thought you'd want the opinion of your wiser, and obviously more sensible, brother. But then again, you've never listened to me. Why should you start now?" He paused for a second, and Derrick could hear the weight machine in the background. Michael never felt he was large enough. He constantly worked out to improve his already-stellar physique. It drove Michael crazy that even with his two inches of height and twenty extra pounds, Derrick could still pin him. The clang of the steel plate clinking into place echoed through the phone, and his brother's breath filled the line again. "Personally, I don't understand the infatuation."

Derrick rested his head against the cool glass, irritated that he'd even taken the time to call, wishing his father hadn't already left for work, which forced him to converse with his younger brother, who for some reason seemed to think he was in charge. Derrick needed to return to the room before Kristina woke up. She'd be confused, he was certain. "You make it sound as if I have a different woman every week. You know there hasn't been anyone in my sights other than her. I've waited fourteen years for Kristina."

"Freak!" His brother let out a roar of laughter. "Just make sure I'm around when you tell Vic. I don't want to miss that."

Derrick squeezed his eyelids closed, resisting the urge to chuck the phone across the room. For some reason, Michael could roil him up faster than anyone else could. "I've already settled this with Vic. We've had this conversation, and we just don't agree — on anything. And I'm not a freak. I had to protect Kristina all these years, since she didn't have anyone else. I knew she'd mature to be as smart and strong as her mother, whom I greatly admired." Janelle had been one of the smartest women he'd worked with when he was in med school. She'd been trying to better her life while carrying the responsibilities of a single mother.

A snort boomed through the phone's speaker. "Yeah, I saw how much you admired Janelle."

"You know it was never like that," Derrick defended himself. "I had a fondness for her, but I was too young. We worked together, nothing more. Kristina's perfect. She's everything I saw in her mother but with a lot more spunk."

"Well, you obviously have more than a *fondness* for Kristina," Michael responded with a chuckle. For someone who hated humans, his brother sure rattled off plenty of innuendos, making it clear where his mind was most of the time. Of course, Michael had the mentality of a twenty-three-year-old male. It didn't matter what species males were when the hormones were in full swing.

Derrick, on the other hand, had only one woman on his mind, which had been the case for the last few years. He'd just been biding his time. "Kristina is special. She's had a hard life and hasn't dealt with her troubles in the correct way, but she's strong. She's caring and wonderful. And she's smart. She's definitely the woman I want to spend my life with. Even if I end up being alone a few years, she'll be worth it."

"Whatever," Michael grunted, and Derrick could picture him throwing his hands up in frustration. Like Vic, his brother was another person he rarely agreed with. Yeah, they all got along, but when it came to their beliefs, his two best friends, Michael and Vic, saw things differently than he did and weren't shy about voicing their opinions. They harassed him every time he mentioned Kristina. "You don't even know if she'll want you, or how she'll react when she finds out you knew her mother. That'll mess with her head. And then, if she doesn't choose you —" Michael broke off,

not finishing his words. His brother knew Derrick
understood what he was inferring.

Derrick's heart thrashed in his chest at Michael's
insinuation. His hands broke out in a sweat causing his grip
to slip on the phone. "You haven't spoken with anyone,
have you? I haven't told Kristina anything, I swear." The
line was quiet and Derrick squeezed the phone in his hand,
almost crushing it. He had to remember his own strength
sometimes. "Michael, tell me you haven't said anything," he
demanded.

"No, man. I haven't said a word," his brother finally said
through a groan.

Derrick expelled a breath of relief. "Thank you. I just
need a few more days. She's through the worst part."

"Where is she now?" Michael asked. A note of concern
in his brother's tone surprised Derrick. Michael had made it
clear on several occasions how he felt about Kristina, about
most humans for that matter. Why would he even care if
she made it through alive?

"Still sleeping. Her fever was high and her pressure was
through the roof. I almost lost her. As you know, it's not
always safe to bring someone down like that. But she has a
strong heart, and I didn't have time to wait for days or
weeks while I tapered her off slowly."

"Why didn't you just give her Valium?"

"Because the last thing Kristina needed —"

"No!" Kristina's scream reverberated through the
apartment, breaking through their conversation. She'd
woken up several times in the last couple of days with cold
sweats and tremors, but this time, her cry resembled one of
her nightmares. It angered him that she still suffered nightly
from memories of Janelle's murder, memories of what that
butcher had stolen from her. Maybe now he could help her
through them.

"I gotta go," Derrick said, hanging up, not waiting for a reaction from his brother.

He barreled across the living room, but inched open his bedroom door quietly so as not to startle her. Kristina was still out cold, so it'd been a nightmare. He didn't want her to wake before he had a chance to put everything away, but he needed to check her vitals before doing anything else. He sat on the chair beside the bed where he'd spent the last forty-eight hours watching over her. Droplets of moisture still dotted her forehead, but she wasn't as pale as she'd been only hours earlier. He reached for her wrist to check her pulse, and her eyes popped open.

She tried to sit up, but the straps impeded her movement. "What the —"

"Hang on. It's okay," he scrambled to explain.

"*Okay?*" she screamed. "You've tied me up?"

"Restrained you," he countered. "There's a difference." Ignoring her full-on glower, he reached for her wrist again, checking her pulse. It had dropped to a safe level, but it was still high for her age. Of course, being *tied up* could cause that reaction, he reasoned.

He unlatched one restraint, and she immediately drew her arm to her chest. "Why did you *restrain* me?"

"You had the DTs, Kristina. You were hallucinating, screaming at the walls, but I think you're finally safe." He unbuckled her other wrist, his eyes gauging her overall health. Her lovely shade of peach had returned to her face, and her skin was more luminescent than the dehydrated state she'd been in for two days. Actually, she looked better than she had in years. "How do you feel?"

She moistened her chapped lips with her tongue before speaking. "Thirsty. Tired."

"I'll bet." He handed her the bottle of water he'd left on the nightstand. She unscrewed the top and took a long pull, her eyes holding his with a hint of caution. He offered her a smile. Not only to comfort her, but because he was overjoyed that she appeared to be over the worst part. "It's not easy to quit drinking cold turkey, but you did it. You're going to be okay." He hesitated. "Unless you start drinking again, that is."

After swabbing the area on her forearm with alcohol, he removed the IV from her vein and covered the tiny puncture with a clean cotton square and tape, smoothing the area several times with his thumbs, delighting in just holding her hand in his.

When he finished, he looked up at her, wondering why she hadn't spoken more than two words. "You need to call Beth. She's worried sick. I returned her texts as if I were you, assuring her you were okay, but she keeps asking you to call." He paused at the confusion in her eyes then quickly added, "I'm sorry if I overstepped my bounds; I just didn't think it was right to leave her worrying about you." He reached for Kristina's phone on the table and held it out to her, letting her know she wasn't a hostage, since she was staring at him like a trapped mouse. "Please just let her know you're okay, nothing else."

Without offering a word, Kristina finished off the bottle of water, trading the empty plastic for her phone.

Not knowing what else to say, Derrick stood to leave as she continued to gawk at him. He assumed she'd have more to offer than a few words. He'd rather hear questions than nothing. Even though she must have been reeling about everything, he was anxious to talk with her. He'd waited so long. Maybe his brother was right; maybe they weren't supposed to be together. "I'll give you a few minutes. You're probably starving anyway. Please don't mention me," he reminded her.

She offered him a nod, so he left the room somewhat contented. It was something anyway. At least she wasn't catatonic. She just needed to catch her bearings.

Derrick walked out into the hallway and then took the elevator to the café in the lobby to get something to eat. He had plenty of food, but he didn't have any way to cook it, and she needed protein. He also wanted to be out of earshot in case she told her friend about him. The lobby wouldn't be far enough, but he could make an effort to tune out her voice. He didn't want to hear anything that would make him have to turn her in. He would never allow them to kill her; he'd destroy anyone who tried. The only thing he could do was hope she fell for him.

He'd only looked to be in his early twenties when he met Janelle, but they had become great friends. In actuality, he'd already lived more than thirty-five human years at that time, but most of his kind lived to one hundred fifty, so they didn't count their years the same. His family had warned him he was too young to fall for a human and that he should stick to his own kind. He'd heeded their words, but since Janelle and Kristina had lived in such a rough area of Boston and were all alone, he'd always felt compelled to check on them. Something his father and grandfather had done for complete strangers in the early days of America, before everyone had a video camera on their phone.

He was now at the age where he wanted to make a lifelong commitment, and Kristina was the woman he wanted to spend the rest of his life with, something Vic and he had discussed numerous times. No matter how many times Vic or Michael tried to change his mind, he wouldn't bend. Kristina was the woman he wanted.

Derrick ordered a double egg-and-cheese bagel sandwich and a latte for Kristina, and then headed upstairs.

"I brought you a vanilla latte," he called out as he walked inside the apartment. She didn't respond, so he peeked in the bedroom, hoping she was decent. He blanched when he didn't see her. "Oh, Kristina!" he shrieked. "They'll kill you." He loped to the front door and jerked it open, as if she would be standing in the hallway waiting for him. Of course she'd left. He probably scared the heck out of her by strapping her to the bed. But if he hadn't, she would have hurt herself. He needed to find her before they did.

"What are you screaming about?" she spoke behind him. "My head is pounding. Please don't yell."

He whipped his head toward the sound of her voice. "Oh, thank God." He released a deep breath. "I thought you left."

She shrugged. "Why would I leave? I've tried to get your attention for six years." She ambled over to where he stood rooted to his wooden floor, accepted the coffee cup and bag of food, and plopped heavily onto the sofa. "Oh, this smells to die for."

Interesting choice of words, Derrick thought as he sank into a chair facing Kristina, drinking in the sight of her. Her hair was damp and she was wearing one of his T-shirts. She'd recovered faster than he'd anticipated. Of course, he'd always known she was strong.

Fiddling with the paper bag, Kristina stared at her lap as though she'd forgotten he was in the room. Finally making eye contact, she moved her mouth toward the sandwich and then stopped as if she'd decided on what she wanted to say. "So, Derrick ..." She paused, measuring her words, it seemed, then took a bite, chewed, and washed down the food with a swig of coffee. "Why don't you start at the beginning? I think I was still drunk the other morning. I don't remember much. Exactly *what* are you?"

He let out a burst of laughter. There was the girl he thought he'd known. He'd hoped she was somewhere inside that drug and alcohol-saturated body. "I'm so glad to finally meet you, Kristina, but why don't we hold off on the deep inquisition for a while? It's good you don't remember much. Now we can get to know each other under better circumstances."

She ripped off another piece of bagel with her slender fingers, then stood again, walking over to the wall of windows overlooking the harbor. "Nice place. What do you do for a living?"

Good, he thought. She really didn't remember. "I'm a doctor." She turned to face him, and the light from outside made its way through the shirt, illuminating every curve beneath the thin white cotton. "Umm ... Kristina, you're standing in direct sunlight."

She glanced at her choice of clothes and then traipsed toward the sofa, her hands roaming over the soft leather. "Nothing you haven't seen before if you're a doctor," she teased, a lightness in her voice he hadn't detected earlier.

"True," he allowed. She definitely had spirit.

Her eyes roamed over the black-and-white nature prints he'd hung on the wall behind the sofa. "What type of practice?" she asked, making eye contact with him again.

"Family medicine."

Kristina returned to the sofa, plopping down and then tucking her leg underneath her. Resting her elbow on the armrest, she focused a poignant gaze on him. "This is kind of awkward. You know I'm not really suicidal, right? I hate my life, but I knew you'd come. I didn't want to die."

He nodded, nibbling on the inside of his cheek, still a bit perturbed by her stunt that could have killed her. "Did you call Beth?"

"No. I needed a shower, and I wasn't sure what to say. I didn't tell her I was going to jump off a bridge. I just told her I'd be happier wherever I was. Beth, as always, assumed the worst." She took a sip of coffee and then her gold-flecked eyes peeked up at him under long blond lashes. She was even more beautiful than Janelle had been.

"Why don't you call Beth while I get cleaned up, and then we'll go out and get some fresh air? I have the week off work, so we can do whatever you want."

She inhaled a deep breath and then let it out. "Anything I want except leave. Otherwise they'll kill me, right?"

Chapter Four

Kris stared at the stranger sitting beside her in the front seat of his car, surprised he didn't feel like a stranger. It felt as though she'd known him her entire life. And in a way, she had. Since he'd saved her from the same fate her mother had succumbed to by the hands of that thief in the alley, thoughts of her dark angel had consumed her.

Every night since that day, he'd occupied her dreams. His leading role had turned more seductive since she'd become a woman, though. As a child, she'd thought he was an angel sent from God, an angel dressed in black. But now that she was able to stare into his fathomless dark eyes that seemed to go on forever, she realized he wasn't an angel, but a man. A man she wanted to get to know better, fully. She wondered for a second if he was real this time or if she'd wake up any minute, realizing she'd taken her fantasies to another level.

Derrick pulled up in front of her apartment and turned to her. "You're so quiet. What are you thinking about?" he asked, reaching for her hand.

His warm touch sent a surge of pleasure through her body and she smiled softly at the feel of his hand around hers and his comment. "I'm not quiet. Actually, my friends, teachers, and employers have always called me a blabbermouth. Said I just spouted off whatever I wanted without thinking." She curled her hand around his, loving the intimacy she already felt, even though he was hiding something from her. She'd never experienced familiarity with any man, even if they'd dated a few weeks, which was about the extent of her relationships. But just in a few hours — well, days, but she'd been unconscious most of the time — she believed she could trust Derrick. "I was thinking about you. Wondering if you're really here."

He returned her smile, but then frowned. "That's what you were thinking again? If I'm real? How can I prove I'm real?"

This time an even broader smile lifted her cheeks. "I'm sure I'll think of something. But first off, I guess I should get into my own clothes. Not that I don't feel all warm and snuggly in the sweatshirt you insisted I wear, but what will your family say if they see me wearing your clothes?" She opened the door and hopped out, noticing her Grand Am was sitting in its normal parking spot. She spun toward Derrick and caught him with his mouth open, as if he were ready to speak, but she interrupted him. "How did — did you bring my car here?"

"I had my brother ..." He shook his head, throwing his hands up. "What do you mean? How do you know about my family?"

"You said something the other day I remembered. About choosing." She glanced up and down the road as she walked around the front of his Navigator. "Come on up. I suppose you have my keys."

He pulled her key ring out of his pocket and handed it to her, a look of concern on his face. But then he followed her up the couple of flights of stairs to her apartment without speaking.

Kris opened the door and stepped inside. Her home looked exactly as she'd left it, but it felt different, as if there was a subtle alteration she couldn't place. She wondered if Derrick or his brother had searched it. Not that they had any reason, but still, it felt strange standing in her doorway, as if someone had been here.

It wasn't as though she had anything to hide, and even if she did, she certainly didn't have any place to hide it. Her home consisted of three small rooms, shaped in an almost perfect rectangle. The front door opened into the living area, no foyer; and off to the left, sat a galley kitchen with its tiny dinette. Her bedroom was directly on the other side of the living room. Again, no hallway, just one door that led to her bedroom. She had an end unit, though, so all three rooms had windows overlooking the alley, and then the bedroom had a second window overlooking the street.

The wood floors and walls were whitewashed white. She loved the solid alabaster color; it felt clean and fresh. The only color she'd added to her simple décor was green by the way of plants. She enjoyed the tropical feel of her apartment with its exotic foliage, sheer curtains, and sparse furnishings and wall decorations. Everything she owned, other than the plants, was white, tan, or black, as she'd seen in home magazines. She'd mimicked Caribbean cottages with their simplicity and inexpensive furniture. She'd made sure the warmth she couldn't find in Somerville was always present in her home.

Derrick looked around appreciatively, though her place was nothing like his high-rise apartment with its dark walnut floors, chrome appliances, and leather furniture. In fact, if she compared their homes to their personalities, she realized, they'd have nothing in common. She hoped that wasn't the case.

Kris gestured to her tiny couch with its white jacquard slipcover she'd found on eBay. "Make yourself comfortable, Derrick. I'll only be a minute."

He sat as directed, looking completely out of place. *Like Adonis himself in a peasant's home*, she thought. She skipped off to her bedroom, her heart pounding. Kris went directly to her full-length wicker-framed mirror, a bargain she'd found at a thrift shop. She twirled once as she inspected her body, marveling at the way her skin glowed and her hair appeared glossy, healthy. Amazing what a couple of days of no alcohol or drugs could do. But there was more ... She looked good mentally too, happy even, an unusual occurrence.

She tugged Derrick's sweatshirt up around her face and inhaled. The scent took her back to when she was a child, curling up next to her mother on the loveseat as they'd watched a Disney movie. Derrick used the same fabric softener her mother had used. Somehow, envisioning him using fabric softener made her laugh.

Deciding to keep his sweatshirt on a few more minutes, she removed her slinky black dress from the other night. When Derrick had left his bedroom this morning, she'd yanked off the blankets to reveal that she was in her undergarments. She didn't remember undressing, so she could only guess that she'd finally passed out after hours of pleading for a drink, and he'd undressed her. She didn't know how she felt about him undressing her, but then again, her clothes had been soaked. He'd washed her clothes and had them sitting out for her, but the sheer, low-cut, backless dress wasn't appropriate for the daytime. Heck, it was hardly appropriate for the nighttime, the reason she'd sifted through his closet for the T-shirt.

Anxious to get out to Derrick before he disappeared, Kris rummaged through her closet, selecting a pair of faded capri jeans and a long-sleeved black T-shirt. The simple attire would complement Derrick's tan khakis and plain white button-down oxford. She could picture him with a white jacket over top and a stethoscope around his neck. Although the image that popped into her head was of a doctor on a soap opera, not any of the physicians she'd ever seen.

If Derrick had been her doctor, she never would have fussed about going. In fact, she probably would have made up excuses for regular examinations. His brooding eyes, dark features, and onyx-colored hair over light olive skin gave him a Mediterranean look. But then again, she'd dated several Portuguese and Lebanese men over the years with similar skin tone, but none of them had Derrick's high, prominent cheekbones, slender nose, and square jawline. And of course, his striking almond-shaped eyes with their immense depth. Somehow, he looked to have a touch of American Indian, Mediterranean, and Asian appearance all at once. He resembled no man she'd ever seen in person, or a celebrity.

Was he real? He'd asked how he could prove it to her. And right now, she could only think of one way. Since she'd only used her finger and toothpaste to brush her teeth earlier, she darted into the bathroom to brush her teeth before she tested his tangible existence.

Taking one long look at herself in the mirror, she drew in a deep breath, steeling herself. *Would he agree?* she wondered. He seemed attracted to her. He'd called her beautiful, after all.

Determined, she marched out of her bedroom, but then stopped when she entered the living area. He was holding up a picture of her mother and her, taken a few months before her mother was murdered. Her mother had taken her to see Santa Claus and then they'd jumped in one of those photo booths. They'd taken silly and serious photos. Kris had enlarged and framed the serious one.

A wave of longing to see her wonderful mother again hit Kris hard, but she sucked it down. "She was beautiful, wasn't she?"

Derrick turned in her direction, his expression surprisingly solemn, and if she wasn't mistaken, his eyes looked glassy. "Yes. Very." He set the frame on the window ledge and crossed the room, taking her hand in his. He led her to the couch, pulling her down beside him. "Kristina," he paused as he lifted his hand to her neck, "I can't introduce you to my family today."

"Why not?" she demanded, attempting to put power behind her question, but a trace of defeat filled her tone and she was certain he'd recognize it. She'd assumed since she had to choose, as he'd said, that they'd want to meet her. "You said your brother moved my car, so he obviously already knows about me," she continued before he could answer, adding validity to her petition.

"Listen to me, please. I'm different. My family's different." He shook his head. "We need to make sure —"

"Derrick," she moved his hand to her lap, "I am sure."

"But you don't even know me. You —"

"I jumped off a bridge to get your attention," she interjected. "Do you think I would do that if I wanted anyone else?"

"You were sick. Under the influence of —"

"I knew what I was doing —" she tried, but this time he cut her off by placing his fingers over her lips.

The edges of his mouth quirked up, but she could tell he tried to resist smiling. "Please stop interrupting me. I was wrong," he said. "I guess you do like to talk." He raised his hand when she started to interrupt again. "Kristina, you heard me. They'll kill you if you ever try to leave. Let's just take a few days, get to know each other. And if ..." he lowered his head to look into her eyes, "if you decide to be with me, then yes, I would love for you to meet my family." He stopped as if it were okay for her to speak again.

"But your brother knows ..." she said, undeterred by his suggestion that his family was dangerous. She just couldn't imagine that anyone related to him would harm her.

"Well, he's my brother. He's allowing us time. But he wouldn't hesitate ..." he trailed off, not wanting to say that his brother would be willing to kill her, she assumed.

Kris' heartbeat kicked up a notch, wondering what was so secretive. "So tell me then, and I'll decide."

He pursed his lips, obviously determined to keep her in the dark as long as possible. "No. But I'm glad you finally believe I'm real. I wasn't sure how I was going to prove my existence to you, but I had an idea."

A thrill shot through her system, watching the way his eyes melted into hers, the ever-so-slight tilt of his head. Her heart thrummed beneath her ribcage as she realized he'd had the same idea she had. She licked her lips, letting out a soft sigh in anticipation. Her Dark Angel was going to kiss her.

Derrick glided his fingers along her jawline as he inched his head closer. "I've wanted —"

She bolted upright as her cell phone rang. "Oh, God!" She threw her hand over her chest and peered down at the caller ID. "Beth," she whooshed out her friend's name, not certain why she'd jumped.

"You need to take her call," he said softly.

Kris shook her head wildly, refusing to break the moment, even though it was already lost. Derrick picked up her phone off the coffee table and hit *answer* before she could object again.

Beth's voice immediately came over the speaker in a frantic rush. "Kris? Oh, dear Lord, are you there, Kris?"

Kris lifted the phone to her ear. "I'm here."

"You scared the death out of me. You left me that message and then wouldn't answer my calls. I thought ... I thought you'd ..." Obviously, Beth couldn't form the words.

"I was leaving town," Kris lied. "It was a spur-of-the-moment thing, and I didn't want you to change my mind. And then I sort of just hid. Cleaned up my act, you know?"

"Oh, thank goodness, Kris. I just ... I didn't know what to think. So, you're not leaving then, right? You'll still be my maid of honor?"

She couldn't help but laugh at her friend's question. If she didn't love Beth so much, she'd think the only reason she was upset was because she'd have to find another size three to fit in the dress that had been custom-made to fit Kris. "Yes. Of course. What are best friends for?"

"Okay, then. I have to go. My mom's here. We're going wedding shopping today. I'll call you later, okay?" Her *okay* sounded like a question of whether Kris would really be around or not.

"Yes," Kris assured her. "But if I don't answer, it's just because I'm busy." She looked up at Derrick, who hadn't moved from in front of her. Her heart started pounding double time as soon as he smiled. "Don't worry. I'm not going anywhere. Bye, Beth." Kris hung up the phone and switched off the ringer. She didn't want any more interruptions.

Derrick reached for the phone and set it on the end table behind her. The heat of his body caressed hers as he moved past her. Instead of pulling away, he trailed his hand down her back, wrapping his arm around her waist. "No matter what happens, I'd hate myself if I never kissed you."

Kris licked her lips again. The anticipation was killing her. Most guys were so sloppy and quick, almost falling forward, missing her mouth. But Derrick measured his moves, planned his approach. His other hand moved behind her neck. And with both hands, he pulled her closer as he moved in again. His eyes held hers as his lips brushed against hers ever so softly. Then he kissed her tenderly on the corner of her mouth, and once again, sweeping his lips back over hers, delicately kissed the other side of her mouth. Her mouth fell open a fraction in submission, as if he'd coaxed her to open up. He drew her toward him and this time encompassed her completely, his mouth closing over hers. He took her top lip, then her bottom lip, venturing inside and exploring. Her entire body felt weightless as if under a spell by just his kiss.

For some reason, she had to break the spell. As good as it was, she felt possessed. "Derrick," she spoke his name under his warm and moist lips. Not wanting to stop, but wanting to maintain control.

"Yes?" he asked, his kisses trailing across her cheekbones.

Her mind almost felt free from his enchantment. Though, somehow, she knew she'd never be free. She'd always been his. "What took you so long?"

"I'm here now." Capturing her mouth once again, he kissed her deeply with a passion she'd never felt.

Not that she'd dated much, but even the few boyfriends she went out with hadn't made her skin heat, her heart pulse, and her soul long to be possessed. Sexual activity had always been about power with her. About what she could obtain. For the first time in her life, she wanted to give. And she didn't even know him. Yes, she did, she refuted herself. He was her Dark Angel, and in some ways, she had a feeling he understood her better than anyone ever had.

Derrick released his hold and Kris wilted against the arm of the couch. "Okay. I believe you. You're obviously real."

He laughed. "As are you. Funny. Beautiful. Real. I want to add more, but I don't want you to think I'm a sap."

She sighed as she met his warm gaze. She didn't need a week; heck, she didn't need a day to decide. She'd been waiting her entire life for him, but she'd play his game, she decided. "I don't think you're a sap."

"Good! So ... what do you want to do today?" He sat up and changed the subject as if flipping a switch.

Had he not felt the same passion she had? Evidently he'd been accustomed to the same kisses that had left her breathless. For some reason, this tidbit annoyed her, wondering what woman he'd been practicing with.

"Hmm ... I don't know." She leaned against the arm of the sofa, attempting to convey the same relaxed, carefree attitude. "Whatever."

He tilted his head a fraction, as though dumbfounded by her attitude that mimicked his. "How about we go to Quincy's Market, stroll through downtown Boston, maybe the Aquarium?"

"Sounds like fun," she offered in the most casual manner she could muster. Despite her irritation, it really did. She liked those types of days. Most guys suggested dinner and a movie. Boring. When a man proposed the movies on their first date — especially a chick-flick — it was usually their last.

Still irritated their kiss hadn't meant anything to him, she stood to leave.

Derrick didn't move an inch. Instead, he clutched her hand, directing her back down to the sofa. "After one more kiss, though. I don't know how long it'll be before I can kiss you again, so we'd better make this one last all day." He pressed his lips against hers again, opening her and exploring as if he hadn't just been there minutes ago. He slipped his hand around her neck and through her hair, a low groan emanating from his throat as he drew his lips away a few inches. "We'd better go," he murmured, but his lips found hers again. "So long," he said under light kisses. He lifted her from the couch, his mouth still working its magic.

He finally pulled away and Kris was happy to see that even with his olive skin, Derrick looked a little flushed. *That's more like it*, she thought. She couldn't be the only one swept off her feet. That wouldn't make for a good start of a relationship. A thrill soared through her body at the thought. Yes, she was decided; she wanted a relationship with Derrick. And she was positive nothing would change her mind.

Chapter Five

Derrick headed east, away from Somerville, to catch the highway into Boston. "You know ..." He looked at Kristina as he waited at the light. "We could head over to Broadway."

She tilted her head. "Why? I like Downtown better than South Boston."

"Do you know what today is?"

Kristina scrunched up her nose. "Yes ... I'm not that out of it."

"I mean the date. It's the seventeenth ... St. Patrick's Day. There's a parade."

She laughed. "Oh ... that's okay. I did that last year. It was a strange collection. Other than the fact that there was a lot of green, I didn't see how it had anything to do with St. Patrick's Day. The funniest thing I saw was the Sith Lord — I think that's what they're called — and Darth Vader from Star Wars. What they had to do with St. Patty's day is beyond me. Listening to him talk about *the force* with a Boston accent cracked me up, though."

Derrick pressed on the gas pedal as the light changed to green. "I guess that would."

"Hey ... how come you don't have an accent?" she inquired abruptly.

"I didn't grow up here," he answered simply.

"Where did you grow up?"

He glanced at her, determining whether to answer. He could answer, he decided. He just couldn't give her details. "England."

"Really?" She didn't elaborate, so he hoped that would be the end of her query, but her *really* had hung out there, as though she were thinking what to ask next. "So, why don't you have an English accent, then?"

Bingo. He'd presumed she wouldn't leave it at that. Kristina was extremely inquisitive. "Umm ... it's a private school," he offered as an explanation. "The professors ... they're all handpicked. They don't have accents, so the students don't have accents."

"In other words, it's another secret you can't share," she retorted.

"Yes." He peeked at her and she was tilting her head, staring at him. Everything she did was endearing. "I'm sorry," he offered, a pathetic apology, but it was for her safety. Everything he'd ever done was to keep her safe.

"Let me ask you a question you can answer, Derrick. How am I supposed to get to know you if you won't answer any questions about yourself?"

He spurted out a half-laugh. "Fair question. How about we just enjoy this day? I'll answer anything you want to ask tonight," he rambled without thinking.

"Okay," she agreed, though hesitantly as if she didn't believe him. Actually, he didn't know why he'd just said that. He couldn't tell her everything tonight.

Their first stop was The Freedom Trail. Kristina listened in earnest as he spouted off his knowledge while they walked the 2.5-mile brick-lined route. Kristina, like him, was most interested in the Old North Church.

With its 191-foot steeple, it'd played a major role during the American Revolution.

Derrick glanced down at Kristina. "Have you ever heard the saying, *One if by land, two if by sea?*"

Kristina nodded. "Vaguely. Something about a warning. Was that here?"

He rested his hand on the small of her back as he ushered her inside. "Haven't you been here before?"

"Unbelievably, no. You would think growing up in Boston I would have. But it seems foster parents aren't interested in that sort of stuff. And I haven't been thinking about America's history in the last few years, as I've been too caught up in mine." She ran her hand over the intricate white wood of the pew, her eyes darting around, absorbing everything. "I like the white and black. Some churches have such gaudy colors. I like simple."

Derrick also loved the ancient architecture, the chandeliers hanging from the high ceiling. He especially appreciated that all the glass was clear, giving the church a light and airy feeling, instead of a dark and gloomy one, which never made sense to him. Why would a church want to convey a depressing image instead of life? After all, wasn't that what churches communicated, life everlasting? "I noticed you like simple. Your apartment. It's nice, comfortable."

"Yes. I always wanted to move someplace warm ..." she trailed off, shaking her head as if changing her thoughts. "Remind me what *One if by land, two if by sea* meant."

"It was a signal. The Sons of Liberty had devised a plan to warn the countryside. You've heard of Paul Revere's famous ride across the countryside." She nodded. "Of course what most people don't know is that there were three men riding, and Revere never finished. The Regulars, as they would have referred to them, detained Revere and William Dawes. Dr. Samuel Prescott was the only one to reach Concord and deliver the warning, and when the Regulars arrived, the Americans were ready."

Kristina shook her head, chuckling quietly. "Well, thank you, professor."

He shrugged. "You asked."

"I didn't expect a history lesson. I just think it's pretty in here. Why do people care about what happened over two hundred years ago?"

"Two hundred years isn't that long," he demurred, strolling around the five-foot-high boxed pews. How strange to think that they segregated parishioners inside the church. Wealthier families' boxes were closer to the front, of course. He sensed Kristina move up behind him. "Pretty, you say?" he asked, turning to her and resting his hands on her waist. She was so tiny he could practically wrap his hands around her waist, but then again, he had big hands. "Did you know there are thirty-seven crypts below the church containing the remains of over a thousand former members?"

"Eww ... really? Can we see them?"

He laughed. "If we return and take the official tour, but all you see are the walled-up tombs." Dropping a twenty in the donation box, he wrapped his arm around her waist and escorted her outside. "Come on. I'm getting hungry."

"I was wondering about that. You haven't eaten anything."

Biting his tongue from responding, he glanced down at her. "Do you like oysters?"

"Love them!"

That was good, he thought. A woman who could eat oysters could understand his dietary needs; at least he hoped. "Let's go eat."

Though warmer than usual, the weather was perfect. It was seventy-two degrees, clear and sunny. Other than a few evergreens that dotted the lawn of the park, the trees were mostly barren, with only a few sprouts visible. But it didn't detract from the beauty of the wharf with sailboats moored one after another in the harbor, their predominantly blue and white sails rustling in the breeze.

The constant squawk of the seabirds as they vied for scraps the tourist left behind filled the air with a vacation-like appeal. Sounds he'd remembered hearing as a child while chasing the white-winged fiends away from his lunch on Old Orchard Beach in Maine. The salty air, laced with the hint of shellfish prickled his tongue, and his stomach growled in response.

Derrick handed his keys to the valet, slipping the gentleman a healthy tip before glaring at him. "No smoking, no scratches, and I'll be leaving it here a while. I'll have another tip ready if you can manage that." The man gulped, but nodded in acquiescence. He didn't like to come off as a brute, but he hated to have his vehicle returned scratched, and he couldn't stand the smell of cigarettes. Thank goodness Kristina didn't smoke in addition to her drinking. He wouldn't have been able to deal with that. It was much easier to wean someone off alcohol than cigarettes.

He turned to Kristina to escort her inside, but noticed her eyes were wide and round. She'd seen him when he'd been ready to kill. Had she forgotten, or had she conjured up a different memory of him? He winked and smiled, hoping her features would relax. It almost worked; she looked slightly relieved, but two little lines still creased the area between her eyebrows. He rushed to explain, "Last time I let a valet park my car, they returned my vehicle with a long scratch and the stench of cigarettes. I'm very sensitive to smells," he added, hoping she wouldn't read too much into his comment, but understand that he had a reason for his severe tone. The last thing he wanted was for Kristina to be afraid of him, even though she should be frightened, since he'd admitted that under certain circumstances members of his family would be willing to kill her. She should have run in fear at that moment, but that was his Kristina, brave to the core.

"Oh," was all she said.

Craving her touch, Derrick held the crook of his arm out to her and she looped her smaller, daintier hands around his biceps, giving him a soft squeeze. He exhaled the breath he'd been holding, thankful she seemed comfortable with him.

They approached the four-story brick warehouse that had been an institution on Long Wharf for over forty years. The inside walls of the late-1700s building continued the red brick of the outside while light from lanterns and lavish chandeliers highlighted the original broad wooden beams and floors. Black iron railings lined the stairwells and landings, adding to the historical appeal of the eatery.

It was quaint, but Derrick motioned to the cast-iron tables with black umbrellas. "We can stay inside if you like, but it's so beautiful outside. Would it be okay if we ate on the patio?"

"Sure," Kristina agreed in a hushed voice. Too quiet. She'd been prattling away inside the vehicle on the drive here about the last time she'd been to the wharf. How she'd loved watching the harbor seals, since she couldn't afford to go to the aquarium. She'd been so perky and excited only minutes ago, and then he had to frighten her. It wouldn't have killed him if he'd gotten a scratch on his vehicle or had to deal with the smell of smoke.

Derrick glanced down at Kristina as the host directed them to a table. Two days ago, she had been dying under his hands and now she was on his arm. It felt surreal, and for a moment, he also wondered if it was real. The day had been going great, until he'd gone and offered that he'd tell her everything later and then practically growled at the valet, that is. Even though she didn't seem uncomfortable touching him, he felt like a moron. He could only hope that his tiff wouldn't fuel her alarm when he told her the truth.

He pulled out a chair for her to sit and then took a seat across from her. "I'm sorry, Kristina. I didn't mean to be harsh with the valet."

She shrugged. "I'm okay," she said in a soft whisper, leaning forward. "He just looked so scared that it sort of took me by surprise. I've never thought of you as scary. Though, I guess I should have."

"I'm sorry," he repeated.

Kristina reached across the table and ran her fingertips across his hand, sending a thrill through him, and surprisingly, an ache in his heart. *It was already happening*, he thought. He'd been with women before. It shouldn't be happening from a simple kiss. Of course, the kiss wasn't simple. He'd tried to play it off, but it had unlocked something within him. And for some reason, he would have sworn that she had felt it too.

She tilted her head as if to get his attention, but waited to speak until he locked eyes with her. "I'm not afraid of you, Derrick."

He nodded and turned his arm so he could take her hand in his. "Thank you."

The waiter bounced over to the table. "Top of the day to you. Will you be starting off with a cocktail or beer?"

Derrick glanced up at the rail-thin college kid with a white shirt and green bow tie. Ah, right. St. Patrick's Day. "Water's fine."

"Umm ..." Kristina looked over the menu and his eyes jolted to her. Certainly she couldn't be thinking about drinking. It could kill her. She'd be able to drink again, but not after drying out in just two days. "Water for me too, please," she finally answered, allowing him to relax.

"And two orders of oysters on the half-shell," Derrick added before the waiter skipped off.

"Two?"

"I'm hungry." He rubbed his thumb across the back of her hand. "Can I ask you something?"

She nodded.

"Were you thinking about drinking?"

"Only fleetingly. I remember what you said. But I don't need it. I know I drank a lot. Every night for the last few years, in fact. But I'm pretty sure I'm not an alcoholic."

"People often confuse binge drinking with alcoholism," he said. "They don't understand that your body becomes reliant on it. It doesn't mean you can't ever drink again — if in fact you aren't an alcoholic — but you need to wait."

"I'm fine," she said as a dismissal, glancing toward Long Wharf and then to the aquarium. Everywhere but him.

Derrick squeezed her hand to get her attention. "I won't ask again." Though he'd been her protector, he wasn't her guardian. And he didn't plan to treat her as though he was, but he was still concerned for her health.

She retracted her hand under the guise of unwrapping her silverware, but he could hear her irritation as she ground her teeth together. "Something else I remembered from the other day has been bothering me, Derrick. About how you always knew where I was. Something about tracking my cell phone?"

"I only did it when you didn't come home. It's not as though I watched you every minute of your life. I *do* work," he snapped, a bite in his voice that he had no right to have. She had every right to be nervous. He softened his tone and tried again. "I'd just got in the habit of driving by your place. And if you didn't come home, I looked for you."

"I want you to turn it off," she snapped.

"Okay."

She bit down on her lip, nodding as if pleased, even if somewhat confused. "That was easy enough."

He reached for her hand again. "You're here. You're safe. Maybe you'll stay with me, maybe you won't. But I don't need to watch you anymore. You're a grown woman." She nodded again, a small smile lifting her cheeks. Had she thought he'd argue with her? "I'm not a controlling type of man, believe it or not. And even when I say *stay with me*, it doesn't mean you can't live your life. It just means we'll always be together." He lowered his head and stared into her eyes. If he was going to tell her everything, he might as well start with an important factor. "Explanation one, Kristina. My kind doesn't separate. Once — rather, if you decide to stay with me, we will be together forever."

Her eyes sparkled, a playful gleam lighting inside of them, and he could swear they turned greener. She pulled her free hand up on the table and leaned her chin on her fist, staring at him. "But what if someone like me, liked someone else of your kind. Is that allowable?"

Derrick jerked upright in his chair as if she'd plunged a knife between his shoulder blades. Now that she was with him, the thought that she'd even think ... "Never," he said seriously. "It just doesn't happen."

"Oh, I understand."

"Do you? Once we —"

The waiter brought their waters and appetizers out on the same tray, halting their hushed conversation. He placed everything on the table and then pulled out a pad and pen to take their order. He looked to Kristina first. "Ready to order?"

"Yes. I'll have the Chicken Romano."

The man turned to Derrick, and he spilled out his entire order without giving him a chance to ask any questions. "I'll have the chopped salad to start. No croutons. Vinegar only. Then, I'll have a double order of the Ahi Tuna. Only, don't sear it. And no side dishes or sauces. Just the tuna, please."

The server wrote everything down without comment, but as every waiter had ever done before him, he gave him a confused look as he turned to leave. Derrick had learned to answer every question with finality before they asked, which saved him from a lot of additional queries. Thankfully, sushi had become so popular in the last few years that most people no longer questioned his eating habits.

"Two orders again? Raw?"

"Explanation number two," he said in a low voice so only she could hear, one of the reasons he wanted to eat outside. "I can't eat cooked foods."

She absorbed that, filing it away, it seemed, and then she whispered across the table, "At least you don't drink blood."

"Not quite," he rejoined, watching as her eyes bulged as he met her playful comment head-on. "People only thought we were."

Chapter Six

Kris bolted upright. Her phone buzzed on the table, jolting her out of the trance she'd fallen into after Derrick's remark about people thinking they were drinking blood. She glanced at the caller ID. "It's Beth. It's after three. She's back from shopping," she babbled incoherently in her frazzled state. "I should talk to her."

Derrick reached across the table, covering her hand and the phone. "Please —"

"I remember," she interrupted, gulping the lump in her throat. "Don't say anything about you."

"That isn't what I was going to ask." He squeezed her hand. "Please don't take her call. Beth knows you're okay. She just wants to talk, and you want an excuse to walk away so you can clear your head, but I don't want you to leave yet."

Tears filled her eyes and she didn't even know why. She didn't care what he was; Derrick wasn't dangerous. She just felt — she didn't know what she felt. *Scared*, she thought. Frightened of the unknown. Kris glanced at his warm and gentle gaze. She wasn't afraid of Derrick. She needed to snap out of this. The phone stopped ringing, and she glanced at it, feeling as though she'd let go of her lifeline.

As if she'd be content in letting Derrick's mysterious dark waters engulf her, absorb her, providing her life-sustaining oxygen from now on.

"Kristina, you asked me to tell you ... and I don't think I have a choice now. When we ..." He paused as if collecting his words. "I don't know how to explain this ... without pressuring you. No. Not now, not here." He shook his head again. "Can we just eat? Then we'll go somewhere and talk, okay? I promise I'll explain everything."

"Yeah," she choked out. Her mouth was so dry. She picked up her water glass, removed the lemon, and drained it. As he watched her warily, she picked up an oyster, deciding to try to relax and enjoy their date. She doused the shellfish with horseradish, then slurped it out of the shell and threw her head back. "Whoo! Love that rush!"

Derrick grinned, seemingly more at ease that she wouldn't bolt. He dropped an oyster right out of the shell into his mouth. No toppings, of course, as everything else he'd ordered. So he ate raw foods. Many people did. He was just joking about the blood-drinking comment, she realized.

Kris glanced at her phone's screen as it lit up. Beth had left a long message. But then she noticed there were two more messages. She picked up the phone and glanced at the three missed calls and messages. Her work was one. That wasn't a surprise; she'd already assumed they'd fired her. But the other message was from an unknown caller. "Hmm ..." she pondered. "I don't get many wrong numbers. I've had the same number for six years."

Derrick rubbed his hand across his chin. "I'm sure it's nothing." He finished off his oysters within seconds and then his eyes flicked to her plate. "Are you going to eat yours?"

She laughed. "No. Go ahead. I guess it takes a lot to fill a man your size." She pushed her ice-filled tray toward him. "How big are you anyway?"

He raised a brow. "You mean, how tall am I?"

"Mm-hm."

"Not so tall. Six-four. My brother's six-six."

"That's tall. I'm only five-four."

"I know. You're cute. Dainty. I like it."

The waiter interrupted them again to remove their dishes. She almost wished they'd decided on pizza so they could just sit and talk. But then it hit her. No cooked foods ... that meant no pizza. Say it wasn't so. How could someone live without pizza?

Derrick ate every last morsel of his salad, and when their meals arrived, he finished off both portions of his fish. "I'd offer dessert, but I think we'll find something more appetizing at the market," he said after the waiter cleared their plates.

"Deal!" She grinned wide. Dessert was her favorite part, and she just wanted to leave anyway, anxious to hear more about the unusual man in front of her. She stood and he rose with her. "Let me take a quick bathroom break, and I'll meet you up front."

He bobbed his head, but a look of concern washed over his features.

Kris stepped toward him, resting her hands on his chest. "Derrick, I'm not going to disappear, and I won't say anything to Beth. I promise."

He dipped his head and rested his hand on hers. "Would you do me a favor, then?"

"Anything." She owed him her life on at least two occasions she was aware of.

"Could you not listen to your messages until we talk? I know who the unknown caller is, and I'd like a chance to explain."

Chapter Seven

After purchasing gelato for Kristina and fresh fruit for himself, Derrick walked inside a gift shop and bought the first two afghans he saw. He escorted Kristina across the street to the Christopher Columbus Waterfront Park. It was much nicer when the wisteria-covered trellis was in bloom and the trees were full and green, shading the red brick walkways, but even winter had its appeal.

The season was ending, and so would the quiet and peaceful nights. Warmer evenings meant more people would be on the street, which meant more crime.

It was only four-thirty, but the sun was fading behind the buildings and the temperature was dropping fast. Most tourists had already left for the warmth of their hotel rooms, so he and Kristina would have the park to themselves.

Derrick located a secluded spot under a deciduous tree overlooking Boston Harbor. He spread one of the afghans on the grass and then held his hand out to Kristina. Lowering his body to the ground, he pulled her down beside him. He folded the other blanket around her shoulders and then wrapped his arms around her. The warmth in his body cranked up a notch as she leaned against him. For several minutes, they stared out over the water.

In a matter of moments, the nighttime sky had transitioned from the pastel periwinkle color of the day to a deep indigo. Only a sliver of the moon rested above the horizon, as if an artist had used the smallest brush he owned and just whisked a thin white line onto his canvas.

Sweeping Kristina's hair off her shoulder, Derrick pressed his lips against the side of her neck and inhaled the fresh clean scent of her skin. She rarely wore perfume, which was fine with him since he had such an acute sense of smell. He appreciated her natural aroma along with a hint of raspberry, which must come from her body spray. He'd always been able to pick her out among a crowd, even if she was out of his line of sight.

"I have something for you," he whispered. "No matter what you decide, it's yours, and I want you to have it."

Kristina turned in his arms, pulling her knees up in front of her and wrapping her arms around them. She lifted her head to look at him, and he couldn't resist kissing those delicate pink lips. Just a soft kiss, but it sent a shockwave through his system again. What would he do if she left him? His kind didn't fall twice. Yes, there was no doubt he loved Kristina. And his heart would break if she didn't return that love. She was human. Capable of loving and leaving. His parents had warned him, his brother had cautioned him, even Vic had begged him to reconsider when he'd even mentioned Kristina in passing.

Kristina pulled her head back abruptly. "Are you okay?"

He nodded, realizing a tear had fallen. He'd never cried in his life, had never shed a tear. Even when Janelle had died in front of him, all he felt was hatred. But the thought of losing Kristina ... the worst possible loss for his kind. "I'm fine."

"Derrick. No matter what your secret is, I don't care. I want to stay with you."

"But you don't even know me," he countered.

"Yes, I do. And I feel something I've never felt. For anyone." She lifted his hand and pulled it to her lips. "Talk to me please."

"There's so much ... I don't even know where to start. But first of all, I have something for you." He reached inside his jacket, pulled out the tiny black box he'd had for six years, and held it out for her.

Kristina eyed it warily. "Um ... well ... this *is* fast."

A laugh shot out of his throat before he could contain it. She was just so darn cute, and again, he couldn't help but wonder why it had taken her jumping off a bridge to send him into action. How had he lived so long without her beside him? "It's not an engagement ring. Besides, marriage isn't what matters in my world anyway. A commitment is a commitment. A piece of paper means nothing."

She reached from under her blanket and opened the velvet box. Her eyes widened as she recognized the ring. "Oh, my God! How did you —" Tears burst from her eyes. "My mother's ring — actually, my grandmother's ring. I sold it when I was sixteen."

Derrick brushed her hair away from her face and kissed her forehead. "I know. I made sure no one could beat my bid."

Laughter and tears erupted again. "Oh, God. Thank you. I've regretted selling it every day of my life." She slipped the ring onto her right-hand ring finger and then moved to her knees in front of him. "Thank you, Derrick. Thank you for everything. What would I have done without you?"

"Kristina," he said, his tone serious, wondering where to start. He tilted her face to him, holding on to her. He'd jump right in, he decided, hoping she wouldn't hate him, or think he was a freak as his brother had teased. "I knew your mother. Janelle and I worked together. She was so sweet, so kind." Kristina's eyes grew wide again, so he rushed to continue. "We were just friends." He inhaled a deep breath as he watched a tear roll down her cheek. He rushed to get his explanation out before she ran away from him. "We were in med school together. And I'd been held up that night. I'd been fighting with my brother. I should have been there, stopped that man. I should have killed him —"

She pressed her hand against the side of his face. "It's not your fault." She shook her head as she obviously tried to make sense of everything. "You *knew* my mother? Did you ... were you —"

He shook his head fiercely. "No. Nothing. Just friends. I'd made a commitment to protect her, though, and I failed." He lifted Kristina's hand to his lips. "When my kind *fall* ... in love, I mean ... we fall completely. It's not like a human falls in love. It only happens once. When we *decide* that we want to be with someone ... and then make love, there's a connection. Because of that, though not completely uncommon, casual sex is rare. We only pursue someone we want to be with forever."

She narrowed her eyes, tilting her head. "So you've never *fallen* for a woman."

"Not in that way ... until now."

Her mouth dropped open a fraction. "But we haven't ... or did we?"

"No, no. God no. The kiss. Just our kiss. It's unusual, but I've heard it happens. If the desire is strong to be together." He sighed. "So much to explain. We got off track. You're not upset that your mother and I were friends?"

Kristina gave a dismissive shrug. "I always thought you knew us. The way you looked at me in the alley, the way you were so upset when you pulled that man away from my mother. I recognized you weren't a random stranger."

He released a breath of relief. "Okay ... well, that takes a load off my mind. My brother insisted you wouldn't be able to handle that, let alone the rest of the details." He brushed her hair back and rested his hand against her cheek. *Just maybe*, he hoped. Perhaps she'd be okay with everything else he had to confess to her. Although his brother thought she'd be upset, Derrick assumed she could live with the fact that Janelle and he had worked together. The rest of his secrets, however, might not be as easy to accept.

"I've always known you're different, Derrick." She ran her fingers down his jawline, a feather-light stroke that sent his heart soaring, ready to take flight. "Will you talk to me now?"

He nodded and decided just to spill it all out at once. "We call ourselves creatus. From the Latin word meaning *created*. When my kind came here, there was a lot of confusion about what we were and where we came from. But the fact of the matter was, even we didn't know. We came to this world about four thousand years ago, on what you might call an ark, in an attempt to escape our world, we theorize. According to my elders, we were directed to this planet. Only two elders escorted hundreds of toddlers and then destroyed all evidence of our arrival and our technology, taking up residence among humans.

"Everything seemed fine, according to our history, which we are taught in our private schools. Until our diet and strength became known." Derrick paused to let her catch up with his earlier comment about their eating requirements. "Cooked meats and grains are poisonous to our system, as they are to humans. But for some reason, the carcinogens don't affect humans the way they affect us. It takes years to kill you in the form of heart disease and other maladies, but for us, we get deathly ill and usually die within weeks.

"When humans witnessed us eating raw red meat, they assumed we were blood drinkers and began to hunt us as demons. In order to protect ourselves, we had to kill and go into hiding."

"Derrick," Kristina cut in, "are you telling me you really are a vampire?"

Derrick drew her hand to his chest and held it there without saying a word for a couple of seconds. "Do you feel that?" She nodded. "The myths are just that, myths. I have a heart; it pumps blood through my system. Just because we eat raw red meat, people assume we drink blood. Have you seen anyone eat a rare steak?"

"Yes ... ewww ... "

He blew out a breath, and a white puff of mist encircled them, as the temperature was dropping fast. "Can you handle this, Kristina?"

She bobbed her head. "Yes. My mother actually ate her steak pretty rare."

"I know ..." He sighed and continued, "We are a peaceful race, and contrary to popular belief, we are not immortal, and a bullet will kill us just as any other being. We are, however, extremely strong. We estimate that most creatus are approximately ten times stronger than the average human. We hear better, see better, and we live twice as long. Hence all the stories that we are immortal.

"According to my family, when the new world opened up, my kind was the first to arrive. We'd already had relatives who had lived with the Cherokee Indians for centuries. It was a chance at a new life where all the superstitions of the old country would be laid to rest. Everything was great at first. We worked and lived side by side in a new unbiased country without all the superstitious ninnies.

"When crime began to increase around the turn of the century, it was my family who attempted to curb the corruption. We took to the streets at night as vigilantes, ridding the cities of the degenerates. It is from my grandfather and father that your superhero stories came about." He tilted his head. "It may sound unbelievable, but Superman, Spiderman, Batman ... they were all one type of man: my family. But then, it wasn't an angry mob we feared; it was the government. The military has been searching for us for more than seventy years."

"Why?" she asked, an innocent gleam lighting her eyes.

"It started with some of my kind during World War II. A rumor had spread that immortals who had lived in the mountains had come to protect the innocent. We'd been here all along, but someone had remembered tales of their childhood about how my kind would protect humans and nurse them back to health." He shrugged. "We've always been in the medical field; it makes forging documents easier. Anyway, my family had to tone down the protection, as sad as that is. In 1947, a division under the National Security Council got wind of the stories and got very close. We hide well, though. We have our own schools, medical centers, and spies within the government, enabling us to stay one step ahead. It is the one area our entire race agrees upon; we must stay hidden at all costs."

Derrick stopped and glanced around the darkened park, thinking they should be getting home, but knew he needed to get to the scary part. The detail about his kind that fed the nightmares. "We protect our own no matter what. Until there's a rogue. As I said, we are mostly peaceful, but we do have our psychos, as humans do. The only problem is when members of my kind are homicidal, they eat their victims." She shuddered and he rushed to assure her. "Don't get me wrong. We don't crave humans. Humans don't even smell like food. Believe me, if my kind really craved humans, the human race would have been extinct a long time ago."

Chapter Eight

Kris shivered again. She gathered the blanket tighter around her shoulders, hoping Derrick wouldn't think she was afraid of him. Because she wasn't. "So your family is concerned if you and I don't work out ..." she trailed off, understanding what Derrick had been trying to impress on her. *Forever.* One man, well ... one creatus, *forever.*

Derrick pulled her to his chest, his hand running the length of her back. "I would never let anyone hurt you, Kristina. No matter what. I'd die first."

"But then we'd both die," she whispered.

She felt the subtle movement of his head. He'd nodded without realizing, she was certain. "I trust you, Kristina. If you'd rather walk away now, I'll let you go. No one will ever know, and you can live out your life as if you'd never proved I existed with your death-defying stunt."

Kris huffed out a chuckle. "As if that were even possible." She turned in his arms again. "I'm not going anywhere, Derrick." She gazed up at his face, struggling to make out his features in the dim light. "You said you've fallen, and that you don't fall twice." She felt his chest fill and release. "Is it possible I've fallen too? Can that happen?

Because I swear when you kissed me, I felt something. But then we stopped ... "

"Yes," he murmured. "You'll feel it inside. It's painful at first, as if something wants possession of your soul. But when you accept it, when you open up to it, the warmth surges through your body. An electricity flares through every nerve ending, and you feel light, as if your body could just float away on its own."

"Do you feel that way now?" she asked, hoping he did, but frightened of what that might mean. What if it didn't happen to her? Was it even possible for a human to *fall* as he had said? She'd never felt anything like she'd experienced when he kissed her in her apartment, but was that just the anticipation of a first kiss from the man she'd dreamed about nearly every night?

"Yes. I felt it fighting to take control. And I'd blocked it until you mentioned being with another man." A burst of air left his lungs. "It enveloped me then. Because the thought of you —"

"Then how could I ever leave you?" She lifted her head to his, wanting to give in to the feeling.

Derrick dipped his head, brushing his lips across hers as he'd done earlier. "I don't want you to ever leave me. I want you to stay, but I'm afraid —"

"Kiss me, Derrick. Possess me," she whispered. "Make me yours. I want to stay with you."

Without hesitation this time, his mouth parted, taking hers completely. The tip of his tongue touched her lips and her mouth fell open, accepting him. He lowered her onto his lap, his arms folding completely around her, cocooning her to his body. He moved his hand behind her neck, locking her in his embrace.

Every nerve ignited as if she were on fire. Red-hot heat radiated through her body, singeing every molecule without actually burning her. Instinctively, she started to pull back against the fiery emotion, but Derrick held her tightly, refusing to let her go as the fire soared through her veins, radiating under her skin. Her body felt as if it would combust. His mouth pressed harder as her body writhed with a somehow joyous pain. She wanted to contest the burning in her stomach, in her loins, but her mind told her it was a good pain. Her heart raced, pounding out a vicious rhythm, and Derrick pulled her even closer, refusing to break the kiss.

Her muscles seized then tingled, and she realized what her body was experiencing. The most intense orgasm she had ever felt — from a kiss. She gave in to it then, feeling the blood rush through her system, an intense heat radiating throughout every molecule in her body. And then she felt a magnificent high. A surge of pleasure she'd never experienced from any man, drug, or alcohol. Her body melted as Derrick finally pulled back, but the fullness of his drug remained in her veins, completing her, making her his. "Wow ..." was the only word she could push out of her mouth.

Chapter Nine

That was some kiss."

Derrick whipped his head to the sound of his brother's voice. He focused his eyes on the top of the Chart House, knowing that's where he'd be hiding. Away from human eyes and ears, but still able to see and communicate with him.

"Excuse me, Kristina." Derrick stood and gestured that she should stay sitting when she bounced up next to him. "I'm sorry. I'll be right back." Her eyes spoke volumes: sadness, rejection, fear. He lifted her hands to his lips. "I've *fallen* completely. I will never leave you now, nor will anyone ever take you away. But ... we have a visitor I need to handle." He lowered her hands. "I'll only be a few feet away. Okay?"

"Okay," she said on a sigh, confusion clear in her eyes.

When she settled herself down on the blanket, he sprinted to the end of the park. It was too dark for her, but he could see her straining to see where he'd gone.

Michael landed in front of him with a soft thump. "Did you fall?"

As usual, no pleasantries. His brother had the personality of a doormat. Did he really think Derrick would ever allow anyone to hurt Kristina even if he hadn't?

"Yes. Completely," Derrick admitted, even though he didn't want to tell him. The experience was personal. Something he'd waited his entire life to experience, but instead of enjoying the moment with Kristina, he had to address his brother's queries. Michael was lucky he hadn't already knocked him to the ground so that he could return to Kristina.

His brother closed his eyes and shook his head. "More importantly ... did she?"

"I'm pretty sure, but you sort of interrupted us, you perv. Couldn't you have waited for me to call you in the morning?"

Michael huffed out a silvery breath in the cool night air. "No. There's a problem and you know it. When were you going to tell me about the detective?"

Derrick grabbed his brother's shoulders and shook him. "What the hell, Michael? Are you bugging my home? I know you have your spies, but you have no right to defile my personal space."

Michael shoved his hands off him and backed up a step. "I don't need to bug your house. I have my own sources. If you'd been paying attention to the news and not your girlfriend for the last few days, you'd know we have some major problems other than the detective. I've been handling everything while you're off playing with your new toy."

His blood pressure rising, Derrick stepped toward his brother again. "That's enough! If you speak disrespectfully about Kristina again, we'll finish everything here." When Michael bobbed his head in understanding, Derrick continued, "What problems?"

"We'll discuss it tomorrow. I assume you'll be introducing your bride to the family."

Derrick nodded.

Michael raised an eyebrow, a sideways smile lifting one side of his rounder cheeks. His brother was the only creatus he'd seen who actually had dimples. It sort of detracted from his bad-boy guise, which Derrick never minded pointing out. "You want me to tell Vic?" his brother taunted.

"No, I don't want you to tell Vic," Derrick growled. "I'd rather do it in person."

"You're going to risk Vic seeing Kristina?"

"Do I have a choice?"

Michael shook his head. "Not really. It'll happen eventually. I'll just let everyone know you're coming. We need to gather to discuss what's been going on anyway. Make sure you watch the news when you get home. I'm sure there'll be another one tonight."

Derrick narrowed his eyes, shaking his head. "Please tell me you're wrong."

"Wish I could tell you that. But there's no doubt. We have a rogue creatus."

Derrick took his time walking back to Kristina. Only officially in his life a few days, and he'd have to remind her that his kind were the most dangerous of all serial killers. He definitely didn't want her out of his sight either, which he was certain would turn into an issue. Especially since he'd just insisted he wasn't controlling and that she could do as she pleased.

The problem was that if there was a rogue in Boston, more than likely they were acquainted with his family, which meant they'd eventually meet Kristina. It couldn't be anyone in Boston, though. Other than a few who'd come to live with their group over the years, most of the creatus he'd known since he was a child. None of them were capable of such atrocious acts. Sadly, it usually wasn't about food when there was a rogue among them, but about hatred and a thrill. They enjoyed the chase, reveled in the fact they were superior.

With their heightened senses and strength, the chances of a human detective catching them were nil. They'd hear or smell authorities a mile away, and then they'd outrun them.

Thankfully, that's where Michael came in. His brother was a true detective. He'd hunt down the rogue and dispose of him before he created a nightmare they'd have to clean up.

Derrick stepped in front of Kristina, startling her. "It's okay. It's me."

She jumped to her feet. "Oh, thank God! I've never been in the park this late. It's scary. Every shadow seemed to come to life." She glanced to the left. "I swear I heard someone breathing."

He smiled to assure her, but then glanced in the direction she'd looked. He saw nothing, but that wasn't unusual. If it were the rogue, he'd know how far to stay away, and he would have bolted the moment Derrick approached. He'd have to keep an eye out for the perpetrator.

Unfortunately, although creatus shared some common features, they didn't look or smell any different from humans. A human and creatus' chemical makeup were so alike that his kind often wondered if the same superior being had created both species. Many of his human patients often questioned his heritage, inquiring if he was of Mediterranean or Asian descent. He would simply answer that he'd been born in Boston, and they usually stopped their queries for fear of offending him, he assumed.

Derrick wrapped his arm around Kristina's waist. "Let's go home."

Kristina leaned against him without a word, content, it seemed, just to be with him. The idea sent a thrill through his system. He'd worried for six years for no reason. Kristina had accepted him without question. The one nice thing about falling was that it could not be faked or forced. Lord knows he'd tried. He'd attempted to fall for one of his kind, but it'd never happened. Now they could move ahead with their lives without any concerns. His family couldn't argue since she'd fallen too.

After the valet brought his vehicle around — with no scratches or reek of cigarettes — he exchanged the keys for a generous tip and then closed Kristina inside.

"Derrick, when you said, *Let's go home* ..." Kristina started as soon as he sat down in the driver's seat. "Um ... what exactly did you mean?"

"Well, I have a spare bedroom, if that's what you're worried about."

She cleared her throat. "I'm not worried, but I have to go to my apartment."

"Of course. We can get your things —"

"No ... that's not what I mean. I have plants that I need to take care of."

He laughed, but then stopped when he realized she was serious. "Plants?"

"Yes, plants. They need water and they need air. They've been closed up in the house for days."

"You're kidding, right?"

This time Kristina crossed her arms over her chest. "No, I'm not kidding."

He turned in the direction of her apartment. *Plants?* He'd understand a kitten or a puppy, but plants?

Derrick parked in front of Kristina's apartment and hopped out. With a quick glance around, he dashed to her side of the vehicle to open the door.

She glanced up at him, eyes wide. "You're such a gentleman, Derrick. I'm not used to this."

He took her hand and led her to the doors of the building. "Get accustomed to it; it's who I am." He pulled her close as they stepped in front of the door. "Would you please water your plants and come home with me?"

"Derrick, I like my bed. I know you have a fancy apartment, but I like my place. I haven't been home in days. My plants need my carbon dioxide too."

"The point is ... my condo is safe." He shook his head. "I can't believe ... plants. I never would have guessed." He nudged her chin up with one finger. "I'll worry about you all night."

"I know it's not the best neighborhood, but I've never had any problems." She curled her body against his. "You could stay here ..." she hedged. "I have a comfy sofa."

He lowered his head and narrowed his eyes. "If I stay the night, there's no way I could remain on the sofa."

Kristina licked her lips in response. "Works for me."

Derrick opened the door and pulled her through the doorway. Anxious to get to the third floor, he moved to the middle of the stairwell and listened for a second. Nothing. He was familiar with each tenant's voice. They were all doing something other than traveling the corridors. "Works for me too." He pulled Kristina up in his arms.

She whooshed out a breath in response. "Um ... you're going to carry me to the third floor?"

"Nope. I'm going to jump to the third floor. Ready?"

She bit down on her bottom lip, but nodded.

Derrick knew the exact force; he'd done this many times in the last two years, since she'd moved into the building. He softened his knees and propelled himself off the concrete, soaring upward and over the railing, landing in front of her door.

He felt Kristina's heart pound against his chest, but she smiled. "Well, that was different." She laughed. "Whew! The blood is rushing to my head. Give me a second to get my bearings before you let me down. I think my feet are still on the ground level."

Derrick continued to hold her in his arms as she handed him the keys. "I can hold you as long as you wish. You weigh practically nothing, and I rather like having you this close." He unlocked and pushed open the door.

As he stood in her tiny living room, he dipped his head to hers. Her lips parted and he sealed his mouth to hers. Walking to the sofa, his lips still pressed to hers, he sat with her in his arms.

Kristina wrapped her arms around his neck, her hands moving through his hair. It felt so good. He didn't ever want to let her go. How did people function? He couldn't imagine having to go to work or eat, or anything for that matter.

He wanted to lie down beside her and never leave her side. His father had tried to explain to him once, but it was difficult to understand. Hard to comprehend how you could want one person forever. He'd liked women before, thought he could make it work, but the couple times he'd mentioned to his father that he thought that maybe he'd felt something, his father had laughed. He'd bellowed, *"When it happens, you'll know. It's like nothing you've ever felt."*

His father had been correct. Derrick had been a fool to think he could have forced this with anyone other than

Kristina. He'd been in love with her spirit for too long. His soul had known all along what it wanted.

Kristina pulled back, smiling. "As much as I don't want to stop kissing you, Derrick. I really need to take care of my plants."

He sighed, ran his hands through his hair. "Tell me what we have to do, please. I never thought I'd be upstaged by plants."

She scooted off his lap and sauntered toward the kitchen, shaking more than she had to, he was certain. Unable to resist, he followed. As she filled the pitchers in the sink, he nuzzled against her. Her body squirmed beneath him as the heat of his breath tickled her neck. He moved his hands down the length of her arms, pulling the first pitcher up to the counter. He pressed his mouth against her skin and she cooed in response.

He lifted the second vessel out of the sink and she turned in his arms, inching her fingers up his shirt, unbuttoning it along the way. When she had it completely undone, he allowed her to move it off his shoulders, throwing it over a chair at the dinette.

Kristina ran both hands over his chest and down his arms. "Are you trying to distract me?"

He smiled. "I was filling water pitchers. You're the one who started undressing me."

"Maybe they can wait until morning," she said, slowly drawing out her words in the sexiest voice he'd ever heard.

"Oh, no. We're watering these plants now." He drew up one of the canisters and headed over to the first window, then whooshed through the house before Kristina could move toward the first plant. He appeared in front of her, an empty water canister in his hands. "Done!" He whisked her off her feet and carried her to the bedroom.

"Aww ... you didn't show them any love. You have to talk to them so they can get their life-sustaining carbon dioxide —"

Derrick pressed his lips over hers, cutting off her words. He lowered her to the bed and hovered over her. *Stupid plants*, he thought. Thankfully, Kristina seemed to forget about her foliage as her hands traveled over his shoulders and across his back. He groaned with pleasure, wanting her fully. His body lit up, ready to partake, but he pulled away. "We're not going to do anything tonight, Kristina."

She crinkled her eyebrows together. "What do you mean? Why?"

"It's just not right. Not yet."

"But you said —"

He rested his fingers over her lips. "I know. We're committed. But it's still our first night together. It just doesn't feel right. I want it to be more romantic, more of a buildup."

She sighed. "I don't understand. How can there be more of a buildup than we've already experienced? What I felt was the most incredible sensation ever."

He smiled and warmth seared through his chest at her words. "Thank you. But trust me; it'll get better. Right now, I just want you to kiss me again."

Kristina lifted her head and parted her lips, allowing him access to taste her again. The same feeling as before soared through his system. He couldn't imagine ever tiring of kissing her.

He jerked his head up at a sound outside and saw a shadow pass by the window. "You don't have a fire escape on this window, do you?"

She squinted in the dim light. "No. It's outside the kitchen window."

"That's what I thought." Derrick jumped up and peered through the wood slats. The shadow moved across the roof of the next building. No way would he catch the perp. They'd heard his words and had moved for cover. Definitely a creatus based on the speed. He could only hope it was not the rogue, but someone from his family checking up on him.

Kris stared at her reflection in the wide chrome-framed mirror while Derrick stood behind her. "Are you sure this is okay?" she asked for the hundredth time, checking her makeup in the unnatural light of his vanity mirror. Her bathroom, though smaller, had soft natural light. Her entire apartment was warm and sunny, even in the dead of winter. It was how she preferred it.

Now, due to his insistence, she'd lined up all her plants in front of Derrick's wall of windows in the living area of his condo. And now she was attempting to figure out if her makeup looked acceptable in his master bath, which had no windows.

Derrick touched the collar of her sweater, which rested at the edge of her shoulders, pressing his lips to her bare skin. "You look beautiful. What are you worried about?"

"I just want to make sure they think I'm good enough for you."

He hummed out a breath, smiling. "It doesn't matter what they think. I love you, and that's all that matters."

Kris gulped, tears forming in her eyes. He hadn't said those words. He had said he'd *fallen*, but in her language, those three little words meant everything. She turned to him. "I love you too, Derrick. I always have."

He brushed her hair away from her face. "Then why are you crying?"

She actually didn't know why she was crying. Overwhelmed, scared, a million reasons why, she assumed, but mostly because she felt his love in an almost palpable way. "Hearing you say that ... it feels real. You're real. And I'm so scared they'll hate me and try to tear us apart. I've been alone since I was eight and the thought of losing you —"

Derrick placed his hands on either side of her face and kissed her softly, then moved his fingers under her chin, directing her head up to face him. "You've never been alone, my love. I've always been here."

"I know." She sighed. "It's what kept me going, what kept me in Boston. But what if they —"

"They can't," he cut in softly. "Believe me. This is the one thing my family — all of them, even my brother — understands. Even if they are not happy, they know there's nothing that will change. And my mother will love you. Another *woman* around ..." he trailed off, as if not wanting to finish his sentence.

Kris inhaled a deep breath and whooshed it out, appraising the cold tile and metal around her. If she were in her home, she wouldn't feel so out of sorts. "If you're not worried, why did you insist we pack up my house in the middle of the night and come here?"

He dropped his hands to her shoulders, fiddling with the soft threads of her sweater. "I just wanted you with me. In a safe place. Your apartment is too easy to break into. All of my doors and windows have extra security, with reinforced steel and glass. Even a creatus couldn't break in here."

She narrowed her eyes. "You think one of them will try to hurt me?" she deduced. "This all happened after you jumped up last night. What did you see?"

Derrick shrugged. "Just a shadow."

Kris presumed he wasn't telling her everything, but she also had a feeling he wasn't going to either. He'd whisked her out of the house so quickly last night her head had spun. Not that she minded being with him all the time, but one minute he was insisting they needed to do something romantic before they went further, and the next he'd had all her plants in the rear of his Navigator. He had helped her pack a duffle bag of clothes and toiletries, but he'd paced the entire time, as if he were all of a sudden in a hurry.

Once they'd arrived at his house, though, he'd carried her items into the spare room. She'd walked right into the room behind him, snatched up her bag, and moved it to his master bedroom while he watched.

After that, they'd cuddled in his bed together, but he'd refused to do anything but kiss her. She'd finally fallen asleep, but had awoken to discover he'd left the room. Following the muted sound and flickering light of the television, she'd found Derrick sleeping on the sofa, remote still clutched in his hand.

Knowing he wasn't going to confess any more than he had last night, she stepped out from under his hands. "I'm ready."

"Good. Let's go," he said, drawing her toward the door.

Derrick's trek away from the city surprised Kris. She'd assumed his family — as he continually referred to them — all lived nearby. Instead, they drove north, then headed west on 495 toward the city of Harvard. She'd been through Harvard a few times. It was a quaint but beautiful town. They passed the town hall on their route, and Kris couldn't help but giggle. It looked as though someone had torn the building out of a Norman Rockwell painting and planted it on the main thoroughfare next to the general store and fire department.

With its whitewashed exterior, front porch, and even a crow's nest on the roof, Kris wanted to pull out her charcoal and tablet and draw for the first time in years. Other than her sketches of Derrick, she hadn't felt like drawing in years.

Her trained eye gobbled up the scene, searing it into her memory. Several apple orchards and farms with riding stables lent a down-home feel to the small town. It was hard to believe such a place existed so close to Boston.

About a half an hour after they'd left his apartment, they turned north again. After several miles of rolling hills, he finally turned onto a dead-end street as indicated by the *no outlet* sign. They passed six chalet-style houses on large plots of land. When he reached the end of the road, he turned off to the left, traveling down a gravel driveway. Derrick finally pulled to a stop in front of another tri-level house, nestled between several species of evergreens. A large barn sat off in the distance adjacent to what looked to be a vacant vegetable garden.

Kris lowered her head, gazing out the window to absorb everything. "This place is enormous. Whose house is this?"

"My parents," Derrick said simply, opening his door and hopping out of the vehicle.

Her heart thrummed in her chest, her earlier nervousness returning, only worse than it had been, as she was now here.

Derrick opened her door and took her hand. "It's okay, Kristina. No one's going to bite you."

"Are you sure?" she fretted, gnawing on her bottom lip. "Maybe we should just go. Give them a few years to get used to the idea of us being together."

He stepped in front of her, lowering his head to her eye level. "Everything will be fine. You're strong, independent, and feisty. Feel free to be yourself. Don't let them scare you, especially Vic."

"Who's Vic?"

Derrick kissed her quickly. Then, taking her hand, he pulled her into the house. He opened the door and stepped inside. The area they walked into was a den of some sort, with an older, seventies-style brown sofa and console television. Derrick led Kris through that area and up a small flight of stairs, passing a hallway leading to several rooms. When they reached the first landing, Kris could see another living area off to their right, only more modern than the room below them. Derrick ignored that area too and walked out a door leading outside again.

As soon as they stepped onto the porch, Kris saw a hundred or so people — creatus — standing in loose circles. Everyone stopped to look — and glare — but then, other than one group of four people, most went back to their subdued conversations, as if not the least bit concerned. She released a short breath of relief as Derrick took her hand and led her down the steps. Her previous nervousness started to melt away at the warmth of his hand wrapped around hers. He wasn't embarrassed of her, so what was the worst thing that could happen? Even if his brother or parents didn't approve, it didn't mean he'd leave her. He had said he'd never leave her and he'd never let anyone take her away. So she had no reason to fret about losing another person in her life.

Derrick made his way to the smaller group, but the entire time they approached, a woman shook her head, her beautiful face contorting with every step they neared. Her hair was long and raven black. Her features, like Derrick's, were striking, and Kris realized immediately where the myth of Wonder Woman must have begun. She, along with most of the other women, looked like Amazons, tall and utterly beautiful. Kris hoped that she was a sister Derrick had failed to mention. Because if this woman had a romantic interest in Derrick, she might just kill Kris on the spot by the look of things.

The Amazon took a step forward. "I can't believe you'd bring that tramp —"

"Victoria!" Derrick barked, causing Kris to cringe behind him. So much for being strong and feisty.

A man standing next to the woman patted her arm, whispering something Kris couldn't hear.

Victoria's lips drew back, and if Kris wasn't mistaken, she growled. "You bitch!"

The man, who Kris noticed looked more like Derrick than any of the other men around her, clamped his arms around the woman, and Derrick rushed them, taking the woman's other arm. Both men dragged the woman away, kicking and screaming obscenities, before Kris could even blink. Kris stood there with tears stinging her eyes, wanting just to seep into the ground. What had she done? She didn't even know the woman. A chill started at the base of her neck and rushed through her body, immediately making her shiver. Wrapping her arms around her body, she attempted to calm her nerves before she bolted up the stairs toward the safety of the Navigator.

An older woman with lighter hair than the rest approached and Kris quivered, knowing Derrick wouldn't be able to protect her. "It's okay, Kristina." The woman wrapped her arms around Kris' shoulders. Her warm chocolate eyes instantly soothed Kris, making her feel as though she were gazing into Derrick's eyes. Her features were soft and round, nothing like the other women now gawking at the commotion she'd caused. "Welcome to the family, honey. Tori — I mean, Vic; she doesn't like being called Victoria or Tori — will get over it; she doesn't have a choice and she knows it."

Kris gazed up into the kind woman's eyes, noticing there was something different about her. Although Derrick had said there was no way to tell, every one of the persons around her looked as though they were related to one another, other than this woman. "You're human, aren't you?"

"Yes. I'm Sabrina. Derrick's mother."

Chapter Eleven

What is wrong with you, Vic?" Derrick roared, wondering if it was safe to release his grip on her arm. "Was that you last night? Huh? You think you can scare her away?"

Victoria lifted her head, ignoring his question. Tears trailed down her cheeks. "I loved you, Derrick. How could you?"

He closed his eyes to break off the pain of her declaration. He'd always known that she loved him, and he loved her too, but they'd never be anything more than friends. Well, maybe not anymore, which made his heart hurt. She'd been his confidante as long as he could remember. He'd hate to lose her friendship. "You know I tried. We both tried. I've been trying for fourteen years. It wasn't ever going to happen, Vic. You know that."

She dropped her head to her hands, and Michael patted her shoulder. Sometimes Derrick wished she would just leave. He had a feeling that if he could have fallen for her, she would have instantly reciprocated. It was his hang-up, he knew; his love for Kristina wouldn't allow it to happen.

"I'll stay with her," Michael said. "Go take care of your woman. She's probably scared to death."

Derrick stared at his brother in disbelief. Again, Michael's actions baffled him. Even though they had a human mother, he'd never hidden his distaste for humans. Even their mother knew how Michael felt. Michael knew if the military ever found out about the creatus, especially him and Derrick, they'd use them as guinea pigs. He and Derrick were an anomaly among the group, but no one dared mess with them. As strong as the creatus were, they were stronger. For some reason, a human and a creatus didn't make a half-anything. Derrick and Michael were twice as strong as their full-bred cousins were. Neither his grandfather nor his father could explain or come up with any rational theory, even with their combined medical expertise.

Derrick glanced at Victoria, feeling horrible, but he had no choice. He was in love with Kristina, and he finally understood that he'd been in love with her for the last few years, the reason he could never fall for another woman.

As if she'd read his mind, Vic's eyes smoldered with hatred. "How could you? You're supposed to protect us. As the overseer, you're supposed to keep the humans away, not bring them inside."

He narrowed his eyes. "Careful, Victoria. My mother happens to be one of those humans."

"Your mother's not a drunk!"

Derrick sprang across the barn floor, landing in front of her, fuming. "Back off."

Michael bounded between them, both hands held at arm's length. He turned to address Victoria, "Vic, he's fallen. End of story. Nothing you can say or do will change that. You need to set your sights on someone else for once."

"You're right, Michael. But the only other man I had an interest in left. Maybe I'll hunt down Jonas."

"Vic," Derrick cautioned. "You know better than that."

She glared at him. "Really? Why shouldn't I, Derrick? You don't like anyone around who questions your rules."

"They're not my rules —" Derrick shook his head, not wanting to revisit this same argument. A woman scorned was a woman scorned; it didn't matter if she were a human or creatus, evidently. "Do what you want, Vic. Just stay away from Kristina. She's one of us now."

"She'll never be one of us," she sneered.

Derrick decided he'd better leave before he did anything he'd regret. "We'll discuss this, along with your appearance last night, at the meeting." He charged toward the door, needing to get as far away from her as possible. He'd always cared deeply for Victoria, but the moment she'd threatened Kristina, he felt as if he could kill her without a second thought. As he'd told Kristina repeatedly, nothing could ever come between them after they'd fallen. Not even a lifelong friend.

He stepped outside again to get away from her and his brother.

The moment he saw his mother's arm draped around Kristina's shoulder, introducing her to everyone, his irritation moved to the recesses of his mind. Kristina did the obligatory nodding and smiling, but he could tell it was forced. She was rightly nervous. All of his assurances that she was safe and she'd nearly been attacked within seconds after their arrival.

He darted to the other side of her, kissing her cheek. "Hi. Sorry about that."

Kristina turned her head, glaring at him. "You should have told me," she hissed in a low whisper.

He didn't want to embarrass her, but he had to remind her. "Um, Kristina, just so you know ... Everyone heard you. There's no such thing as whispering in my world."

Kristina's eyes widened. As she looked around the property, her eyes filled with tears, but she lifted her head to restrain them. "I'm sorry."

"Don't be. It's a lot to take in, I know. And you're right; I should have told you. We'll talk about it later though, okay?" He wiped a tear off Kristina's cheek. Knowing Victoria could hear him, he stated clearly, "Vic won't bother you again, I promise."

He heard Victoria harrumph from inside the barn, but suppressed a snarl in front of Kristina, since she obviously couldn't hear her. He'd never imagined that Vic would turn violent. Upset, yes, he assumed that. But if Michael hadn't restrained her when he had, and she'd launched across the lawn, she could have killed Kristina with one blow, and then his life would be over. Creatus didn't recover after losing a partner. They usually ended up moving away from the family, wishing for death. Suicide wasn't common, but they begged death to take them.

Kristina nodded and attempted a smile. "Your mom has been introducing me to everyone. How come you didn't tell me?"

"I didn't want to influence your decision in any way." He picked up his mother's hand. "I'm sorry I didn't get to introduce you properly. Mom, this is Kristina Heskin."

His mother released an airy laugh, squeezing her arms around Kristina's shoulder. "Sabrina Ashton, as you already know."

"Actually ..." Kristina laughed, pink tinting her cheeks. "I didn't know your last name was Ashton. I like that."

"Oops." Derrick shrugged as his mother glared at him. As a distraction, he glanced over his shoulder for his father, who stepped toward him immediately, a smile on his face. He didn't think his father would be upset once he saw Kristina. Their only concern was her drinking, but Derrick had assured them she'd want to clean up. Derrick knew she wasn't an alcoholic; she'd just been looking for a means of escape. And if she hadn't said anything about him all these years, why would she start now? "And my father, Lynford Ashton, but everyone calls him Lyn."

Kristina flashed a genuine smile. "Nice to meet you. Both of you. And didn't you mention you had a brother?" Kristina asked.

"Yes, well ... Michael's —"

"Right here, Bro," Michael called, landing in front of Kristina, not concerned with showing his ability, which most of the group rarely demonstrated. Of course, Derrick had shown off the previous evening too.

"Oh!" She recoiled, but then seemed to catch her bearings. "Um ... is everything all right? I didn't mean to cause derision in the family," Kristina offered, beaming at his younger brother.

Derrick felt a pang of jealousy surge through him because of her words about being with another of his kind yesterday, even though he knew nothing could ever come between them. But his brother was a good-looking, *and younger*, man. He actually looked the same age as Kristina, since he was five years younger than Derrick was. And he looked more human with his slightly rounder cheeks and lighter shade of hair with just a hint of curl. More natural, anyway, than the hard sculpted faces and raven-straight hair most creatus had.

Michael lifted her hand to his lips. "Everything is fine, Kris. Welcome to the family. I hate to do this to you, but Derrick and I have to talk. Do you mind if I steal him away for a moment?"

Kristina withdrew her hand, subconsciously wiping it on her jeans. Derrick couldn't help the laugh that threatened to escape. Michael would be devastated that his charms hadn't worked on her. He was obviously testing whether she'd actually fallen. Few women were able to resist his brother's magnetism. Even though he supposedly didn't like their species, he had no problem taking what he wanted from a human woman.

"Kristina, why don't you and Mom take a tour of the house and get to know each other while I talk with the family?" Her face dropped. "We'll be fifteen minutes at best," he rushed his weak explanation.

She inhaled a breath, turning to Sabrina. "Okay, I guess. I would actually love a tour of the house. It's lovely."

Sabrina wrapped her arm around Kristina again and strolled off toward the house.

Derrick walked toward the barn. "Let's get this over with," he called to the rest of the group.

His father, brother, and every other creatus, men and women, except those who remained with young children, followed Derrick inside the barn. The barn, which was actually an office, served as the center for all their meetings.

Victoria balanced on a rafter, but dropped when he rolled his eyes. She made a wide loop around him, plopping down on one of the chairs closest to the door. "First off, Derrick, what is it you keep accusing me of?"

Derrick ignored her while everyone found chairs or empty railings to sit on, or leaned up against posts. Derrick perched on the edge of his brother's desk, while Michael stood beside him.

Every eye focused on Derrick.

Even though they knew Michael would discuss news of a possible rogue, it seemed most of them had more interest in a new human family member.

"So, I assume you all met Kristina," he started. Heads nodded, most respectful, a few not so much. "This should come as no surprise as I've discussed her with you several times."

"You also said you'd wait until she was older, more mature," Dean, an elder he'd always thought of as an uncle, reproached. "She's a liability, Derrick. You should have talked with us before bringing her here. If you want to endanger yourself and your family, that's one thing. To have her see us without our consent is another."

Derrick pursed his lips, nodding in assent. "Fair comment, Dean. And I apologize. In hindsight, I guess I should have met you alone."

The group glanced around, nodding in agreement, and Derrick noticed an overconfident grin spread across Vic's face. Did she think they'd banish him or Kristina because of it? That wouldn't help matters. He'd always gone with the idea that it was better to beg for forgiveness than to plead for permission.

Dean leaned back in his chair and jutted his chin in Derrick's direction. "That said ... Kristina seems like a wonderful girl. If she hasn't mentioned any of your peculiar antics in fourteen years, I'm certain she won't start now."

Victoria's arrogance fell flat and she twisted in her chair as if wanting to make her escape.

Derrick tore his eyes away from the woman who used to be his best friend. He'd told Victoria everything, had always been upfront with her. They'd shared stories, experimented with life and love. He shook the thoughts from his head, feeling as if he'd been using her. "Kristina won't talk to anyone. She has fallen for me, as I have for her."

A few surprised gasps and audible grunts traveled throughout the barn, echoing in the rafters.

His father stood up and approached the front. "It's over. You all act as if this doesn't happen. Might I remind you I married a human. Sabrina has lived beside you, prepared food for you, adjusted her entire life to be one of us." Lyn glared at his youngest son. "And still, we treat humans as though they are a subspecies. Just because we are stronger, doesn't make us better." He shrugged. "Besides, we have more important things to discuss than my son's love life. According to Michael, we have a rogue on the loose. And that, my friends, is more dangerous to our way of life than one young girl." Lyn walked back to his chair and sat down, crossing his arms in finality.

At a hundred years old, his father was still a force to be reckoned with. No creatus, himself and Michael included, would dare challenge him. Yes, Derrick was stronger, but his father had seen more life. He'd met his mother when she was twenty-two and had fallen within days, he'd said, ignoring his parents' concerns. Now his mother was seventy-three, and his father looked to be in his early fifties. His father would live another fifty years. But more than likely, his mother would survive another twenty at best. The creatus' diet of all whole and natural foods made her appear younger than her years, but facts were facts. And nothing they could do would change the reality that his father would spend roughly thirty years alone, something he'd admitted on numerous occasions that he accepted fully.

Derrick knew he too would be in the same situation, but also identified with his father's avowal. Nothing would cause him to regret his decision to spend his life with Kristina.

Michael stepped forward and took his father's place at the front of the room. "I'm sure you know the reason we asked you to be here today."

Nods and sniffs among the family assured they understood, even though there were no comments.

"The police are being careful," Michael continued. "Nothing has been leaked to the press, which is unusual. They're keeping a tight lid on this one, as they are baffled."

Derrick scanned the room, watching for any indication that someone they knew could be committing the crimes. If it were someone in the family, they'd still come to the meeting, he was certain. The news Derrick had watched last night revealed nothing that hinted at a creatus attack, but if Michael believed it was true, that was good enough for him. He always had an inside track on this sort of stuff.

Ryan, a younger member of their family who'd just returned home from England a few years ago, stood. He was smaller than Derrick, but strong as an ox. They'd wrestled a few times in fun, and Derrick had always liked him, thinking he'd be someone they could bring into their inner circle of leaders. He was forty-two now, the perfect age. But lately he'd been spending a lot of time with Michael, frequenting places they shouldn't, looking for quick hook-ups.

Ryan looked to the family and then back at Michael. "I've been watching the news, and I don't get it. How do you know it's a creatus?"

Michael sighed. He didn't like anyone to question him. He may only be forty-four, but he was a born leader. "I've studied our past, that's how," he said, no inflection of his irritation, which Derrick sensed was teetering just below the surface. His brother also had a temper. "Creatus are smart, as we all know." Michael looked to his father, as if challenging his earlier assessment. "Even the so-called crazy ones. One of the signs of a rogue kill is separating the body so the authorities won't have any identifying marks. They take what they want and leave the rest. Unlike an animal that rips a human to shreds and leaves the carcass, a creatus will pull the human apart with his bare hands and take the parts he wants."

Collective gasps filled the room.

"Okay, Michael," Derrick interrupted. "I think we get the point." Derrick, as he assumed a few others felt, was glad he hadn't eaten lunch yet. He didn't like to think that there were animals that would do such a thing.

"He asked," Michael defended his repugnant answer. "But here's the part that baffles me. Whoever this is, they want us to know."

"How's that?" Dean spoke up again, curiosity lighting in his eyes.

Michael moved backward toward the desk, resting on the edge as though he were a professor addressing his students. "Even though a creatus is smart enough not to give any indication of how the person was killed, they usually hide the victim, bury them. These victims have been left for authorities to find." Michael paused for effect. "The rogue wants us to know."

"So, as Michael and I discussed earlier, there's only one answer," Derrick cut in. "We need to start *watching* again."

Vic burst to her feet. "What? What happened to *the rules*? Isn't that why you banished Jonas?"

Derrick shook his head, casting a glance in Ryan and his mother's direction, wondering if they had thought the same thing too.

Michael also stared in the direction of Ry and Margaret and then hopped off the desk to answer. "We didn't banish Jonas; he left on his own. Jonas was a good friend of mine, but he used watching as an excuse to fight. He didn't care about humans any more than you or I, Vic. He was only looking for a fight. And he was sloppy."

"So we're supposed to put our existence in jeopardy because a few humans are dying?" Vic raised her hands in the air and paced. "Derrick's just worried about his new precious human."

"Sit down, Victoria, or leave," Derrick ordered. "Your choice."

Vic inhaled a deep breath as though she would argue, but then flopped down in her chair again.

Derrick held up his hands in a silent request to the rest of the group. No one as much as breathed. "They are the rules, and I intend to keep them. As for Kristina, she's my concern." He leveled his eyes on Victoria. "No one will get near her; I will make certain of that. As for the rest of you, we will set up a perimeter around Boston where the killings have occurred." Derrick glanced around to see if anyone else dared to question him. "Per *the rules*, as Vic pointed out, I do not want you to get involved with a crime; we're only looking for the rogue. Only interfere if the rogue is involved. And make sure you are always dressed in black with a knit ski mask so that you can shield your face if need be; we don't need to start any vigilante investigations again."

His father stood again. "So, if we see a human getting attacked, you want us to stand by?"

Derrick's stomach plummeted. No, he didn't want that. What would Kristina think of him saying such a thing? But, it was the only way. "We don't have a choice, Dad. It's not like it was when you were protecting the streets. Humans are busy 24-7. They never sleep, it seems. Also, everyone has a video camera on their cell phone. We'd be on the front page of *The National Enquirer* the next day."

Chapter Twelve

After Michael presented the map and the schedules of where he wanted everyone stationed, the barn cleared.

"Hang on a second, Vic," Derrick called as she made her way toward the massive doors that were big enough that a tank could fit through them.

She threw her head back in disgust, acting like a spoiled child. He almost expected her to stomp her feet and stick out her tongue at this point. "Now what?" she whined.

Michael stopped his departure as well, which was probably a good thing. With Vic's attitude, no telling what they'd end up saying to each other. Besides, Derrick needed to question his brother as well.

So as not to accuse just Vic, he addressed both of them with a razor-sharp scowl, "Which one of you was outside Kristina's window last night?" he asked point-blank.

Vic rolled her eyes and Michael's brow furrowed almost imperceptibly, clearly digesting this information.

Smoothing her hair with her hands, sending him the image of a cat preening herself, Vic laughed. "That was fast, Derrick. Didn't waste any time getting with the human, did you?"

Derrick huffed out a breath. What a one-eighty her personality had taken. Again, he hated to keep thinking she was the typical scorned woman, but he now understood all the colloquialisms. There clearly was a thin line between love and hate. "You didn't answer my question, Victoria."

"I have better things to do with my time than spy on your little girlfriend. Besides, I didn't know you'd decided to bring her into our humble family until you showed up with her on your arm." Vic bit her lip, her tough façade seemingly melting. He knew she was heartbroken, understood that her antagonism was directed at the situation, not him. She had to know he'd tried to make it work with her. "Thanks for that by the way," she said sharply, attempting to hold onto her anger. "You could have warned me instead of blindsiding me, making me look like a fool."

Derrick rubbed his chin. "I'm sorry. I guess you're right." He walked toward her and she stepped backward, away from him. "I was worried you'd leave without me having a chance to explain."

"What's to explain, Derrick? I always knew you loved Kristina, even if you denied it. You've been spellbound by her for years. I figured it would happen when she got old enough, when you finally saw her as the beautiful woman she is." The corners of her lips turned up, and a semblance of a smile dawned on her face that he hadn't expected in the middle of her rant. "She is beautiful, by the way. I still hate her, mind you, but I can see the attraction. I guess being half-human makes you boys want a weak shell of a woman —"

"Not me, Vic," Michael burst into the conversation. Derrick was surprised he'd kept his mouth shut as long as he had. An unusual occurrence for his brother. "I love a tough woman."

She laughed, and for a minute, Derrick wondered if they could be the trio they'd been all these years.

"That's the problem, Michael. You'll love just about anything with legs," Victoria teased.

Michael's bravado dropped, looking as if she'd slapped him. "That's not true. You've just been too busy to notice what I do."

Victoria waved her hand in dismissal. "I'm just messing with you, Mike. Chill. You know you'll always be my number one guy."

His brother smiled, but Derrick could see he hadn't been placated. Not wanting to embarrass him, Derrick decided to drop the subject. He'd revisit it later. "I hate to interrupt you two, but let's get back to the purpose of our little soirée here. Neither of you paid Kristina and me a visit last night at her apartment?"

They shook their heads in unison.

Michael rolled his eyes. "Last I saw, you two were playing kissy-face in the park. I actually met up with Ry after we talked and went clubbing."

"What time was that?" Derrick asked.

Michael looked toward the roof of the barn as if the answer would be dangling from the rafters. "Hmm ... I went to dinner. Had a few glasses of wine for St. Paddy's Day. You know we have an Irish heritage by way of Mom, right?"

"Michael ..." Derrick chided. His brother could be so juvenile sometimes.

"Oh, right. I don't know. Ry called me. Asked if I wanted to hang out."

Derrick rubbed his fingers across his eyebrow. "So ... six, seven, eight?" he prompted.

"Honestly, I don't remember. I guess I had a few too many glasses." Michael laughed, but Derrick didn't find it funny. A rogue creatus was stalking Boston, and Michael was out getting drunk after chastising him about his choices. "Wait? What are you thinking, Derrick? You don't think Ry —"

Victoria huffed. "That's just rich ... Who're you going to blame next, Derrick? Your father? We all went to school together, for God's sake. Ry even stayed with us after his brother left."

Derrick paced the room. "All I know is someone was hanging outside Kristina's window last night. By the time I caught a glimpse, they were on the next building. No human can move that fast. So, yeah, I'm perturbed, to say the least. I'd be happier if it was one of you and not the rogue." They both shook their heads again instead of appeasing his concerns.

Michael hopped up from his desk where he'd been perched. "I'll make sure I take the section near your apartment. And I don't know if you're up for it, but I was thinking ..." he trailed off, his dark eyes lighting a shade in his apparent excitement. Derrick didn't like when his brother got that gleam in his eyes. It'd gotten them into plenty of trouble as teenagers. Even though they were five years apart, they'd always gotten along. "If the rogue is interested ... "

"Don't even think about it, Michael. No way will I allow you to use Kristina as bait."

"I'm just saying —"

"No!"

"Man, you're awfully testy. I thought you were supposed to be all lovey-dovey after falling." He laughed. "Oh ... I get it. It's because you haven't consummated your relationship."

Victoria jumped up. "What? You fell without —"

Derrick sighed, cutting her off. "Honestly, you two are like a couple of college kids. Can we get back to the point here? Kristina's not bait, and we still have the other issue I'm dealing with. I managed to delete all the messages on Kristina's phone, but he's not giving up. What do you think he has?" He peered at Michael for an answer.

"The detective doesn't know what he has. He's actually worried about her, believe it or not. You'll never guess who he is ..." Michael trailed off as if Derrick could actually guess. "Give up?"

Derrick resisted rolling his eyes at his immature brother, and instead just stared at him as he sat down. His brother had been alive for forty-four years, but acted as if he were twelve sometimes. The problem with aging slowly was that most of his kind also matured slower.

Michael pulled up a chair in front of Derrick and straddled it, leaning over the backrest. "You're going to flip. He's the uniformed cop who was first on the scene of Kris' mother's death, but now he's a homicide detective."

Derrick whipped his head up. "You're kidding?"

"What are the chances, huh? Small town. Evidently he got the *jumper* call. He ran her tags, since her car was left on the bridge, and realized who she was." Michael shook his head. "You should have called me sooner. We could have avoided all of this if I'd moved her car immediately." He smiled. "But I understand you weren't thinking clearly. I jacked it from the impound yard, pulled all the records as you'd requested. So far, they haven't even figured out it's missing. But Murphy, that's his name by the way, Murphy O'Brian, doesn't seem to want to throw in the towel. He wants to make certain if she's dead or alive. I think your best bet is to have her speak with him, and maybe he'll back off."

Chapter Thirteen

Kris gathered the coat Sabrina had given her tighter to her chest as she watched Derrick shove the canoe off the shoreline of the lake and jump in gracefully.

He was amazingly lithe for such a large man. She'd always imagined a man of his size would move like an oaf, but his movements, as well as his actions, were smooth and methodical. Her insides warmed as she imagined some of those movements. Though he'd been nothing but a gentleman, she found herself imagining all sorts of future actions where she could test his physical abilities.

"Why are you smiling?" he asked as he paddled.

With every stroke, they moved the length as if he'd dipped the paddle in the water ten times instead of just once. And yet, as with everything, there was barely a ripple in the water. Smooth as silk, he was.

"You," she admitted, a warm rush of blood filling her cheeks.

"What about me?"

Kris shrugged. "Still wondering if I need to pinch myself."

He laughed. "You're incorrigible."

Derrick stopped paddling, and Kris scanned her surroundings to see they were already in the middle of the lake. The tree line bordering the water's edge emphasized Harvard's rolling hills, pleasing the eye with a subtle rise and fall instead of a straight line. The sun had begun to make its final descent, casting an orange glow at the center of the horizon with swirled hues of peach and pink adding to the remarkable sunset. The image reflected onto the pond, encompassing their canoe with a picturesque setting for a nighttime boat ride.

"It's beautiful," she whispered. The lake was so peaceful that it felt as if even the vibration of her voice would cause the glass-like surface of the water to ripple in response.

"It is. I've been coming here since I was a boy." Derrick glanced around at the vast lake that even had small wooded islands in the middle. "It's one of the largest lakes in this part of the state, and in the summer, you'd think you were at spring break in Florida with the amount of beachgoers. But what I enjoy are the peaceful evenings this time of the year and the privacy of being off land, away from prying ears."

"I guess you would. With your family's ability to hear you from several blocks away, you can't say anything aloud you want to keep private."

Derrick laughed. "Nope. Thankfully my parents installed soundproofing in their bedroom, which helped some."

Kris burst out a laugh. "Oh! I guess, um ... that would be awkward, huh?"

"Very," he agreed.

"So, why are we hiding?" she whispered conspiratorially.

Derrick shrugged. "I just wanted to bring you here, and we do have a few things to discuss." He inhaled a deep breath and then reached out for her.

Hesitantly, afraid of tipping, she moved to her feet, keeping herself in a crouch. Before she could even attempt to balance herself, he swept her onto his lap. "You need to start warning me before you sweep me off my feet, Derrick. You keep taking my breath away."

He pressed his lips to the side of her neck. "Isn't that what I'm supposed to do?"

Leaning against his chest and into his kiss, she murmured. "Yes."

"Is it okay if we talk like this?" he asked. "I mean, instead of eye-to-eye? There are a few things I need to tell you, but I've been aching to have you in my arms all day."

She turned her head to look at him. "Can't we talk later?"

Derrick took her mouth with his and she felt her body melt in response. She'd missed this too. They'd ambled around the property earlier, making chitchat with the family, but the entire time, Kris had been thinking the same thing. She had to admit it was an interesting afternoon, though. Surprisingly, the buffet of food Sabrina had set out didn't look much different from any other banquet spread. Derrick's mother had learned how to make their diet pleasing to the eye and palate for creatus and humans.

He released her mouth and sighed. "I love kissing you. It feels so right."

She burrowed her head between his chin and chest, reveling in the feel of his chest as he breathed in and out, completely content in his embrace. For the first time in her life, she felt safe. Maybe sharing a bed with Derrick would even chase away her nightmares; she could only hope. Reliving her mother's murder night after night, attempting to rewrite the past, unsuccessfully, had nearly driven her to madness. "It feels right for me too," she confessed. And it did, as nothing in her life had ever felt. She kept teasing him about whether he was real when, in fact, her time with Derrick had felt more real than all her previous twenty-two years, as if she were finally home.

Derrick withdrew one of his arms from around her and reached into his pocket. "It's too beautiful right now to talk, and while you can still see ..." He lifted his hand in front of her, holding up another black velvet box. Though he'd said *forever* repeatedly, she gasped in a mouthful of air, hoping this time it was what she thought it was. Using his thumb and forefinger, he flipped open the tiny case. "I know what I said, and it's still true, but ... I do have a traditional human mother, and I know how much it excited her when my father proposed." He stopped and pressed his hand to her cheek, turning her head, so he could see her face. "Kristina, will you marry me? Officially."

Tears poured down her cheeks, and she hoped he didn't get the wrong impression as she tried to find her voice. She gulped the tears away the best she could and gasped out, "Yes! Without a second's hesitation, yes!" She kissed him quickly as he lifted her hand and slipped the ring onto her left ring finger. The vintage-style ring had a beautiful center diamond, but as large as it was, it didn't look gaudy. The band had a crisscross of diamond paves, shanking the center diamond. It was simply breathtaking; she'd never seen anything like it. Though she'd never been one to peruse bridal magazines, she'd listened to Beth enough to appreciate this masterpiece. "Oh my, Derrick. It's so beautiful. When did you —"

"I ordered it online and had my mother pick it up."

"So they knew?"

"My mother did ... she's always known."

A chill traveled the length of Kris's spine. Sabrina had been so kind to her today, but she'd assumed she was just comforting her after Victoria's rude comment. "I don't know what to say."

He pulled her tighter against him. "You already said it. *Yes*, was all I needed to know."

"But you already knew that," she teased, resting her head against his shoulder, luxuriating in the feeling of his broad chest as he breathed in and out, the refuge that just his closeness provided.

He trailed his fingertips down the side of her face, twisting a strand of her hair around his hand when he reached her neck. "You're human; I'm sure you could break the spell if you so desired. If something repulsed you enough. Like the way Vic reacted. I'm sure that must have frightened you."

"A bit." She crossed her arms over his and tilted her head back to him. "But, I don't scare easily. I've been through worse."

He exhaled a breath. "Yes, you have. About that. Not to ruin the mood, but we really need to talk."

"If you insist," she said on a sigh, not wanting to ruin the beautiful evening.

"It's about the calls. We never finished that conversation."

She shrugged under his embrace. "I trust you, Derrick."

"Well, I'm not proud about this, but I deleted several messages from your phone. I won't do it again. I just thought you needed a moment to digest everything without throwing several barbs at once."

She squirmed under his arms. "Okay ... I'll forgive you this time, but you promised to delete all the tracking devices. I don't want to feel like a hostage in our relationship."

Kris felt Derrick nod his head. "Of course, and I said you were free to come and go as you please, but there's been a new development, so please don't be upset if I'm extra careful."

This time she turned in his arms so she was facing him. Seeing what she was doing, he pulled her sideways on his lap. He lowered his head to her ear. "I came out here for a reason. As I mentioned, away from prying ears." She nodded in understanding. "When you were eight, you told the police officer on the scene that a dark angel had rescued you."

Her eyes bulged. "I did? How did you know?"

He nodded again. "I never left you unprotected. I waited until the police came. I couldn't leave you alone in that alley. I would have killed anyone who approached you, though."

"I'm sorry. And here I thought I'd never told anyone."

Derrick touched her cheek. "It's okay. You were in shock. And the police officer chalked it up to a child's fantasy. The murderer had already jumped up by the time they came, and as much as I wanted to follow him, I couldn't leave you. Instead, he got away with murdering Janelle."

She shook her head, trying to make sense of his comment. "I'm confused. You think the family will be upset at me now? For something I did when I was eight?"

"The officer's name is Murphy O'Brian. He's a detective now. Homicide. He got the call about your jump, and he's been trying to reach you to make sure you're okay, since they never found your body."

Kris clasped her hand over her mouth, a wave of nausea washing through her. Dampness spread over her skin, and for the first time in days, she wanted a drink to calm her nerves. *The same officer who worked her mother's homicide,* she digested, her head spinning for some reason at this revelation.

"Are you okay?" Derrick's words came out in a rush.

"No. I think I'm going to be sick."

Derrick picked her up and set her on the opposite side of the canoe. Within seconds, they were on the shore. He lifted her from the boat and set her on a weathered bench. "I'm sorry. What can I do?"

She moved her head back and forth sluggishly, unable to speak, attempting to restrain the bile in her throat. What was wrong with her?

"You're having withdrawal symptoms again, Kristina," Derrick answered her unspoken question. "Just breathe through it — slowly. And if you have to get sick, do it. I've seen it all before so it doesn't bother me."

Her mouth filled with saliva, and she nodded, in fear that if she tried to speak, she'd puke right in front of him. How romantic would that be? She concentrated on short shallow breaths, willing the clammy wetness on her skin and the queasiness in her stomach to subside. She shook off the coat, appreciating the coolness of the evening.

Since the sun had set, the temperature had dropped by at least ten degrees, which she would normally hate, but right now the brisk air soothed her skin.

Derrick sat down beside her. "Better? Your color has returned. You were pale white a minute ago."

She nodded again, still concerned with her speaking ability.

"You feel like moving to the car? You really shouldn't be out in the air while soaking wet."

Kris patted her hands against her body. Sure enough, the perspiration had soaked right through her clothes. "Okay. Give me just a second."

"Take all the time you want," he said, but then layered the coat she'd discarded around her shoulders again.

"What else?" she asked. "Though, I feel silly. I don't know why that affected me that way."

"Maybe we should wait on the other information."

"No. Talk to me. No more secrets," she insisted.

"Okay. The reason I ripped you out of your home last night ... It was my brother in the park. Michael came to check on us and let me know that we have a rogue."

She tilted her head. "A rogue?"

"Yes. A serial killer of the worst kind is terrorizing Boston — one of my kind. The police will never catch the perp; it is up to my family." Derrick pursed his lips as if not wanting to reveal everything.

"And this *rogue*? You think he was the one outside my window last night?"

"Yes. He or she. Though, Vic swears it wasn't her."

"Why would you think a rogue would come after me?"

Derrick closed his eyes for a second and then swallowed loudly before answering her question. "To get back at me."

Chapter Fourteen

Derrick scanned the trees, feeling eyes watching them. That was the answer. One of the creatus he'd banished for one reason or another was out for revenge. He'd never exiled anyone for a crime of this magnitude, but he'd sent many of his kind away for other indiscretions.

Creatus, as humans, had their dissenters. The only difference was that his family — and most creatus families — didn't put up with them. If you couldn't live and work as a family, you were sent on your way. It'd been three years since he'd asked anyone to leave, and the family had run smoothly since. In fact, other than holidays, they rarely even had to gather.

"Get back at you for what?" Kristina asked, a crease between her eyes revealing her concern ran deeper than she'd let on.

Derrick curled her hand in his, really wanting to get her inside the vehicle where it was warm, but he could understand that the fresh air probably felt good in her condition. "We live in a sort of utopian society. My family was one of the first families to settle in Harvard. In fact, other groups had tried to mimic our lifestyle. I'll take you to

Fruitlands Museum someday. It's popular because in the early 1840s, a faction attempted a society based on transcendentalist principles, which failed miserably. Although they failed for multiple reasons, their foremost mistake was the lack of food. They'd planted, but the harvest wasn't plentiful, and since they were vegans in the truest sense, even excluding milk and egg products, there was nothing to sustain them through the harsh New England winter. They'd refused to use animal labor and even restricted wool, since it came from sheep. They wore only linen clothes and canvas shoes. How they kept warm is beyond me. Imagine trying to work the fields?" Kristina shook her head. "Anyway, the experiment ended only seven months after it began.

"Our lifestyle now is different from when my family settled in the 1700s. We can live where we want, do what we want. But we still stick together. Mostly we work together, have our own schools throughout the world, and when there's an issue, we pull together. Though we live by the law of the land, we also have our own government. And in our region of the world, which is all of New England, I'm what you might call the president, and Michael is the vice-president. If someone breaks our laws — which aren't much different from America's laws — they're on their own. So, unfortunately, I have enemies, I'm sure. But I've never had a rogue creatus."

She scrunched up her nose. A habit Derrick found endearing for some reason. "And you think this rogue will try to murder me?"

He squeezed her hand, rubbing small circles on her soft skin. It was to comfort her, but also, he was checking that her temperature and heart rate had returned to normal. "I don't know, but if you'll bear with me while I find out whomever it is, I would be especially appreciative."

She leaned against him, evidently feeling a little better. "That's understandable."

"I have to ask, Kristina," he started, suppressing a chuckle. "How is it that a homicidal creatus doesn't worry you, but the detective does?"

She peered up at him with those sparkling green and gold eyes. "Because I know you'll protect me from a murderer. But I don't know how I'll protect you from the government. If what I said or did causes that detective to seek out your family ... "

He pulled her closer, cutting off her words, a contented groan escaping his throat at her statement. Kristina loved and cared about him, regardless of what some of his kind were capable of. Then again, even humans perpetrated heinous crimes. Even he, unlike his brother, couldn't condemn an entire species because of a few.

"Thank you, my love. But you don't have to worry about me. I, along with all of my kind, have managed to stay hidden for four thousand years. One detective isn't going to bring us down." He stood, then held out his hand to his bride-to-be. "Let's get you into some dry clothes."

Kristina rose from the bench and leaned against him, allowing him to wrap his arm around her. He made his way to his Navigator, helping her up to the passenger seat. After locking her inside, he walked to the water's edge and picked up the canoe.

A pebble hitting the water's surface on the other side of the lake caught his attention, and he turned to the sound. He surveyed the surrounding trees for any sign of a threat, wondering if he should investigate while Kristina was locked inside the vehicle. Deciding against it, he walked toward the truck again. He hoisted the canoe on top of the SUV, strapping it down on both ends.

A branch *cracked* from the opposite direction, and he realized what had happened. He hadn't imagined the pebble, just the origination of the toss. Nor had he imagined the eyes he felt on him. He turned to the sound. No creatus who knew him would attack while he was on guard, as they knew they couldn't win. So he decided to let them know he was aware. Whispering low enough that Kristina couldn't hear, he made his intention clear, "I know you're there. And let me make myself perfectly clear. You touch her, and I'll rip *you* apart limb by limb."

"I'm coming for her, Derrick. I'm coming for Kristina."

A shiver swept through Derrick, but he shook it off. The words were faint and garbled, so he couldn't decipher if it was a man or a woman, but the threat was unmistakable. The rogue's intentions were clear as well. They were at war.

Chapter Fifteen

Murphy O'Brian parked a block away from Kristina Heskin's apartment for the third day in a row. The Grand Am he'd impounded still sat in the same spot where it had been the day after it disappeared from the impound lot, along with all the documentation.

When he'd arrived to search the vehicle the next day, the operating manager of the facility not only didn't have any clue the vehicle was gone, but also had no signs that there had been a break-in. When he searched the files, everything on Kristina was missing, as if he'd never submitted it as evidence.

It was past nine and he had to get to the station. A missing jumper was a low priority on the city's list — especially when there were no frantic calls from family, insisting the police locate her — so he had to investigate on his off-time. So far, nothing had changed in the last three days, and he'd been on her street every morning, during lunch break, and on his way home from work.

Once back at the station, Murphy fished through the expanding file folder he'd made eight years ago that he brought from home. He had a separate file for every year he'd been a cop, but he'd also made files for specific cases he'd worked. His wife had complained that even the IRS didn't require documentation after five years. Courts had subpoenaed him to testify on crimes even older than that, though, and he liked having his handwritten reports.

Now his home office had hundreds of the brown recycled expanda files, but he'd brought this one he'd made eight years ago because of a common thread among many reports. He pulled out the manila folder with her name on it and the one with the vigilante cases.

Something had been bothering him ever since he'd read off Kristina Heskin's name as the owner of the Grand Am. An encounter he'd had with the little girl when she was about eight years old bubbled to the surface as if cued. For some reason, his brain tried to connect her situation with a vigilante case that had started eight years ago, but then had abruptly stopped three years ago.

In every situation, the victim had claimed that in one minute they were being attacked, and the next, the attacker had disappeared. One woman had caught a glimpse under the light of a streetlamp. She'd said that a man dressed in black had pulled the man off the ground from above her. Even though she laughed while uttering the words, she remarked that it was as if Batman had appeared and saved her.

The other victims hadn't a clue what happened to their attacker because the alley had been so dark. But each one of them insisted that their assailant had mysteriously vanished. Some even cited that it must have been their guardian angel.

Most cops had gone to just inputting their reports into the computer on their patrol car's dash, but he liked to have a hard copy. And at times as these, he didn't have to cut through bureaucratic red tape to get copies.

Murphy reclined in his chair, kicked his feet up on the desk, and sipped black sludge from a Styrofoam cup. He scanned his report, skimming through a lot of the description of the poor kid's dead mother. O'Brian dropped his feet to the floor as he found the passage that had tripped his memory: "My Dark Angel saved me." He'd put the little girl's comments in quotes, because even though she'd only uttered a few words, she'd seemed entirely lucid of the situation.

Riffling through the other vigilante scenes, he found two similar entries. "It was as if an angel had pulled him off me." He found the report from the lady who'd made the Batman comment. "It was like Batman; he'd even been dressed all in black."

He'd entered all of these comments into the database, but nothing had come back other than in his area, and none of his superiors had been interested in chasing down a vigilante. As long as his captain didn't have any dead bodies to deal with, he didn't seem to care about a man ridding the streets of a few thugs.

Murphy set the files aside and fished through his briefcase for the disc the boater had given him on the *jumper* case. The man had been filming for a blog piece he was working when he saw Kristina's body drop. He'd followed her descent to the water, but then another figure had dropped right behind her. As he was starting the boat to rescue them, the other jumper had broken the surface and was on the shoreline in seconds. The boater had shaken his head and then reiterated, "Less than seconds" to Murphy when he'd recounted the scene.

O'Brian popped the disc into his laptop and watched the scene unfold in regular speed. At least based on the first body's rate of descent, it looked as though it were in regular speed. Unless the boater had screwed with the recording, he was correct; the second jumper had had Kristina's body on the riverbank almost faster than Murphy could blink.

"I'll take care of this, sir." A man leaned over Murphy's desk and ejected the CD drive, removed the disc, and then quickly shoved it into his attaché case.

Dumbfounded, Murphy bounced to his feet. "Excuse me. Who the hell are you?"

The man, who was about six-four, had a commanding appearance. Everything about the man, right down to his sunglasses, was dark with the exception of his short spiky hair, which was blond. A spook if he ever saw one. Murphy slumped in his chair as the man exited his office without comment, and he was certain there wouldn't be an explanation even if he caught up with the man.

Murphy picked up the phone and dialed the number he'd scribbled on his desk calendar three days ago. After several rings, the photographer picked up. "Hello?"

"Hey, Bruce. Murphy O'Brian. We spoke the other day and you gave me a copy of video you'd recorded of the Tobin Bridge. I was wondering if I could get another copy."

"Sure, if I had one," he replied with an irritated edge. "I had months of work on that flash drive and a man showed up this morning and asked if he could get a copy as well, said he worked with you. No problem, I told him. But as soon as I pulled out the flash drive to make a copy, he snatched it out of my hand, said thanks, and walked out of my office. I would have chased him down, but he looked scary. I was just getting ready to call you and ask if I could have the copy I gave you."

"Military looking guy with blond spiky hair?" Murphy asked.

"That's the dude."

"He's not my partner. I'm sorry, Bruce. I'm afraid you won't be getting your copy back." Murphy hung up the phone and reached for the files. He sighed as he searched all around his desk. The man had taken them too, it seemed.

Scratching his head in confusion, Murphy picked up his cell phone, deciding to make one final attempt at speaking with Kristina. The phone rang a few times and he was sure, as the last six times, it'd go to voicemail, but it didn't. He heard the click of a connection and waited for a response.

"Hello?" A woman's voice filled the line, and for some reason, he exhaled in relief. From minute one, he'd only wanted to make sure she was okay.

"Hi, Kristina. I've been trying to reach you for days." Murphy used only her first name, hoping she'd assume he knew her.

"Who's calling please?"

Oh well, he should have known better. "Are you Kristina?" he asked this time.

"Yes."

Warmth filled his insides; she was okay. He didn't know why; he'd just wanted her to be okay. "Kristina, my name is Murphy O'Brian. I don't know if you remember me, but we met when you were eight, and I just so happened to witness your acrobatic maneuver off the bridge a few days ago. You're not in any trouble. I just want to speak with you, if that's okay."

"Hang on." She muffled the phone and he could only hear low mumblings, nothing discernible.

At this point, he just wanted to make sure she wasn't in some sort of trouble. Maybe the man hadn't been a spook, but had illegal reasons for wanting the video. The bulge under his jacket proved he had a concealed weapon, so he was still leaning toward spook, as most civilians wouldn't get past the front door of the police station.

"Where would you like to meet, Mr. O'Brian?" Kristina asked.

"Your apartment is fine, if that's okay with you?"

"Sure, I mean, you're a cop and all, right?"

Murphy smiled. He could picture the cute little blonde with a ponytail. "Yes, ma'am. Detective, actually."

"I have to meet my friend at the high school around three, but I'll be home by five if that's okay?"

"I'll see you then." As he hung up the phone, the real image of that day filled his vision. The eight-year-old girl covered in her mother's blood. He'd never escape the nightmares of all he'd seen in his thirty years as a cop. He was looking forward to retirement.

Chapter Sixteen

Kris covered Derrick's hands, which were on either side of her face, with her hands as she stood in the doorway of his apartment. "I'll be fine. I'm running to see Beth after school, we're going to the bridal shop for measurements, and then I'll head directly to my apartment to meet the detective at five." She pulled a canister of pepper spray out of her purse. "I'll hold the bottle in my hand as I move from car to building, okay?"

He closed his eyes as he shook his head and then, opening his eyes again, dropped his hands from underneath hers. "O.C. spray will do little against a creatus; it'll just tick him off."

"And you think he's going to attack me in the middle of the day — in the schoolyard? That'd be stupid, and I thought creatus were supposed to be smart." He rolled his eyes, but didn't comment, so she continued, "And then once I get to my apartment, the detective will be there. You insisted I could come and go as I please." She crossed her arms and jutted her bottom lip a tad to convey she wouldn't allow anyone, a detective, a creatus, or even her fiancé to interfere with her freedom. He'd just have to get used to the fact that she could take care of herself.

"You can. It's just —" He stopped talking and blew out a breath as if understanding that arguing with her was futile, which it was, of course. "Just be careful, okay? I don't want anything to happen to you."

Content to get her way, she smiled. "I promise to be extra careful." She reached up on her tiptoes, wrapping her arms around his neck. "And you're sure you don't mind me using your vehicle?"

"Of course not. It's more reliable than the car you drive. We'll go out this week and get you a new one. Okay?"

She dropped her heels to the floor in shock. "You don't have to buy me a car. I don't expect —"

He stepped forward and picked her up, bringing her lips to his for a quick kiss. "I don't have to do anything I don't want to either." He grinned, seemingly cheerful to throw her attitude back at her. "I want to, so you'll have to deal with my wants too. Fair enough?"

Kris lifted her head, beckoning another kiss, and Derrick complied with a sweeter and longer goodbye kiss. "Mmm ..." she murmured. "That's more like it. So, when exactly will we get married ... so we can fulfill all our wants? One second you tell me we're connected for eternity and that marriage doesn't matter, and now you want to wait until our wedding night." She sighed longingly. "It's not as if we haven't been with other —"

He kissed her again, breaking off her words. "Shh ... I just want it to be special is all." Derrick lowered her to the wood floor. "And it depends on what type of wedding you want."

"I don't want much. I've never been into all the fluff and frills." She fiddled with the new ring on her left hand, loving the way it felt. Like a link in a chain, uniting her with him forever. "Besides, after dealing with Beth today, I'll probably want to run straight to the courthouse."

He harrumphed. "My mother would never allow that. She's always wanted to adopt you."

Kris sucked in a mouthful of air, her playfulness coming to a halt at his words. "What do you mean? Not literally, right?" Ever since she was orphaned, she'd prayed a real couple would want to go through the trouble to adopt her. Instead, she'd been tossed from house to house.

Derrick moved his hand to her neck, wrapping her hair around his hand, which he seemed to enjoy. Every time he did it, the action instantly soothed her. "Yes, literally. She thought since you'd already seen me that it would only make sense. To protect you from the others."

Appalled at the thought, she stepped away from him. "Your family would have killed me when I was only eight?"

"No, no, God, no. I would never ..." he stammered to retract his comment, stepping forward and closing the gap she'd made between them. She was against the door now, so she couldn't withdraw again, even though she felt anger pulse through her. He drew in a breath. "Yes ..." he conceded, "there was talk, but everyone knew that never in a million years would I, my father, or the other elders allow that. And of course, they would have had to commit my mother if anyone in our family had ever hurt you."

She stared at him in shock, still disbelieving that they could ever do something so heinous. "Let me guess. Your brother and Vic." He dropped his head, confirmation enough. "I understand you have to keep your secret, but —
"

"They'd just come home from school. They were young and stupid — well, I guess they're still immature," he lifted his hand to her cheek, "but, Kristina, never at any time was your life in danger. I wouldn't have allowed anyone to harm you then — or ever. But I also wanted you to be able to live a normal life ... as a human. So I convinced my family that I would watch you ... that I didn't think the police would believe your story. And I was correct. But then, you never told another soul." He tilted his head, as if just working through it. "Why?"

"Because you were mine." She rested her hands on his chest and gazed up at him, knowing he would never have allowed anyone to hurt her. "I didn't want to share you with anyone. To let them convince me you didn't exist. I wanted to believe."

Her husband-to-be ran his fingers across her forehead, sweeping her hair away from her face. "And do you finally believe, my love?"

"In you? Always. Even if you disappeared tomorrow, I'd always believe you existed."

Derrick dipped his head and took her mouth once more, pulling away after a few seconds with a sigh. "Be careful. I love you."

This time Kris turned and opened the door before she could get lost in his eyes, his kiss, his arms. Everything about him. They needed to elope. That way they could spend an entire week doing nothing but filling themselves with each other. Maybe then the fire would smolder a fraction so they could carry on with life away from each other. Because even as she closed the door behind her, her heart felt as if it would shatter into a thousand pieces. Like one of those jigsaw puzzles where all the pieces were the same color and she'd never figure out how to put it back together if something happened.

Inhaling a deep breath, she stepped into the elevator, still feeling his warm arms around her. Then she remembered, she hadn't told him she loved him too. She lifted her hand to touch the button for the next floor so she could go back up, but then smiled as she spoke aloud, "I love you too, Derrick. Forever." Thankfully, she had the elevator to herself; otherwise, her neighbor would think her insane.

Her phone buzzed, so she pulled it out and read the text: *Always and Forever! So, be careful. Yours, Derrick.*

She inhaled a deep breath and forced the stupid grin off her face as the elevator opened to the parking garage.

Remembering her promise to be careful, she pulled the O.C. spray out of her purse and held it at the ready. She hadn't been attacked in years, but she had a feeling Derrick had always been close, ready to kill anyone who tried. With a click of the key fob, the Navigator's headlights beamed across the concrete, lighting her way.

Driving the Navigator through the narrow streets of Boston felt like maneuvering a tank through a minefield. Not that she'd ever driven a tank, but she imagined it had to be similar. Kris constantly checked her rearview mirror, side mirrors, blind spots, anywhere a compact car could hide — or a semi-truck for that matter. On her third peek over her shoulder, she noticed a car she'd seen earlier. Not that she was a car enthusiast by any means, but this vehicle stood out because of its intention not to stand out. Everything on the sedan was black with the exception of the blue Ford emblem in the center of the matte-black grill. The tinted windows were way over the legal limit, and even the windshield had some type of film, restricting her view of the driver.

Already nervous after Derrick's concerns, Kris veered for the next exit, changing lanes and jerking the car to the right at the last second. She traveled the service road for several streets until she found a cross street that took her under the overpass and into the neighborhood of her old school.

Feeling ridiculous, Kris pulled into the visitor parking area. She willed her heart rate to slow as she made a slow track of the schoolyard. The parking lot was mostly empty other than a few cars parked in the teachers' area, which had been off-limits to students.

The visitor area was vacant, and she remembered how the women in the front office locked down and left almost seconds after the final bell rang too. No other cars had followed her onto the school grounds and into the student parking lot. She laughed at that, realizing she'd parked in the student section. Habit.

Checking her surroundings before exiting the SUV, she made her way across the parking lot and into the corridor where the teachers' lounge and dean's office were located, knowing that'd be the only open exterior door. She inched open the door and slid through, holding it so it didn't slam shut. She really didn't want to run into the dean, as he'd have plenty to say to her, since they were on such friendly terms — not.

She skirted the wall, ducking under the glass, and made a beeline to Beth's classroom. It was only a few minutes after three, but other than the sounds of a basketball game going on in the gym, the students had already cleared the building.

Walking through the corridor, Kris' gaze fell on all the posters and announcements. The junior class was already reminding students about this year's prom theme, encouraging teenagers to buy their tickets now. The posters weren't fancy. Mostly just black font on white poster board with glitter and confetti pasted over the words to add a splash of color. Students in this neighborhood didn't have the money to have printed posters as she'd seen in teenage movies.

Feeling melancholy, Kris dropped her head. She'd skipped prom. Not because she hadn't been asked, but because as much as she'd tried to play off the attack by that college kid, he had scared her. Never again had she accepted a drink from a man, or anyone for that matter. She'd switched to bottled or canned alcoholic drinks. She was especially fond of *Mike's Harder Lemonade*. The regular stuff filled her up before she even felt a buzz. But the *harder* brand did the trick and went down smoothly. Her mouth watered thinking about it. She'd told Derrick that she'd only thought about a drink in passing, but truly, on more than one occasion in the last few days, she'd longed for it. Only because she believed it would settle her nerves. She was strong, though; she had no doubt she could abstain as long as she wanted.

Stopping at her old English classroom, Kris peered through the rectangular window on the drab-brown door. Beth sat behind a desk in the front of the schoolroom, her head leaning over a stack of three-ring binders in every color of the rainbow. Portraits of classic authors: Shakespeare, Dickens, and Twain — lined the walls, along with posters spouting motivational clichés with images of kittens and puppies.

Like Kris, Beth had always been a contradiction. Probably the reason they got along so well. Kris smiled at the picture of a kitten hanging off a tree branch with the words "Never Give Up" written across the top in large, bold typeface. She was almost certain the faded and curled-at-the-edges poster had been there since her mother attended high school.

"Hel-lo, Ms. Witters ..." Kris drew out her words in the sweetest schoolgirl voice she could mimic as she opened the door.

Beth jumped up from her stack of folders, her reddish-blond curls bouncing on her shoulders. "Kris!" Her friend ran around the desk as if she hadn't seen her in a year, even though it'd only been a little over a month. Beth grabbed and squeezed her, holding on a good twenty seconds before leaning back to appraise her. "Oh, my God! You look so good. Where did you disappear to, a spa retreat?"

Kris chuckled. "No. What do you mean?"

"You can't tell me you don't see it. You're practically glowing," she squealed. "You're not pregnant, are you?"

"No, I'm not pregnant. Sheesh!" Kris smacked her friend on the shoulder. "Are you?"

Ignoring her, Beth lifted Kris' hand with her one hand and fanned herself with the other.

Oops ... she'd forgotten to remove Derrick's ring so she wouldn't have to explain. Beth lowered her head, but lifted her eyes with a penetrating gaze. She must have been practicing on the students, because even though Beth was an inch shorter than Kris' five-foot-four stature, all of a sudden she felt as though she were fourteen again.

"Really?" Beth challenged. "This is some major bling. What gives? I didn't even know you were seeing someone."

Kris licked her dry lips, not wanting to lie to her friend, but knowing she couldn't betray her new family's trust. "I've known him for years, but we met up recently, and we just ... clicked. I'd always known he was the *One*. But since he wasn't from here, I didn't think we could ever make it work." *There, that was all true*, she thought.

"Is he from Boston?" Beth asked, her brow still lowered. "And how come I've never heard about him?" She shook her head, obviously unable to make sense out of the fact that her best friend had kept something from her for years.

"He went to school in England," Kris announced happily. Another truth. "It'd been almost six years since I'd seen him, and then one day, he just showed up." Inside, she cheered at her cleverness. She was good at this. It was all truth. Nothing she could get in trouble for revealing.

Beth pressed her lips together in a straight line, clearly not buying her story, but she nodded anyway. "Got a picture?" she asked offhandedly, seemingly uninterested as she reached down and picked up Kris' right hand. "This looks familiar, though. Didn't you sell this ring when you were sixteen?"

"What are you, a detective?" Kris snorted, hoping Beth would drop the interrogation bit.

Beth planted her hands on her hips. "No ... I'm your best friend." She grabbed her purse off the desk and threw it over her shoulder, marching off without a glance backward.

Kris followed, smiling, happy to know that Beth did care. In fact, she was beginning to realize more people cared about her than she had known. Heck, even a detective she'd met only once, fourteen years ago, cared. He could have filed the attempted-suicide report, but he actually wanted to see her. People — creatus included — cared if she lived or died. The thought made her want to smile as much as it made her want to cry. She'd never been alone.

Chapter Seventeen

As soon as the elevator doors closed Kristina inside, Derrick shoved through the stairwell door and bounded over the railing to the ground level.

He would not get close enough to hear her, he decided; he'd just stay nearby in the event he needed to protect her. He hadn't told her about the rogue's words, as he hadn't wanted to upset her, but now he wondered if he should.

The rogue was obviously targeting Kristina, rather, targeting him by threatening the most important person in his life now and forever. A creatus knew the worst thing you could do to another creatus was kill the one for whom they'd fallen.

Derrick slammed through the steel doors into the parking garage, racing toward his BMW HP4. He had arranged special parking for the motorcycle with his condo's proprietor, so that it'd be right up front. Kristina hadn't asked, and he hadn't bothered to tell her it was his.

Normally he loved the extravagant multi-color finish in metallic blue with silver and white accents, but today he wished he'd had it specially ordered in a solid black. He quickly pulled his full-face helmet over his head and backed the bike into a dark corner, waiting for Kristina to emerge from the elevator.

He watched gratefully as Kristina surveyed her surroundings before stepping away from the doors. Then she clicked the key fob, lighting the parking area as she rushed to the Navigator's door, locking herself inside the cab. She acted tough, but he presumed the fact that she'd been attacked twice in her life — the first time watching her mother die — had to mess with her head.

Once she left the garage, he followed. He knew her destination, so he had no concern about losing her in traffic. He made a detour via an exit ramp then returned to the highway a few blocks later, ending up behind her again. Far enough that he could just see his truck's medical parking pass on the rear window.

Derrick watched a black sedan trail Kristina by three car lengths, changing lanes within a minute or so when she did. Though the car looked simple enough, Derrick knew better. It was the new police Interceptor. The dead giveaway; it didn't have the vehicle model stamped on the rear of the vehicle. He doubted the local Boston police department footed the bill for the new Taurus SHO, so this had to be a Fed of some sort. His brother had been right.

He clicked the Bluetooth on his helmet and spoke clearly, "Mike." The line connected and his brother picked up, sounding bored with his simple "Yeah" as an answer. "I need you to run a tag," Derrick told him.

"Fire away," Michael chirped.

He figured that'd cheer up his brother. Derrick read off the numbers as he watched Kristina jerk the Navigator at the last second to take a different exit than she should have. The anonymous driver of the sedan stepped on the gas immediately, surging forward with the vehicle's two turbochargers. Derrick followed the sedan; he knew where Kristina was heading.

"Nothing," Michael said. "A spook, I'd guess. Please tell me this guy isn't following Kris."

"Okay, I won't."

"Just what we need, Derrick!" His brother spewed a sentence of obscenities masquerading as adjectives and ended his tirade with a vulgar noun. "My girl told me that O'Brian was ticked because some guy with spiky blond hair had come into his office, taken the disc out of his drive, and then walked out without a trace. I assumed it was another spook."

"The video from the Tobin Bridge?" Derrick inquired.

"One in the same. Moron," his brother grumbled under his breath, knowing Derrick could still hear him. "What were you thinking?"

Derrick resisted doing some cursing of his own. Though it was impossible to change Michael's ways, he still tried to influence his younger sibling. "I wasn't thinking about anything but Kristina."

"That's obvious. You think what I do is a joke, don't you? Do you know how many times I've thwarted an investigation?" As his brother rambled on about security and I-told-you-so nonsense, Derrick took the next exit, drove back in the opposite direction, and scanned the roads for the Interceptor. Nothing. The driver must have backtracked. He'd obviously discovered Kristina was staying with him. Probably the night he'd driven her home and then packed half of her belongings into his vehicle. So he'd probably head there and wait for her return. Oh, well, he won't see anything to alert him, so eventually, he'll get bored and drop the investigation, chalking up whatever report he'd found as bogus.

Derrick made a pass by the high school. He saw his Navigator, but no black sedan. He circled the neighborhood a couple of times, waiting for the young women to exit. After a few minutes, they came outside arm in arm. He couldn't keep the smile off his face. Beth was good for Kristina, well, except for inviting her to that frat party when they were sixteen. But then again, how could she have known that her boyfriend's suitemate would attempt to date-rape a sixteen-year-old girl? She couldn't, and for that, he couldn't be upset with her. In fact, Beth was marrying her high school sweetheart, Jason. According to Kristina, he'd proposed to Beth her junior year of college.

After the ladies drove off in separate vehicles, Derrick headed over to Kristina's apartment. He wouldn't follow her to the bridal shop. No one, even a creatus, would attempt to attack her in a public location in the middle of the day. No, they'd go to her apartment and wait, and so would he. Blood rushed through his system at the thought. He didn't want to kill anyone, but he would, without a thought, to protect Kristina.

Derrick parked his bike behind the decrepit apartment building and busied himself with his iPhone while he waited. Thankfully, he had vacation time saved up; otherwise, his father would start to get ticked. The medical center ran well with the staff they had, but they needed him for emergencies. Even though they treated humans and creatus, the employees were only creatus. That way any records that needed forged never came under the scrutiny of human eyes.

Creatus weren't declared born until their tenth year and were schooled at private institutions. Then they'd spend the first ten years of their adult life after college, teaching in their private schools. When they finished and were ready to enter the earthly world between the ages of thirty and thirty-five, depending on their maturity, their records would indicate they were twenty-five, which gave them years to catch up. With their smooth olive-tone skin, most humans couldn't tell their age anyway, so they always looked younger than they were.

After answering a few emails and texts, Derrick started to get antsy. It was past five, and he hadn't heard his Navigator pull up. He paced the alleyway behind Kristina's building, looking up at the red brick walls, contemplating whether he should just go up and meet her there.

He trailed his hand along the chain-link fence and walked back to the side, under her fire escape. He poked his head around the corner of the building. Not much had changed. A few more cars, but that made sense. Neighbors returning from work.

Deciding he'd go up to her floor the easy way, he strolled to the side of the building, surveying the area to make sure no witnesses were nearby. He'd be ready in the event anyone unexpected arrived.

Chapter Eighteen

Kris parked in front of her apartment building and glanced around before jumping out of the Navigator. Derrick had her frazzled with all his worrying, and that black car following her hadn't helped.

The entire time the seamstress fitted them in their dresses, Kris' mind had wandered. Beth rambled about her bachelorette party, the wedding, the reception, the honeymoon. But most of her words just hung in the air, never seeping into her brain. Thankfully, enough tidbits registered so she could utter an appropriate "Mm-hm" or "Oh" when necessary.

She'd been right. A day with Beth cured her of ever wanting a big wedding. Beth had spent over a year and thirty thousand dollars for one night. Of course, the honeymoon sounded wonderful. A week in Bora Bora, in a hut, over crystal-blue water, with nothing to do but eat and make love all day and night. Where could she sign up? She'd have to make sure she reminded Derrick that she didn't want the fairy-tale wedding, just the happily-ever-after honeymoon.

Trudging up the three flights of stairs, Kris sighed. Derrick had made this so much easier. She could use a lift about now. A quiver of longing fluttered in her stomach as she wondered if he missed her as much as she missed him. The day had been tortuously slow. As much as she enjoyed her girl time with Beth, her relationship was too new with Derrick. She found herself never wanting to be away from him.

Finally making it to her door, she rustled in her purse for the keys. She'd forgotten to keep them in her hand as she'd promised Derrick.

Kris scanned the hallway, wondering where the police detective was. She'd expected him to be here, one of the reasons she hadn't been concerned for her safety. She looked at her phone as she pushed the key into the deadbolt. Five-fifteen. Maybe he'd left already, since she was fifteen minutes late. Oh well, she'd grab a few more things she needed and head back to Derrick's.

As she pushed open the door, she remembered the pepper spray. She positioned her foot between the doorjamb and the door, propping it open. Kris fiddled inside her purse, untangling her earphones from around the metal ring at the top of the can. How the dang things ended up so twisted was beyond her. No matter how carefully she stored her headphones, she swore tiny gremlins tied them in knots.

Pepper spray finally in hand, she pushed open the door the rest of the way and stepped inside her frigid apartment. Somehow, it didn't feel like coming home anymore.

Cold and dark eyes stared blankly up at her, causing a shriek to escape her throat.

Derrick bolted over the man's body, lifted her off the floor, and carried her into her kitchenette. He set her down after darting his eyes around the tiny room and ascertaining there was no threat.

"What —" she tried, but he placed his fingers over her lips, hushing her. In a flash, he was gone. Kris heard doors open and close throughout the apartment, and then he was in front of her again, eyes wild.

He grabbed her hand and drew her through the apartment to her bedroom. "Get whatever you need; you're not coming back. I'll have my family move the rest."

"But ... that guy ... he's dead?" she asked, stuttering.

Derrick nodded as he helped her shove clothes into a gym bag she'd had stored under the bed. "*That guy* is Detective O'Brian, and his neck has been snapped," he said point-blank.

She gasped in understanding, but then wondered again. Had Derrick — she shook the thoughts from her head. "Why are you here, Derrick?"

"I was here to make sure you were okay, and I'm glad I was. The rogue was probably waiting for you in the other room, but went out the bedroom window when he heard me."

"But you were inside ..." she trailed off, her voice nearly nonexistent.

"No," he said in a calm tone. "I heard you scream and I came in through the open window."

"But you were there ... immediately. I didn't leave a window open."

Derrick stopped shoving clothes in the bag and glared at her. "What are you insinuating, Kristina? You think I snapped a man's neck. You think I'm capable of that? Obviously the rogue came in through the window and left it open."

Kris ran her hands through her hair, tears filling her eyes. "No, no, of course not. I'm just confused. Why would anyone kill him? He seemed so nice." She sniffed back the tears. "When he showed up on the street after my mother had died, he was so kind to me. I remember him asking me what happened, but he never pressed me for details. He'd handed me a tissue and told me he had a daughter too, but she was grown." The tears poured freely now as Derrick walked around the bed and wrapped his arms around her. "That was fourteen years ago, so he's probably a grandfather," she continued babbling. Unable to stop crying, she burrowed her face against his chest.

Derrick ran his hand through her hair. "We have to go, Kristina. We have to inform the police, but we have to get you out of here first. We'll go in person."

Kris lifted her head and stared at him. "Why do the people around me always have to die?"

He just shook his head. "I don't know, love. Sometimes it just happens that way." He picked up her bag and pulled her against his side. "Let's get out of here. I'll have everything packed up tonight."

Unable to do anything but cry — for herself, for others, for all that had gone wrong in her life — Kris rested her head against Derrick's chest, wondering again why anyone would kill the innocent detective. Had he known something he shouldn't have?

Chapter Nineteen

Derrick directed Kristina to the passenger side of the Navigator, helping her up. Hearing the whine of fuel injectors as a key turned in an ignition to "alt" mode, he flashed a look without lifting his head in the direction of the sound.

Parked six spaces away was the Ford Interceptor from earlier. A man with spiky blond hair, as his brother had described, sat behind the wheel. A film on the windshield diminished the view for a human, but he could see the man clearly.

The driver didn't look like a creatus, but he could never be sure. Some of them dyed their hair to look more human than their raven coloring, typical of their kind, but he also had a strong jawline and olive features.

Derrick whispered, *the detective is dead,* but saw no reaction. So he decided to try another sentence, knowing if it was the rogue, he'd want to taunt Derrick. *You'll never touch Kristina,* he growled in a low breath only one of his kind could decipher.

Nothing, which meant that he wasn't as bold as he had claimed the other evening, afraid that Derrick might attack him right now, or somehow, a Fed of some sort had gotten wind of them again. No normal agency would care about an attempted suicide or even a homicide for that matter, unlike Detective O'Brian, who wanted to know what was going on and how it affected Kristina.

No, if he was an agent, he had to be under the National Security Council. There were so many initials and different agencies they never knew where to look, but there was always one division tracking paranormal activity.

Agents searched key words in police reports such as: *angel, guardian, vigilante, superhero, alien*, and any other words indicating that something supernatural had protected a citizen. Contrary to popular belief, according to Michael, they didn't seem to bite on UFO sightings; they left that for the military branches. They were more interested in anything involving superhuman strength, continuously searching for the next weapon.

His brother had someone working in every branch in the government and would always stay one step ahead of them for creatus everywhere. Any family, whether across the nation or overseas, would call Michael if they thought an official was investigating them. And if Michael found any evidence, the entire family would disappear in a matter of days or weeks, depending on the severity of the examination.

Locking Kristina inside, Derrick trotted off to get his bike, sprinting once he was around the side of the apartment building. When he returned to his vehicle, he acted as though it were a struggle to lift the almost-four-hundred-pound bike and load it into the rear cargo area of his SUV.

He clicked the key fob to lower the lift gate then climbed into the driver's seat. He turned to Kristina. Her eyes were bloodshot, her normal contented expression cast downward. He lifted her hand and it was ice cold, as if she might be in shock.

Derrick took her other hand and rubbed both her hands to warm them up as he stared into her eyes. "We need to go to the police station, and not that you or I have anything to hide about the detective's murder, but we need to get our stories straight." He lowered his head to hold her eye contact. "So they don't look at me too closely. We don't allow authorities to retain or arrest creatus; we take care of our own. Okay?"

Kristina choked on a breath, but nodded.

"I have to make one quick call first, though." Derrick pressed the SYNC button on the steering wheel and listened to the female voice ask for a command. "Call Mike," he spoke, squeezing Kristina's hand.

His brother answered, and Derrick spoke fast and low enough that Kristina could probably only catch a few words. He didn't want her to worry.

The drum of his brother tapping on his keypad resounded through the phone before he spoke. "Take me off speaker," Michael said before commenting on the situation. "I just texted Matt. He'll be at the Somerville police station within the half hour. Be cool, brother. We'll find this guy. But you know, he actually did us a favor."

Derrick huffed out a breath in disgust instead of commenting on his brother's callous remark.

Michael sighed through the phone. "I know how you feel about humans, but it's true, Derrick. Sometimes I think you forget what our ancestors went through. They should have killed the lot of them before they almost murdered our kind to extinction."

"That's enough! Sometimes I think *you* forget our mother is human," Derrick seethed, though swiftly and quietly so Kristina couldn't understand. "*Where are you, Michael?*"

"What the hell is that supposed to mean?" his brother spat in response.

"I asked you a question. I want to know where you, Vic, and Ryan are. For that matter, I want to know where every member of the family is when I get back from the police station. Do you hear me? Unless you ran off your mouth, no one else knew about the detective but you and Vic. And if someone is trying to fill your role as cleaner, I suggest you find the culprit before I assume it's you." Derrick stopped and pulled in a breath. "No one is to act without my authority. Do you understand me? Not even you."

The connection was silent for a moment. "Yes," Michael spewed. "Loud and clear, sir."

Derrick clicked *end* and, feeling Kristina's gaze, turned to her. She'd evidently heard enough to understand the gist of the conversation. "I'm sorry," he said. "Maybe this is a bad idea."

A sheen of moisture glassed over her eyes, obviously understanding that he was referring to their relationship. Too many factors to consider. Too dangerous for her. Maybe they could just go away. Being the overseer of his family didn't make it easy. If Michael was in charge ... No. He couldn't do it. Not yet. His brother was too immature, hated humans too much. If he left, he could only imagine his brother amassing an army and taking on humankind.

Derrick brushed a tear off Kristina's cheek. "No ... I can't let you go," he said to her as much as to himself. He pulled the vehicle to a stop and parallel parked outside the station. It would take Matt a while to get here anyway. He pressed his palm against her face. "Kristina, I didn't murder him, I swear." She nodded, and he could see she believed him, so it was his other comment. "I'll never leave you.

Please don't worry. You'll never be alone again." She blinked, and he understood that was it. She loved him, he knew she did, but she was terrified of being alone again.

Derrick turned her face so she was looking at him fully. "Listen, you are going to go in there and tell the entire truth with one exception." She nodded as if listening to whatever he had to say. "Tell them everything that happened. The only difference is when you saw his body, you came downstairs, and I showed up at the same time, since I was going to meet you and the detective at your apartment. Okay?"

Kristina nodded again, but Derrick needed to hear her voice, make sure she wouldn't break down inside the station.

He picked up her hands and rubbed them between his, attempting to get her circulation flowing, so she could think. Not only were her hands cold, now they were shaking. "Kristina, they won't understand that I came through the window three stories up when I heard you scream, and there are no phone records to corroborate that you called me to come get you. So, I have to have shown up right after you ran for safety. Okay? You were scared and you ran, and then I met you on the street. Understand?"

"Yes ..." she choked out. "I understand ..." She bobbed her head, her breathing almost returning to normal. "I was scared when I saw him on the floor, afraid whoever killed him could still be in my apartment, so I ran downstairs. Right before I got to the car, you showed up."

"Very good, love. It's almost exactly what happened. They wouldn't understand anything else."

She gave him a weak smile, but then tears began to flow again. "I need a drink, Derrick. To calm down. I can do this if I could have just one drink to calm my nerves."

Derrick shook his head. "You're strong, baby. You don't need a drink. I'm right here. You can do this."

She gasped, attempting to hold back tears. "I'm so tired of death. His eyes ... "

"I know." Derrick pulled her closer, caressing her hair. "I'll take you away. We'll go away until they find out who did this."

Kristina peered up at him through glassy eyes. "You can't just leave."

"I already told you; I can do anything I want."

Her mouth turned up, but she couldn't force a smile.

Derrick's phone buzzed at the same time Matt's name and number lit up on his radio's screen. He answered on his phone instead of the SYNC system. "I'm here. She's ready." He hung up and jumped out of the truck, making his way around the vehicle to Kristina. Opening her door, he helped her down and pulled her to his side. "Matthew Ashton is my uncle. He doesn't usually come to family gatherings; he prefers to stay out of the loop of most things. He only comes when we need an attorney."

Matt stood next to the first set of red brick steps leading to the small station, his briefcase resting on the squat concrete wall. "You're lucky, Derrick. I was heading home from a meeting in Boston when Mike texted me." His uncle stepped forward and hugged him. "This must be Kristina. I've heard a lot about you, young lady."

Kristina glanced up, but squeezed on to Derrick, as a child would hang on to her mother.

"She found him, Matt. As if she hasn't been through enough." He lowered his voice. "It had to be one of us, his neck had been snapped, but there were no signs of a struggle or defensive wounds. It was clean and swift, a planned attack. Somehow, the rogue knew the detective would be there. And I can't help but wonder if he's trying to set me up."

Kristina leaned back, her eyes wide, as if that hadn't occurred to her, but clearly revealing that it *had* worked. She obviously had thought for a second that he might have murdered the detective.

Matt stepped closer. "But this isn't how the other murders —"

"Exactly," Derrick interrupted. He looked down at Kristina. He didn't want her to hear his next words, but he also didn't want her to think he was keeping anything from her. "He — the rogue — spoke to me the other night. Heck, it could have been a *she* for all I know. The voice was low and garbled, but he said he was coming for Kristina, and he called me by name."

Kristina threw her hand over her mouth and stumbled backward as though she would be sick again.

Derrick held his hand out to her. "I'm sorry. I didn't want you to worry."

She shook her head, more tears falling, and Derrick felt as though his heart would break. How much more could she take? How could he expect her to live like this?

Matt pulled in a breath, nodding. "So it's someone we banished, but they're blaming you," he speculated. "Is Mike tracking down everyone we've exiled in the last ten to twenty years?"

Derrick shrugged, thinking that would have been a good start, but he doubted it. As Michael had suggested, they'd taken to the streets, assuming it was a psychotic rogue, not a vengeful creatus. But what if they weren't actually eating humans, only wanted it to look as if they were.

"Call him and tell him to get started," Matt continued. "I'll go in and start the ball rolling." He looked at Kristina.

"You think you can talk if they request? You don't have to, of course."

"As soon as I saw the man, I ran out the door in fear. When I came downstairs, Derrick had just pulled up," Kristina babbled off, just as he'd told her with only minor variances.

"And why was Derrick there?" Matt asked.

"He's my fiancé; I'd asked him to meet me there when I spoke with the detective."

"Good. Nothing else is any of their business. Not why you jumped off the bridge or whether Derrick followed you. Nothing. Do you understand? The only thing you know is that the detective had some questions." He lowered his head and looked at her. "You don't know what his questions were. It would only be speculation. Understand?"

"Yes."

"Okay." He offered her a smile. "You saw, you left, Derrick was waiting on the street. Anything else they ask I will object to as not relevant. Understand?"

"Yes." She sighed, crossing her arms. "I understand."

Kristina had reached her max, and evidently, Matt had realized it too, as he raised his hands in surrender. "Derrick will not be talking to them, as he was never in the apartment," he added for good measure then turned and walked away.

Derrick pulled Kristina to a stop when she started to follow. "You okay?"

"No!" she said, a frustrated huff escaping her throat. "But, yes. I'll survive. I always survive!" She pulled her hand loose and stomped off.

Chapter Twenty

*R*ogue. Was that the best name they could come up with? The world had no idea what *this* rogue was capable of.

At one time in history, humans revered creatus as gods, superheroes, idols.

Creatus had been on the earth almost as long as humans. But because those self-important hominids didn't understand the creatus' eating habits, his ancestors had slithered into the shadows, not allowing humans to see their strength and power until they became myths — fairy tales.

Ridiculous!

Creatus weren't anomalies; they were superior in every way. Even the fact that they'd landed on this planet some four thousand years ago proved their superiority. Too bad their ancestors had destroyed all evidence of their supremacy.

The only way to become great again would be to start a war, to hint to the humans of their existence. Once the humans knew that creatus existed, they'd have to protect themselves, which would start a battle between their species. And when the creatus banded together — around the world, in every nation, in every government office —

the world would once again worship and fear them, as they should.

Derrick was just one of many leaders who didn't understand this. And since New England was one of the largest and most powerful sects, and Derrick was one of the strongest creatus, he had to be dealt with first.

Until then, the name *rogue* would have to suffice. Tonight, a calling card on the woman would elicit a notable name from the media anyway. The wax seal wouldn't prompt the correct name, but it would hint at an ancient myth. Even if humans didn't believe the fairy tales and horror stories, they'd know something was different about these killings. They'd never figure out why every victim suffered a different death, but was found in the same condition, as that wasn't standard serial killer M.O. Their textbook investigations will fail, and then the media will scream for justice.

Every superhero had a name, and so did the superhero's archenemy. The press could make up any name they wanted. But they'd probably come up with something ridiculous like Count. Maybe leaking *creatus* to the press would be the way to go. Creatus would know with certainty after this attack, and they'd be angry. The seal meant unity, but also anonymity, and now humans would once again question the existence of beings who were smarter and stronger, and they'd be afraid, as they should be.

After tonight, *Rogue* would work well within the family, as it was the one crime the family wouldn't tolerate. The name was starting to sound tolerable. *A mischievously playful person, one who lives apart from the rest of the group — naughty.* The depiction was sounding better all the time. *Uncontrolled*, though ... never!

The human woman walked down to the river a while ago and had been just looking out as if in a daze. Her hair was fair, as was her skin. Weak, pathetic, hardly even worth the effort, but it was fun when they knew a predator was stalking them. Like watching a rabbit attempt to evade a cougar, only a rabbit had more skills than a human did.

Just when the prey thought they might escape was the time for the real attack. The lightning strike they didn't see coming, when their breath whooshed out of their body at the suddenness. How they tried to comprehend that their feet were on the ground and now they were on the rooftop, the predator staring down at them.

That was the best part.

Even better, the attack would enrage Derrick.

Chapter Twenty-One

Kris stares at the calm water of the harbor. It is so peaceful that she wonders how she can feel fear. But she does, wondering why Derrick left her, and whom he went to see.

She remembers the detective's eyes, cold and dark, lifeless, staring up at her. Death is always near, taunting her. The rogue is coming, she knows. His breaths are louder as he approaches. To finish what the thief attempted when she was eight. She screams Derrick's name, but he doesn't answer. *Why?* she wonders. He said he'd protect her, but now she's running for her life. Not knowing who or *what* is chasing her, wondering if she can trust anyone, she tries to find her assailant. She hears a *crack* and whips her head around, seeing nothing.

Arms latch around her, restraining her. She screams as her feet leave the grassy knoll below, knowing he has her, but she can't see him.

"It's okay. I have you. It's Derrick." His words broke through her nightmare.

"The rogue ..." Her voice sounded ragged even to her. "He ... he ... had me. He pulled me off the ground ... He —"

"I won't let anyone touch you, Kristina," he promised, pulling her closer. He ran his fingers over her forehead attempting to soothe her.

Kris let out another breath and rested her head on Derrick's chest. It felt so good, but the dream had been so real. She'd felt the attack, saw the solid earth disappear from beneath her as her body had been ripped from the ground.

Derrick's phone buzzed on the nightstand. He turned to it and looked at the number. "It's Michael. If he's calling at two a.m., there has to be a reason. Maybe he caught the rogue."

Kris nodded at the hopeful look in his eyes. She'd never been so scared. Even after her mother's attack and the nightly bad dreams, a part of her assumed it wouldn't happen twice. But this *thing* had marked her for death. As a payback for something Derrick had done as overseer, he'd explained when they came home after the police station. He'd wanted to move away, but she had refused. They couldn't leave permanently. If the rogue wanted her, he'd track them down, she was certain. And who knows how many innocent people he'd kill while they hid somewhere. How could Derrick expect her to sit around while innocent people were slaughtered? No, she'd told him. She agreed with Michael; she would become bait.

Derrick answered the phone and then sat up quickly. "Where?" He listened for a second and then hung up. Derrick turned to her, his eyes grave.

Kris shook her head, knowing it was something awful. News that would hurt her again based on his expression. She opened her mouth to speak, but no words came out.

He picked up her hands and held them. "Beth is in the hospital."

She gasped, throwing her hand over her mouth. Tears seeped down her cheeks, as if someone had turned on a spigot. "The rogue?" Kris pushed out the words, praying they weren't true. But if Beth had been hurt any other way, they wouldn't be receiving the news from Derrick's brother. If Beth had been in a car accident, Kris would have heard from Beth's mom — eventually. Beth's mother had never liked Kris, so she wouldn't be first on the list, she knew.

Derrick nodded, pulling her into his embrace. "Michael thinks so. The police aren't releasing any information, but his source gave him enough to go on."

"But ... she's alive?" she mumbled against his chest.

"Yes, but she's in ICU. I doubt they'll let you see her. But as a doctor, I can get to her. Her parents won't know I'm not just another doctor checking on her. The nursing staff won't question me; I've visited patients there." Derrick peered down at her. "Do you want to come with me? Or, I could get my parents to come and stay with you."

Kris' eyes darted up at him in response. "Of course! Even if they won't let me see Beth, I want to be there."

He pulled her off the bed and to her feet. "I'm sorry —"

"Stop it!" she shrieked. "This has nothing to do with us." She shook her head as she darted into his walk-in closet to grab clothes. "This is ... *that rogue*, as you call *that thing. That animal.*" Kris pulled her hands to her head and released more sobs. "Beth's so little. So sweet." Derrick wrapped his arms around her without a word, comforting her with just his touch. She leaned against him. "How could anyone hurt Beth?"

"I don't know," he said, turning her in his arms. "But we'll find out. This stops now. I swear to you —" He sucked in a breath. "I won't let this continue. And whoever's responsible ... will pay."

When Kris rushed through the doors of the emergency room, only a few people sat in the black vinyl chairs in the waiting area. As predicted, they wouldn't let her see Beth, since she wasn't family. Derrick had dropped her off at the ER entrance so she could walk in by herself, and he'd taken the rear entrance, keeping in touch with her via text messages.

Now, she sat anxiously, awaiting any word. The room was surprisingly quiet other than a few moans and groans here and there, reminders to the nurses and receptionists that the people were in pain, she imagined, since no one seemed to be in a hurry to attend to the new arrivals.

A few minutes after she sat down, the locked double doors to the ER opened, and Derrick, wearing a white jacket over his khakis and oxford, leaned his head through the doorway. "Ms. Heskin?" he called without making eye contact with her.

Truly surprised, since he hadn't texted her he was coming to get her, Kris jumped up. Maybe that's why he hadn't warned her. "That's me!" She tossed a glimpse at the receptionist's desk, but they didn't seem to question the fact that a doctor was calling her to the secured area. Kris ran across the gleaming-white floor of the emergency room toward Derrick while he held the door.

"Right this way, Ms. Heskin." He placed his hand on the small of her back and escorted her along the corridor, stopping before he turned to walk them into a room. He lowered his head to speak, without looking as if he knew her. "She's going to be okay, I swear. But she looks really bad. Are you sure you want to see her?"

Kris gulped, restraining her tears. "Yes. Please."

"Okay ... but try not to upset her. If she wakes up and sees you crying, it will only make it worse for her."

She bobbed her head. That made sense. She didn't know how she could restrain the tears, but she would. For Beth, she'd be strong.

Kris walked inside the room quietly, doing her best to hold her audible sobs as she took in her surroundings. Where were Beth's parents? Jason? Why weren't they here holding her hand? Speaking to her, telling her she'd be all right? Kris stepped to the hospital bed, looking up at the monitors to the left of Beth and the IV fluids to her right. *Was that a normal beep?* she wondered. *Was Beth in danger of dying?* Derrick slid up beside Kris as she placed her hand over Beth's, and she remembered that as a doctor he would know if anything wasn't normal. But would he tell her? He'd sworn that she'd be okay, so Kris had to have faith that he wouldn't say it if it weren't true. He just wouldn't have said anything.

She restrained the audible cries that threatened to burst from her throat, but she couldn't impede the stream of tears sliding down her cheek. Beth had looked so lovely in her dress today. Her strawberry-blond curls had bounced beautifully around her shoulders, and Kris had told her she should allow plenty of tendrils on her wedding day. Beth had looked like a princess and had even tried on some tiaras, but in the end decided to go with a stunning white lace headdress with rhinestones that didn't look as if she was pretending to be royalty.

Now Beth's light peach-colored skin was red with splotches of yellow and blue forming around her eyes and cheeks. Kris choked back the tears, imagining what that beast had done to her.

"It was a message, Kristina," Derrick whispered in her ear. "She looks worse than she is. He could have killed her, but he just smacked her around a bit. He wanted her to live."

Kris turned to him. "How do you know it was the rogue? Maybe it was a mugger."

Derrick shook his head. "The 911 call came from her cell phone. There were no words, just the open line. The police triangulated the position from the signal. She was on a rooftop. But worse ... He used our kind's insignia. Before phones, when creatus needed to meet, they'd use a courier to deliver a note card with a red wax seal on the front. Nothing else, but it told family members that there was an emergency. The meeting had always been held in the same place at the same time, so creatus knew to show up that night. Obviously, we don't need to resort to those methods nowadays, but it's something we've kept from our heritage, reminding us how we used to have to hide, and that our anonymity was our greatest strength." Derrick dropped his head and sighed. "Since he wasn't eliciting a response from the media, I guess he decided to leave a calling card. Sick S.O.B. This isn't about food or a thrill; he's trying to let humans know we exist."

Chapter Twenty-Two

Reece Buckley leaned forward, resting his chin on his fist as he examined the video feed from the hospital. Catching a glimpse of his own image on the monitor, he flinched; he still hadn't adapted to the short spiky cut. But, *high and tight*, they'd said, just like when he was a SEAL.

He'd been UC for so long in Miami, he'd gotten used to wearing it long. But that's why the government wanted him, he imagined. He cleaned up well. He could go undercover as a druggie or infiltrate the Russian mafia if need be. With his nonspecific features and olive skin tone, he'd been able to pass for almost any nationality, and it didn't hurt that as an army brat he was able to speak several languages. The government agency had solicited him; he'd been content traveling back and forth from Miami to South America. DEA had sent him south numerous times to bust a newbie drug cartel before they got out of control like their counterparts.

This was Reece's first classified investigation, which he was certain they'd sent him on because he was a rookie in their eyes. A simple Google search by a homicide detective had attracted his office's attention, but now Murphy O'Brian was dead.

The scene on the flash drive was interesting enough to keep Reece investigating, but certainly not worthy of the detective's execution. The detective hadn't done anything but mouth off to a few other detectives that some agent had walked in and taken his evidence.

As always, Reece's orders were to do his job, so he didn't question his superiors' motives. From now on, though, Reece decided he'd keep all the information he gathered to himself before forwarding it to his boss. He wanted more time to interview potential witnesses before they needed silencing.

When Reece had been parked outside Kristina Heskin's apartment earlier, waiting for her to come home, her boyfriend had looked in his direction. The film on the government-issue vehicle's windshield was similar to the advertisements on busses, except that the outside image was clear instead of having a print on it. Reece loved the anonymity it gave him. But for some reason, he would swear that the man had looked him dead in the eyes. The same man who'd jumped off a hundred and thirty-five foot bridge and pulled up the girl who'd jumped.

Reece examined the image on his phone. Just a red wax seal with a *C* stamped into the middle, but it meant something. Why use a relic as a calling card? When his boss indicated that the stories might be connected, Reece didn't see it, but then the same man he'd been tracking had shown up.

"Who are you Derrick Ashton? Or *rather*, what are you?"

Chapter Twenty-Three

S o why can't I be a part of the meeting?" Kristina asked again from the passenger seat.

Derrick moved his gaze from the highway to her and smiled at her pout, her arms crossed over her chest, her lip jutting out a fraction. He resisted smiling, knowing it would only irritate her more than she already was. "It's not that I mind, but there's a very good reason other than the family just feeling uncomfortable, which I tried to explain to you earlier."

Kristina cocked her head and shrugged her shoulders as if to tell him she didn't care what the family thought.

Derrick decided to continue with the rational reason why. "If authorities discover us, we can escape; you cannot. We — okay, I'd rather you not ever be put in a position where you would have to lie more than you already have to."

She released a sigh as if she understood but still didn't buy it. "So, I just sit around and wait while you discuss using me as bait?"

He squeezed his fingers around the steering wheel. He should never have told her that Michael wanted to draw out the rogue by leaving her unattended. "We are not using you as bait, Kristina," he said. "Besides," he continued, not giving her an opportunity to argue, "my mother has never been involved. She understands that she isn't a superhero."

A burst of laughter shot out of Kristina's mouth. "A superhero? Is that what you are, Derrick?"

At that remark, he found himself pouting slightly. There wasn't a UFC fighter, boxer, or creatus that could take him out with their bare hands, but somehow, this tiny woman could bring him to his knees. "Some would say so," he offered. "I don't go around trying to act like one, and I may not be able to fly, but I can leap tall buildings with a single bound."

Kristina leaned over the center console, draping her arm around his waist and resting her head on his shoulder. "You're my superhero, Derrick. Always have been."

Pacified, he kissed the top of her head, breathing in the raspberry scent which he'd discovered was the shampoo she used. She could also uplift him faster than anyone else could.

After pulling into his parents' driveway, he drove around to the rear of the house this time. He threw the gear in park and jumped out, anxious to get the day over with and get home.

Kristina hopped down when he opened the door and marched off toward the house without a glance backward. She was such a firecracker. Spunk. As he'd always known, the girl had spunk.

He heard his mother greet Kristina when she walked into the kitchen, and then the kiss she'd certainly placed on her cheek. *"Don't forget they can hear us, sweetheart,"* his mother said, *"but if you want to go for a walk, we can go down to the lake, out of earshot. I'd love some girl time."*

"I'd love that too," Kristina said. *"And I love you, Derrick, but I'm going to go find out all I can about you."*

Derrick shook his head and walked off toward the barn, smiling, listening as his two favorite women walked out the front door chattering to each other. He was thrilled they were getting along so well, even if they planned to talk about him.

He stopped in his tracks. No. They couldn't go off on their own, he realized. He took off in a sprint and leapt the house, landing in front of them.

His mother threw her hand over her heart. "Oh, my word, Derrick. You scared the — I'm not used to you showing off, and you know better than that," she lectured.

"I'm sorry. I really am. And I swear you can talk about me all you want. I promise I won't listen, but you can't walk to the lake by yourselves."

"Why on earth not?" Sabrina retorted, folding her arms over her chest in defiance. His mother wasn't the type of woman you told what to do, he knew.

"The rogue was here, Mom. At the lake when Kristina and I went for a paddle. He'd like nothing better than to take the two most important people in my life away from me, I'm sure."

"Oh ..." his mother said, and Derrick exhaled in relief, thankful that she didn't plan to argue with him. Sabrina focused on Kristina and nodded. "He's got a point, sweetheart. We'll walk down together later, the four of us."

"Okay, Derrick," Kristina conceded. "But I'm taking a sign language course, and then I'm going to teach your mother."

Derrick leaned in and kissed his mother on the cheek and Kristina on the lips. "Works for me." He took off in a hurry, listening as his mother locked up the house. He'd make a conscious effort to tune them out, except of course if they were in danger. But he doubted the rogue would come anywhere near the house. Unless he or she was already in the barn waiting.

Michael intercepted Derrick at the door. "Good call on Mom. I'd hate to think she was in danger just because she was next to Kristina."

Derrick crossed his arms, tucking his fists beneath his arms, resisting the urge to punch his brother. Michael was really getting on his last nerve. "So, you couldn't care less what happens to my future wife as long as Mom is okay?"

Michael rolled his eyes. "You know that's not what I said. Man, you're in an awful mood these days. Still haven't had sex, I take it."

Rolls of laughter emanated from inside the barn.

Unable to resist, Derrick smacked Michael upside the head. At least he hadn't punched him. "I don't think you said that loud enough for the Midwest family to hear you. Want to borrow my phone so you can call them?" Derrick stopped talking as he heard a familiar voice. "Jonas is here?" He slammed past his brother, understanding why he'd met him at the door.

Michael hurried up alongside of him. "Chill, Derrick. He's cool. It's not as if we banished him. Jonas left because he wanted to leave."

Then why is he back? Derrick seethed. *And how long had he been back?* he wondered. He knew he was his brother's best friend all through high school and college, but Derrick had never cared for him. Unlike his brother, Ryan. Derrick had always liked Ryan. Ryan was about seven years younger than Derrick, but they'd gotten along well over the years. Probably because Ry wasn't a hothead like Jonas. They'd wrestled when they were younger, but it'd been good-natured, a chance to blow off steam.

Jonas lifted his head in acknowledgement, a cocky smile lifting one side of his mouth. "Hey, Derrick," he called. "I heard you need help."

"We don't need your help, Jonas." His words had come out almost in a snarl and also a reminder why they'd asked him to leave in the first place. His gaze bolted to Vic sitting next to Jonas. "You called him, Victoria?" She'd been fond of Jonas for years, ever since he and his family moved here. Derrick had always thought she'd fall for Jonas if she'd take her focus off him. Looks as though she decided that's what she needed to move on. Derrick just wished it'd been anyone but him. Jonas was a loose cannon. Yeah, he'd protected humans, but he'd also left witnesses, and that was something his family couldn't allow. Humans wouldn't care that most creatus protected them; they'd only see them as a threat. Michael and he agreed on that one issue anyway.

Ryan stood. "I called him, Derrick. We needed help, and my brother is one of the best."

Derrick narrowed his eyes at Ry. It was bad enough that he had Michael and Vic questioning his every move, but now Ryan was giving him a hard time. So much for liking the kid. Not wanting to lose his temper, Derrick walked toward his desk without responding. His father and Dean followed behind him.

Lynford raised his hands to get everyone's attention, and the entire room fell to a hush. "In all the years we've lived here, we've never had a problem," his father started, "because we've always elected an overseer, and we've adhered to our rules. Nothing has changed. As head of the council, Dean, Matthew, and I will continue to stand behind Derrick and his decisions. Anyone who does not want to abide by the same rules can leave. Is that clear?" His father sat down on a chair, waving for Derrick to continue.

Internally, Derrick wasn't certain how he felt about his father stepping in, but he was still head of the council, even if Derrick was overseer.

Deciding to get right to business, Derrick made eye contact with Jonas. "The rules haven't changed, Jonas. We are not going out on the street as vigilantes looking for a fight; we are seeking a serial killer. The rogue has an agenda, and it's personal. What started out looking like a rogue creatus now looks as though he has a plan. And I use *he* only because it's easier. This creatus could be male or female. I've seen his shadow and heard his voice, but he's kept his distance. It's clear that he knows me personally." A murmur swept through the barn, and Derrick was grateful to see that some of his family actually cared. "The last murder was a police detective inside Kristina's house. My guess is that he wanted to make me appear guilty. But as you know, this endangers all of us. If they start questioning me, no telling how close they'll get to the family. And the last thing we want is to relocate."

Collective whispers and nods traveled around the room in agreement.

Now that he had everyone's attention, he continued, "He also attacked, but didn't kill, Kristina's best friend, Beth. This time, though, he used our creatus seal. He pressed the red wax seal on her forehead, which as you know will have humans searching for any similar uses of the seal throughout history and leaves no doubt in our mind that this is a creatus attack. And as far as attacking Kristina's friend, my only guess is that he's taunting me. Which makes me believe it's someone we banished in the last ten to twenty years or ..." he paused a moment, knowing he was going to catch flack, "someone here who disagrees with my decisions."

This time a few harrumphs shadowed the mutters of surprise. Derrick wasn't surprised to see that the disagreements of his assertion stemmed from Victoria, Jonas, Ryan, and sadly, even Michael.

Chapter Twenty-Four

Kris sat across from Sabrina, sipping a cup of hot tea. According to her future mother-in-law, she grew all the herbs in her garden. The creatus' diet was so restrictive of any proteins, oils, and grains heated to high temperatures, causing high levels of toxins, that they couldn't take a chance on any processed foods.

"So you grow everything you eat?" Kris asked.

"Practically," Sabrina answered. "I do buy fresh fruit and vegetables from vendors, but mostly we just stay away from anything processed or pasteurized."

Kris shook her head. "It sounds like a lot of work."

"It's not so hard. We all work together. Every family specializes in something different, so the bartering system works well. And look at me; do I look seventy-three?" Sabrina said proudly, lifting her head.

Kris blinked in shock, her grin spreading wide across her face. "Actually, no. Not at all. You're seventy-three?"

A beautiful pink spread across Sabrina's cheeks, making her appear even younger. "Yep. Lyn and I married when I was twenty-two, and we had Derrick almost two years later."

Kris leaned in, excited that Derrick and she would be the same age as her in-laws had been when they married. Though she hadn't married yet, she was ready. "How did you meet?" Kris asked excitedly, wiggling on her chair in her eagerness to hear the entire story of their romance. Her future mother-in-law's mouth turned down, and a wash of sadness spread over her round and kind-looking face, and Kris was instantly distressed that she'd asked, since obviously it wasn't a story Sabrina wanted to share. "I'm sorry," Kris instantly excused her careless question. She should have asked Derrick first, knowing that it might have been a tragic meeting, as Derrick and hers had been. "I shouldn't have pried."

Sabrina waved her off. "It's okay." She took a sip of her tea before continuing, as though trying to collect her strength. "It's actually similar to how you and Derrick met, only I wasn't a child. My father was involved with the Irish Mob. He'd turned evidence on one of the gang leaders. In retaliation, they killed him and then came after my mother, brother, and me. Regrettably, I was the only one to survive."

Kris pulled her fist to her mouth. "I'm sorry. I didn't know."

Sabrina patted her hand that still rested on the table. "It's okay, sweetheart. How could you have known? I know Derrick wouldn't have said anything." She took another sip of her tea and continued, "Anyway, after killing my mother and brother, they decided I was too pretty to kill immediately. I'd been holding a knife I had hidden under my mattress when they found me. I swung the knife at them, slashing both of them at once, but it wasn't enough to stop them. It gave me enough time to get away from them for a few minutes, but then they caught up with me in the alley behind my house." Sabrina closed her eyes for a second then opened them. "No one did anything while the men beat me on the street. And then, something changed, I couldn't feel the gravel beneath me anymore. My eyes were too swollen to see, but I'll never forget his voice as he whispered that everything would be all right."

Kris' eyes filled as she listened, thinking about her mother — and herself. "You would have died and no one would have stopped them?" she asked, unable to believe people would stand by and watch.

"Yes. The neighbors were afraid of the mafia, and it was dark. People didn't know I was the person the thugs were beating up; they just knew that someone was paying for betrayal. My assailants repeated those words over and over. Perhaps so that no one would interfere." Sabrina clasped Kris' hand in hers. "Of course, unlike you, I was an adult, but things were different then. It wasn't easy to find a job that paid the bills on your own. Without a family to support me, I would have ended up on the street. Luckily, Lynford took me home, which of course was against the rules, but he didn't know what else to do with me. If he'd taken me to the hospital, more than likely the mob would have killed me." Sabrina stared off dreamily around the kitchen as she continued, "His parents were furious when he'd announced that he'd fallen for me. They didn't believe it was possible for a human to *fall* for a creatus, but I did. As far as they'd known, it'd never happened before."

Kris smiled. "Like us." And then a thought occurred to her. "That's why you wanted to adopt me? Because I was all alone, as you would have been?"

"Yes." Sabrina smiled sweetly. "Oddly enough, Lyn was okay with it. It was Derrick who wouldn't allow us to adopt you."

"Why in the he — ?" Kris spouted, perturbed at once, but then pulled her expletive before she offended Sabrina.

She could have been living with this great family her entire life instead of a new foster home every six months. With people who loved her and didn't think she was an imposition in their lives.

Sabrina's lips turned up again. "I don't think Derrick wanted to ever think of you as a sister. He was crazy about your mother, but he knew he was too young, so he never let it go beyond friendship. Although, we were hard on him about their relationship too, especially Michael. We constantly warned him that he was getting too close, and that it could only end badly." She sighed. "He tried to date other women over the years, but I think your souls were already connected; it was just a matter of you growing up. And now, you are perfect for each other."

Kris did the mental math in her head, since Derrick had never mentioned how old he was. He was about forty-nine, and he'd live another hundred years. If she were lucky, Kris had another seventy years at most. So, he'd be alone for thirty years or more. More years than she'd already lived. That didn't seem fair.

Sensing her distress, Sabrina touched her cheek. "He loves you, Kristina. Neither you nor anyone else will ever change his mind, so stop thinking whatever you're thinking."

Kris' eyes popped open, wondering how she'd known.

"I've been there. At a hundred years old, Lyn hardly looks a day over fifty, and I worry sometimes, but he still gazes at me as if I am the only woman on the planet."

"You *are* the only girl on the planet, my bride." The deep voice belonging to Derrick's father broke through their conversation, and Kris observed a beautiful blush spread across Sabrina's cheeks again. Her soon-to-be father-in-law swooped in and pressed a kiss to his wife's neck, causing her to giggle.

Derrick's warm arms folded around Kris, instantly comforting her. The thought that they too would always be so happy was worth everything. "You ready to go home?" Derrick whispered in her ear. And though Derrick's father didn't as much as raise an eyebrow, Kris felt her cheeks heat up, knowing he could hear everything.

"Almost," she responded. "I have one thing left to discuss with your mother." The three of them stared at her as if confused, so she continued, "Derrick mentioned you wanted to plan a wedding ceremony with all the frills." She raised her hand to her chest, battling the tears that threatened at the notion they wanted to take care of her as if they were her parents. "Thank you from the bottom of my heart, but I don't want a big wedding, Mr. and Mrs. Ashton. In fact, it may sound strange, but I don't want a wedding at all, especially with all that's going on." Derrick's eyes widened and he started to protest, so she raised her hand, silencing him. "Let me rephrase that. I want to get married, but I don't want a wedding. I don't have any family — other than all of you — so I think it would make me sad."

"Oh, honey." Sabrina stepped forward and wrapped her arms around her. "Don't think we would ever push you into doing anything you don't want. I just want you to be happy."

Kris accepted the hug, reveling in the feeling of Sabrina's arms around her. She hadn't felt parental affection since she was a child. She'd forgotten how good it felt when her mother tucked her in at night, read bedtime stories, pressed her lips to her forehead to check if she had a temperature. All the tiny gestures that she'd taken for granted prior to her mother's murder.

She leaned back and smiled at her new family. "I know, and I am. I just didn't want you to feel disappointed if I talked Derrick into eloping."

They all laughed and Kris relaxed. Already, she felt at home with the Ashtons. Of course, she wondered if Victoria was still within hearing range, listening to their conversation, waiting for an opportunity to kill her. The woman petrified her as no man ever had. Something told Kris that she wouldn't feel safe until Vic fell in love with another man.

Chapter Twenty-Five

Today?" Derrick asked as he situated himself behind the wheel, elated at the thought of marrying Kristina.

She stared at him as if she hadn't a clue what he was talking about. "Today, what?"

"Do you want to get married right now?"

She jumped onto her knees in the passenger seat. "Can we?"

Derrick couldn't help but laugh. "If we hurry, yes! It's still early. Massachusetts has a waiting period, but New Hampshire is only forty-five minutes away and they don't." He ran his hand up her cheek. "And I know a beautiful place we can stay afterward." His heart thumped loudly in his chest, so loud he could hear it, and at the moment — well, always — he was thankful Kristina was human and couldn't hear his heart race. It was amazing how something as simple as that gave away one's feelings.

As creatus, they'd learned to control their heart rate and pulse when near a possible threat. Around Kristina, however, Derrick never had to worry about anything. He'd never felt so alive as he did since he'd been with her. And marrying her would just make them more complete.

Though most creatus didn't care about the act of marrying, he knew his mother — and even Kristina, although she didn't want to admit it — wanted to go through all the traditions. And he did too, really. Something about taking official vows made it feel all the more tangible.

Kristina glanced at her clothes. "Like this?"

"I think you look beautiful," he replied. "I happen to love simple attire of jeans and T-shirts, but we can do a little shopping afterward. The place I want to take you has an amazing restaurant that overlooks a mountain. We'd have to backtrack to go home, so let's just go. It'll be romantic, exactly what I've been waiting for. Plus ... since no one knows where we are going, for at least a few nights anyway, we can feel completely at ease."

"I feel at ease now, Derrick. After all, you are the superest superhero of them all, right?"

He laughed as he pulled out of the driveway. "Have you ever been to White Mountain National Forest?"

Kristina sighed. "Derrick ... "

He stopped in the street and looked to her side of the car because of the way she sighed and said his name. "Yes?"

Tears flooded her eyes. "Do you have to ask? You've known me since I was eight. I've never been anywhere."

He rested his hand behind her neck at her distressed look and his careless words he'd uttered out of habit. It's just what people said, but perhaps he needed to be more thoughtful. No, she'd never been anywhere. He knew that. "I'm sorry. That was insensitive, but I'll think before I speak in the future. And, get ready, my love. We're going to have fun this week." He stopped for a second. "Do you mind driving? I can make all the arrangements over the phone on the way."

Kristina swiped away a tear as she nodded. Derrick jumped out of the vehicle and she crawled over the center console. He typed the address for Manchester, New Hampshire into the GPS as their first stop and then went to work on his iPhone.

"Derrick ..." Kristina pulled him from his thoughts a few miles down the road. "Do you think Beth will be okay? I mean, he won't go after her again, will he?"

"No." He shook his head. "He won't. The rogue just wanted to make sure I knew he was targeting me; he's made his point and he knows I know it. Plus, Michael promised to keep an eye out." He paused before continuing, not wanting to tell her the truth, even though she already recognized what was going on. "He wants me, Kristina ... which means he wants you too. He'll go after you first, though, I think. To hurt me."

She nodded, but didn't comment on his blunt statement. She was tough. Of course, he'd always known that about her. "So, is that why you want to go away?"

"Hey, it was your idea to elope," he reminded her. "I just thought it sounded like a perfect plan. We get away for a few days, get married, and give Michael a chance to catch a killer."

She released a nervous chuckle. "When you say it that way, it doesn't sound quite as romantic."

He leaned over to her side of the cab. "Keep your eyes on the road, beautiful." He brushed his lips down her neck and shoulder and peered up at her, making sure she kept her attention on the road. He trailed his hand along her arm. "I promise to make it the most romantic weekend you've ever experienced," he whispered in her ear.

She squirmed as a shiver must have swept through her. The idea that he could make her wriggle with just whispered words sent a thrill through his own body. "That won't be too difficult, Derrick," she said through a chuckle.

He collapsed in his seat, sighing. "You went out on plenty of dates over the years, Kristina. I know ... I had to clench my teeth as I waited for you to get home safely."

She crinkled her nose and then chewed on her bottom lip. "Hmm ... not sure how I feel about the fact that you know every guy I've ever dated."

"Not every one of them. I tried to ignore them for the most part. I only followed you to the frat party because I knew it wasn't a good idea."

She peeked at him out of the corner of her eye. "Did I thank you for that, by the way? He would have raped me."

Unable to comment through his gritted teeth, he nodded his acceptance of her gratitude. The only thing that had mollified him was the fact that when he sought the degenerate out a few days later, he was happy to learn he'd broken both his legs and his arm when he'd thrown him against the brick wall after pulling him off Kristina. He'd also been expelled for contributing to the delinquency of a minor after Derrick handed the Dean of Students papers on Kristina's condition, courtesy of his medical office. "He got his reward," he said flatly.

Kristina's mouth turned up slightly at the edges, which caused a smile to spread across his face as well. "So I heard."

She should have known her Dark Angel wouldn't have let him get away with hurting her.

Seemingly content, Kristina played with the radio controls on the steering wheel, finding a soft rock station that he'd preprogrammed. Within seconds, she sang along to an eighties Phil Collins song, surprising him. He wanted to comment on the fact that he thought she only listened to new age music, but held his tongue. She had a beautiful voice. How had he never known that? He'd known her for fourteen years and didn't know she could sing like an angel.

Derrick turned his attention to his iPhone while Kristina's voice filled the vehicle, surrounding him in an almost palpable warmth that flowed through his body. He was definitely looking forward to the next few days.

Yes, he almost shouted. He couldn't believe his luck. They had a room. The luxury tower suite. It was eight hundred fifty dollars a night, but it was the only package that included a king-sized bed. But it also came with a spa treatment per adult per day. Kristina would enjoy that. He made the reservation and then researched all the activities he'd surprise her with later.

And then, he had the best idea. He found the contact information and typed out a quick email.

Kristina pulled up outside the Manchester City Hall, and Derrick looked up at the gray and beige building and then smiled when he saw the business next door. "Let's run into Pearson's first," he suggested.

She peered in the direction he was looking, at the jewelry shop next door. "Oh, perfect. I was wondering about that."

As they walked up to the red awning, he turned to her. "Are you sure, Kristina? It's not too late to change your mind."

She patted his chest and huffed out a breath. "Um ..." she trailed off, shaking her head. "Do you not know how I feel? You described it perfectly before our incredible kiss in the park. How can you think for a second that it's not too late?" She removed her hands from his chest and rested them on her hips. "It's way past too late, Derrick. We've been linked as long as I can remember. This is just the next step."

Chapter Twenty-Six

A few days of peace, Derrick? Not on your life, the rogue mocked silently as the running lights of the Navigator faded in the distance.

Like hunting prey, it would be fun to attack when the newlyweds thought they were safe. The lovely couple could have their honeymoon, but then it was time for retribution.

The new groom thought he was special, but Derrick wasn't the only one with a human for a parent. Why they were stronger didn't make any sense, but then again, neither did the hatred. Humans were the only beings more repulsive than Derrick. And as a human and Derrick's wife, Kristina topped the list. Orchestrating and watching her die would be enjoyable. And after her death, Derrick would be putty. He'd no longer be able to function as overseer.

And then, the army would amass, ready to fight. No doubt when creatus realized someone was willing to take on humans, they'd want to join. Why would they want to continue to live in the shadows as they'd done for four thousand years? It was time creatus took over this planet and lived as they wanted, ate as they desired, killed anyone who stood in the way.

They were more powerful for a reason, and as one of the most powerful of their kind, it only made sense to lead.

Chapter Twenty-Seven

As Derrick hung a left onto Fairway Drive, Kris saw the red rooftop and white stucco of the resort, which backed up against a snowcapped mountain range. He still hadn't given her the name and refused to let her peek at his phone even when she said she was just going to search his music list.

When he rounded Mount Washington Hotel Road, she gasped, throwing her hand over her mouth at the same time tears poured from her eyes. It was like no place she'd ever seen in her life; even her dreams of her fairy-tale honeymoon had never looked so incredible.

The sun had started to set, but the rays reflecting off the snowy landscape made it seem brighter around the hotel, casting the magnificent structure in a globe of light. The sky was a royal blue, and the horizon looked as if the sun had just melted into layers of yellow and pink streaks across the mountain peaks.

The Omni Mount Washington Resort was breathtaking. It resembled a chalet she could only envision seeing in Sweden or Colorado. She had no idea places such as these existed within a couple hours of Boston.

It was a good thing they'd stopped at the Mall of New Hampshire in Manchester, because she didn't think she'd ever want to leave. Derrick had practically purchased her an entire wardrobe along with all her toiletries and luggage, since she'd admitted — after much prodding — that other than a couple gym bags, she didn't have any suitcases. And yet, he had only purchased a few things for himself.

She was thankful, as she peered out of the vehicle, for the long wool coat they'd chosen together. Every square inch of the property that didn't have evergreen trees had a blanket of white.

After parking, they strolled through the entrance, careful to take their time to absorb all the beauty that surrounded them. Massive rows of white pillars atop wood floors covered by area rugs greeted them as they entered the lobby.

Chandeliers, ornate crown moldings, and intricate woodwork adorned the great hall. As her eyes traveled up to the twenty-some-foot ceilings, she relished the lavishly, but tastefully embellished hotel, from the white wainscoting to the cherry wood banisters and gold draperies that contrasted brilliantly with the pale-yellow and cream-colored walls.

Soft light filled the immense room from the lamps on tables scattered every few feet next to cozy wingback chairs waiting for readers to curl up with a classic novels.

Before they headed to their suite, they meandered through several more rooms. Each destination had its own flair, whether it was small and cozy with a stone fireplace or grand and open, as the great hall. He trailed her through a small pub typical of New England with its deep-stained wood and plush chairs and then into a nightclub that the hotel had dubbed *The Cave* due to its granite and stone-clad walls. Kris imagined they could stay a month and not see every nook.

They lingered along a high porch overlooking Mount Washington, stopping to take in the last of the day's light as it liquefied behind the mountain range. Kris rested against the railing and peered out at the majesty and splendor sprawled before her.

Derrick moved up behind her, wrapping his arms around her waist as he dipped his head to her ear. "What do you think?"

She leaned against him and he tightened his grip, molding her to his body. "I think it's incredible; you're incredible." She inhaled a mouthful of the brisk mountain air and then released it in a soft sigh of delight. "Thank you."

"My pleasure, my bride." He pressed his lips to the bottom of her neck, working tiny kisses up toward her ear. "Ready to find our room, Mrs. Ashton?"

Kris turned in his arms. "Oh, yes."

He raised her hand with the new wedding band to his lips and then led her to the elevator.

"What? No soaring up the stairs?" she teased.

Her new husband lifted her up against the wall of the elevator and nuzzled her neck, "I think I'll save my strength for later," he murmured into her ear, sending a buzz through her body, lighting her on fire from head to toe.

When the elevator reached their floor, Derrick released her, but only until they reached their room. He swung open the door then lifted her up in his arms, carrying her over the threshold of their honeymoon suite.

A large, but comfortable room similar-looking to a bed-and-breakfast with its high back cushioned chairs, country patterned drapes, and bedspreads greeted them. Two walls of the suite had windows overlooking the snow-capped mountains, and bright orange and red flames licked gently at an iron screen in front of a fireplace.

Her groom carried her to the king size bed but didn't set her down. Instead, he held her in his arms as he sat on the bed. "Kristina, I want you so much right now, but I'm afraid we'll never make it out of the room if you even allow me to kiss you."

She laced her hands around his neck. "I guess we'll have to take our chances then, because I've been aching for you to kiss me since we said, *I do*. That wasn't nearly a long enough kiss."

"Well, I couldn't very well attack you in front of the Justice of the Peace, could I?" Derrick laughed.

"No one is here now," she suggested.

Derrick wasted no time in lifting her to the center of the bedspread and sliding down beside her. "I do love this dress; it'd be a shame to wrinkle it." He moved his hand around her back, and his fingers went to work unzipping the dress, but he paused. "Do you mind?"

"Of course not!" she burst out. "At this point, I wouldn't mind if you ripped it off me."

He smiled. "I couldn't do that. It's too beautiful, and then you'd think I'm an animal."

Actually, she was thinking he was too gentle. Her body longed to feel some of his power. Every nerve ending seemed heightened with arousal. Their foreplay had gone on too long, and she was ready.

Kris moved her hands to his standard oxford, unbuttoning it as he continued to unzip her dress. She traced his tanned olive skin with its thin cropping of soft black hair over his chest; it felt incredible, the way a man was supposed to feel. His chest was firm and sculpted, and her heart raced as she ran her hands over his shoulders to remove his shirt.

He helped her at the end, and then she witnessed the restrained desire crumble in his dark eyes. There was no turning back at this point. His gaze spoke volumes without opening his mouth.

A longing filled his eyes, and she knew hers probably mirrored his. She'd dreamt about this moment so many times, even though she never imagined it in a honeymoon suite of a chalet with a fire crackling in the background. Somehow, Derrick had managed to fill even her unknown fantasies. She would never have thought to ask for this, never have believed it was even possible.

He ran his fingers over her collarbone, trailing a line up her neck and under her chin, lifting her head and kissing her softly. He moved toward her neck, his mouth working its way to her earlobe, stopping and nibbling there. "This is so different, Kristina. I've never experienced this."

"Me neither," she said on an exhale. "It's always just been cold." She moved her hands up to his wide shoulders, pulling him down on top of her. "We have all weekend. Please don't make me wait too long."

He chuckled against her neck, his warm breath tickling her. "Why are you in such a hurry? Are you hungry?"

"I'm starving!" she yelped, throwing her head back to give him complete access. Derrick took advantage of her position, lowering her dress off her shoulders, exposing her. He trailed his hand over her shoulder and around to her back again, deftly unclipping her bra. He may not have *fallen* or made love to a woman, but he'd definitely had sex. She shook the woman's image that flashed through her brain from her head, knowing Derrick was with her, not Victoria — forever.

Chapter Twenty-Eight

Which dress should I wear tonight?" Kris called to Derrick, who was cleaning up for dinner. She laughed internally, remembering she didn't need to yell.

"The white one. The restaurant is very formal," he responded.

Kris pulled out the tea-length dress Derrick had helped her pick out that afternoon. She had felt as though she were looking for a prom dress. He kept picking out formal wear with lace and silk, dresses that were appropriate for weddings and balls, not dinner at a ski lodge. But he'd been here before, he'd said, so she trusted he knew what he was looking for.

When she'd seen the price, she shoved it back on the rack. But he pulled it back out, insisting she try it.

Kris whirled in front of the mirror, realizing she looked like a bride, not a teenager going to a prom. She decided to pull up her hair instead of leaving it long and straight as she usually preferred. It was official; she looked like Cinderella heading off to the ball. "All I need now is a fairy godmother to bring the pumpkin coach." She chuckled under her breath, then clamped her hands over her mouth.

"I won't do?" Derrick said through a laugh.

"That's not fair —" A knock on the door broke off her complaint.

"Wait!" Derrick yelled, stopping her. He darted out of the bathroom, a towel wrapped around his waist. "I'll get it." He shooed her away.

Only the fact that he looked so good in nothing but a towel kept her from arguing. And then she wondered, *Was he worried? Did he think someone had followed them?*

Derrick grabbed his wallet off the credenza as he opened the door. He exchanged a tip for a garment bag and a box, seemingly unconcerned that he was standing in the doorway covered only by a towel. The giggle that escaped curbed her irritation, until he turned and stared her down. Then she just flashed him a what-the-heck-are-you-up-to look.

After closing the door behind the room attendant, Derrick disappeared into the bathroom again, so Kris continued to get ready.

A few minutes later, he stood behind her dressed in a black and white tux, holding a box. "This is for you."

Kris appraised him before lifting the lid. "Wow. You dress up nice. I've never seen you in anything but khakis."

He smiled. "As do you. Let me see."

Kris twirled in front of him, reveling as his eyes gobbled her up. They'd better get to dinner before they wrinkled another dress.

"Beautiful, absolutely stunning." He leaned forward and placed a delicate kiss on her lips. "You're only missing one thing." He lifted the lid of the box, revealing a white ribbon hand-tied bouquet with a tight cluster of about eighteen cream-colored roses surrounded by lemon leaves. It was simple and elegant.

"Derrick," she gasped in a breath, "that's a wedding bouquet?"

"I couldn't manage a pumpkin coach, but I figured you deserved a wedding night, my love." He held out his arm for her. "Shall we?"

Kris fought to hold back the tears that threatened to overtake her, which would ruin her makeup. Unable to speak through the emotion choking her words, she nodded and accepted his arm.

Derrick led her to the elevator without uttering a word and then pressed the button for the top floor. When it stopped, he led her to a private room decked out like a wedding reception.

A crystal chandelier and candelabras cast subtle light over a lone table covered with a white tablecloth, a centerpiece of more roses off to the side, and two beautifully adorned chairs with gossamer and ribbon. Soft piano music played in the background as moonlight streamed in through the glass windows, which once again offered a magnificent view of the mountains.

A host greeted them, escorting them to the table set just for them.

"Oh my ..." Kris fanned her eyes. "This is amazing."

Derrick pulled out her chair and helped her scoot forward. "I'm glad you approve."

"How did ... you do all this?" Her voice cracked, faltering with the love she felt enveloping her as though it were a tangible ribbon, interwoven through both of their souls, cinching them together forever.

He moved his head back and forth only slightly. "Every girl should have a fairy-tale wedding, even if it's just for two."

Kris leaned forward as he took his seat. "This is so much better than a formal wedding, Derrick. Thank you."

Her husband dipped his head. "My pleasure, my bride." Reaching across the table, he took her hand in his. "Thank you for marrying me, Kristina. I plan to make all your wishes come true."

She smiled. "You already have."

Derrick had taken it upon himself to pre-order their dinner, so there were no inquiries. He'd ordered her Filet a la Oscar, and she thought she'd died and gone to food heaven. She'd never thought of pairing filet with crabmeat, asparagus, and béarnaise sauce, but the result was delectable. It pained her that he could never sample such fine sauces. And pizza! Even with the incredible food she'd eaten with him, she was starting to crave pizza. She needed to see if she could sneak off and get a fix one of these days. There had to be somewhere in the hotel that served it.

After dinner, Derrick twirled her across the floor, teaching her all types of dances. She started to ask where he'd learned all the styles, but then remembered he'd been alive since the sixties, so he'd seen a lot. And his father had been alive since the early nineteen hundreds. It baffled her to think that he'd actually been alive during World War I.

As they danced, the waiter cleared their plates, and when she needed a respite, they returned to their table to see a wedding cake for two in the center of their table.

Kris giggled as she sat. "I'm starting to think I'm dreaming, Derrick. You may have to plant one of those mind-blowing kisses on me again."

"Gladly," he offered, pulling her out of the chair and into his arms before she could blink. He spun around in a circle, kissing her, unconcerned with the onlooking staff.

Kris dipped her head to his ear when he finally released her lips. "Okay. I believe again." She glanced around to the door. "Aren't you concerned they'll wonder how you did that?"

He laughed. "Kristina, you weigh all of a hundred and twelve pounds. I'm sure even a human man of my size could do this."

She crinkled her nose. "How do you know how much I weigh?"

"My senses, all of them, are ultra perceptive."

"Hmm ... all of them?"

"Everything."

She thought about that for a second, her brow furrowing. That could be uncomfortable at times.

He smiled. "No need to worry. You'll get used to not talking to yourself." He set her down and walked her to her chair.

"I was thinking of other things actually."

"Such as?"

"Your sense of smell. I'll be concerned."

He laughed full and deep and nuzzled her neck, inhaling a deep breath. "No need. I think you smell incredible. All the time," he clarified.

They finished their cake, and then Derrick guided her around the hotel again, asking if she wanted to dance in the nightclub. She refused, wanting to return to their room. She hadn't gotten her fill of him yet today, and she was starting to get tired. Derrick never seemed to tire.

When they made it back to the room, Derrick was content to sit on the loveseat. For a long while, they just snuggled and stared at the fire. His fingers trailed over her skin, seeming to memorize every square inch of her body. Occasionally he would plant delicate kisses on her hand and neck.

"Derrick," Kris asked, pulling his hand to her lips. "What happens if I die?"

He huffed out a breath. "What kind of question is that to ask on your wedding night?"

"I'm curious. Can you *fall* twice?"

He shook his head.

"So if I die, you'll be alone for a hundred years?"

His eyes narrowed, wondering, she guessed, how she knew his age and how long he'd live. He'd hinted, but he'd never come out and told her directly. "Yes. Though, it is unlikely I'd live that long without you."

Her eyes widened. "What do you mean?"

"It is from creatus that humans coined the term, *died of a broken heart*; they just don't know it. When you see a story on the news where a couple has been together for sixty to seventy years and they die within days of each other, often it is one of us, though they are usually much older than humans know. Creatus simply do not want to go on living after their partners die, and a creatus who is widowed very young will usually leave the family and become a hermit. Again the reason you hear stories of the old lady or man in the neighborhood who never comes out of their house."

A moan escaped her throat. "What if he —"

Derrick raised his finger to her lips. "He's not. Let's drop this discussion please."

Kris nodded and rested her head against his chest, swiping away a tear. She'd have to be extremely careful so that nothing ever happened to her. Because the thought of Derrick living in pain — she simply couldn't imagine putting him through that agony. Their connection was so strong now. She couldn't bear the thought of having him ripped from her life. She couldn't imagine the anguish.

Chapter Twenty-Nine

Vic sat next to Jonas on the high-rise building's ledge, lazily surveying the city, not really concerned with what was going on.

Even sitting next to this wonderful specimen of a man, all she could think about was Derrick, wondering if he and Kristina had really fallen. Maybe he'd lied to protect her from the family. As cool as the night air was, she couldn't help but feel the heat radiating off Jonas' body. How wonderful it would be to want another man. To have the comfort of a hot body on a cold night.

Even though she was only forty-four — young by creatus standards — she wanted to fall. It was every woman's dream, well, creatus women anyway. Meeting that perfect man, gazing into his eyes, and knowing that you'd be together forever. She shook the ridiculous thoughts from her head. If it hadn't happened with Derrick, a man she'd loved for years, how would it happen with anyone?

She turned to Jonas, who'd been content to sit beside her quietly, even though he had to know how she felt about all this. "Why did you come back, Jonas?"

He glanced up without lifting his head. His catlike orbs sparkled in the limited light from the surrounding buildings;

he'd always had the prettiest eyes. Even though they were a dark sable, they had flecks of gold in them. "I heard Derrick finally made a decision," he answered easily, as though he'd been prepared for her question.

She narrowed her brows. "A decision on what? *Watching*?"

"*Watching*?" he repeated, spurting out a laugh. "No. I can *watch* and get into a fight anywhere. I didn't need to come back to New England to *watch*. Besides, humans are hardly worth battling. Even when they have a weapon, they're usually poor fighters. And unlike our grandparents, I have no desire to protect them."

Vic flinched. She hadn't believed that Jonas had been *watching* just so he could fight, but his comment sounded as though maybe he had been.

He rested his hand over hers, and she immediately withdrew it, tending to an itch behind her head.

"So, what, then?" she prodded, even though she now had her suspicions, wondering why she'd felt the need to remove her hand. Hadn't she been thinking she'd track him down? Hadn't she said she needed to move on?

"A *Kristina* decision," he said. "I knew once Derrick made his choice, you would be open to someone else. I couldn't compete with him around for some reason." He shook his head. "What is it about him anyway? Why are you drawn to him?"

She shrugged. Honestly, she didn't know, and now that Derrick had made his decision to move on, her heart should feel free to pursue other men, but she didn't feel as if their relationship was real. There was still a chance. If Kristina were out of the picture —

"Victoria ..." Jonas' voice pulled her from her thoughts.

She hated the name Victoria. It wasn't as bad as when her family had called her Tori, but it was close. It sounded weak. Derrick had only said it when he was mad at her or when he pleaded with her.

"Stop it, Victoria. Look at me," Jonas demanded.

Vic huffed out a breath. "What?"

"Stop thinking about him. He's on his honeymoon in Mount Washington."

She whipped her head to him. "How do you know where they went?"

"My brother and I overheard them. They were going to get married in Manchester, and then he said there was a nice place he'd take her. Where else would they have gone?" He stopped, obviously taking in her hurt expression. "Oh, that's right. You two used to ski there. I forgot."

She bit down on her lip until she tasted blood. "You forgot nothing, you twerp. Besides, it wasn't just the two of us. We all went there as a group."

He wiggled his eyebrows at her. Jonas could be so maddening sometimes. "Yeah, but I seem to recall Derrick and you curled up on the chairs outside by the fire pit."

Vic punched him in the shoulder. "Only because he was drunk. We only succumbed to our desires when he was drunk ..." she trailed off, her heart wrenching. He hadn't used her, she knew. They had used each other. They were the right choice for each other. He would have chosen her if it weren't for Kristina.

Jonas grabbed her fist and clutched it between his hands. "And you call me a twerp. Come on, Victoria. Let's get out of here. I don't need a drink to want you. What are we waiting for anyway? The rogue isn't going to strike. You heard Derrick; the rogue is after *him*."

She sighed. "It's not going to happen, Jonas."

"Why the hell not? Who else you pining for? Michael?"

A burst flew out of her mouth. "What would give you that idea? We're just friends. We'd kill each other as a couple. We hate each other's quirks more than I hate Derrick. And I hate Derrick a lot right now," she emphasized.

Still holding on to her fist, he pulled her toward him. "Michael doesn't hate you. Not even close. He's wanted you since we were in high school. We've both wanted you since we were teenagers. But you can't seem to imagine yourself with anyone but Derrick. If you could just see —"

Vic pulled her hand free. As much as she wanted to flee, she couldn't make herself leave, but she didn't feel comfortable with him holding her hand. She knew she had to forget Derrick. And she had always liked Jonas ... but Michael? She'd never seen it. She'd actually thought Ryan was interested in her.

Seeming to witness her emotions, Jonas moved closer.

No, she couldn't. She shot her hand up in front of her, creating a barrier. "I'll think about it, Jonas. I really will. But I'm not ready."

He threw his head back, sighing dramatically. So melodramatic. Maybe that was what she liked about Derrick. He was a steady rock, rarely easy to upset. In fact, the only time she'd ever seen him upset was over Kristina. It was Derrick's passion she admired — craved. Her soul longed for a man to want her like that. The other men were moody, irritable, childish.

Jonas. She rolled his name around in her head. He'd always been in the back of her mind. Since they were kids, she'd found him attractive. But somehow, she'd never pictured him as a husband, as wanting anything other than a fling. Of course, that was common for creatus men. If they didn't take things too seriously, they didn't risk falling.

Even though they all wanted to find the perfect partner, they were still men, and they still liked to play.

"I'm sorry," she said, patting his hand platonically, letting him know she wasn't against his touch entirely.

Jonas had been leaning back, his eyes shuttered, but he opened one eye and smiled. "It's okay," he said, turning his hand over so hers rested in his. His thumb made a small circle on the back of her hand, and Vic was surprised to feel a faint flutter inside her. Jonas exhaled a deep breath and stared into her soul. His eyes looked lighter than before, almost a deep dark hazel as he studied her. And though he had the silky raven hair, his and Ry's had more curl than most creatus. He moved his hand up her arm and she didn't move this time. "But I really thought we had something before I left. My brother said you mentioned me in the meeting, said you were gonna to come find me. Was that just to get Derrick riled up?"

She nodded. "I was going to call you, but yes, I was trying to rile him up."

Without warning, Jonas hopped up, huffing out a breath as he marched away. "See ya 'round, Victoria," he drawled in that seductive southern tone that she'd always liked. Few creatus had accents, but Jonas' family had lived in South Carolina before moving here. She remembered the first time she'd seen him when they were in middle school. A new boy, someone who hadn't known her since she was a toddler. She'd been intrigued from the first time she'd cast her eyes on him, even though he'd paid her little notice. Typical of boys and girls that age, regardless of the species.

"Wait!" Vic jumped up and landed in front of him, blocking his exit to the stairwell. "Don't leave."

He shifted on his feet. "Why? It's obvious that there's nothing for me here, as I'd hoped."

Vic leaned in, her eyes closing, hoping he wouldn't embarrass her by leaving her hanging.

Immediately, Jonas wrapped his arms around her, tugging her to his chest. She'd always known he was strong, and for a second, she realized he was too strong. If she'd wanted to escape his embrace, it didn't feel as if she could. His heart pounded loudly in his chest, a rare occurrence. Most creatus were experts at hiding their emotions. His mouth clamped over hers, demanding and powerful, taking what he wanted. At first, his forcefulness surprised her, and she wanted to withdraw, but then his lips softened, coaxing her to join in the kiss.

Seemingly without her consent, her body melted against his, accepting him, reveling in the feeling that a man wanted her, really desired her.

But then, Michael popped into her head. They'd been best friends since they were children. Even as she kissed Jonas, moving her hands through his silky hair, traveling over his muscular arms, she couldn't get the image of Michael out of her mind.

Michael's words rang through her head from the other day ... that he wanted a strong woman. *Had he meant me? Had Michael wanted me?*

Chapter Thirty

Anything?" Derrick asked Michael over the phone.
"Nothing. Not even an attack on a human."
Michael was obviously tapping away on his iPhone
as he used the earpiece, because the annoying tap came
through the phone like a bass drum. His brother knew he
hated it, but Michael never put the phone down; he was an
addict. "Of course, we patrolled the city well," he
continued. "I'm starting to wonder if maybe you're right.
Maybe it's someone we know, and they're just looking to
destroy you."

"My bet's on Jonas, Michael. You need to see what he's
been doing the last few years."

"He just got back a couple of days ago; these attacks
have been going on for weeks," Michael protested. "We've
been best friends since he and his brother and mom moved
here. Heck, we spent more time in high school together
than you and I did, Derrick."

Derrick inhaled a deep breath, not wanting to argue. "I
know, Bro, but people change. And just because he hasn't
been hanging out at family gatherings doesn't mean he
hasn't been in town. Ry could have just been looking for an
opening to get him back inside family matters."

"I'll do some research. I already tracked down everyone who's left in the last ten years, so I'll work on that today." Michael stopped talking for a second and then chuckled. "You know, you sound pretty chipper, considering all that's going on. So, everything's good? You two warm and cozy up there?"

"Actually, it's freezing."

His brother let out a loud guffaw. "I'm not talking about the weather, dude."

"Oh, that warm and cozy ..." Derrick let his words trail off. "I'm not talking to you, man. Besides, what do you care? You hate humans. So you certainly don't want to hear any of my *boring* details," he drew out his words and then lowered his voice, "You want a strong woman who'll rock your world, right?"

Michael laughed again. "Yeah. I guess I do."

"So, when exactly are you going to tell her?"

"Tell who?" he grumbled, giving away that he knew *who*.

"Victoria," Derrick chided. "Come on, man. You practically crawled across the floor the other day, telling her what you wanted in a woman. She was just too angry to see it, but she will. You two are perfect for each other."

Michael huffed. "We would end up destroying each other. We're too much alike."

"Ah-ha, so you are interested."

"Yeah," he conceded. "I've always been interested in Vic, but she sees right through me, as if I'm just an apparition. Jonas wanted her too. At least he did in high school. I wouldn't be surprised if she's the real reason he came back. You know, we always assumed she wanted you because you were the strongest." Derrick rolled his eyes even though Michael couldn't see him. "So, where's Kristina? You let her out of your sight?" his brother asked nonchalantly as if he didn't really care, just changing the subject.

"Not really. She's having a spa treatment. We'll be meeting in about fifteen minutes in the couple's area."

"Have fun, loverboy, while I persevere here with no warm woman to keep me company on these chilly nights."

Derrick laughed. "As if you've ever had a problem finding a warm body."

"Yeah well, sometimes we grow up."

A huff threatened to pop out of Derrick's throat, but he restrained it. Maybe his brother really was growing up. "All right then. I'll call you tomorrow," Derrick said and hung up. He made his way to the lounge. He was looking forward to another incredible evening with his wife, but he had a day of outdoor activities planned today.

Derrick found an open loveseat and sat down to wait for Kristina. He pulled out his iPhone, checking the weather to see what the ski conditions were for tomorrow, as he'd already made reservations for zip lining today. If conditions weren't good, he had back-up plans of sleigh rides, hiking, or horseback riding. Heck, even staying inside all day would be fine with him, but he wanted their makeshift honeymoon to be something she'd remember forever, since she hadn't wanted the huge wedding as most women did.

He glanced at the time. Kristina was late. He pulled their reservation receipt out of his wallet and confirmed the time. Only five minutes, which wasn't unusual for her, as she was habitually late. But still, the hotel filled every slot; rarely did they get behind.

Derrick made a loop outside the area. He glanced at the hot tub and pool, thinking maybe she'd assumed they were supposed to meet there. Coming up empty, he sought out one of the employees to see if her appointment had been rescheduled for a later time. The woman whom he had spoken with earlier was on the phone, explaining the different services they offered to a prospective customer. She peeped up at him and smiled, but returned her eyes to her computer. The woman droned on, detailing every massage and facial treatment that was available.

"I'm sorry, miss," he interrupted, and her eyes flashed to him, irritation now overshadowing her previously friendly smile. Ignoring her glower, he asked, "Did my wife change the time of her treatment?"

"Excuse me," the woman said into the phone and then glanced at him. "Could you give me a minute, sir?"

"No. It'll just take a second. My wife was supposed to meet me in the couple's area ten minutes ago, and she's not there."

The woman sucked on her teeth. "One second, sir, and I will be happy to look up that information." She returned to the caller. "Yes, ma'am. We can schedule you in tomorrow." She clicked her mouse, scrolling down the computer screen. "Hmm ... let's see."

Derrick had lost all patience. Even though it wasn't the woman's fault, her unwillingness to understand his concern aggravated him. He understood someone was on the phone, but shouldn't the person standing in front of her take precedence? He stormed toward the lounge area again to see if Kristina had returned.

Pulling out his phone, he checked the time again. Fifteen minutes. His blood raced through his veins. He glanced at the women's locker room, wondering how quickly he'd get the staff's attention if he sought out his wife himself.

Clearly, fifteen minutes meant nothing to them, but if the rogue had found Kristina ... He whooshed out a breath, his hands trembling. Decided, he opened the door to the women's locker room. He didn't care what they thought; he only wanted to know if he needed to seek his wife. And if she was embarrassed, so be it.

"Kristina!" he shouted into the vacant corridor. All the rooms were private, so it wasn't as if there would be naked women wandering the halls. They all wore robes, courtesy of the hotel. He stepped inside, letting the door close behind him. "Kristina," he repeated, louder, and he could be very loud. His voice had a tendency to carry if he so desired. And right now, he had only one concern: finding his wife.

Chapter Thirty-One

Reece Buckley sifted through the files, dating back fourteen years. He'd been surprised when he searched Kristina Heskin's records and discovered she'd been the victim of a brutal attack that had left her mother bleeding on the street, and yet she'd been able to walk away, unharmed.

"My dark angel saved me," Detective O'Brian had written in quotes on the now-faded police report, but thankfully, as with most cops, all his reports were scribbled in bold black ink, standard procedure for officers. O'Brian had also made a file he'd titled as *Dark Angel*. Too bad O'Brian was dead; he probably could have picked his brain.

Reece pulled out the stack of reports he'd lifted from the dead detective's office. Most cops didn't bother to keep paper copies, but O'Brian was old school, just like Reece's dad. Reece remembered how his old man would never trust computers, had repeatedly said, *"What're they gonna do when they all crash and burn? Or terrorists take out the Internet?"* He missed his father; he was the one man Reece could trust with his life. Even in the military, Reece hadn't felt completely comfortable. Things weren't the same as they'd been when his father was a cop, as he'd always complained, and Reece had to agree. Reece was born in the Deep South where loyalty meant something. Even the men he'd met overseas and in Miami would stab you in the back, metaphorically, as quickly as a punk would stick you with a blade on the street, if it meant they'd advance in front of you. He'd kept his nose clean while he served his country and his head down when he returned to the U.S. His promotion had nothing to do with the good-ole-boy system; he was where he was because he had a knack for finding missing links.

The reports under the "Dark Angel" tab dated back eight years, but then stopped a few years ago. Some of the reports hadn't been O'Brian's, but they all had one thing in common. Every report was of an attack on a citizen where a vigilante had intervened. Although said in different ways, each victim had claimed that one second the thief had been on them, and the next it was as if they'd disappeared. One woman had gone on to say that she was sure it was Batman who had protected her.

Reece reclined on the hard mattress of the cheap hotel room his agency had reserved. What happened to the plush accommodations he'd seen in the movies? James Bond had never stayed in a fleabag hotel. Apparently holding a license to kill didn't mean the same as it used to.

He stared up at the water- and smoke-stained ceiling, wondering how the incidents connected. Fourteen years ago, this supposed *dark angel* protected an eight-year-old girl. Six years later, he saved others, but then disappeared until the Tobin bridge event, nearly three years after the last report.

Reece logged into the Massachusetts police database, courtesy of his boss' security clearance. After a rudimentary search, he returned a few situations where a vigilante had stepped in to help a civilian in the last eight years. However, none of those incidents included any mention of supernatural occurrences. Maybe that was why O'Brian had left them out of his file. Again, he thought about what a waste it was that O'Brian was dead.

Clicking through the crime reports, he ran across a slew of homicides in the last couple of months. No mention of a vigilante stepping in, but the crimes in and of themselves were interesting. Every corpse had been *torn* in pieces. The ME's report had used *torn* for a reason, he was certain.

Sawed, ripped to shreds by an animal, axed, hammered, and pulled apart by two cars — that wasn't a pretty sight, even if the dude was a drug dealer — were all terms Reece was accustomed to from his investigations in Miami and South America. But he'd never run across the term *torn*.

Reece clicked on the images from the medical examiner's office, zooming in on the screen to get a better look. *Torn* was the correct word. Pieces of flesh and muscle hung from the appendages, indicating the body had in fact been torn apart.

Had the Dark Angel in fact gone dark? Could Derrick Ashton have finally had enough with society and, instead of helping, decided to punish?

Chapter Thirty-Two

Michael sat across from Rebecca at the sushi restaurant they always ate at when he came to see her for information.

Rebecca twisted a lock of her short hair as she leaned toward him. "I deleted all of O'Brian's computer files, Michael, but I can't find the hard copies, and I know he kept them."

"So you think the same guy took them?"

She bobbed her head. She was so cute, not nearly as intimidating as some creatus women. Her decision to cut her hair short had surprised him, though. She already looked so young. She'd only been home from school for a couple of years, but she was a genius when it came to computers. He'd had Rebecca earmarked for a position in Boston's PD immediately. It wasn't hard to do. The man who'd interviewed her for the position had fallen in love with her looks, and her mind was sharp. All she needed was a position where she had access to a computer, and she could get Michael anything in the state. Of course, he had intentions of getting her to a government office in Washington, but at thirty-seven — twenty-seven to the rest of the world — she barely looked as if she were drinking age. So he had a few years to mold her.

Rebecca took a bite of her tuna, careful to scrape off the rice. "I also tracked down the guy who recorded Kristina's free dive off the Tobin, but he doesn't have another copy."

Michael cocked his head. "He gave the original to O'Brian, right?"

"Uh-uh," she said, taking a sip of her water. "He'd given him a copy, since he had material he needed on it. When I told him we lost the copy and needed another, he said he'd gladly give us another disc, but he'd already told O'Brian that someone else from the department had taken his only copy. He said if he gets it back, he'll call me."

"Do you think he was telling the truth?" Michael asked.

She shrugged. "Why would he lie? He's the one who came to the PD and offered it to O'Brian in the first place."

Michael bit down on his lip and glanced around the restaurant. Derrick continually complained about everyone else doing things to screw up, and here he'd screwed up twice. And now, as always, Michael had to clean up behind him. Derrick had thought that no one would believe a little girl's claim of seeing a *dark angel*, and yet, O'Brian had held on to the report for fourteen years. "You got the copies for me?"

Rebecca dug in her briefcase. "Yep. All of them."

"All? I thought there were only two," Michael questioned.

"When I searched his computer, I found more reports filed under *dark angel*; I assumed you'd want them all."

Michael smiled, and if he wasn't mistaken, pint-sized Rebecca gave him a little wiggle. He was flattered, but she wasn't his type. And she was too young. Granted, she was only twelve years his junior, but — who was he kidding?

He'd never had a type. Until Victoria came on the market, that is.

Now, his days and nights were inundated with thoughts of her. And clearly, Jonas wanted her too. So after waiting years for Derrick to make up his mind, Jonas strolls back into town and makes a pass at her. Michael had decided not to mention to his brother about Vic and Jonas' pow-wow last night, as he certainly didn't need to add any additional fuel to Derrick's animosity against Jonas. At first he'd been overjoyed when he watched Victoria fend off Jonas' advances, but the moment Jonas had turned to leave, she'd bolted after him.

He did have to be thankful to Jonas for one thing, though; he'd told her that both of them had liked her since high school, so maybe she wouldn't be blindsided when he confronted her.

"Michael?"

Michael lifted his head to see Rebecca's eyes as they bore into his. "I'm sorry, what?" He'd heard her speak, but had lost total focus on the issue at hand as his mind battled with how to approach Victoria. All of a sudden, he felt as though he were out of time, realizing if he didn't do something quickly, he'd lose her forever.

Rebecca batted her long black eyelashes over her liquid-ink eyes that reminded him of a fawn in their innocence. "I asked if you'd like to meet me after work."

"Oh." He gulped, not wanting to offend such a pretty little thing. If he couldn't get Victoria's attention, perhaps Rebecca could be his type. He flashed a sideways smile, the one his mother always told him would get him his way. "I can't tonight. Raincheck?"

She chewed on the tip of her nail as she stood. "Sure. Let me know if you need anything else." She tromped off, obviously knowing he had no intention of taking her up on her proposal. There weren't many secrets within the family. If Derrick and Jonas had known he was in love with Victoria, more than likely everyone did.

Michael threw a fifty on the bill and left the restaurant. He had one more stop to make before he did anything else.

Before exiting his Dodge Charger, Michael grabbed his ID from the glove box. Though technically he was a medical doctor by degree, he'd stepped away from the profession, seeing a need elsewhere within the family. Derrick was skeptical at first, but he'd realized in this day and age, they needed his expertise.

In the last twelve years, Michael had situated creatus in high-level positions around the globe. So if anything ever got out of control, the evidence could disappear with a couple of clicks.

He used the designated entrance, positive no one would stop him; of course his ID was up-to-date if they did. He smiled as he passed the nurses' station, listening to their whispers. Probably the women who didn't know his brother personally would mistake him for Derrick.

Sure, he had two inches and about twenty pounds on his older brother, but most women only saw the tall, dark, and handsome doctor. *Why couldn't Victoria see that?* he wondered. Though he knew why. To Victoria, he was just another creatus, a brother-in-arms. She'd grown up with him, had fought most of the males. She'd been the only female near their age, so she didn't hang out with girls. She played football and basketball with them. It wasn't as if they'd complain; they needed players, as they certainly couldn't play with humans.

Michael stepped into the hospital room, pleased to see that she was alone. He'd rather not have to explain to a parent or fiancé why someone other than her regular doctor was here.

Beth's face had cleared up some over the last couple of days. Such a shame. She really was a pretty girl. He'd always been a fan of strawberry blondes. Derrick thought Michael hated all humans. He didn't. He just wasn't willing to let any human jeopardize their way of life, nor would he let a creatus for that matter. He planned to do his job to the fullest, whatever it took.

Chapter Thirty-Three

Kris grabbed the plate of pizza as soon as the man threw it on the counter. She shoved bites into her mouth as she ran the long stretch of corridor, which she was positive had doubled in length. Not as enjoyable as she'd imagined when she had to keep checking the time.

At a couple minutes late, she was fine. Ten, she'd started to tap her foot in exasperation. Fifteen, she'd demanded they just give it to her as it was.

She rounded the hallway and saw Derrick coming out of the couple's lounge, his white robe still wrapped around him. He made eye contact, and at first, a look of utter gratitude washed over his features as he pulled to a stop, both of his hands running through his hair. But then, if looks could kill, well, when she'd thought Victoria was dangerous-looking, she'd been way off.

"I'm sorry ..." She almost fell into him, the paper plate still clutched in her hand. "I'm so sorry. I was running to get back before we were supposed to meet."

He exhaled a breath as one arm latched around her body and his hand cupped her face. Kris stared up to see his eyes completely glazed over. He pulled her against him. "I thought —" He ran his hands through her hair and kissed her forehead. "Please don't ever scare me like that again. Any other time I wouldn't freak out that you're late, but right now, with that maniac —"

"I'm sorry," she said again, her words disappearing into his chest as he squeezed her tighter.

"Pizza?" he groaned, pressing his lips to the top of her head, as if just happy she was with him. "All you had to do was order it. They would have brought it to you."

She peered up at him, feeling like a little girl. "I didn't want to eat it in front of you."

"Why on earth not?" he demanded, his voice rising a fraction.

"Because you can't eat it."

Derrick swiped his hand across his forehead. "Kristina, I've never even tasted pizza, so I don't miss anything. But oddly enough, it doesn't appeal to me. It'd be like offering a great white shark ice cream."

She covered her mouth to restrain a laugh. "Yesterday a superhero, today a great white?"

"I'm not comparing myself to a shark. I'm just saying pizza isn't in our food group. We don't crave food the way humans do. We eat when we're hungry, simple as that." He lifted her chin. "And you're in trouble, so stop trying to change the subject by laughing."

She dropped her head. "I really am sorry. I knew you'd be worried, but I thought it'd only take a few minutes."

Derrick scooped up her hand and led her to the couple's area so they could change and be on with their day. "We'll find him, Kristina. I promise. And then I won't go insane when you're fifteen minutes late. It's just —"

She pulled him to a stop before he opened the door. "I understand, Derrick. This is serious. I know you're not being ridiculously obsessive. I saw Beth; I know this is real. I just figured I was safe here."

He nodded and pulled her against him again. "You are safe, but I can't take any chances. I can't lose you. I just got you."

She smiled, even though he couldn't see it. She felt the same way. She'd been irresponsible. "I promise. I'll never cause you to worry again."

Obviously comforted, he lifted her chin and kissed her again. "Okay. So, since you've already eaten lunch, how about we go change before we head off to our next adventure?"

"Maybe we can take a little nap before getting ready," she said suggestively, hoping he wasn't too upset with her. Though, oddly enough, he didn't seem angry at all. It's as though he'd gotten over his frustration in seconds.

"Well, our reservation is at two, so I'm sure we can fit in a nap if you're tired." He raised his eyebrows in question, but then continued, "But first off, I have to go in and settle our bill and make certain the staff doesn't have us thrown out for disorderly conduct."

Kris bit down on her lip. "Um ... exactly what did you do?"

"I was looking for you the last place I saw you — the ladies' locker room. They don't like men in there, it seems."

Catching the gist of his confession, Kris mashed her lips together to keep from laughing again, even though she knew it wasn't funny. "You think? It's not as if you can sneak in and out."

He shook his head. "There wasn't any sneaking going on, believe me. I'm surprised you didn't hear me from the other side of the hotel."

She nibbled on her bottom lip, her head lowered. She'd have to be extra nice to him when they returned to the room. He was being kind, but evidently, he'd been more upset than he'd let on. "Okay. I'll go get my stuff out of the locker while you make amends."

"I'm sure there will be a hefty tip involved." He pushed open the door and stopped, peering into the eyes of the woman who'd checked them in earlier. He shrugged. "Found my wife."

Kris cringed and then slunk off toward the ladies' room, knowing Derrick would take care of everything.

Two hours later, Kris stood bundled in a harness and helmet, ready to take on the largest treetop zip line, approximately 165 feet off the ground. It didn't sound high when she was on the ground, learning how to zip line five feet above the snow. But now looking over the expanse of the hemlock canopy below her to the platform over eight hundred feet away, she knew she'd been utterly insane to think she could do this. She was sixteen stories up; even Derrick couldn't fall from this height and live. Or, at least she didn't think he could. She'd never actually asked. The guide had mentioned that some of the trees were two hundred and fifty years old, dating back to The Revolutionary War. So they were strong and sturdy. The zip lines consisted of two vinyl-covered cables, assuring they were completely safe, and she'd been okay on the first few zips. Even the sky bridges they'd crossed had been okay. But getting a bird's-eye view of Rosebrook Canyon, she was having second thoughts.

"You okay?" Derrick asked, encircling her waist with his arms.

She afforded him an unconvincing nod, gulping in the process, her hands sweating. She knew she didn't have to hold on, but the instructor had told her to be careful that no part of her skin touched the line. So what if her hand slipped out of the glove?

The guide stepped in front of her. "It's no different than the others, Mrs. Ashton. Just let the harness do all the work. Lean back in the cannonball position we showed you, point your toes downward, and have fun."

Kris gave another nod and stepped forward, but then turned to Derrick. "Maybe you should do this one first?" she suggested.

Derrick pressed his hand to her cheek. "You'll be fine, love. Just keep your eyes forward. Focus on Mount Washington." He gave her a wink. "Pretend you're gazing out at the trees from our suite."

She smiled and huffed out a breath. "Maybe I'll just rappel down. I handled the rappelling okay."

"But how would you get to the next platform?" Derrick suggested.

"You go first," she insisted again. "That way you can catch me if I fall — I mean, come in too quickly."

The guide laughed, so obviously he thought nothing of her blunder. Of course, who would imagine that her husband was capable of jumping off a building and saving her?

Derrick stepped toward the front of the platform. "Okay, Kristina." He chuckled along with the guide. "I'll be waiting to catch you."

The guide checked Derrick's straps and, using the carabiner, hooked his harness onto the line. After getting an "all clear" from the guide on the opposite platform, Derrick whooshed over the expanse of trees, letting out a thrilled whoop for her benefit, she assumed.

After a few minutes, the other guide's voice came through the radio, signaling it was safe to send her down. Even though her heart pounded fiercely in her chest and her hands were still sweaty, Kris took a deep breath and let it out and then said through gritted teeth. "Okay. I'm ready."

The guide didn't respond. She turned, but saw nothing as a cloth covered her entire face. Unable to control her need to take a breath, she inhaled the ether-like odor, a sweet taste prickling her tongue. She tried to pull the glove-covered hand away, but to no avail.

He'd found her. The rogue had obviously been watching for the first moment she was alone.

The world seemed to wobble before her eyes, and her legs felt non-existent. For a second, she wondered if she was even standing. Then the trees whooshed by her, but she heard no sound as if she'd gone deaf. Was she falling? Had the rogue just dropped her? She tried to scream for Derrick, but nothing left her throat, at least she didn't think so, remembering she hadn't heard the trees that looked as if they jumped over her either.

Now the entire forest bobbed up and down, and she just wanted it to stop. Dizzy and feeling sick, she closed her eyes and just waited to hit the forest floor and die. Unfortunately, Derrick would not be able to save her this time.

Derrick. Tears burned her eyes, or maybe it was the chemical on the rag. Her husband would be alone forever. She attempted to lift her head, tried to fight, but it seemed her body wouldn't obey. Then the sun flickered off and on, as if it were the fluorescent bulb in her kitchen. Dampness spread over her entire body, or was she drowning? The icy dark water engulfed her.

That's right, she remembered. She'd jumped off the Tobin Bridge, and she would die. It had all been a dream. None of it had been real. *Derrick* ... his name ... her Dark Angel had a name. He was real. *Derrick*, she repeated.

Though again, she wasn't sure if the word escaped her lips. She had to believe; she had to hold on for Derrick.

Chapter Thirty-Four

Michael called Victoria, but she didn't answer. Next he called Jonas, ready to confront him. He didn't have a problem with him being back, but they needed to make a decision. He had no intention of fighting with his best friend over Victoria's affection. And Ry, well, he could just give it up. He was too young anyway. Vic thought of him as nothing but a kid brother. Hell, she probably thought of Michael as a brother too, but he could remedy that.

Jonas' cell phone went to voicemail as well. "Damn!" He hated thinking what that might mean. He searched his phone contacts and found Ry's number and touched the name.

"Yo, what's up, Mike?" Ryan answered. "I was just in the middle of something."

Michael heard Ry's car door slam. "Have you seen your brother?"

"Nah. Not since last night. We pulling same shifts tonight?"

"Yeah," Michael answered. "How about Vic? I can't reach her either."

Ry laughed through the phone line. "Oh, I get it. You think they're together. That maybe Jonas is comforting her after telling her where the newlyweds went."

Michael stopped walking toward his vehicle. "How do you know where they went?"

"We overheard them yesterday after the meeting. I think since Derrick is with a human, he forgets that we can hear him."

Continuing his tread to the car, Michael hopped in, irritated. "Hey, you want to go out tonight, Ry? I have one thing I have to handle, but then I can meet you downtown around ten-ish."

"What about watching?"

"I don't think we'll see any action tonight, but come dressed, though."

Ry clucked his tongue. "I'm in the middle of something. I'll call you later this afternoon if I have time."

"Sounds good," Michael told him. "As I said, I won't be available until ten-ish anyway." Michael looked at the time on his phone. One-thirty, he had just enough time.

At ten o'clock, Michael turned his phone on. He had several missed calls from Derrick and his father, but he wasn't in the mood. It'd been a long day. He tried again to reach Ry, Vic, or Jonas. *What the hell were they doing*, he wondered. He needed company, preferably of the female persuasion. He lifted his phone and searched through the contacts again; Rebecca would do well. She was fun, cute, and she generally wanted to be with him.

The thought that Victoria could be off with Jonas somewhere burned his insides. He thought he could just let her go if Jonas wanted her, but now he felt otherwise. The current situation he was in allowed no time for screwing around, he knew, but if he didn't act quickly, he could lose her forever.

Would jealousy work? he wondered. Jonas had told her last night of both their interests, so maybe …

Rebecca picked up on the first ring. "I was hoping you'd call," she drawled. He wasn't certain where she'd picked up her slight southern drawl, but he had to admit, he liked it.

"Hey, Rebecca," Michael responded simply. No sense in getting her hopes up too much by turning on the charm. He just needed her with him for a few minutes. Fifteen at the most. "You still up for that drink?"

"Sure," she answered without hesitation. Too hastily. No challenge. He sighed inwardly, wondering why he needed a challenge.

"Meet me at the pub at ten-thirty."

"I'll be there."

As soon as he hung up, he clicked Victoria's number again. No answer, of course. Maybe she and Jonas had skipped town together. "Hey. Meet me at the pub round ten-thirty, so we can discuss this evening's route." He clicked end, ran his vehicle through a car wash, and then headed to meet Rebecca. He hated even the slightest bit of dust on his Charger. She was his baby, the one woman who could do no wrong.

Chapter Thirty-Five

Vic sat across from Jonas, thinking how good he looked, wondering why she couldn't fall. They sure gave it a good shot. And it's not to say that she could never fall for him, but evidently, she had to get her head screwed on straight first.

Still, she did appreciate what a good-looking man he was. She hated to think it was true, but after her attraction to Derrick, and Ry's confession, she had to believe that their heritage is what drew her to them, even though a human man had never turned her on. She could never be attracted to a man who was weaker than she was.

"Ry told me about you —"

His gaze bolted up from his plate. "What? About us?"

"Yes. It's okay."

Jonas shook his head. "No, it's not. He had no right."

Vic raised her hands in confusion. "I don't understand. Why is it such a big secret? Everyone thinks Derrick and Michael are anomalies —"

"And yet, Ry and I also have a human parent. In fact, I think Ry is stronger than Derrick. He's younger and doesn't know as many moves, but he's strong."

"So, why don't you want anyone to know? What's the big deal?"

Jonas pursed his lips, staring out the window for a few seconds before turning back to her, his eyes cold and blank. "Because our father hated us when he found out we weren't *all* human. My parents had been together for years, but my mother had hidden what she was." He bit down on his lip. "But she didn't think about kids, about the fact that she couldn't hide the eating habits and strength of a creatus child. He'd been in the military, so he missed a lot of our rearing. But when he was stationed in the states permanently, he saw me." Jonas inhaled a deep breath. "Ry had thrown a ball up on the roof by accident, and I, being the big brother, went up to get it. When my father saw me jump off the roof, he flipped. Scared at first, but then he was excited. Thought he had some superkid for a child. My mother assumed that as many years as they'd been together, he'd accept her."

Vic reached across the table and squeezed his hand. Ryan hadn't told her this part of the story. Maybe he hadn't known since he was obviously younger.

Jonas shook his head. "He — my father — treated us like pariahs. He didn't think twice about picking up the phone right in front of my mother. She had no choice. That S.O.B. was going to call his superiors in the army and turn us in as aliens. Can you believe that?"

"No," Vic responded. She'd never been fond of humans, but his own children?

"She killed him. Right there in front of me. She snapped my father's neck. Then she brought us here, where she said we had family. The family forged papers for us, and she stayed out of sight from all authorities."

"I'm so sorry, Jonas," Vic said, but he pulled his hand out from under hers.

Jonas pushed his chair away from the table and stood, throwing his napkin on his plate. "Don't feel sorry for me. I don't want your pity. I think I made that clear last night." He skirted the table and pulled her to her feet. "Did you think about it? Are you gonna try? Will you leave with me and start a new family?"

She exhaled a deep breath. "I —"

"Enough said, Victoria. I get it. You're still hung up on Derrick. Fine." He stormed off, slamming the door behind him.

Jonas had left so quickly that his absence seemed to leave an empty vacuum in her apartment, dead space that needed filling. She just couldn't think. Yeah, she loved Derrick. She wanted to believe that this was all subterfuge to protect Kristina, but it wasn't Derrick's face that she'd seen when she was with Jonas last night; it was Michael's.

Still, she had to know. Vic glanced up at the clock: eleven a.m.

Chapter Thirty-Six

The guide called up for a second time and still there was no answer.

Even if Kristina had chickened out, the guide would have called before rappelling down and trekking toward them. Derrick glanced up at the man in front of him. He hated to do it, but he didn't have a choice. Chances were, the man wouldn't even know what happened. Derrick just had to decide if he should choke him out or hit him. It wouldn't take but a couple seconds for him to drop. The movies had it all wrong. If you knew what you were doing, a man would drop in less than three seconds.

He decided not to hit the innocent man; instead, as the guide stared up toward the higher platform, Derrick used his hand to compress his carotid arteries, hence causing cerebral ischemia, a temporary hypoxic condition in the brain. The guide dropped before he could even lift his hand to Derrick's arm.

After lowering the man to the deck and strapping his carabiner onto the cable in the event he rolled over, Derrick grabbed his rappelling gear and hopped off the platform, hitting the ground and leaving a deep pit. He quickly covered his tracks and took off in the direction of the first platform.

As he ran, he attempted to listen to all surrounding sounds, but it was no use; there were too many tourists on the property. Every direction he turned, he heard skiers, hikers, and animals scurrying through the underbrush.

Keeping his focus, he remained within the trees so he could run. It only took him a few minutes, but he knew it'd be too late. He was faster than most creatus, but Kristina would be barely more than a backpack to the rogue, and he had the benefit of a head start and three different directions he could have taken. The only thing that Derrick could pray was that he was wrong. Nothing had happened; she'd just been terrified and rappelled down the tree instead. The other guide just hadn't heard the transmission.

When he reached the bottom of the platform, all his hope melted. There, lying at the bottom, his neck twisted in an unnatural position, was the other guide. Granted, the guide could have fallen, but this appeared to be the rogue's M.O., when he wasn't ripping their bodies to shreds to attract the family's attention, that is.

Derrick dropped to his knees and felt for a pulse. Nothing. He held his breath and listened for anything. Any sound. His gaze dropped to the forest floor. Nothing.

As with Janelle, no tears fell. His heart ached, but he had no time for sorrow. Only hatred filled his veins — and guilt. Just like Janelle. He'd failed to protect Kristina, just as he'd failed to protect Janelle.

Moving on instinct, and because his mind wouldn't allow him time to grieve, he jumped to the platform, grabbed the rappelling gear, ripped the harness as if it had broken, and dropped it over the platform. Then he darted back to the tree stand and watched as the other guide rappelled down the tree.

"What happened?" the guide called as he dropped a few feet at a time.

Derrick gave a noncommittal shrug. "I came down to find my wife, but I haven't seen her. She must have walked back to the hotel. Probably furious with me for forcing her to go zip lining."

The man shook his head. "I mean, how did you get down?"

"I rappelled down," Derrick answered, as if it was the most obvious answer. Why would he have thought anything else? He dropped his gear and turned away. "I have to go find my wife."

"Wait," the man called. "I woke up on the deck. What happened?"

Derrick shrugged again. "You were fine when I saw you. Maybe you're diabetic." He bolted off before the man could ask any more questions, charging his way through the woods the moment he was out of view. He had no time to waste. He needed to contact his family, track down all the people who could have been responsible. There was no doubt anymore. Someone in the family was the rogue.

He'd left his phone in the room. He never left his phone, but he'd wanted the day to be about Kristina and him. Derrick struggled to keep his expression passive as he walked as swiftly as was humanly possible to his room, but instead of taking the elevator, he took the stairs, knowing few humans bothered. He paused only a second to listen for any sounds and then shot up to his floor.

As soon as he unlocked the door, he made a beeline for his phone. Four o'clock. Michael first, so he could track down the others. He hit "call" and then buzzed about the room, packing up everything. As much as he wanted just to run, leaving everything behind, he had to be sensible. He couldn't give the authorities any more than they already had. Of course, who would possibly think that someone as small as Kristina could push the guide off the platform? No. They'd have to assume that the guide was in a hurry to rappel down and the harness broke. And they couldn't blame Derrick because he had been with the other guide who, as he'd assumed, hit the deck so fast that he had no recollection of what had happened.

So, as always, he'd leave no trace. And his story would be that his wife was livid with him for making her go, and he couldn't find her afterward, so he'd hiked back to find her.

The call to Michael went directly to voicemail, so Derrick systematically dialed all his top suspects. When none of them answered, he made his way to the Navigator. As soon as he was inside, he called the only other person on earth who would understand his pain — his mother.

Tears stung his eyes the moment she answered.

"Derrick?" she screeched his name in panic after he hadn't answered the first three times because he couldn't find his voice.

"He got her, Mom," he choked out. "And I don't know where to start looking."

Sabrina screamed his father's name, and Derrick had to extend the phone away from his ear. After all these years, she still forgot. He switched the call to the hands-free SYNC and peeled out of the parking lot. His only hope would be that the rogue wanted Kristina alive, wanted Derrick to somehow witness her death. And wouldn't he know if she were already dead? If the rogue had wanted her dead, wouldn't he have left her on the ground for Derrick to find her?

Yes, he knew she was alive. She had to be alive. He would find Kristina and, man or woman, friend or foe, he would tear the culprit apart with his bare hands if he so much as put a scratch on her. He was finished with being nice.

"Derrick?" His father's deep voice filled the line. "Dear God, your mother is ready to have a heart attack. What's going on?"

Derrick relayed the story as he sped across the highway about ninety, not concerned with getting a ticket. Not that he would stop, even though he did have a get-out-of-jail-free card as a doctor. A state trooper would more than likely just chase him at ninety. Any more though, and he'd have a roadblock waiting for him, and that definitely would waste time. He'd do better to run, but then how would he explain his vehicle left at the hotel?

His father listened intently without interrupting and then Derrick relayed his greatest concern. "Dad, I've been trying to reach Michael, Vic, Jonas, and Ry, and I can't find any of them. Will you get on the horn and track them down? I'm going straight to my apartment, as the house would be backtracking, and I have a suspicion that this *rogue* wants me to watch Kristina die, or he would have left her body in the mountains. I have no doubt that he plans to murder her, as he thinks that would kill me. But, he's partly wrong." Derrick steeled himself, knowing his father hated violence and loathed vengeance; after all, that's how his mother's family had died. "If he hurts her ... I'll use every waking minute of my life to track him down. I will not die or wither away; I will never give up until he dies."

Chapter Thirty-Seven

Every time Kris stirred, a quick whiff of the rag and she was out again. But that would only work for so long. Too much would cause cardiac arrest, especially with her history of drug abuse and just detoxing. And Kristina couldn't die. Not yet.

Derrick needed to watch her die, needed to know that nothing he did could save her. And Derrick needed to die too. The plan was flawless. Easy actually, since Derrick lived in one of the tallest condos in Back Bay. Even the *all-powerful* Derrick wouldn't be able to survive a drop from the roof. Then the poor star-crossed lovers would die together, exactly what Kristina had wanted.

Based on her history, no one would question that Kristina jumped off the roof, and no one in the family would doubt that Derrick would jump right after her, attempting to save her, as he'd done for the last fourteen years.

Derrick was too weak to lead their family, and so he would die too. Shame, though. His intelligence and strength would have been invaluable. But choosing Kristina over the family had proven his weakness for humans. The rest of the family would have no problem with the plan to start

moving key creatus into top-level positions in the
government, something they'd never done in the past.

Notoriety was something creatus had always shied away
from. If you were famous, humans started to wonder why
you were still alive when everyone else was dead. But now,
they'd use their heritage to their benefit. Outliving their
peers would work to their advantage as they infiltrated all
branches of the government.

"Oh, my ... head ..." Kristina moaned from the
passenger seat.

Enough was enough. She obviously had a high tolerance
to drugs. Pulling the vehicle underneath an overpass before
she awoke completely, the rogue sifted through the bag of
medical goodies on the floor. "You like drugs, Kristina?
You are going to like this drug, lovely. Propofol will give
you a high like you've never known." With a slight squeeze
of the pump, all of the milky substance disappeared into
Kristina's vein. That would keep her knocked out until
everything was ready.

Escorting Kristina to the parking garage was easy; no
one seemed to care that a half-drunk woman was being
assisted to her apartment. Of course, sleeping beauty
wouldn't be receiving a princess' welcome.

Chapter Thirty-Eight

After hours of knocking on doors, and knocking some down, Derrick had no more information on Kristina's whereabouts than he'd had since she'd been kidnapped from the zip-lining stand.

He knew he should have just returned to his condo, but he wanted to be in control, to catch the rogue off-guard. He'd questioned — rather, demanded — the whereabouts of the creatus he suspected from every family member he reached. No one had seen Jonas or Ry, Vic, or even his brother since yesterday. The only hope Derrick had at this point was that the rogue wanted to confront him, so he headed back to his apartment, assuming he'd have to wait for a call.

Derrick ascended the stairs to his apartment, knowing that anyone waiting would more than likely be watching the front door. As much as he wanted to scour the city for Kristina, he knew all he could do was wait for the rogue's next move. It was painfully clear that he wanted Derrick to suffer. And so, the rogue would stage an event where he would have to watch Kristina die, he was certain. His father had promised to keep searching for the others, rally a group of watchers who would ferret out the rogue once and for all. Although his father and mother had only known Kristina from a distance, his parents loved her as if she were one of their own. His mother had always wanted a daughter and grandchildren. It would kill them, too, if something were to befall his wife.

Inching through the emergency-exit stairway door, Derrick saw a figure hunched over in a seated position, arms wrapped around their knees, sitting in front of the entrance to his apartment. His heart skipped a beat, wondering if it could be Kristina, but then he saw a strand of black hair sticking out from the knitted ski cap, standard watcher protocol in the event they needed to shield their faces.

Padding his way along the corridor, he approached as quietly as possible, but her head jerked up off her knees when he was two doors away. "Derrick," she said on a sigh. Vic's eyes were barely visible beneath her swollen eyelids. Crimson ringed her irises as if she'd been crying for days. He'd never seen her cry.

He shook his head, not believing she could have done anything to hurt Kristina, knowing that he could never fall for anyone again. Surely, Victoria loved him enough not to cast him into a lifetime of torture.

"Please, Victoria ..." He plummeted to his knees in sheer agony, remembering her scornful remarks the other day, her utter hatred for what he had done. His stomach twisted, pain seared straight up to his heart at the thought that she could have left Kristina for dead. "Please tell me you didn't hurt her. Just tell me where she is, and I'll do anything you ask. Kristina and I will leave. You'll never see either of us again, I swear." The thought that he'd have to kill his best friend to avenge his wife hurt almost as much as the thought of losing Kristina. He knew he wouldn't be able to live with himself, but hatred surged through his veins. "I love her. Please tell me she's alive."

Confusion shaded Vic's eyes. "What?" she asked, shaking her head. "You think ... you think I'd hurt your wife?"

A wave of relief washed through him as he lifted himself and her off the ground. "Kristina's missing. Why are you here? *Crying?*" Hope flickered like a candle wafting in a draft, but it just didn't make sense that she'd come here. If Victoria hadn't heard that his wife was missing, why would she have come here?

"I wanted to confront you, Derrick. Find out if your relationship was authentic." Victoria raised her head, releasing a breathy groan, seemingly restraining a cry. "But I guess you just answered my question."

Grateful that Kristina might still be alive, he ran his hands over his head, pressing his temples. But now he needed to find the next suspect in his mind.

"Where's Jonas?" he demanded. "Have you heard from him or Ry, or Michael? Someone kidnapped Kristina, and it has to be one of them."

"You'd accuse your own brother ..." She pulled her hand to her mouth, chewing on a fingernail. "You think your brother, or someone in the family could do such a thing?" She closed her eyes in exasperation, shaking her head again. "Why would they kidnap her?"

Derrick grabbed her shoulders, resisting the urge to shake her until she understood. "I told everyone he threatened her, but no one seems to be taking this seriously. I don't know why, dammit. I don't know anything. All I know is he murdered another innocent man, and Kristina is missing." He choked out a breath. "Now, where's Jonas?"

Vic knocked his hands away and stepped out of his reach. "Last time I saw him was eleven this morning. We ate breakfast together."

"*Breakfast*, at eleven a.m.? That doesn't sound like you."

Her eyes cast downward. "We spent the night together."

Odd that that tidbit hadn't even fazed him, and she'd clearly thought it would. Or maybe she was just embarrassed. "And you haven't seen him since?"

She wagged her head in a jerky action. "No."

"Where have you been all day?"

She shrugged. "Just thinking. I've been smacked upside the head with a lot of stuff in the last few days, and I'm not sure —" She released a long sigh. "It doesn't matter. You've got more important things to concern yourself with."

Derrick released a groan. "I do care, Victoria, but I don't have any time to think of anything but finding Kristina at the moment." The problem was he didn't know where to start. He had hoped that the rogue would call or show, make demands. Obviously he wanted something, but for the life of him, he couldn't imagine what. Even if it was one of the three men, what could they gain? What had he ever done to them? And then it occurred to him. Maybe his position? They wanted to be overseer? Well, they could have it. He'd leave. He didn't even care about the position. It wasn't as if he'd ran for office. The council chose the overseer.

Derrick unlocked the door and held it open for Vic, but she didn't step inside.

Vic shook her head. "I have to go, Derrick."

He took a step toward her, resting his hand on her shoulder, gentler than he'd been before. She'd been his best friend since they could walk. He'd confided in her more than he had Michael. "You know I never meant to hurt you, right?"

She nodded. "We both knew. We've always been honest about our relationship. But now, I have to go after someone before I lose him."

"I need your help, Vic," he said. She was dressed in black jeans, long-sleeved shirt, and a heavy leather jacket over her arm. Obviously, she'd planned to be on watch tonight for him — for all of them. But he knew it must kill her to know she was protecting his wife. Vic was an excellent fighter, and they'd sparred many times. If he had to go up against the rogue, he'd want Vic even before Michael. She may not be as strong, but she was fast, and she knew all his moves, since the same person had trained them. Actually, he'd trained all of them.

"Name it. Tell me what to do, and I'll do it. But until then, I have to find him."

"Who?"

She turned away, ignoring him. "Call me when you know what you're going to do." She pushed open the door to the stairwell and walked out, letting the door slam behind her. Like him, she couldn't be bothered with the elevator.

Derrick stood motionless for a second, confused, wondering if Victoria had really given up her supposed claim on him that easily. He couldn't think about it. He picked up the phone and dialed Michael again. He'd been trying to reach him all day.

Chapter Thirty-Nine

Kris woke up with a stabbing pain shooting through her skull, reminiscent of the worst hangover she'd ever had. It was dark, so dark, but then again, she could feel a rough material against her face, so maybe it was daytime.

She had no idea how long she'd been out. Her body was in a fetal position atop a scratchy blanket, but the cold dampness seeped through to her bones. Her arms ached from the unnatural position behind her back, and the restraints cut into her wrists. Her fingers tingled from the lack of blood flow.

She stretched her top leg out and pushed up with her bottom leg until she was in a seated position with one leg underneath her. She repositioned her body so that she was on her knees, and then propping one leg up and then the other, she managed to get herself to an upright position. The ties were so tight on her wrists that she couldn't pull her arms down the back of her legs as she'd done when she was a child with play handcuffs.

She took tiny steps forward, not certain where she was. In just a few strides, she bumped into a wall. Moving her head back and forth carefully against the solid wall, she realized in fact, that there was a shroud over her head. A rough burlap material scratched against her face.

Now would be a good time to scream, she thought, but whatever was over her mouth prevented her from getting any volume. She wiggled her lips, attempting to get the sticky substance free.

As she worked at moving her mouth up and down and sideways, she skirted the room cautiously, measuring the width and length, tripping over a bucket of some sort every few steps. The stench of oil, grease, and bleach assaulted her nostrils, and she struggled to scratch her nose against the hard cold surface of the wall. The tiny room was only about three by six feet, she guessed. A storage unit, or a maintenance closet, maybe? It was cold, but once she was off the concrete floor, her body felt better, since she still wore her jacket from the hike and zip line trip. But her face was freezing — Derrick! The memory crashed into her consciousness.

The hike, the zip line. She hadn't dreamed up Derrick. She wasn't in a riverbed. The rogue had kidnapped her. *Was Derrick okay?* Derrick had said that the rogue would kill her first to hurt him, so he was probably okay if she was still alive. But that also meant the rogue had something ruthless in store for her.

She chewed furiously at the tape. If she could get free ... if Derrick was anywhere nearby, he'd hear her. Kris turned to the sound of wood scraping across the floor.

"Ahh ... we're awake," the rogue whispered in a guttural sneer. The same voice she'd heard on the platform for a brief second after the rag had been placed over her face. "Now, here's what's going to happen, Kristina." The voice was so low it was hard to recognize. She wasn't sure if maybe it was because the rogue knew Kris would be able to identify the voice or if Derrick was close enough to hear. "Listen very carefully because I don't like to repeat myself."

Kris nodded, since she couldn't speak or scream anyway with the tape over her mouth.

"I'm going to take the hood and tape off, but if you as much as utter a word, I'll kill Derrick. Do you understand?"

She nodded again.

"I don't want to kill Derrick. I just want him to go away and you are the key. Derrick will do anything for you."

The rogue turned her, and the sound of a switchblade snapping open caused her to jump. But then she heard the knife break through the tie around her neck, and felt the sack release from over her head. She still couldn't see, so obviously she had a blindfold over her eyes as well. A few seconds later, the tape she'd been gnawing on was ripped from her face, leaving a stinging sensation behind.

"Walk forward," the rogue commanded, and Kris obeyed, as if she had any choice in the matter. "Remember, not a peep."

Kris gulped, wondering if Derrick was nearby, wanting to scream with all her might, but if she caused his death knowingly, she could never live with herself. A few seconds later, her hands were free, but then the rogue pulled them up over her head, cinching them together with another zip tie. Well, at least that was something, she reasoned. At least her arms didn't feel as if they would snap behind her back. Now they just ached from the position they'd been in for God knows how long.

"Move." The rogue's hand nudged her forward. "Careful, though, not too fast. I don't want you to fall."

The concrete disappeared below Kris, and she gasped at the pain now in her wrists and shoulders, as all her weight suspended from just the tie around her wrists. Her legs dangled below her, scrambling to find purchase with anything to release the pain of the plastic digging into her skin.

"Lift your right leg. There's a ledge just above your foot," the rogue commanded.

Kris did as instructed, feeling the rope remain taut as she inched herself onto the ledge. Only the tips of her toes connected, even as she pushed her foot directly against the wall.

"Now, feel to the right with your hands as I direct you," the whispered words continued, tugging the rope to her right until her hand hit another ledge. "You better do it quickly before I cut the rope."

Kris grappled for the ledge, finding the cold niche as it scraped the tips of her fingers.

"I'm just kidding." A cackle came from above her. "I'm not cutting the rope yet. Now, I need you to count to one hundred and then scream for Derrick."

"But you said ... "

"And I meant it, and you've done well. But now if you don't call for him, I'll just have to kill him. If you do as you're told, however, you can both leave and live happily ever after. Remember the rules, Kristina. Don't call for him until you count to one hundred, so I can be on my way."

Something didn't make sense. Why would she have to count to one hundred? She was in a no-win situation, she realized. If she didn't call, Derrick would die. If she did call, Derrick would probably die. But ... at least if she called, they both stood a chance. Derrick was the most powerful, but she doubted the rogue wanted a fight. But why one hundred? To be prepared?

With no other choice but to trust that Derrick would save them both, Kris started to count, quickly, hoping she wouldn't fall from the ledge. Her hands were still bound and secured by the rope, but she wouldn't be able to climb the wall. It wasn't like rappelling down, which was easy. She couldn't walk up a wall. Or at least she didn't think she could. She continued to rattle off the numbers as she thought of any solution.

As soon as she hit one hundred, she screamed as loudly as she could, "Derrick!"

Chapter Forty

Michael glanced at his phone as it lit up. He looked at the map and smiled. *Time to go.*

When he'd spotted his vehicle earlier, he put a GPS tracker on it, so he'd know when he was leaving. He'd left messages for everyone to meet him later tonight, so they wouldn't wonder why he was dressed for watching. He'd decided the only way was to make it look like a creatus attack. That way no one would question his decision to take him out. He hated doing it, but he didn't have a choice. It was him or the entire family, and he simply couldn't allow anything to interfere with everything he'd put in place in the last few years. He'd strategically placed creatus everywhere to protect them if the time came. And he wasn't about to let one person within his reach ruin everything.

"Rebecca, I hate to drink and run, but something just came up. We'll do this again soon." He bounded up from his chair, grabbed his leather jacket off the backrest, and headed for the door. "By the way, if Victoria, Jonas, or Ry show up, tell them I'll call them in a little bit."

"But you just got here," she called after him.

He turned and ambled back to her, leaning over the chair and planting a kiss on her lips. A test. She tilted her head back, accepting him. He pulled himself upright after a moment and peered down at her, enjoying the starry-eyed gaze she shot him. Yep, he still had it, even with a creatus woman, and they weren't as easy to seduce as humans were. "I'll see you later, okay?"

She didn't question him again, so he walked off.

Nope. She wasn't his type. The kiss had confirmed that, but it'd still been fun to see her melt beneath his lips.

He waited for him to show, and when he did, he came up behind him, surprising him.

***

Vic heard the scream and ran. When she saw him, she bounded up behind him, latching her arm beneath his neck, attempting to cut off blood flow to his brain. It was hard to gain purchase with her leather jacket on, and within seconds, he'd freed himself.

She heard a grunt behind her, but refused to take her eyes off her target, knowing he could kill her easily. She flipped around and landed a roundhouse kick to his head and watched as he dropped to the ground. Before he could stand up, she landed another. This time, he grabbed her leg, dropping her to the ground.

All the creatus had been trained by the same person, so they all had learned the same moves, which was good — and bad. She knew what to expect, but so did he. The only difference was that she was faster and lither, even if he was stronger.

She'd trained hard for this moment, though. She'd been wrestling creatus men for years, and she had flexibility on her side. Rarely could they pin her. She was back on her feet faster than he could grab her. He reached for her, but she ducked and landed a solid punch to his kidneys, sending him to his knees.

And then she heard the *crack*.

***

Derrick heard the scream as clearly as if she'd been in his apartment. *From the roof?* Kristina was on his roof? Unmistakably it was a set-up, he knew, but he had to go.

He charged out of his apartment and darted toward the stairwell. He was on the rooftop of his condominium within seconds, her voice clearer as she called his name. Derrick ran toward her voice, but only saw a thin rope tied to one of the roof vents. "Kristina!"

"Derrick," her voice rang out in relief. "He's waiting, Derrick! It's a trap, I'm sure."

He peered over the side and she gazed up at him, even though she was blindfolded and couldn't see him. *Thank God she was* — An arm latched around his neck, pulling him backward. Derrick tore at the leather jacket. The attacker had trouble gaining purchase as Derrick pulled his chin down in response to the threat. Derrick freed himself and prepared for battle with the rogue, who was dressed as a watcher, of course, full black leather and ski mask.

Kristina grunted as if trying to come up, but he couldn't take his eyes off the threat. He'd have to pray that the tiny rope and ledge held.

The rogue flipped around and landed a roundhouse kick to his head and Derrick dropped to the ground. Before he could stand up, he landed another. The rogue was stronger than any other creatus he'd fought, and he was fast. The next time the rogue kicked, he grabbed his leg, dropping him to the ground. But in a flash, he was back on his feet again.

Derrick swung, but he ducked, landing a solid punch to his kidneys, sending him to his knees. And then he heard the *crack* of concrete.

"Derrick!" Kristina cried.

Derrick came back up, grabbing the rogue and pulling his arms behind his back. He threw him to the concrete, pinning him with his arms strapped behind him. Derrick glanced to the rope holding Kristina. It was unraveling. He watched as individual strands popped.

"Kristina?" he called to her. "Are you still on the ledge?"

"No ..." she cried. "The one below my feet is gone, but I think I can hold onto the ledge above me."

"I already whittled them away, Derrick," the rogue growled in a raspy, unrecognizable voice. "The ledge will give way the moment the rope breaks."

Derrick slammed the rogue's head against the concrete, hoping it would knock him out, and ran toward the sound of the snapping rope. He launched, but the rope slipped out of his reach. He darted to the edge of the rooftop, thankful to see Kristina holding onto the ledge, but he could see the hairline cracks and knew it'd only be a couple of seconds before the ledge gave way. He glanced over his shoulder at the rogue, who still remained unconscious on the concrete, but would probably be up in a second.

As he tried to decide whether to go back and immobilize him, he heard the *crack*. It was too late; he had to make a choice. Save Kristina or secure the rogue.

***

Vic turned to the sound of the *crack*. The man she'd protected had a gun in his hand and had shot the rogue she'd been fighting.

"Victoria," the rogue called behind her. *No, not the rogue,* she realized. "Michael?" That's why he hadn't fought back, only tried to stop her advances. She darted to his side, falling to her knees beside him. "I don't understand. You're the rogue?"

Blood seeped out of his mouth. And she realized the man had shot him. "No ... for you. Everything for you. I love you ..." he gurgled out. "The agent ... get the brief ... case." Michael collapsed on the ground.

Vic pulled off her jacket and pressed it to his side, layering his hand over the top to stop the blood. She stood and launched herself at the human she'd been trying to protect. He was still on the ground. Evidently he'd put up a fight against Michael. She grabbed the briefcase and then hovered over him.

Pulling off her belt, she latched it around the man's wrist several times. "If he dies," she growled in his ear, "I'll kill you myself."

The blond-haired man's eyes were wide, but he didn't look scared; he looked to be in shock.

Vic raced over to Michael and pulled him up, allowing him to rest against her side. She walked back toward the man and dragged him by her belt. She obviously couldn't let him go now that he'd seen her. Derrick would know what to do, but first, she needed to get Michael to the center.

After she threw the agent in the cargo area of her vehicle, latching him to the seatbelt and strapping Michael in the front, she called Lynford on his cell.

He answered immediately. "Derrick and I have been looking for you, Vic. Where are you?"

"Lyn, there's no time to talk. Meet me at the clinic," she panted out. "Michael's been shot."

Lyn hung up the phone without a word. It was the same characteristic she'd admired in Derrick. He thought quickly, no questions asked.

Vic stomped on the gas and headed toward the clinic.

Michael? Why now? Just when she'd thought ... Why had Michael told her to meet him at the pub if he'd planned to confront the agent? *Everything for her*, he'd said.

As soon as she pulled up in front of the clinic, there were several nurses waiting. Lyn had apparently called, notifying them of her arrival. She watched as they pulled Michael out, transferring him to a gurney. She parked the vehicle and then opened the rear hatch, pulling the agent out on the concrete, not concerned whether she injured him.

The man looked up at her again. His eyes and mouth were swollen. A mere human had given Michael a challenge, but she was certain that Michael had never meant to hurt him; he only wanted whatever was in the case.

"What ... are ... you?" the man slurred.

She punched him, knocking him out cold, and then carried him into the rear entry of the clinic.

Chapter Forty-One

Derrick bounded over the side of the building at the same time the ledge gave way. He grabbed Kristina's arm and then attempted to grasp on to anything he could.

He couldn't secure a grip. All he could do was slow their descent as he held onto her with one arm, pulling her against his side, and groping at the wall with the other.

"Hang on to me, Kristina!" he yelled.

She latched her arms around him tightly, freeing his other hand. He clawed at the wall, slowing their fall. Derrick peered below them, making sure they had a clear path before he dropped. Skin had already ripped from his fingers, and he didn't know how much longer he could dig bloody flesh into the building and still maintain his grasp.

At two hundred feet, they were within dropping distance, so he swung her up in his arms and dropped, his body taking the force and allowing his arms to fall further to lessen the jolt on her body. After all, his body was made for this; hers wasn't. He removed the blindfold and realized the impact had still knocked her unconscious.

He heard a man's laugh and glanced up to see the black-clad figure leaning over the wall. The rogue saluted and took off.

Derrick glanced around the alley, praying no one had witnessed his stunt. Thankfully, one thing had gone right. Well, two; his wife was in his arms, which was more important than anything else in his life. But the rogue was gone, and it was clear he wasn't going to give up.

He stood with Kristina, cradling her like a child, and then walked inside the lobby of his building, ignoring the shocked face of the doorman as he strode toward the elevator to the parking deck. He was sure the blood dripping from his fingertips and an unconscious woman in his arms were enough reason to call the police, but as always, he'd come up with a story. He hadn't been prepared, nor did he care at the moment. He just wanted to get Kristina to his vehicle and drive her to the clinic so he could check to make sure she didn't have any internal injuries.

After reclining the front seat and strapping her in, he vaulted over the vehicle to the driver's door. For the first time in his life, he didn't care who saw him; he only cared about his wife.

He hit the *call* button on the steering wheel and clicked *recent calls*. The clinic's nighttime receptionist picked up, rattling off her name.

"Roseanne, it's Derrick. I need you to call my father. Tell him he needs to meet me at the clinic. Let him know I'm bringing Kristina. She may have internal injuries."

"Um ..." She paused, making him want to crawl through the phone, as if she had any right to question him, but he held his tongue, waiting to hear her great excuse. "Um ... Dr. Ashton ... Your father, excuse me, Dr. Ashton is already here ... for your brother."

"What?" he asked, confused, thinking he'd misunderstood. "Why? What happened?" he choked out. Derrick had hurt the rogue, but not that severely, and he wouldn't have been able to get there that quickly, so that was good. His brother was clear of any suspicion.

"Dr. Maher brought him in," Roseanne responded.

"Victoria Maher or her father?" he pressed.

"Dr. Victoria Maher, sir."

Hanging up, Derrick smashed the gas pedal to the floor, weaving through the narrow streets of Boston, ignoring every streetlight. Kristina groaned from the passenger seat, and he realized he needed to take it easy with the potholes. He touched her arm, but kept his eyes on the road. After a few seconds, her hand covered his and he breathed a sigh of relief, glancing down at her. Her eyes were still closed, but she was alert enough to recognize his touch.

"Where do you hurt, Kristina?"

"My ... head," she said in a shaky voice.

"Did you hit it?" He was certain jostling her around while keeping from falling couldn't have helped her.

"Don't ... think ... so," she sputtered, and he wondered if she'd passed out again. "He ... drugged ... pungent, alcohol-like ... thirsty."

Chloroform, Derrick thought. A common person couldn't get it, but anyone associated with the clinic could, simply by showing a hospital ID, as it was still used in lab work.

Derrick pulled into the parking lot and jogged around to the passenger side, pulling Kristina out. He was careful not to bounce her as he carried her through the ER doors and back to the procedure room. It was small, but they had everything the larger hospitals had, if not more. Being a private organization had its benefits. There was no board of directors. If something new came out, Derrick or his father ordered it.

Derrick shouted to Roseanne as he walked Kristina to the back where they housed an MRI. "Tell my father I'm here, please." An MRI was the fastest way to see if there was any internal bleeding. In public hospitals, they screwed around with cheaper tests, but he didn't see any need in wasting time with x-rays or ultrasounds. As he trudged along the corridor, he scanned the rooms for his father or Michael, but saw no one.

After the tests were completed, Derrick went to move Kristina from the platform, but Victoria appeared behind the glass wall, streaks of tears running down her cheeks. Derrick checked on Kristina, who was still out, and then went to the door. He needed to get Kristina IV fluids, as it appeared there were no internal injuries. She was just dehydrated.

As soon as he opened the door, Vic fell into his arms. "Michael's in the O.R. He was shot. I was beating the crap out of him, thinking he was the rogue, and then the agent shot him —"

"Victoria," Derrick cut her off, "slow down. Michael was shot?"

She nodded.

"You were beating him up?"

She nodded again. "I ... I thought he was the rogue," she stammered. "I heard the man yelp, and then I saw Michael, only he was all in black, fighting him. I just assumed ... "

"Agent? Does he have spiky blond hair?"

"Yes."

"Where is he?"

"I have him cuffed to a bed upstairs in the psych ward since there's no one there."

"Is Michael okay?"

She exhaled a deep breath and more tears fell. "I don't know. The man shot him."

"Okay," Derrick said, steeling himself. "Stay with Kristina. The rogue used her as bait to lure me to my roof, but then I had to make a choice to save her or chase him. So he's still out there. He drugged her with chloroform, I think. So she needs IV fluids and something for nausea." He stopped and stared at her, then lowered his voice. "Give her eight hundred milligrams of ibuprofen for her headache. Nothing stronger, okay?"

"You'll go assist with Michael?" She swallowed hard, shaking her head as if embarrassed. "I couldn't. I couldn't pull myself together. Some doctor I am, huh?"

"That's normal, Victoria." He rested his hand against her cheek and then pulled her into his arms to comfort her. "He'll be okay. Dad won't lose him," he said, as much to convince himself as her. He stepped over to Kristina and kissed her on the head. "Please protect her."

"I will, Derrick. I understand. I saw your pain earlier. I don't ever want to see you like that again. Do you hear me? We need you. You're strong. The family can't afford to lose you."

He closed his eyes and released a shaky breath. He didn't feel strong at the moment. He felt as though everything in his life was unravelling. He turned and exited the room, heading toward the O.R.

Derrick scrubbed up and entered the surgery area, but his father had just finished, it appeared.

Lynford turned to Derrick and gave him a quick nod. "He'll be okay." He motioned for Derrick to leave, so Derrick followed. Once outside the O.R., his father turned to him. "We have another patient. God only knows how, but Vic took out both of them. Evidently, Mike had injured the human before Vic showed up, so we need to tend to him. Of course, then I don't know what we'll do with him." His father ran his hands through his black hair that had only a sprinkling of gray, but right now, he looked older than usual. His normally olive skin was pale, and it looked as though someone had sponged a soft purple shade underneath his eyes. "Do you have any idea what's going on? Why Michael would attack a human?"

Derrick chewed on his lip a second and then nodded. "Unfortunately, yes. We think he's a government agent. I called Michael with his tag number the other day because he was following Kristina. Michael must have tracked him down. The man has the video of my dive off the bridge to rescue Kristina, and who knows what else." He paused and whooshed out a deep breath, running his hand over his mouth. "But I'm sure Michael didn't plan to kill him. I'm certain he just wanted the file."

His father dropped his head, seemingly exhausted by the entire situation. "Let's go see what sort of medical attention he needs, and then we'll decide what to do with him."

Derrick shook his head at his father's comment. He had to remember his father was around during two World Wars and several smaller ones. The mindset for that generation was to heal a prisoner of war, not dispose of him. Not that Derrick could ever hurt an innocent person, but if he'd seen Vic and Michael dueling it out after already witnessing his swan dive off the bridge, he'd know that they weren't normal. So they'd definitely have to question the man. But then what? They couldn't keep him prisoner in the psych ward forever. Someone would come looking for him.

Chapter Forty-Two

Michael glanced up from his hospital bed as the door inched open ever so quietly. He forced a smile when he saw Victoria, but inside, his stomach wrenched.

"Hey ... you're awake," she whispered.

"I was hoping I was dead," Michael groaned.

She sat on the edge of his bed, pressing the back of her hand to his forehead, obviously checking if he had a temperature. "Why would you hope that you were dead?" She lifted up the pitcher from the bedside table, poured him a cup of water, and held it out to him. "You need to drink more; your temperature is still hovering above a hundred." She glanced up at the antibiotics in his IV drip. His father must be concerned with the bullet causing an infection.

Michael accepted the Styrofoam cup, grazing her hand with his fingers in the process. It wasn't his stomach wrenching, he realized, it was his heart. "Because I'm pretty sure if the bullet wound doesn't kill me, I'm going to die of embarrassment."

The edges of Victoria's lips turned up and she playfully wiggled her eyebrows at him. She always liked it if she thought she'd beaten him in anything. Only she didn't know that he let her beat him in sports and running, just because it made her happy.

"You mean when everyone finds out I kicked your ass?" she teased.

He choked out a laugh, but then winced at the pain. "No ..." He took a sip of water to gather his thoughts and then narrowed his eyes at her. He couldn't let her think she'd won this match, though. He had to assure her he'd never hurt her purposely. "I wasn't fighting you, Vic, so it doesn't count."

He attempted to reposition himself on the pillow, which had fallen too low when he took a sip of water, but he grimaced in pain again. *What the hell did the bullet do, play pinball inside of me?* he wondered. It felt as if every internal organ hurt.

"Here, let me do that." Victoria moved the pillow so it was directly beneath his head and then propped her hand up against the mattress on the other side of his body and leaned into it, staring at him. "Why are you embarrassed then?"

He pursed his lips and huffed out a breath. "You heard me. You heard what I said when I thought I was dying."

"So?" she said, shrugging. "It didn't mean anything. Of course you love me. We've been best friends since we were toddlers, for heaven's sake."

With every ounce of effort he could muster, Michael reached for her hand. Thankfully, she didn't fight him. "I didn't want to be lying on the ground, gushing blood when I told you, and I certainly don't want to discuss any of this while I'm an invalid on a hospital gurney, but I have to beg one thing of you."

She gave him a gentle nod, but didn't respond.

"Please don't leave with Jonas, Victoria." He squeezed her hand in his and pulled it to his chest. "Give me a chance before you go away." He paused, letting his words sink in, hoping that she understood this wasn't a friend request. "I've waited too long for you —"

"Shh," she hushed him, placing their linked hands against his lips. "I'm not going anywhere, Michael. And I'm definitely not going anywhere with Jonas. He and I would never work. He's too much of a hothead. One hothead in a relationship is enough, don't you think?"

Michael forced a smile. "You're not a hothead. You're opinionated and tough; there's a difference."

Vic pulled back her hand and folded her arms over her chest. "Yes, I am, but that's the difference. You know me, and we're comfortable together."

He pressed his lips in a straight line, holding back his words. He didn't want to be *comfortable* with her. He was so far past wanting to be comfortable with Victoria, his arms ached to pull her against him right here on the tiny hospital bed.

Out of nowhere, the realization that he'd known her his entire life and had never once been able to feel her lips on his drove him mad. He'd never longed for anything this much in his life. But, as long as she wasn't going anywhere, they could have this conversation later. Preferably over dinner ... with candlelight, red wine, and a bubbling Jacuzzi in the background.

All these years he'd just been fulfilling his needs elsewhere, waiting for her to notice, when he should have just demanded her attention.

"When can I get out of here?" he blurted out.

Vic patted his hand in a very platonic way, causing his heart to wrench again. "That's up to Dr. Ashton. I'm not your doctor."

He smiled, thinking that could be fun. He pulled her closer, but she hovered over top of him, moving both her hands beside his head to support her upper body. "Will you go out with me then, as soon as they let me go? Alone. Just the two of us."

"Sure, Michael," she agreed offhandedly. "But right now, why don't you concentrate on getting better? I'm not going anywhere at the moment."

"That doesn't sound too promising. You're going to give me one pity date to let me know you're taking off with Jonas?"

She leaned lower and pressed her lips to his forehead. "I won't go anywhere until we talk. That's all I can promise right now."

Well, that was something anyway, he thought, feeling his body drift off.

Chapter Forty-Three

Reece opened his eyes and glanced around at what looked like a hospital room. Unlike most rooms, though, it was empty. Other than the bed he was lying on, there was only one chair.

The black vinyl chair held a woman. The same stunning woman who had kicked the hell out of the man who'd kicked the hell out of him. He wasn't quite sure how he felt about that, but she was breathtakingly beautiful.

Of course that angel with long onyx hair had then kicked the crap out of him. One second he'd been so taken with her beauty that he was asking *what* she was, certain she had to be a goddess or an angel, and then the last thing he'd seen was her fist coming down against his face.

She was just staring out the window, so he watched her instead of letting her know he was awake. Her hair fell over the back of the chair and it took every ounce of strength he had not to reach out and touch it. It looked like black silk.

Her features were strong, but attractive. She was tall, close to six feet, he remembered. And her eyes ... they were a dark sable, the richest and deepest eyes he'd ever seen. Her skin was smooth with a light olive complexion. To say the woman was exotic-looking would be an understatement; she was the most unique woman he'd ever laid eyes on.

As she'd glared down at him in the alley, assuring him she'd kill him if the other man died, all he could do was gaze into the depths of her lustrously dark eyes. Never had any woman caught his attention completely, and yet, he wondered if she was actually a woman or some type of cyborg.

In his thirty years in the military and police, he'd never seen a woman fight like she had. And he'd seen some bad mammas in the military and when he'd work UC in Miami and South America.

He attempted to remain quiet as he cleared his dry throat, but she whipped her head toward him and glared at him, those mysterious eyes gazing into his.

"Finally!" she spouted. "I wondered if you were ever going to wake up."

Reece couldn't help but smile at her venomous attitude. "Is that man okay?" he asked, knowing that was why she'd been so upset with him. But he'd thought that the man was going to hurt her. He saw the man that had fought him for his briefcase lift his hand to her, so he assumed he had a knife or a gun.

She huffed out a breath. "That's none of your business. Whom do you work for?"

"That's none of your business," he retorted, smiling at her perfect grammar. Who said *whom* anymore? "*Whom* do you work for?"

She sighed, exasperated. "Well, we obviously aren't going to get anywhere."

He tried to sit up, but she held up her hand. Beautiful, long fingers attached to deadly hands. "Move, and I'll kill you right here. I unlatched you from the bed only because my boss told me to. But I'll lock you right back up."

Reece grinned at her, watching as it only caused her scowl to crease her lovely skin even more. "I need to go to the bathroom. So unless you're willing to help me with that or are willing to clean up a mess, I'd suggest you let me up, Ms ... "

The woman rolled her eyes, stepping back and leaning against the only exit. She motioned her hand as though it were okay for him to proceed to the only other door in the room, which must be the bathroom.

Reece moved his legs to the side of the bed closest to the exit, not the bathroom, and she crossed her arms defiantly. "You sure you want to take me on, Reece?" she sneered.

He smiled again, standing up, unable to resist admiring her boldness. "I managed okay with your friend."

She raised one eyebrow. "When I found you, you were on the ground."

Reece stopped within a few feet of the amazon-looking woman. He'd been right; she was just about five inches shorter than his six-four. He glanced at her throat, making sure she didn't have an Adam's apple. That'd be embarrassing, considering the way she was waking up long-dormant parts of his body. He decided he'd better take a bathroom break before challenging her.

He edged alongside the bed, pulling the sheer cotton robe around his body. Would they ever stop using these stupid things that left your backside hanging out for the world to view? But then again, maybe it would distract her.

It wasn't as if he had a bad build either. The man who attacked him on the street was a couple inches taller and had a larger build than he did. But Reece had spent years doing cross fit, which not only gave him a muscular build, he was fast and nimble and could outrun anyone in the military academy or on the street. When he was a cop in

Miami, he was the first officer other cops wanted for back-up. This woman was serious, though. Just her stance told Reece she was ready for a fight, so he'd have to wait until her guard was down. He kept his distance as he turned toward the bathroom door.

"Smart move," she said mockingly.

Reece relieved himself, taking extra time to formulate a plan. He'd already noticed that the window was solid and high off the ground. Even if he threw a chair through it, he wouldn't want to climb down. He searched the bathroom for a weapon, and found nothing usable. Shampoo was his only option, but how could he get it in her eyes? He decided to reserve that feeble option for later. Right now, the chair was his best weapon.

After a few minutes, he opened the door to see her in the same position. He stepped to the opposite side of the bed this time, leaning as if he planned to get back onto the mattress.

He didn't.

Instead, he snatched up the chair and hurled it at the woman, surging toward her immediately.

She deflected the chair with one hand and then grabbed him by the shoulders as he lunged, throwing him on the twin-size mattress as if he weighed no more than a sack of flour.

His breath whooshed out of him as he hit the bed perfectly. Even her aim was spot-on.

"Okay, then." She stepped toward the bed, grabbing his wrist and latching him to the railing. "I'll be sure to let your doctor know that you can't be trusted."

The door opened, and an older man of about fifty stepped inside, eyes darting from him to the woman. "What's going on, Vic?"

Vic, Reece repeated to himself. Probably *Victoria*, but she was too tough to go by that lovely name.

"I warned him," she growled, crossing her arms over her chest, which only accentuated how well built she was — everywhere.

The man shook his head and stepped toward the bed. "I'm very sorry we have to keep you here like this, but there's no sense fighting, Mr. Buckley. You're in a completely sealed off ward. Even if you got out of the room, every door is secured, and as you can see, you won't be able to overpower my staff."

"What are you people?"

The doctor sighed. "Just a peaceful group you won't leave alone." With that, the man turned and left him with Vic.

Reece looked back up at the woman and flashed his best smile, the one the women always loved, knowing it would tick her off. "So, Victoria, since we're going to be here a while, do you play cards?"

She narrowed her eyes and moved her head slowly from side to side. "Don't ever call me Victoria again." She opened the door, following the doctor out, and slammed it behind her.

Chapter Forty-Four

*U*gh! Men! Vic grumbled inwardly. She couldn't complain aloud, of course, because even the creatus on the first floor could hear her. They were all so damned infuriating. And arrogant. And pompous. And ... *Ugh!* She needed to go away to some deserted island where she wouldn't have to ever see another man in her life — creatus or human.

What really enraged her was that she was attracted to that stupid weakling of a human. *What was wrong with her?* First Jonas, then Michael, and now Reece Buckley. Was her biological clock ticking? In human years, she'd only be about twenty-three. Much too young to be thinking about settling down, and yet, she craved it with a passion. Although she hadn't really been interested in Jonas, even though he'd begged her to go away with him. He'd wanted to start a new family, he'd said. With like-minded creatus. She had just wanted to make Derrick jealous, but that had backfired, and she'd ended up spending the night with Jonas. No wonder she couldn't fall. She'd have to make up her mind whom she wanted before she could fall.

Stupid human, she thought again. She'd planned to head directly to Michael's room after someone swapped watch with her, and tell him she understood what he was implying and that she was open to a relationship with him.

But that stupid human had gazed at her with such wonder in his eyes. It had been what she'd wanted to see, what she thought she could force with Jonas. What she'd wanted from Derrick all these years. Reece didn't even know her, but he had regarded her as if she were a prize to behold, as if he'd wanted her.

So she threw him across the room. Served him right.

Secretly, she had hoped he'd try to escape. She'd been looking forward to putting him in his place, and still, he had ogled her as if there were no other woman in the world.

Maybe he was into whips and chains. The thought repulsed her. Though she'd thrown him across the room, she'd much rather hold a man than fight him.

Vic stood in the middle of the corridor, battling with her feelings, wondering how she'd ever get her life in order if her hormones kept raging as if she were in high school.

At the last second, she turned in the opposite direction of Michael's room. As Michael had suggested, she'd wait until he was healed and back home, and then they could go out as a couple and attempt to make a relationship.

In the meantime, she'd stay as far away from Reece Buckley as she could. Unfortunately, since she hadn't been wearing her ski mask, he had seen her face, so now the responsibility of silencing the human would fall into her hands.

Chapter Forty-Five

Kris felt her mother's warm hand check her head for fever. She'd always loved when she'd come into the room in the middle of the night when she was sick and just check on her.

Even if Kris wasn't sleeping, sometimes she'd pretend to be asleep so she could just enjoy her hands as they caressed her head and hair. Though on occasion, she'd open her eyes and her mother would question why she was still awake, and then she would sing to her until she fell back asleep.

The knife flashed in front of Kris again, then everything in the room turned blood red, and she remembered that her mother was dead. The rogue had killed her mother. No ... the rogue had killed *her*, not her mother. She had stood on the tiny ledge, listening as Derrick and the rogue had fought, and then she'd heard the *crack* of the ledge below her feet and seconds later had felt the shelf beneath her fingertips bend as she'd tried to grab onto the wall. She'd clawed nothing but air as she fell.

"Derrick!" she screamed.

"It's okay, Kristina. You're safe." A woman's voice.

Kris tried to open her eyes, but they were heavy, and an annoying beep filled her head, which throbbed. That voice. She recognized that voice. Victoria? Was she the rogue? No. The rogue had a male voice, she remembered.

"Where's Derrick?" she tried to push out, but she wasn't sure if she'd spoken audibly. *Had the rogue killed him*? No ... Derrick had told her to hang on to him, and then she'd passed out again.

"I just rang for him when I heard you waking up," the woman said. "But I'm sure he's running after he heard you scream."

Kris attempted to turn her head to the voice, but every muscle in her body ached. "Vic?" she tried.

"No, sweetheart. It's Sabrina." The woman touched her face again, and Kris forced her eyes open, knowing she was safe. "Don't cry," her mother-in-law said, kissing her forehead. "Derrick will be here in a moment. You're safe, honey."

Kris hadn't realized that a tear had escaped. She wasn't sad, however; she was happy. Her mother-in-law was here, and she'd said that Derrick would be here soon, and that was all that mattered. Her body felt so sore though, and she was thirsty. She licked her lips, attempting to get moisture.

"Here, sweetheart." Sabrina held up a spoon of ice chips for her, and Kris accepted gratefully. They tasted so good. Kris opened her mouth and Sabrina offered her another.

"Kristina," Derrick said on an exhale, appearing in her line of sight. "Thank God."

Kris attempted to smile, but even that hurt. Why did her body hurt so much? "What ... happened?"

Derrick ran his hands through her hair and kissed her forehead. "Honestly, woman. You've been through more stuff than any person I know, and still, you greet me with a smile. We'll talk later. You're okay, and that's all that matters. Just extremely dehydrated, and your body took quite a shock. Humans aren't meant to drop thirty stories."

"No ... I guess we're not." She closed her eyes, just wanting to sleep, but she didn't want Derrick to leave either. "Please don't leave me."

A soft chuckle escaped her husband's throat. "Baby, I will never leave you. It's you who needs to promise that."

She released a labored breath. "I'll never leave you, Derrick." And the world faded to black again, but this time she knew everything would be okay.

Epilogue

He bolted down the stairs, watching that Derrick didn't come through the building after him. But he was certain that Derrick had been too preoccupied with Kristina and had completely lost focus on him. Maybe he'd just go to another family. He didn't need New England to make his plan work. He'd find another family who was tired of living the way they had for centuries. Together they would build an army and take on Derrick's family. And when they were gone, they'd have control.

The familiar truck pulled to a stop in front of him. The window lowered and the driver stared out at him, as if he knew. "Hop in."

The rogue — as he'd become quite comfortable thinking of himself — hopped in the cab. He turned to the driver. "You knew?"

"Yep. I've always known."

He nodded and then smiled. "Where to?"

"You're the boss, brother. Just say the word."

"What about Mom? Won't she be upset?"

"Who do you think told me to call you? We'll pick her up on the way. After what Dad did, she hates humans more than you and I put together."

He dropped his head, not sure how he felt about dragging his mother and brother into his plan. Of course, he had said *start a new family*. Well, they were family. "Okay, Ry," Jonas said. "Let's go get Mom and decide what we need to do next."

Ry squealed out of the parking lot and headed north. From there, who knew? He'd have to come back to Boston, of course. The one thing he wouldn't leave behind was Victoria. She'd be his, one way or another. He'd make certain of it. As soon as they were settled, he'd come back for her. Hopefully, she'd come willingly, but if not, he'd take her anyway.

And then, he'd deal with the Ashtons and anyone who stood with them. Creatus were meant to rule this world, and he'd make certain his kind did just that, once and for all.

And now, turn the page for a sneak peek at *Creatus Rogue*, the next book in the Creatus series, or hop on over to my website, www.CarmenDeSousaBooks.com.

Sneak Peek

Creatus Rogue

Ancient myths, superheroes, vampires ...

Forget everything you've heard.

Chapter One

You want me to do what?" Vic threw up her hands, turning her back on the man she'd once loved. If she were being honest, still loved. She peeked over her shoulder, hoping he'd admit that he was joking.

Derrick said nothing, just waited, as he always did, calm, cool, and collected. Not one strand of his silky black hair was out of place, even though she knew he'd been at the hospital for more than twelve hours already.

As she stared out his office window that overlooked Boston Harbor, she tried to comprehend how he could ask her to do such a thing. Afternoon clouds had rolled in, seeming to match her dismal mood, and even though it'd be another hour before sunset, she could tell by the lack of boats on the waterway that the temperature had already started to drop.

Turning away from the window, she walked back to Derrick's desk and plopped down in the chair. How dare he suggest such a thing? Just because he didn't want her didn't mean he got to choose her destiny. "You're kidding, right? I said I was sorry. I told you I wouldn't bother you or Kristina."

A burst of air popped out of Derrick's mouth as if she'd said or done something funny. There was nothing humorous about this situation.

"Vic ..." He sighed. "We don't have a choice."

"What does Mike have to say about this?" she asked. "I bet your brother wouldn't agree."

"Of course he wouldn't agree, but when has Michael ever agreed with me? He'd be happy to take care of this issue. The last thing he wants is for you to be anywhere near Reece Buckley."

"And yet, you want me to *fall* for him, as if that's even possible."

"It's possible. You seem to forget that my mother and my wife are human. My mother reciprocated when my father fell, and Kristina fell for me. It's clear we have more in common with humans than we thought."

Vic jumped up from her seat again. The idea of Derrick falling for a human wasn't something she liked to think about. All the nights they'd spent in each other's arms, all the deep discussions they'd had, and they'd never fallen for each other. If it couldn't happen with Derrick, then it certainly wasn't going to happen with a human.

"He's human. How could I fall for a man who's weaker than I am, a man who wouldn't be able to protect me if the need arose?"

Derrick laughed full and deep this time. "As if you need protecting. You beat the crap out of my brother and then went and took out Reece."

"Yeah, well. Michael wasn't fighting back; he only defended himself, and Reece is human, so he doesn't count."

Derrick got up from behind his desk and crossed the room to stand in front of her. Her body heated up about ten degrees as he got closer.

Even though she knew they were over, that after he'd fallen for a woman he'd never fall for another one again, she still found it hard to move on with her life.

She didn't wish any danger to befall Kristina, but she couldn't help but wonder what would occur if something did. If their histories were wrong about humans being able to fall for creatus, then maybe a creatus could fall more than once in a lifetime.

Kristina was still in danger. And she was human. It wouldn't take much for her to die.

The killing spree had stopped, at least in Boston. Nothing in the last few days resembled the previous murders anyway. But she was sure the rogue hadn't given up that easily.

The rogue — she couldn't bring herself to believe that Jonas was capable of all the things he'd been accused of, so she'd continued to refer to the culprit as the rogue. She'd known Jonas almost her entire life. She'd even thought that maybe he was the *One* at one point. They certainly had made a good go at it. The night she'd spent with him had been powerful. Of course, she'd been trying to fall, trying to get Derrick out of her head.

Derrick rested his hand on her shoulder. Even through her clothes, his touch felt as if it would burn her skin. "He saw you, Vic. He saw Michael. And then you threw him across the room, again reinforcing your abilities." Derrick shook his head. "Why did you do that? We might have been able to talk him out of believing that we're different."

"Why did I —" She huffed out a breath. "You started this, Derrick. The reason Reece even began this investigation was because you felt compelled to save a *human*. Michael had been trying to clean up your mess. We all were." She stepped out from under his hand and walked back to the window, wishing she were anywhere but here.

A few months ago, she never would have believed that Derrick would demand she fall in love with another man — a *human* man. "I can't believe you want me to fall for a mere human."

"That mere human put up a fight against Michael. Michael is one of the strongest creatus on the planet. We both are. No one denies that. No one understands why being half-human makes Michael and me stronger than the average creatus, but we are. So how do you explain that a mere human put up a fight?"

Vic turned to look at Derrick and shrugged. She really didn't care. No way was she going to get romantic with a human. No matter how good he looked. No matter what he did to her insides every time she stepped within ten feet of him. She hated humans, and she was starting to hate half-humans like Derrick, Michael, and Jonas too. For that matter, she was starting to hate men in general — all species.

"Mike probably wasn't trying to hurt him," she said. "He just wanted the evidence in Reece's briefcase. Again, evidence you provided the government of our existence. For four thousand years we've managed to stay hidden, but you go and do a swan dive off the Tobin Bridge and bring some division of the National Security Council down on us."

Derrick casually leaned back against his desk. "My saving Kristina isn't what made the Feds aware of us. They've been tracking supernatural events since 1947. You can blame that on our parents and grandparents for trying to be superheroes and save the world."

She laughed without humor. "Yeah, well ... You're still at fault more than I am. Why don't you see if you can get him to fall for you?" She raised an eyebrow at him, challenging him in her juvenile wordplay. She couldn't help it; that's how she felt, and it felt good to release some of her pent-up anger. "Or, you kill him. You're the boss." She plopped down in the chair again and crossed her arms. No way was she going to come on to Reece Buckley. If Derrick wanted him dead, he could handle it. She didn't care about a stupid human.

"Is that what you want, Victoria? You want me to approve the assassination of an innocent human?" Derrick asked.

Unable to keep up her charade, she sighed and dropped her head into her hands. "No."

Derrick sat down beside her. "Vic, Michael would take him out without a second thought. I love my brother, but even though we have a human mother, he treats humans as if they are a subspecies. As though their lives mean nothing. And some of Reece's comments haven't helped the matter. I know my brother can be cold-hearted, but as you said, he hadn't hurt him in that alley. Now all of a sudden he's willing to kill him."

Vic whipped her gaze to him. "What do you mean? What comments?"

"Reece keeps asking about you. Every time Michael or I take a security watch, he asks questions about you."

"Me? What types of questions?"

Derrick sighed again. "Victoria, honestly, are you trying to tell me you don't see the man is enamored with you?"

She shook her head, even though she had noticed. Never had a man gazed at her the way Reece had. It didn't matter. She didn't want anything to do with him. Him or any man for that matter, human or creatus.

"I asked him," Derrick continued, "When I realized we couldn't change his mind on what he saw, what he believes we are, I asked him why he didn't fight you." Derrick smiled. "You know what he said?"

Vic gulped, shaking her head again, unable to find her voice for some reason. She didn't want to know what he said.

"He said you were the most beautiful woman he'd ever seen. He admitted that he threw a chair in your direction, but he knew he wouldn't hit you. And there was no way he could ever hit a goddess."

Vic snorted. "I bet you rolled with laughter at that comment, huh, Derrick?"

"Victoria, why do you do that to yourself? You know my falling for Kristina had nothing to do with you. You know you are one of the best-looking women on this planet. Reece even made a comment that you look like a modern-day Wonder Woman."

"What the hell? Are you guys best friends now?" she asked.

Derrick shrugged. "He's a nice guy. What else is there to do when I have to take four hours out of my day to sit with him? We play cards and talk."

"I just don't understand why we can't leave him handcuffed to the bed," she said.

"Because it's inhumane, and even if we aren't human, we are not mindless cold-blooded beings, as some would believe."

"We have him locked up in the psych ward. The lock was probably broken when he escaped the first time."

"The lock wasn't broken, and Michael admitted that Reece put up a decent fight. Something he hadn't been prepared for. If being half-human makes Michael and me twice as strong as most creatus, imagine what having any creatus blood, even hundreds of years ago, would mean to humans."

Vic narrowed her eyes. "What are you saying, Derrick?"

"I think there's a reason some humans are ridiculously stronger than other humans. Why some can dead lift more weight than other humans, why some are Olympians. I believe there were more interspecies relationships — or, would interracial be a better word? — than we knew of in the past. I'm pretty sure Reece Buckley has creatus blood running through his veins."

Thank you for reading this sneak peek of *Creatus Rogue*.

Visit my website, www.CarmenDeSousaBooks.com to find links to the Creatus series.

Before You Go ...

I hope you enjoyed the start of the Creatus Series. *Creatus Rogue* and *Creatus Eidolon* are already available, and *Creatus Animus* is on the way. If you purchase the boxed set next, please know that I will update it to reflect any new books in the series, so you never have to worry about buying it too early. Simply stop by my website, CarmenDeSousaBooks.com, and click on "NEWS" on the top right-hand corner of the page to receive notifications of the new release, promotions, and giveaways.

If you enjoyed reading *Creatus*, please check out my other books while you wait for the next installment. Although all of my stories have a common thread — romance, mystery, and suspense — not all my stories have supernatural elements. If you haven't read any of the books in my Southern Romantic-Suspense collection, all of the novels are stand-alone stories — NO CLIFFHANGERS — but a couple of them should be read before the follow-up novels, so as not to run into spoilers. You can read them in any order, as long as you read Charlotte 1 before Charlotte 2 and Nantahala 1 before Nantahala 2.

The Lucky In Love collection will be a series of women's fiction / chick lit books. *Unlucky In Love* is the start of the series and is FREE where allowed. While there isn't a cliffhanger, it is only part one of Jana's Story. *Some Lucky Woman* includes all three-parts of Jana's story, no cliffhanger! After that there are several novels in the works. All stand-alone stories featuring characters from the first two books.

If you'd like some more supernatural, this time with a ghostly edge, please check out my two short story mysteries, which are free through most retailers, and then the follow-up novel.

The Watermen Series
A Solstice with Jacky Waterman

You can find all my books on my website:
www.CarmenDeSousaBooks.com

If you enjoyed this book, please leave a review. It doesn't have to be fancy, just a few words to let other readers know if they should download it too. It means so much to an author to hear what readers loved — even didn't love — about a book. It's how we grow and learn what you want to read next time ... and in the case of a series, which characters you want to see more of in the next books or which ones we should knock off. :)

Thank you again!

Carmen

Acknowledgements

My journey as a writer has been a long one. Although my first book only took two years to write and publish, the story took twenty-five years to compile, as life tends to get in the way of dreams. But since then I've met an amazing group of readers and authors I now call friends. Without their support and encouragement, the last eighteen months wouldn't have been possible. There is no way to name them all, but there are three women who have been my constant cheer squad from the beginning: Jaime Rush, Bernadette Marie, and MJ Kane. These three women have suffered through my first drafts and listened to my whining and crying over technological issues and just plain life. Thank you, ladies. Not only are you all amazing authors, you are wonderful friends.

Of course, if it wasn't for my wonderful, supportive husband of twenty-six years, my writing would not be possible. He truly made me believe in a happily-ever-after. Without my husband and two wonderful sons, there would be no reason to write.

And lastly a thank you to my biggest fan — my youngest son — he has stood by me longer than any other person, championing me constantly through every rough turn in the road. He is also the creator of the Creatus seal and title, which I hope will someday be recognized across the book community.

I love you all.